ACCLAIM FOR ALTON FLETCHER

Based on actual events, *Hear the Wind's Voice* transports the reader to 1857, just after the Dred Scott decision was released by the United States Supreme Court, which tested the very foundation of liberty upon which the republic was founded.

Though fiction, the story explores the quest for freedom by an oppressed element of the population against the backdrop of the abuses of freedom by those who already had it. Alton Fletcher's deft use of compelling characters, vivid imagery, and a nail-biting plot bring this story to life in a way that will not disappoint. It is a fitting sequel to *Find the Wind's Eye*.

—Jim Jordan, Author of *The Slave-Trader's Letter-Book*

Other titles by Alton Fletcher: *Find the Wind's Eye*, Book One in the Andrew Gunn Trilogy

HEAR THE WIND'S VOICE

A NOVEL

BOOK TWO IN THE ANDREW GUNN SERIES

ALTON FLETCHER

Aldebaran Press

4196 Merchant Plaza #528

Woodbridge, Virginia 22192

ISBN-13: 978-1-7361668-2-6 Paperback

ISBN-13: 978-1-7361668-3-3 Kindle ebook

Library of Congress Control Number: 2025902299

Cover art: Patrick O'Brien, Annapolis, Maryland

— EPHESIANS 6:12 (KJV)

~

1

With the dim gray light of dawn came the passing of a two-day gale. In the morning twilight, Second Lieutenant Andrew Gunn surveyed the weather deck of the ship, her entire length swept clear of anything not nailed shut or lashed down. The *Dobbin* had tried to run before the storm, heading far out to sea to escape its wrath, but in the end, it had overhauled her. Throughout the heavy blow, the shrieking wind had shredded the cutter's storm sails and rigging. One monstrous black wave taken over the bow had crushed the ship's dinghy into splintered staves and flushed the detritus over the side.

The gale abated without much warning, just as it began a day earlier. Subdued now, but still biting, the wind whipped the parted rigging overhead and taunted the ends of tattered sails. The North Atlantic could be merciless, especially at the height of a late winter nor'easter.

Up forward, the larboard watch crew huddled near the foremast around the dinghy's empty cradle, their sou'westers bent against the wind, oilskins dripping cold rain. By twos, the sailors took turns seesawing the pump handles in an unceasing attempt to keep the ship afloat. The activity afforded the added benefit of keeping them warm.

The wind veered to the west, and Gunn ordered a change in course to meet it. He shouted to the cutter's boatswain through cupped hands.

"Look lively there, Blake. Trim the sails. Send the watch aloft. Let's see what can be salvaged. And send Walters to me."

The boatswain nodded and barked orders that launched the seamen —cold, wet, and reluctant as bilge rats—scurrying into the rigging on both the mainmast and the foremast.

They all had lived through it to see another dawn, which brought Gunn another day closer to realizing his eventual return north to New England, the land and people of his birth. Though fierce, the impact of the waning gale, one of dozens like it that he had known in his years at sea, seemed far less severe than the raging manmade tempest that had swept him away from home and family more than two years earlier. By his reckoning, nothing before or since had equaled the consequences of that hellish disaster.

Yet, even in the darkest hours of the past thousand or so days, he'd had a singular comfort, which was the steadfast assurance of his eventual return home. The captain's solemn promise to him had acted as an occasional inebriant, providing a sporadic, mercurial hope that this one burning desire, which never completely left his thoughts, would surely come to pass. Now, after more than two years of exemplary service aboard the *Dobbin*, arrangements at last would be made for his transfer to a cutter somewhere up north—subject to the needs of the service, of course. He could leave Savannah and go home to live once more among his friends and family in Boston, or at least somewhere closer to them. Soon, he and Elizabeth could be married, provided he continued to serve well and kept his own word to the captain, the unwritten terms of his redemption. The thought warmed him even now, despite a gust of chill wind that blew the rain sideways.

An hour ago, after assuring himself with a final look at the glass that the storm at last was subsiding, Captain Dawes had gone below to rest for a while, saying that he felt rather tired.

"I'm going to catch a few winks," he'd said, with a pat of his hand on Gunn's shoulder. "I know we're all in good hands with you on watch. Keep a weather eye, Mr. Gunn. If anything changes, let me know. Otherwise, wake me when the wind shifts." Nothing meant more to Gunn than having the confidence and trust of an expert seafarer in his ability to keep a tight watch.

A finger of frigid rainwater, seeping beneath his upturned collar, traced his spine to the middle of his back. He shivered and wiped his vision clear of rain, then with numb, trembling fingers untied the rope harness from around his waist and shrugged it from his shoulders. Tethered to the jackline, which stretched from bow to stern for the safety of all who kept watch above decks in the gale, the harness had saved his life several times during the last watch and throughout the past forty hours.

The helmsman at his elbow turned to him, relief sounding in his voice. "Looks like the worst is over, sir."

"Let's hope so, Foster. For us, anyway."

"The old girl, she took a good beatin'. But at least nobody got hurt, or worse, praise be."

"Yes. Thank God."

"It woulda been a cryin' shame if they had, now wouldn't it? Truth be told, Mr. Gunn, these yere so-called winter cruises is for the birds, if you don't mind me sayin' so. Nobody has any sense bein' out yere in such a weather as this, leastwise nobody who dudn't know what they's a-doin'. And them that do, wellsir, they'd have the sense to see theirselves home, now wouldn't they? 'Course they would. 'Course they would. For the life of me, lieutenant, it jes' don't make no sense 'tall to be sailin' around out here gettin' our hides whipped, jes' waitin' for somethin' bad to happen. Sink or swim, is what I say. Sink or swim. Ain't it so?"

Gunn glanced over his shoulder at the helmsman. "Do you even know how to swim, Foster?"

Foster looked at him, open-mouthed. "Well, no, sir. Don't care to get wet, if you must know. Don't even much care for bath night."

Gunn laughed for the first time in a while. "I didn't think so. Mind your helm now."

Summoned by the boatswain, the captain's steward mounted the steps to the quarterdeck. Clinging to the jackline, Walters cat-walked across the rain-slicked deck toward Gunn. He tried to salute, but his feet slid out from under him. He ended up in a heap at Gunn's feet.

"Beg pardon, sir." Walters struggled to get up.

Gunn helped him to his feet. "That's all right, Walters. One hand for you and one for the ship."

"Aye, sir. You sent for me, sir?"

"I did. Lay below and wake the captain. Give him my respects and tell him that the storm is spent."

"Aye, aye, sir." Walters opened the hatch to the cabin and crept down the ladder. Gunn heard him call out. Not a quarter minute later, the steward poked his head out of the companionway, eyes wide with alarm.

"Mr. Gunn, I think you should come down here."

"What is it, Walters?"

"Something's wrong, sir."

"What do you mean?"

"I—I can't seem to wake the captain."

The helmsman chuckled. "Send the bos'n down there. He'll get him up, sure as—"

"Mind your helm, Foster. And your tongue. I'm going below. I'll be gone but a minute."

Foster gave a sullen nod and turned his eyes to the binnacle. "Mind my helm, aye, sir."

Though the watch officer's place was always on the quarterdeck, Gunn couldn't help but respond to the urgency in Walters' voice. He hurried to follow, as usual favoring his game right leg as he eased down the ladder. He paused long enough at the bottom rung to let his eyes adjust to the darkness.

"Give us some light, Walters."

The steward moved toward the brass lamp that swung on gimbals over the captain's table. Gunn felt his way along the table to the cribbed bunk on the starboard side. He swept the canvas curtain aside.

"Captain."

Walters struck a match. The flame diffused a wan light throughout the room, which brightened as the lamp began to glow, casting long shadows that flickered against the bulkhead and across the deck.

"Captain Dawes." Gunn shook the captain's shoulder. "Sir, wake up. The storm's past."

The ship's timbers mimicked the groan of a man awakened from restless sleep. The captain, however, didn't stir. His sightless eyes stared at the overhead.

Gunn felt the man's neck, searching for a pulse. Nothing. He pressed deeper into the cool flesh below the jaw, but the only response was a short burst of air, which parted the captain's lifeless lips.

"Walters, go and wake the first lieutenant. Tell him to come quickly."

"Is he—is he dead, sir?"

Gunn nodded. "Appears so. Go on, lively now."

2

The captain's still body lay face-up on his bunk, legs twisted in the blankets. The purpled facial features held an odd expression of wide-eyed wonder. One hand rested on his chest, grasping a few folds of rumpled nightshirt.

First Lieutenant Desmond Bulloch sniffed and wiped the sleep from his eyes with the heel of his palm. "When was the last time you spoke to him?"

"About an hour ago," Gunn said. "He came up on deck to check the weather and the sails, and he said to call him if anything changed."

"Did he seem ill or out of sorts?"

"No. But you know him. Nothing much bothers old Dauntless Dawes."

"Nothing more ever will, I expect."

Bulloch reached out a hand to close the lifeless eyes. One eye resisted, remaining half-open, as though determined even now to keep watch on the ship. Bulloch pressed it shut.

"You're the captain now." Gunn tugged the tangled blanket free and pulled it over the captain's head, leaving visible only a shock of coarse gray hair.

"Yes, well, at least until we return to Savannah."

"What are we going to do, Des?"

"Good question." Bulloch scratched his head. "Press on, I suppose. After that storm, we're more than likely to find somebody in distress out here."

"What about the body?"

"It won't keep, that's certain. No way to preserve it. Commit it to the deep, as Captain Dawes always said he wanted. Best thing. I'll take care of it."

"Let me tend to him." Saddened, Gunn eyed the lifeless form, recalling how the captain had taken him under his wing. "He was always very good to me."

Bulloch clapped a hand on Gunn's shoulder. "No, Andrew. I'll tend to it. You'd better get back on deck now. We need you on watch. Send word for Doc, will you?"

"Aye, aye, captain."

"Belay that noise."

"Better get used to it, Des—I mean, captain."

Gunn climbed the ladder back into the icy wind, now diminished to a light breeze. The sun's upper limb broached the horizon, where the Madeira sky had cleared.

"Mark your head, Foster."

"East by northeast, sir."

Gunn eyed the sails, set full and by on a close reach. "Very well. Keep her so."

"Is it true, Mr. Gunn? Is Captain Dawes truly dead?"

"I'm afraid so."

"Jessee-e-e." It was the closest that Foster could come to swearing in the presence of an officer.

Gunn beckoned to the boatswain, who stood near the mainmast with the rest of the watch, all facing the stern, hats in hand.

"Boats, come aft," he called.

The boatswain loped onto the quarterdeck, taking the steps in a single bound. He saluted as he approached Gunn.

"Has he pegged out sure, sir?"

Gunn returned his salute. "Aye, he has. Captain Dawes is dead. Lieutenant Bulloch has assumed command. He's our captain now. Let the crew know."

"Aye, aye, sir." The boatswain turned to go.

"Wait. I need you to send Doc to the cabin."

"Right away, sir." He started aft.

"Hold on, Boats. What's the damage to the sails and rigging?"

"We popped the jumper stay, sir. Lost the jib stay, too, when the sail blew out. Also, one of the outer shrouds parted on the main topmast. A few sails need patching. The dinghy's done for, o'course. But nothing we can't handle, sir."

"Good. Need to keep these men busy with repairs to take their minds off what's happened. And we must get this ship moving, Boats. Let's turn to repairing the rigging, then make all plain sail soon as we can."

"Aye, aye, sir." Blake stood still.

"That's all, Boats."

The boatswain took a tentative step.

"No, wait. One more thing. We're going to need a shroud for the captain's body. See what you can find. A spare hammock, perhaps?"

"What about the blown-out jib, sir? We'll need to bend on a new one. Some others will need to be changed out, too."

"Is there enough of it left to make do?"

Blake gave a quick nod.

"Aye, then, he'd like that."

"Yes, sir. A piece of the old girl's skirts wrapped about him. I think he would, indeed."

"Good. Cut a piece and bring it aft to the cabin."

"I'll sew it up with my own hands, sir, with your permission, o'course."

"I'm sure he'd like that, too, Boats."

"Cap'n Dawes was a good man, sir."

"The best of men."

Gunn opened the leather-bound book, labeled *Rough Log of the U.S. Revenue Cutter DOBBIN*. He smoothed the page, headed by the date: Sunday, 15 March, 1857. With his palm, he held the page flat to keep it from flapping in the wind. His hand shook as he made the latest entry—whether due to the cold or to the subject matter, he couldn't say. It was an entry unlike any other he had ever made, so consequential to him that he had never even considered the possibility. He wrote in a shaky scrawl.

Captain Joseph S. Dawes, U.S. Revenue Cutter Service, died aboard this vessel on this date, during the first watch. His body was discovered in his cabin, alone, by the steward, Matthew Walters, at approximately a quarter past six o'clock a.m. Cause of death unknown at present. First Lieutenant Desmond R. Bulloch assumed command as acting captain.

Now it was official. The captain was dead. It had happened, hard as it was to believe. As Gunn finished writing, Third Lieutenant Marcus Grant approached, ready to offer relief of the watch. The look on Grant's weathered, middle-aged face said that he'd already heard the news. Of course, news traveled quick as a shout in such a small ship. They exchanged solemn greetings. Gunn showed him the entry in the log.

"Who would have guessed it?" said Grant.

"I'd have been the last, believe me."

"Does anybody know what happened?"

"No. He was hale and hearty one hour and gone the next."

"How are you taking it, Andrew?"

"What do you mean?"

"It's no secret how much you thought of him. And he of you. He took a shine to you from the time you first stepped aboard. Leastwise, I've always thought so. And I should know. I've been around long enough to have seen a lot of captains. Never had one take to me like he did to you."

"I can't fathom that he's gone. He offered me a safe harbor in a foul wind, that's sure."

Grant smiled. "Not to mention being the only other Yankee onboard, besides you. He was from Massachusetts, wasn't he?"

"New London, Connecticut. I think maybe he still has a brother there."

"Same difference. Well, go on below and get some rest, Andrew. You look like you could use it, if you don't mind me saying so."

"Thanks, Marcus. But I think I'll see if our new captain needs any help."

"Suit yourself." Grant took the logbook from him. "Do we have any idea where we are?"

"About four hundred miles east-southeast of Savannah, by dead reckoning. That storm likely blew us out to sea quite a bit. There weren't any stars last night. Maybe we'll get a sunline or two today."

"We still headed away from the storm, toward Bermuda?"

"Aye, a little less than halfway. East by northeast is the best we can do with the wind right now."

"Looks like the seas are calming down at last."

In the diminished wind, the waves, although still the height of warehouses and jumbled like a busy shipyard, now appeared less menacing with their tops rounded off.

Grant squinted toward the horizon into the rising sun. "Any sign of other ships?"

"Nothing. Nary sail nor scrap."

Once relieved, Gunn went below into the cabin. Bulloch, seated at the table in the captain's chair, pored over a chart, dividers in hand. In the corner on the starboard side, "Doc" Dougherty, the gunner's mate and unofficial ship's doctor, hovered over the bunk. He and Walters worked with great deference to undress the body.

Although the *Dobbin* had no true physician attached, Dougherty did what he could to serve in that capacity, having learned from necessity during the war with Mexico to deal with illness, injury, and death on their own terms, as they came. Officially designated the ship's gunner, he was also called into service on occasion as the crew's dentist, but only when no other possible options presented. Everyone had forgotten his true given name, but Gunn always thought it amusing that Doc's surname in Gaelic meant something like "hurtful."

Dougherty peered at the naked body. "From what I can see here, Mr. Bulloch—er, cap'n—there's nary a mark on him, head to toe." He motioned to Walters. "Let's turn him over. Gentle, now." Doc jerked his head to the side and rolled his eyes. "Oooh, law sakes—it appears he's done shat hisself." He ran a hand down the torso. "No, sir, nothing here, neither. Best guess is heart failure, or maybe a stroke."

Bulloch looked up from the chart. "Are you certain, Doc?"

Dougherty shrugged. "Sure as I can be, cap'n."

"Thank you. See that he's cleaned up, will you? And dress the body in his best uniform. I'm sure Walters there can put one together."

Gunn sat down at the table across from Bulloch. "Anything I can do to help, captain?"

"Ah, Andrew, you've finished your watch. Good. I wanted to ask you something."

"Certainly. What is it?"

"Did anyone visit the cabin from the time Captain Dawes went below to the time Walters found him in bed?"

"No, certainly not."

"Who was the helmsman on watch?"

"Foster."

"Can he testify to that fact?"

"Absolutely so. Nobody passed by us. Sure as I can be."

Bulloch smoothed a wayward shock of blond hair back from his eyes. "Good."

"Why do you ask? Do you think—"

"No, no. I simply must make certain of the facts. There will surely be an inquest when we return home to Savannah. I don't want there to be any unanswered questions."

"Of course. I'm sure there will be no question whatsoever. Nobody on this ship would've harmed a hair on his head."

"Nevertheless, I'll need written statements from Doc, Walters, and you for the record. And anyone else who might have seen or done anything last night in connection with the captain. What did he have to eat for supper?"

"Same as what we ate," said Gunn. "Far as I know. Same as the rest of the crew, like always. You know how he is . . . *was* about that."

Bulloch nodded. "As far as I know, Cookie's mess hasn't killed anybody yet."

Doc grinned. "Come real close a few times."

"Better not let Cookie hear you say that, Doc. Well now, nobody else was ill last night, were they?"

Gunn shook his head. "No, not that I know of."

Bulloch's tired eyes rested on him. "Andrew, I'll need you to get statements together from the crew. You're acting first lieutenant now."

Gunn's gaze drifted toward the bed of his dead captain. "Strange as it may seem, I'd give anything if that were not true."

3

Blake poked his head, silhouetted by the morning sunlight, down through the cabin hatch.

"Beg pardon, sir, and I hate to be the bearer of more bad news."

"What is it, Boats?" asked Bulloch.

"It appears we've sprung a leak somewhere in the bow, below the waterline. We've been at the pumps all through the storm, o'course. But the pumps can't keep up. Seems to be gettin' worser."

"How much?"

"Well, we've took on about three inches in the bilges the last hour, cap'n. Not sure where it's all comin' from."

"Go take a look, will you, Mr. Gunn? See what you can find."

"Aye, captain."

Gunn rose from the table and climbed the ladder to join Blake on deck. The two of them grasped the jackline hand-over-hand and pulled themselves along, timing their progress with the uneasy roll of the ship, while skating on a skim of water across the quarterdeck and down the steps to the main deck. They reached the forward hatch and climbed down the ladder into the forecastle and the crew's berthing.

Blake led the way, crouching beneath twenty or so triced hammocks swinging overhead, as they shuffled forward in the dim light past a pile of soaked oilskins. Ten of the off-watch crew sat on stools at an assortment of trunks and lockers, which doubled as tables for their breakfast of porridge, sorghum syrup, biscuits and tea. Any aroma of food was masked by the dank smell of tobacco smoke mixed with the sweat of men. They stood, best they could, and made way as Gunn and Blake passed through the cramped triangular space toward the forepeak. The floorboards under their feet were slick with seawater.

"As you were, men," said Gunn.

The sailors sat back down to their meals, following the two with furtive, uneasy looks, unaccustomed to having an officer in their midst. The forecastle, hovel that it was, was the only place on the small ship they could call their own.

"Now it's coming in here, sir, but only a tad more'n usual." Blake pointed to a stream of water, seeping through the seams of the strakes with every passing wave. "That's not the worst of it."

Gunn's boots slipped on the floorboards. "It's bad enough."

"You can say that again, sir," said one of the sailors.

"Pipe down, tarhead," said another. "Ain't nothin' we hadn't seen before, lieutenant. Happens every now and again. More often than not."

"She's just like any ship, sir," said Blake. "She can't help but leak a bit. But that's not what troubles me. Let me show you what I mean."

The boatswain shoved aside a trunk that rested over a hatch and yanked on the braided rope lanyard to lift open the cover.

"Hand me that lamp, would you, sailor?" Blake pointed overhead to the lantern that swung on a bent nail. The man got up from his stool and reached to turn the knurled knob, raising the flame. He handed the light to Blake, who knelt on the wet floor.

"Beg your pardon, sir, but you'll have to put your head down in here to see." Blake lowered the lantern into the black void below.

Kneeling beside him, Gunn ducked his head and shoulders into the hole. The sulfurous stench of decaying sea life rose to meet him. It didn't take long to see what Blake was worried about. A steady rivulet of troubled water ran from some invisible source over the shots of chain and anchor cable in the forepeak. Water covered about two-thirds of the mound of cable. Rats swam and scurried about, climbing wherever they could find to get out of the pitching water and the glare of light.

Gunn pressed himself upright and knelt beside the open hatch, gazing into the shadows below. "We've sprung a few plank seams, is my guess. We need to find the source and stop it, if it can be stopped, or we'll be the ones needing rescue."

"Aye, sir," said Blake. "We'll get right on it."

"We have a captain to bury first. Better get the men ready."

An hour later, the ship's company stood to attention. The two watch sections faced opposite each other, flanking both sides of the starboard gangway. The captain's body lay on a plank between them, stretched across a jury-rigged catafalque. The national ensign, draped over the body, ruffled in the mild breeze. Standing at the head of the deceased, facing the slate-gray open sea, Captain Bulloch read from a small, well-used black book.

"We therefore commit the earthly remains of Captain Joseph Dawes, United States Revenue Marine, to the deep, looking for the general Resurrection in the last day, and the life of the world to come, through our Lord, Jesus Christ; at whose second coming in glorious majesty to judge the world, the sea shall give up her dead . . ."

Gunn wondered how that could possibly happen, as he always did whenever he heard that phrase. How would it be possible for the sea to give up a body, long decomposed and devoured by countless sea creatures—all of them dispersed and later dead, themselves decomposed? All the innumerable dead who had been committed to her care since Noah built his gopher-wood ark. No matter. Regardless, Captain Dawes was dead and gone, never again to have influence in this present world. Bootless and dead as Noah himself.

"Well, Mr. Gunn?"

"Sir?"

Captain Bulloch turned to gaze at him. "I asked if perhaps you might like to say a few words."

It was no use trying to distract himself any longer with pointless thoughts. The dreaded moment had come and there was nothing for it. He looked into the expectant faces of the crew and drew a deep breath.

"Some men leave no legacy, save those whose lives they touch. Captain Joseph Dawes was one of those men. He had neither wife nor children. Yet none can deny the many among us who gladly would call themselves his sons. He was not a great man, by the standards of this world. However, those who knew him will forever be impressed with his greatness. He was not a wealthy man, if wealth be counted in coin. Even so, we all owe him our lives several times over. He—"

Gunn faltered. He had more to say, but the words would not come without unleashing a flood of emotion. His vision blurred, and he shook his head.

"Hear, hear," said one of the men.

Another sailor raised an arm. "Three cheers for Cap'n Dawes."

"Hold on," said Bulloch, staying them with his palm. "Though I do share your sentiment, men, let's remember the solemnity of the occasion. Perhaps it would be more appropriate to render a moment of silence, if you will."

The crew uncovered and bowed their heads. The ship's hull, laden with seawater, groaned as she cut through the crest of a passing wave. The sea shushed alongside. The quieted wind whispered a wordless, unutterable prayer.

Bulloch raised his head and replaced the cocked hat on his head. "Sound the ship's bell."

The quartermaster, stationed on the quarterdeck by the mainmast, struck the bell four times.

Bulloch nodded. Four side boys raised the plank by the head, and the dead captain's body, shrouded in canvas and weighted with cannon shot at the feet, slid from beneath the flag overboard and into the briny deep with a heavy splash. The waves tumbled and soon consumed it.

"Man the pumps."

Four sailors bent to the handles of the ship's pumps, resuming with fervor their unending task.

"Listen up, men," said Bulloch. "We, all of us, have suffered a great loss. Captain Dawes was indeed a good and respectable man and the finest ship's captain I've ever known. As your new captain, at least for now, I will strive to meet the high standards set by him. Mr. Gunn is your new acting first lieutenant. I have every confidence in him, as you should. By now, we all know that this ship is soon to be under hatches, unless we reach Savannah to make repairs. We're heading home now, as directly as we can. Meanwhile, I expect every one of you to do your jobs to the best of your ability. If we all do that, I am certain that we'll come out of this just fine."

4

The *Dobbin* turned about and headed for home. Still at least two days out, with a foul wind, there was a lot of water to be covered to reach Savannah and safety.

Three hours later, the ship entered a debris field, comprising all manner of flotsam, spread in every direction. Much of it was charred by fire. A lookout, perched high on the foremast, spotted a body in the water. It was the lifeless form of a young girl, snarled in rigging attached to a broken spar.

The ship hove to next to the girl's body. The motion of the waves lolled her head and arms as though she were stirring from sleep, which might have been the case, had she not lain facedown in the water, her head surrounded by streaming locks of long blond hair.

The crew fished the bound, lifeless form from the sea with a cargo net. They cut away the tangled rigging and gently laid the slight, stiffened body on the deck. She was bundled in a knitted shawl, her nightclothes peeking from underneath. Doc brushed back her hair and examined her blanched face and arms, mottled pink and blue beneath the skin.

"Rigor's setting in. She's been dead less than a day, is my guess," he pronounced. "Probably last night, poor thing. At least nothing's et her. Not yet, anyways."

"Cap'n, I see something out there to starboard," called the lookout, his outstretched arm angled two points off the bow. "Maybe a quarter mile or so. Looks to be an overturned lifeboat. I think there might be somebody holding on. One, maybe two. Could be more."

Bulloch raised his spyglass. "Alive or dead?"

"Can't say, sir."

Motioning in the general direction of the lookout's arm, Bulloch bellowed, "Mr. Grant, head her up. Let's see what we've got."

"Aye, aye, sir," said the watch officer.

Bulloch turned to Gunn. "Andrew, put together a rescue party, will you? We'll use the larboard long boat."

"Shall I take Doc with me?"

"No, just get those people aboard as quickly as possible if they're still alive. If not, then it won't matter whether Doc is with you. I'll need him to tend to this poor little girl's body. She deserves a Christian burial, and we'll see to it that she gets one."

A little more than a quarter hour later, the cutter rounded up near the overturned boat and lowered the longboat on the leeward side. Gunn and four others dropped over the side into the boat and shoved off. The four men pulled on the oars, and Gunn took the tiller, turning the longboat about to skirt astern of the *Dobbin* and toward their target.

Gunn hailed the other boat as they approached, but his call didn't stir any response, not even movement. The forms of two people, a man and a woman, clutched each other in a tight embrace under a heavy cloak draped across the upturned keel of the boat.

"Ship your oars," said Gunn.

The longboat thumped against the capsized hull, and one of the sailors reached out to shake the man's shoulder.

"Sir, are you all right?"

"Course he's not all right," said Foster, rolling his eyes.

The man raised his graying head as though it were made of stone.

"We're here to help you, sir."

"My daughter," croaked the man. "Help her. She's—" His head fell back.

Foster and another crewman stood up in the boat and reached for the woman. Each grasped one of her shoulders and pulled her toward them. Her head lolled back, eyes shut, her jet-black hair clinging to her young face. Her eyes fluttered for a moment, revealing nothing but the whites.

The men dragged her into the boat. Her heavy skirts slapped like a wet swab across the gunnel. They wrapped a wool blanket around her and laid her on the bottom boards, her head toward the longboat's stern, near Gunn's feet. One of the men brushed the matted hair from her face.

"Put something under her head," said Gunn.

Foster grabbed a folded blanket and placed it gently beneath her head. She gave no sign of awareness. Her blue lips gaped open, and the fine, delicate features of her face slackened, as though life had lately departed. Gunn hoped they weren't too late.

They grabbed the man by the shoulders, dragged him into the bow of the boat and covered him with blankets. He raised himself up on an elbow and looked anxiously aft.

"My daughter. Is she—"

"Your daughter is safe, sir," said Gunn. The man searched his face. "We're taking you both to our ship, where you will have every aid and comfort. Are there any others about?"

The man shook his head. "None that I know of, sir. We are alone." He slumped back, his neck against the thwart. The bowman helped lower his head to a more comfortable position.

"There you are, mister," he said. "Rest easy now."

"Man your oars," ordered Gunn.

They shoved off from the doomed, half-sunk lifeboat, the bow of which bore the name of the lost ship, *S.S. Georgiana*. The men bent to their oars. Gunn shifted the tiller and turned the longboat back toward the *Dobbin*.

He glanced down at the woman near his feet and was struck by her appearance. Even in her current condition, wet hair disheveled and cheeks colorless, she was surely one of the most beautiful women he had ever seen. Her eyes flickered open and locked on his for a moment, registering uncertain fear. She stirred and moaned. Her eyes draped shut again, but not before he could see their bright green hue, the color of the sunlit sea after a storm.

In a few minutes, they were alongside the *Dobbin*. Bulloch and Doc met them at the gangway, assessing each one as they brought the pair aboard.

"Are they alive?" Bulloch asked.

"Aye, captain, just," said Gunn. "But not for long unless we can get them warm."

"Put them in the cabin. They'll be more comfortable there."

"Are you sure, captain? We can make quarters available in the wardroom," said Gunn.

"Yes, I'm sure. I'll stay in the wardroom. Truth be told, I miss your company already, Mr. Gunn." Bulloch grinned. "The captain's cabin can be a very lonely place."

5

Seeking refuge from a cold squall that had blown in from the west, Gunn climbed down the ladder into the wardroom. At the table, pen in hand, Bulloch consulted the *Coast Pilot*, making hurried notes as he read. He looked up from his work as Gunn removed wet oilskins, shaking the water from them.

"Sorry to disturb, Des, but there's no place else to get out of the squall that just came up."

"Nonsense. Pull up a chair. I was just finishing."

Gunn sat across from him at the table. "Too late to be studying for exams."

Bulloch chuckled, rubbing a hand across his tired eyes. "I was just trying to gauge the Gulf Stream. We should be upon it soon, by the looks of that squall. Probably tomorrow morning, if my calculations are correct. We'll need to head southwest a bit more. Otherwise, we'll likely end up in Charleston."

"Well, I hope you have answers to the really hard questions. Maybe they're in the back of the book."

"You mean, like whether to spend more time looking for other survivors?"

Gunn nodded. "Tough decision."

"Yes. A few hours of daylight wasn't nearly enough. It weighs on my mind. But with the ship in her current state, we need to get home. I had no choice. I certainly have a better appreciation for every consideration that a captain must make. God bless Captain Dawes. No wonder he never slept."

"I think he slept with his eyes open."

"No doubt."

"Speaking of sleep, any word on our passengers?"

"Doc tells me they are still dead to the world. They haven't taken much food, but he was able to get them to drink a beaker or two."

"It's been nearly twenty-four hours."

"Likely they'll be up and about soon, thank God. I thought the young woman might be a goner."

"She was in bad shape, that's certain."

"It would have been a real shame to lose her. And such a beauty, too."

"I was quite sure that fact would not be lost on you, Des."

Bulloch winked. "Eternal vigilance, my man."

"Aye, the price of liberties, I know. So you've often said. Somehow, I don't think that's what Jefferson meant. The poor man must be spinning in his windings."

"Was it Jefferson? He has said so many things, even those he didn't say."

Gunn chucked his chin toward the open book. "Anything in that book about saving a sinking ship? We're down by the bow, probably another foot in the last four hours."

"The pumps still aren't holding?"

Gunn shook his head. "We've done what we can to stem the flood. The fothering on the hull seems to be holding, and we finally managed to send one of the boys down in the chain locker to shore up inside the hull as best we can. He was the only one who'd fit in the crawl space. But we're still taking on water, I'm afraid."

The new captain sat in silence, all the while studying Gunn's face as though the answer was written there, but he couldn't make it out.

"Right." Bulloch said after a moment. "Let's lighten the load. Have the men start jettisoning anything we don't absolutely need. Save just enough water and rations to get us home."

"Aye, aye, sir."

"You know, it's strange," mused Bulloch. "I don't mind confessing that I keep wanting to go and tell Captain Dawes. I wish he were still here."

"So do I, Des. So do I."

"Of course you do. He treated you almost like a—"

"Like a son. Yes."

"I know he was working to find a way for you to return back north, at least somewhere nearer to Boston and your family and friends."

"Yes. You know how important that is to me, Des. I haven't seen any of them for over two years now. I haven't even been able to take leave at Christmas."

"It's these blasted winter patrols. Lifesaving duty over all else."

"Yes, of course. And I know how important that is. But I ache to the marrow in my bones to go home."

"I know, Andrew. Believe me, I do."

"To see Elizabeth again, especially."

"Have you heard from her recently?"

Gunn pulled the letter from his inside pocket and held it, running a finger along the elegant handwriting, imagining her hands as she wrote it. He could remember her strong yet delicate hands almost as well as her lovely face.

"She's taken a teaching position near her home in West Roxbury. Most of this letter is about how much she enjoys it."

"How often does she write?"

"About two letters a month, give or take. Sometimes a postcard in between. I received this one several weeks ago, just before we left Savannah. They all end the same way, asking when I am coming home. I think she doubts I truly know the meaning of the word *soon*."

"Of course. I understand. Captain Dawes told me not long ago that he thought he had found a solution. I didn't want to say anything because nothing was certain."

Gunn sat up. "Do you know what it was?"

Bulloch shook his head. "No, I'm afraid I don't. He wouldn't say. But I do know that he and the captain-commandant were well acquainted. Former shipmates. Friends, I would go so far as to say. Dawes sent him a letter not six weeks ago, explaining your case in detail."

"Including the charges against me?"

"Well, there were no formal charges from your old ship, as I recall, lucky for you. But yes, I think he explained everything. He wrote that you had served your due parole, your performance had been outstanding in the past two years, and it was time to reconsider your assignment. He inquired as to any open assignments on cutters up north."

"Did you happen to see a reply?"

Bulloch leaned back in his chair and shook his head. "If there was one, I haven't seen it. Nothing in his papers so far."

Gunn sighed. "Well, at least he kept his promise to try."

"Did you expect anything less?"

"No, certainly not. But that's all water under the keel now, isn't it?"

"Come, now. Don't lose heart, Andrew. It may still happen. Certainly, if I have anything to say about the matter, it will."

Gunn pursed his lips and cast a skeptical eye at the rain spattering on the skylight overhead, blurring his view of the gray world outside. Bulloch meant well, he knew. He had no better friend in the world, proven many times over in the years that they'd been shipmates, not the least of which was his role in pressing for Gunn's transfer to this ship from the *Morris*, despite the dark cloud of insubordination hanging over his head from his previous assignment. But there were limits to what a mere lieutenant could do.

He shook his head. "Not likely, Des. Not without Captain Dawes pushing for it to happen. Nobody else gives a short whit about a second lieutenant who struck a superior officer, even if the man deserved it."

"I do." Bullock struck a boxer's pose and thumbed his nose with his right. "Give a whit, that is." His warm smile was certainly welcome but hardly a consolation.

"Be serious. What can you do?"

"I don't know that I can do anything, but I will try. You can count on that."

"You know I would be most grateful if you could. But I'm already so deeply in your debt for pulling me out of high water after the incident on the *Morris*."

"Hogwash, you say. What are friends for?"

6

Stretching away toward the eastern horizon, the cutter's wake was strewn with casks, cartons, and crates of items summarily deemed unneeded, although at any time previous they'd been quite necessary. Losing his first command was not something Bulloch was prepared to do, so he had been quite strict in deciding what should remain onboard. His decision to unship and cut loose one of the anchors had surprised Gunn, but he followed the captain's stern order nonetheless.

"Whaddya think, Mr. Gunn? Shouldn't we wait?" Blake, the ship's boatswain, licked his front teeth. The tobacco-stained overbite marked the defining feature of his face. "Maybe the cap'n'll change his mind."

"Unship it and cut it loose, Blake. Be lively about it."

Blake saluted half-heartedly and headed for the bow. Gunn's dislike for him had grown by a substantial measure since his arrival onboard. As a boatswain, Blake left a good lot to be desired. He most often waited to be told what to do, rather than anticipating what needed to be done. Questioning orders when they came didn't help matters. What Gunn wouldn't give to have Nelson's firm hand to manage things instead. What he wouldn't give to be back with good ol' Nelson and the rest of his former crew aboard the *Morris*.

A moment later, amid sharp axe blows and shouts to stand clear, the starboard anchor tumbled into the sea with a great splash. The men drew back from the rail to avoid a good soaking. The bow lurched upward and settled, like a mare pulling her head free of the reins. From his position as watch officer on the quarterdeck, Gunn followed the foaming patch of waves, the anchor's point of entry, as it passed boiling and hissing along the hull.

The hatch to the cabin's companionway swung open and a tall, distinguished-looking gentleman emerged. Although he was in shirtsleeves, wearing a blanket over his shoulders, his appearance was quite different, much improved from the previous day, when he had been carried aboard unconscious and clinging to life.

Gunn turned to greet him. "Good evening, sir."

The man offered a graceful bow, as though greeting royalty.

"Good evening, captain," he said, smiling.

Gunn returned his smile. "No, sir. You are mistaken. I am not the captain of this vessel. I am Second Lieutenant Andrew Gunn. Captain Bulloch is in command. He is below in the wardroom at the moment."

"Ah, I see. Forgive me."

"Understandable. A moment. I'll ask him to come up."

"No need, sir. I do not wish to disturb him. We've been enough trouble already."

"I am quite certain he will be very glad to greet you, mister . . ."

"Sullivan. Jay Daniel Sullivan, Esquire. At your service, sir." He bowed again, then tugged the blanket closer about his shoulders. "Please forgive my appearance."

"I doubt your frock coat is anywhere near dry, Mr. Sullivan."

"Quite so. My trousers are still damp." He looked down and plucked at them.

"I'm afraid the salt water will prevent them from drying thoroughly. Perhaps we can find you something else to wear in the meantime."

"One of your officers—Mr. Grant, I believe—brought us some dry clothing, but none of it fit me, I'm afraid. You're most kind. Thank you."

"Not at all. Is your daughter awake as well?"

Sullivan smiled. "She is. Just now."

"Your wife. Was she?"

"Ah, no. My dear wife, God rest her soul, departed this world many years ago, when Sarah was a child. Thank goodness she was spared this ordeal. She hated the sea. It frightened her terribly. I hope my daughter will not have the same fear after this awful disaster."

"Was there anyone else traveling with you on the ship?"

"No. Only Sarah. We were returning from a trip to Ireland." Sullivan surveyed the open deck. "Were there any others recovered?"

Gunn shook his head. "I'm afraid not. We searched yesterday afternoon and into the night but found no one else alive. One little girl, but she was drowned. We buried her at sea last evening."

"What a shame. What a terrible shame. All those poor souls." He gazed over his shoulder, aft along the ship's wake. "Is that what's left?" he asked, pointing with his chin to the stream of debris.

"No." Gunn took a deep breath and held it, not sure whether to tell the poor man that their ship of rescue was in danger of sinking underneath them. "We've had to lighten the ship a bit to make better time."

"I see. Well, is there somewhere that I might sit to rest, out of the way? I've come up to get some air. It's rather close down below. And my daughter is in want of . . . well, freshening up. So, I've left her to enjoy some much needed privacy."

"Of course, sir." He called for one of the seamen, who came right away.

"Donaldson, take Mr. Sullivan forward and find him a comfortable seat in the waist. Then go below to the wardroom and inform the captain that Mr. Sullivan is up and about here on deck, should he care to know."

"Aye, aye, sir." Donaldson motioned for the man to follow. "Right this way, sir."

"Thank you, lieutenant."

"Pleasure, sir." Gunn helped steady him as he turned with a tentative step to follow the seaman.

The sun had set. Gunn pulled his watch from a vest pocket to note the time in the ship's log. The western sky blazed orange, red, and indigo, underscored by a band of gold at the horizon, mirrored below on the surface of the sea. The quartermaster struck the bell on the mainmast. Three bells, time for the change of the dogwatch. Good thing. But he didn't need the bells to tell him the hour. His stomach took care of that.

Seaman Dawkins mounted the steps to the quarterdeck and strode aft, arriving on time to relieve the helmsman. He stopped short at the skylight over the captain's cabin and gave a low whistle. A grin spread across his face as he looked down, and his eyes widened.

"Dawkins?"

"Jee-hosaphat, Mr. Gunn." Dawkins wiped a dirty sleeve across his eyes and blinked twice.

"What is it, Dawkins?"

Dawkins took a half step away from the skylight. "You gotta see this, lieutenant," he whispered.

"What now?" Gunn stepped forward, as Dawkins' pointed finger indicated where to look.

"An absolute vision, ain't she?" said Dawkins.

Gunn glanced down into the darkened cabin, past his own warped reflection in the glass of the skylight. The dim glow of the overhead lamp threw a faint circle of light across the captain's table, which was littered with women's clothing, spread to dry. On the floor alongside the table sat a washbasin. In the shadows next to it knelt the young woman, facing them, her head bent to her task. Except for a towel draped over her lap, she was naked, her long dark hair draped over her right shoulder onto her breast. Above the elbow, the otherwise flawless flesh of her right arm bore a dark, banded bruise, perhaps like one that might be caused by the violent grip of a strong hand. Another like it, but fainter, covered her left shoulder.

She squeezed water from a cloth into the basin. Lifting her chin, eyes closed, she wiped the cloth down the side of her throat and over her exposed breast. Her eyes fluttered open and met Gunn's, just as they had the day before in the longboat. She glared, eyes wide and unflinching as a startled cat. Tossing her hair back over her shoulder, she raised the towel to cover her chest and slipped back into the shadows.

Gunn's face grew warm. He shrugged out of his uniform sack coat, and draped it over the skylight, covering it as best he could.

"Get on with you, Dawkins. Go on about your business."

"Did you ever—"

"I said, get on with you. *Move.*"

"Aye, aye, sir."

Gunn turned toward the foremast and shouted through cupped hands. "Boats, get a tarp and cover this skylight. On the double."

Maybe the ship would sink and the sea would swallow him whole before she ever came topside. One could hope.

7

After the end of his watch, Gunn retreated to the wardroom, expecting the evening meal to be well underway. Instead, Bulloch sat at the head of the table, chatting with Mr. Sullivan, seated to his right. Walters, the steward, stood in the far corner, waiting upon his new captain. At the sideboard along the aft bulkhead, one of the ship's boys took care ladling fish stew from a steaming tureen into four bowls to cool.

Bulloch looked up. "Ah, Andrew. I've invited Mr. Sullivan and his daughter to dine with us. They're both feeling much better now. We've delayed our meal until she can join us. I'm sure it won't be much longer. You don't mind, do you?"

"Of course not, sir." Gunn removed his cap and hung it on a hook nearest his stateroom on the starboard side. "It will be . . . a pleasure, I'm sure."

"Come, sit." Bulloch indicated a chair next to the empty one to his left, rather than Gunn's preferential place on his right. "Why don't you sit over here, next to Miss Sullivan's place? She'll be our proverbial rose between two thorns, so to say." He turned back to Sullivan with a smile. "It's so out of the ordinary for us to have female company at dinner. Quite a rare delight, I must say, sir. You understand."

"Of course," said Sullivan. "She'll be quite honored, I'm sure."

Bulloch winked. "I hope she won't feel outnumbered or put upon in such rough company."

"Put upon? *Pish*. I'm certain she's up to it, gentlemen. Sarah won't wilt, that's sure. Actually, you'll find her to be quite comfortable in the company of men. Always has been, much to my dismay of late. You understand a father's cares, of course."

"Well, sir, you've no cause for concern aboard the *Dobbin*, I assure you," Bulloch said.

"Perhaps I should go and see what's keeping her," said Sullivan.

As Sullivan rose from the table, Walters stood aside, making way to the sliding door that separated the wardroom from the cabin. Sullivan rapped lightly on the door.

"Sarah. Are you decent? May I come in, dearest?"

After a moment, a muffled voice came from the far side of the door. "Come in."

Sullivan slid the door open and stepped through. "Are you ready, my dear? We're waiting—" He cocked his head. "What is it?" As she whispered a reply, he shot a subtle glance into the wardroom and nodded. Sullivan shut the door, behind which the muted conversation continued, largely unintelligible. Gunn made out one brief, excited exchange.

"I simply will *not*," said Sarah, her voice rising.

"As you wish, but in that case . . ."

The rest was lost to bated speech and whispers. Bulloch caught Gunn's eye and raised a brow. He shrugged a reply, pretending ignorance, but it wasn't hard for him to guess at the gist of the exchange, given his earlier awkward encounter with the young woman.

The door slid open. Sullivan stepped into the wardroom as Gunn and Bulloch rose to their feet.

"Captain, I beg your pardon, as does my daughter. Unfortunately, Sarah is still feeling quite indisposed, which I hope you will understand. She will not be joining us this evening."

"Of course, sir. Perfectly understandable. We hope she recovers very soon. Perhaps tomorrow morning, then." He turned to his steward. "Walters, please see that Miss Sullivan gets something to eat. Perhaps some soup, at the very least."

"Certainly, sir," said Walters.

"Indisposed, indeed. I am nothing of the sort." Sarah Sullivan swept into the wardroom and stood smiling next to her father, her spirited blue-green eyes shining with a light of their own. Her appearance was stunning. Dressed in the makings of a slightly oversized officer's uniform, wearing her own low-cut button boots, she struck a dignified pose as though standing for a portrait. She took her father's arm. "I am in need of no special accommodations, captain. Thank you kindly. As you can see, your Mr. Grant—who it turns out is quite the gentleman, unlike others perhaps—has graciously lent me some dry clothes, which thankfully are almost a good fit. My frock is regrettably not yet dry, you see. I hope you will forgive my rather unorthodox appearance, though without the benefit of a good mirror, I can't quite tell how it suits me. I trust I will fit into your company nonetheless." She tossed her mane of black hair, pulled back into a sailor's braided pigtail, tied with a bit of cordage. "May I join you, gentlemen?" Looking past Bulloch, her gaze landed squarely on Gunn and met his. She lifted her chin. Her smile flickered for an instant and then broadened. Gunn broke her gaze, looking furtively to Bulloch to answer.

"You are most welcome to join us, Miss Sullivan," said Bulloch. "If it is not too distressing."

"For me?" Her light, appealing laughter filled the room. "Nonsense. Father, where are your manners? Won't you introduce us?"

"Of course. Gentlemen, may I present my daughter, Sarah." He pressed her hand, nestled in the crook of his arm. "Sarah, this is Captain Bulloch." She nodded gracefully. "And Lieutenant Gunn. These are the men who saved us."

"Yes, of course," she said, again gazing at Gunn. "You are the man whom I saw— who was in the boat with us, were you not, Mr. Gunn?"

Gunn cleared his throat. "I was."

"Yes, I thought I had the pleasure of seeing you earlier."

"The pleasure was—"

"All yours. Yes, I thought you might say so."

Sullivan, red-faced, shook his head in disapproval. "Sarah, dear, remember yourself."

"Well, it is so, isn't it, Mr. Gunn?"

Bulloch shot him an odd glance.

"How could it not be, Miss Sullivan?" Gunn managed to say, bowing his head.

"Oh, please. Let's not be so formal, shall we? I feel we already know each other *so* well. After all, gentlemen, you did save our lives. Call me Sarah, won't you? Both of you. We must be intimates now, isn't that right, Father?"

"You'll hear no objection from me, my dear. In the brief time I've had to get to know Captain Bulloch here, I feel we could become true friends. Eh, captain?"

Bulloch smiled. "Desmond, by all means."

"Lovely. There, that's better, isn't it, Jay Daniel?" Sarah, clearly amused, beamed at her father.

He gave a wary chuckle. "Of course, my dear. But Daniel will do just fine."

"I always call him Jay Daniel, especially when I'm angry." She patted his arm. "Which I'm not, by the by." She turned to Gunn. "And you are?"

"Andrew."

"Oh my. How *manly*. I mean, literally. And no less than an officer and a gentleman, to boot. How very lucky am I to have such a savior." Her pleasant laughter teased him, this time with the slightest tinge of animus. "You're blushing, Andrew."

"I . . ."

She affected sincerity. "I'm sorry. I meant no offense, truly. It is a fine, virtuous name, one befitting a . . . well, a saint." Her beguiling lips curled into a sly smile. "Aye, my own Saint Andrew, patron saint of fair maidens to watch over me. How grand."

Gunn feigned a smile in return.

Bulloch sent him another inquisitive glance. "Yes, well. The stew is getting cold. Shall we be seated?" His right arm ushered the others to the table. "Sarah, why don't you sit here, between Saint Andrew and me?"

"Delighted. Thank you, Desmond."

Gunn attended her chair, then sat beside her. Sarah nodded her thanks. Her father seated himself across the table from them, and

Bulloch resumed his place at the head. The steward immediately began serving the bowls of stew.

"Smells delicious. I must admit, I'm properly famished," said Sarah.

Sullivan nodded his enthusiastic agreement. "Nothing spurs the appetite like being rescued from a shipwreck. It's grateful to be alive, I am."

"Yes, Father," said Sarah. "As am I."

"May God bless us and have mercy on all those poor less-fortunate souls." Sullivan bowed his head in silent prayer, then crossed himself and raised his eyes, now troubled and glistening. "I am truly sorry there were no other survivors."

"Yes, and so are we," said Bulloch. He picked up his spoon. "Please enjoy the stew, everyone. It's Cookie's finest, and we should not let it get cold."

"Can you tell us what happened?" Gunn said. "If it's not too much to ask and you're ready to talk about it."

"Yes, Desmond and I were discussing it earlier, when you arrived." He paused for a moment, blinking his wet eyes, collecting his thoughts. "Our ship was caught in the storm."

"The *Georgiana*, was it?" Gunn asked.

"Yes, yes. A steamship out of Dublin." Between mouthfuls of stew, he began telling the story. "On our way from Ireland back home to Savannah, we were. We sailed first to Liverpool and then stopped in Bermuda to resupply and take on more passengers. We left there four days ago. The weather was fine until the storm came up out of nowhere, it seemed. We spent almost two days trying to steam through it, but we weren't making much headway. Then the vessel began taking on water. It happened so fast. We didn't even have time to abandon ship." He stopped and set down his spoon in the half-finished bowl, his gaze fixed upon the saltshaker on the table before him.

Sarah picked up the story. "Daniel and I were waiting at our station near the bow for the crew to prepare the lifeboats. There was a terrible explosion."

"I suppose the boilers must have blown up," Sullivan said.

She continued. "We were all thrown into the sea. The ship caught fire and went down like a stone. Daniel and I were lucky to find each other, and we clung to some wreckage and one another for hours. We got separated from everyone else. At last, sometime during the night, we found the overturned lifeboat and were able to climb on top. I don't know how. It took all our strength. That's where you found us, thank goodness."

"All those good people," said Sullivan, shaking his head. "So many children, too."

"Terrible," said Sarah.

Bulloch pursed his lips. "Indeed. We're so sorry."

"Were you hurt?" Gunn asked, recalling the dark bruises on Sarah's arm and shoulder. "I mean, you must have been. How are your injuries?"

"Not really, no," said Sullivan. "Thank God in heaven, we were both spared even that."

Sarah lowered her eyes and shook her head. "Nothing to speak of. Lucky, I guess." She finished her stew in silence.

8

The evening proceeded on a more convivial note. Bulloch changed the subject several times to livelier, more pleasant matters, complemented by a course of dried fruits and cheese. He apologized for the common fare due to their limited supplies, but the two guests expressed their gratitude nonetheless.

Despite the forgettable meal, the conversation among the four grew relaxed and casual as the evening progressed, rising and falling on various aspects of their daily lives and the current events that had impacted them. Gunn was pleased to note that, on occasion, Sarah Sullivan turned her beautiful eyes to meet his, seemingly without rancor. However, she let most of Gunn's comments go without reply, directing her attention and her conversation mainly to Bulloch, laughing heartily at his charming banter and wit and offering measured ripostes in reply. The two were soon lost in a conversation all their own.

Meanwhile, Gunn turned his attention to her father. He learned that Sullivan was an attorney in Savannah, practicing trade law. They lived in a new house he had just built on Jones Street, near the corner of Bull Street, halfway between Madison and Monterey Squares, where he loved to walk in the evenings. Gunn knew the area well, having often walked there to admire the relatively new stately brick-and-wood frame homes and town-houses, despairing that he would most likely never live in such a dwelling. He told Sullivan so.

"Oh? Have you lived in Savannah for a long time, Andrew? I shouldn't think so. I mean, your speech is rather, well, foreign to the ear. You are a Yankee, I take it."

Gunn laughed. "Is it so obvious? Yes, sir, I am a Yankee and a sojourner."

"Savannah can be rather indifferent to, ah . . . sojourners," said Sullivan, smiling.

"Yes, that's true."

"Not inhospitable, though."

"I would agree. But not exactly welcoming either. Though I must say, it is nigh impossible to be indifferent to Savannah. In the two years since I arrived in the city, I have walked nearly every street or lane, I think, and lingered in every square at least once. I especially favor the Spanish moss hanging from the live oaks. It is a lovely old city. And my family has roots there, so I do enjoy some welcome. My mother is from Savannah, though she moved north to Boston when she married my father. I still have some relatives living in the city. They are my mother's people, her cousins, Josephine and Julia Gryffith—well, Josephine's married name is Moore. She's been widowed ten years. Her husband, John Moore, was a financier until he died. Josephine and Julia live together now in a town-house over on Perry Street. Perhaps you know of them?"

He shook his head. A slight frown furrowed his brow. "Gryffith, you say? I don't believe I've had the pleasure. Have you, Sarah?"

She stopped in mid-sentence. "Have I what, Father?"

"Have you perhaps met Andrew's cousins, Josephine and Julia— Gryffith is it? Of Perry Street."

"Gryffith-Moore," said Gunn.

"Perry Street?" She wrinkled her nose. "Can't say that I have, no." She took a quick breath and resumed her conversation with Bulloch.

Sullivan leaned forward, an elbow on the table. "Well, now wait a moment. The name does ring a bell, after all. I once knew an Alexander Gryffith. Welshman. Shipping merchant. His wife's name was Anwen. Called her Annie."

Gunn nodded. "They were my grandparents. My mother's father and mother."

"You don't say," said Sullivan. "Fine people. Tragic situation. They both died maybe six years ago of cholera, not three days apart."

"That's right."

"Terrible thing. I'm sorry. Were you close?"

Gunn shook his head. "Not really. I hardly knew them. They rarely came north and we never ventured south. My parents had no money or inclination to travel. I did have a chance to get to know my grandfather a bit just before he died. My ship would make port calls in Savannah from time to time. But he was a very private man, not given to much conversation. A man of few words, you might say."

"That's my recollection as well. They had only two daughters, as I recall."

"Yes. Eleanor is my mother. Her younger sister is May."

A queer look crossed Sullivan's face. "Yes, Eleanor and May. Of course. I do indeed remember them."

"Oh?" Gunn said.

"Yes. Your mother, especially, though it's been such a long time." He paused briefly, pressing his lips together. "Small world, isn't it?"

"What do you remember about them?"

Sullivan brushed his question aside. "It's been so many years. Quite stunning beauties, both of them, as I recall. They broke some hearts around Savannah when they married Yankees and went to live up north, I daresay." He shook his head, as though trying to clear his mind. "Never mind. Never mind all that. So how did you come to Savannah, then?"

"Not exactly by choice, I can tell you that."

"Oh, how's that?"

Bulloch stopped chatting with Sarah and scratched his chin, listening. Gunn exchanged glances with him.

"I had a little trouble on my last ship. Our second lieutenant and I didn't quite see eye to eye."

Sullivan looked puzzled.

"Do tell, Andrew," Sarah said, eyebrows arched.

Gunn hesitated, darting a glance toward Walters and the seaman, who tended to the empty plates and dirty tableware, placing them in a wooden tub.

Bulloch turned toward them in his chair. "Would you boys excuse us for a while?"

"Certainly, sir. We'll just take these dishes to the galley," said Walters, motioning to the seaman to hurry.

Gunn waited for them to clear away. When they had climbed the ladder, out of earshot, he continued. "It's a long story. I'm not exactly proud of everything that happened, but I must say that I would do it again under the same circumstances."

Bulloch winked. "Perhaps it's better left untold, Andrew."

Gunn sat silent, collecting his thoughts, unsure whether to say anything.

"Oh, come now," said Sarah. "It can't be quite so scandalous as all that, can it? Out with it, Andrew. Surely, nothing can be more liberating, more freeing than to bare one's breast." Her tongue caressed her smirking upper lip. "So to speak."

Chagrined, Sullivan chuckled nervously. "You'll have to excuse my wayward daughter, gentlemen. She often forgets how to speak and act like a lady."

"I haven't forgotten a thing, Daniel. I simply don't care to. Besides, I only just had in mind that wonderful line from Walt Whitman's new book. How does it go? Oh yes. 'Come I am determined to unbare this broad breast of mine, I have long enough stifled and choked.' Sublime. Do you know it, gentlemen? Oh, I doubt very much that I'm corrupting these two sailors with mere poetry, am I?" She flashed an impish smile. "Besides, Andrew has already achieved sainthood, of sorts." She crossed herself, her hand lingering over her right breast. "Haven't you, Andrew? So have no fear. Go on, tell us what happened."

"The short of it is, we came to blows. I struck a superior officer."

"Well, now," Sarah said with renewed interest. "That's my kind of man."

Bulloch held out a palm. "In fairness, I will submit that he was provoked, well and truly. I was there. I saw the whole thing."

"Pretty serious. Sounds like you could have used a good lawyer," said Sullivan.

"If I'd had a different captain at the time, I might have. As it was, Captain Whitcomb treated me very fairly."

"What was the issue, if I may ask?" Sullivan said.

Gunn told them the story, recounting how he had resisted President Pierce's order to extradite a fugitive slave aboard the Revenue Cutter *Morris*, his former ship, from Boston to Norfolk almost three years earlier. Believing the order to be immoral and unjust, though lawful, he had made his misgivings known to his command. Eventually, after they arrived in Norfolk, his actions had resulted in open confrontation with the ship's second lieutenant, who hailed from Tennessee, which then escalated into a brawl in the muddy streets of Norfolk.

"You two were involved in the extradition of Anthony Burns?" asked Sullivan, incredulous at the prospect. "That event was all over the newspapers at the time. Incredible."

"Not I, only Andrew," said Bulloch. "My ship just happened to be in Norfolk at the time, and I witnessed the fight."

Sullivan scoffed. "Fight? It was more than mere fisticuffs between two men. We nearly had a full-scale war between the states over it. As I recall, Virginia threatened to secede if Pierce hadn't carried through with the extradition. Why, I don't doubt . . . it's my opinion that the rest of the South likely would have followed. Certainly, South Carolina, but I expect even Georgia would have entered the fray."

"I must agree," said Bulloch. "That was the sentiment. It was very intense."

"You're right about that, Daniel. I think Massachusetts would readily have gone to war at the time, too," said Gunn. "It was a near miss all around. Anyway, I was punished for my part in the skirmish by being transferred off the *Morris*. As a former shipmate, Desmond stuck his neck out for me and offered an open position in his ship, the *Andrew Jackson*. I'll always be grateful to him for that."

Sarah looked puzzled. "So how did you both come to this ship, the *Dobbin*, is it?"

Bulloch nodded. "The *Dobbin* is a new cutter, just four years off the ways at Somerset, Massachusetts. She was sent down here from Wilmington, Delaware last year to replace the *Andrew Jackson,* which is a much older ship. The *Jackson* was sent to Eastport, Maine, for lighter duty."

"The *Andrew Jackson*, eh?" Sullivan said. "A ship named for one of my heroes."

"Is that so? My mother thought so highly of him that she named me after him," said Gunn. "My middle name is Jackson."

"You don't say," said Sullivan, musing. "What a coincidence. Isn't life strange that way? Strange, indeed."

"If I can divert your attention from hero worship for a moment, I'd like Mr. Andrew Jackson Gunn to finish his story." Sarah gazed intensely at him.

Gunn was surprised at her sudden interest. It made him wary. He mustered a guarded reply.

"Well, that's pretty much it," said Gunn.

"Quite a story," said Sullivan.

They sat silent, somber for a moment. Then Sarah spoke quietly.

"Gentlemen, would you excuse me? I think this would be a good time to take some air." She rose from her chair. The men stood with her. "Andrew, would you be so kind as to accompany me for a stroll on deck?"

9

The light to moderate westerlies that prevailed after the hurricane had slowed the ship's progress toward land. When Gunn and Sarah Sullivan arrived on deck in the gathering dusk, the cutter sailed a southwesterly course to make ground to windward, against the Gulf Stream. Gunn estimated they were still about seventy or eighty miles from shore. With any luck and another tack or two, they would likely reach the mouth of the Savannah River by daybreak, provided the ship remained afloat. The hourly reports of soundings in the hold showed that the ship's pumps were holding their own. Now that they had lightened the load, the danger of sinking had lessened considerably, though the hull plowed sluggishly through the choppy waves.

Marcus Grant stood watch on the quarterdeck, spyglass trained on the horizon ahead. He lowered the glass and immediately noticed their presence with a smile and an awkward yet gratuitous bow.

"If I may say so, Miss Sullivan, that uniform suits you far better than it does me," he said.

His greatcoat draped over her shoulders like a cape. She drew it more tightly about her.

"Thank you, Mr. Grant. It suffices to keep me warm and dry. I am most grateful to you."

"My pleasure, ma'am."

The two sailors who manned the seawater pumps stopped mid-seesaw and stood up, mouths agape, surprised to see a trousered woman treading the boards of their ship. She smiled broadly and saluted them.

"Back to work, men," shouted Grant. "Quit your lollygaggin'." They exchanged glances, wiped their brows, and resumed their monotonous labor to the rhythmic squeak of the pump handles, keeping their eyes all the while on Sarah.

The breeze had a slight chill to it. Sarah took Gunn's arm with both hands and sidled next to him as they walked over to the starboard rail.

"You're limping, Andrew," Sarah said. "Are you injured?"

"It's an old wound," he said, shaking his head. "It stiffens after sitting a while. Long story."

"I see." Sarah turned toward the western horizon, where an azure band of luminescence divided the sea from the moonless, star-studded sky. She gazed overhead. "What a beautiful evening. Look at those stars, will you? So many of them. I never get tired of looking at them." She pointed almost directly above her. "That red one. Does it have a name?"

Gunn nodded. "That's not a star. It's Mars."

She chuckled. "Ah, the god of war presides. How appropriate. And that bright one nearby? It's a bit reddish, too. Another planet?"

"No, that's Aldebaran. Easy to find. We often use that one to navigate by."

"Aldebaran. Strange. Does the name have a meaning?"

"It's Arabic for 'the Follower.'"

She pulled away, crossing her arms as though to warm herself. "Really? What does it follow?"

"The Pleiades. The Seven Sisters." He pointed to the cluster of stars nearby. "Right there. He chases them all night from one end of the sky to the other."

"One blackguard chasing seven women? No surprise there. Not very bright, though, if you ask me. But I only count six."

He grinned. "One is hiding."

Laughter escaped her lips, somewhat nervous and fettered, quite at odds with her previous demeanor. "Well now, that makes perfect sense, doesn't it? Good for her. Smartest of the bunch, no doubt." She regained her composure. Peering at the expanse of stars in a nearly cloudless heaven, she pointed in front of them, to the south. "And that one?"

"Ah, I see you have a very discerning eye. That's the brightest star in the sky. Its name is Sirius. They call it the Dog Star."

"Why is that?"

"It's part of the constellation Canis Major, or the big dog." He traced the outline for her, head and torso. "He follows someone, too."

"He does?"

"Yes, close on the heels of Orion, the hunter."

"Show me. Where?"

He stood behind her and took her elbow, raising her arm to trace the hunter's form, ending with the drawn bow.

"Yes, I see." She turned toward him, her smiling face illumined by starlight. "Do you know all their names?"

He shook his head and laughed. "No. Just the important ones. The ones that we can easily use to navigate by."

She took a deep breath and exhaled, gazing back at Orion. "With a sky like that, it's not hard to forget that we came through a terrible storm not two days ago."

"I must say, you seem to have weathered it well, Sarah. It's remarkable how quickly you've recovered."

She faced him. "It's not so hard to understand, is it? Despite our recent troubles, I love traveling by ship. The sea always rejuvenates me. And especially after surviving a shipwreck, after being so near death, I feel reborn somehow. Like I've been given a new life. It feels incredible. And I so love being at sea, despite the hazards. I feel as though I can escape everything out here and no trouble can follow me. Do you know what I mean?"

He nodded, acknowledging the feeling of freedom that he often experienced in being at sea. "Indeed, I do. Most of the time. Not always."

She turned, and her eyes took in the entire ship. "I envy you. All of you."

"Why is that?"

"Surely you know."

He shook his head. That anyone would envy the hardships and danger intrinsic to the life of a seafarer, not the least of which was isolation from loved ones, was surprising to hear from a woman.

"Tell me why you like being out here aboard ship," she said. "Why do you prefer going to sea rather than staying ashore?"

He didn't have to think about it very long. "There's just something about being out in the middle of a wide-open ocean, harnessing the elements of wind and waves, sailing a vessel finely crafted by human hands, and finding our way by the sun and stars."

"Yes, of course."

"But it's not just that. It's knowing that I can't take anything for granted. My life depends at every moment on the soundness of the ship, my own abilities, and the skills of the captain and all the men around me. It makes me feel alive and part of something active and living, like nowhere else that I can be."

"Yes, yes, that's what I mean. That's what I want, too. I'd give anything for a life at sea."

"You would?"

"Certainly. Why should I want anything less as a woman than you do as a man?"

"Most women don't seem to like the idea."

"I'm not most women."

"I don't know. Maybe you are romanticizing a bit, as women sometimes do."

"Do tell. In what way, may I ask?"

"Well, life on most ships, especially merchant ships, is fairly rugged, sometimes brutal. Most crews are made up of what might be called a rough and roguish class of men. Some captains have been known to use very harsh measures to maintain discipline. Not exactly the easiest life for a man, let alone a woman."

"No place for a woman. Is that what you're saying?"

"Well, yes, I suppose so."

"I see. Tell me, Andrew, are you familiar with Captain Josiah Creesy?"

"Of the *Flying Cloud*? Of course. Only the most famous clipper ship captain alive. Made the trip around the Horn from New York to San Francisco in eighty-nine days back in fifty-one. The ship set a record that has not been broken since."

"Wrong. The *Flying Cloud* broke her own record by thirteen hours two years later."

"Well, yes, that's right, of course."

"Don't look so surprised. I know things."

"I'm not. What's your point?"

"Do you happen to know who Creesy's navigator was on those voyages, both times he broke the record for sailing around the Horn?"

He thought for a moment. "No, I don't guess I do."

She grinned. "Eleanor, his wife. You're a navigator, Mr. Gunn, are you not? How important is a navigator to the progress of a ship and the speed of her travel, would you say?"

"Well, that's an unusual—"

"How important?"

"Crucial. Essential. Indispensable."

"Exactly. Yet Eleanor is rarely recognized for her skill. Nobody knows her name. Her husband, as captain, gets the credit for setting all the records. I wonder how she ever managed to accomplish such a feat while fighting off those ruffians and rogues that make life so unbearably hard aboard ship? What an amazing woman she must be."

"As I said, she is an unusual woman."

"She is an unusual woman in part because she had an unusual father, who taught her how to use a chronometer and a sextant when she was just a girl. And an unusual husband, who was willing to take her with him. How many unusual women would there be in this world if only they had more unusual fathers? Or unusual husbands? Are you an unusual husband, Mr. Gunn?"

"No, I'm not. I am as yet unmarried."

"Do you have someone who matters to you?"

"I have a fiancée."

"A fiancée. What is her name, may I ask?"

"Elizabeth."

"I'm sure she's as lovely as her name."

"She is."

"Is she unusual?"

"I think so."

"What makes her so?"

"Look, obviously your father has taught you some very lawyerly skills, and very well, I might add. I don't wish to test them any further. And I have no desire to quarrel with you, Mars or no Mars."

"Leave my father out of this. I am no protégé of his, believe me. What I know is what I have learned in spite of him. Thank heaven for his library. As far as he's concerned, he'd like nothing better than to see me married off, which is far from any of my fondest dreams."

"All right, I take your point. I truly do not wish to argue with you, Sarah."

"All right, then."

"Let me ask you something."

"Go on."

"Why did you ask me to come up on deck with you?"

She hesitated. "That story you told. It made me rethink my opinion of you. And I don't think you were trying to do that. I sensed you were in earnest, and I began to see something in you that I value, maybe even like."

"And what is that?"

"I'd prefer not to say. Not right now, anyway. I'm not at all sure. Haven't made up my mind."

"Fair enough. What then, may I ask, was the opinion that you've reconsidered?"

"That you were just another typical example of the male species. Willing to take full advantage of those who are vulnerable or, shall we say, *exposed*." She pointed at the bright star in the southern sky. "Another follower, if you will."

10

Before Sarah retired for the evening, Gunn offered his necessary and most sincere apology for the indignity of their earlier discomfiting encounter. He assured her that the incident was entirely unintentional on his part, and that he had done everything in his power thereafter to restore and respect her privacy. She accepted the apology and asked that they should agree to leave it at that, to put it out of mind, never to be mentioned again. Though he could no longer see her face with any clarity in the advancing darkness of the evening, her voice sounded warm and sincere.

"Shriven and forgiven, Saint Andrew. Goodnight," she said, touching his sleeve as she brushed past him and mounted the steps to the quarterdeck, receding into the night.

Despite his best efforts, however, he could not dispel from the shadows of his mind the image of her bathing over the washbasin. It recurred at the least expected moments, without summoning. Her naked beauty was astonishing, and he had never seen the like, under any circumstances. Always attempting to live his life in good conscience, in accordance with morals that he knew to be right, he had avoided any situations that might compromise his love for Elizabeth and their relationship. He desired to be faithful in thought and deed to the woman to whom he had promised himself heart, mind, and soul, a devotion without question or blemish.

He wished the incident had never happened, but it had. Even worse, and against his best inclinations, it had created an instance of undeniable intimacy between them, an affiliation that he would have preferred to share with Elizabeth alone. He found himself wanting, even desiring to live up to Sarah's newly considered opinion of him, which was oddly confounded by his rather unseemly thoughts of her—though why it should matter escaped him, given they were practically strangers.

The realization saddened, frustrated, and intrigued him. And then there were the unexplained bruises on her otherwise flawless arm and shoulder. He couldn't imagine who or what might have caused them, and he wanted to ask her about them, but a question like that would revisit the incident and require even greater intimacy, which he felt compelled to resist. He fretted about all these things in the solitude of his stateroom that night as he tossed and turned in his bunk, trying to get some sleep before his next watch. Finally, he gave up and rose early to dress and prepare himself to go on watch.

Though now captain of the ship, Bulloch had insisted on remaining in the three-way watch rotation, and he had taken the evening watch. It was an unnecessary gesture, as far as Gunn was concerned, because the need for officers to stand port and starboard watches was not infrequent or unusual, for one reason or another. Nevertheless, he appreciated Bulloch's willingness to relieve the strain of standing duty somewhat, though he doubted the current propensity for an equitable division of labor would last very long if the promotion to captain became permanent.

After walking the weather deck to quiet his nerves and acquaint himself with the set of the sails and the ship's condition, Gunn approached the quarterdeck and saluted Bulloch.

"You're early," said Bulloch, returning his salute.

"Couldn't sleep."

"Shouldn't wonder."

"Why is that?"

"Well, to have spent the better part of an evening with such a remarkably beautiful and intelligent young woman would arrest the sleep of even the most somnolent of men, and right now I include myself squarely in that lot. Not even men's clothing could diminish such an absolute vision. Did you enjoy your private little promenade?"

"We had a lively and memorable chat."

"I'll bet you did. I'm jealous."

"Jealous of what?"

"Her attentions, of course. What red-blooded man wouldn't be?"

"I don't know, Desmond. She seemed most interested in you all evening. I was completely shocked that she asked me to join her after dinner."

"I wasn't."

"Why do you say that?"

"Well, it was obvious from the start there was something between you two. All those side-glances and gibes and intimations—nudge, nudge. You know. Not to mention the constant friction. Where there's friction, my man, there's smoke and eventually flame."

"Nonsense, Des. I'm not the least bit interested in Sarah Sullivan, or anyone else for that matter, other than Elizabeth. You know that."

"Well, you could have fooled me."

"I'm dead serious. She's all yours, if you think you can tame her, that is."

"She is a bit of a wild one, isn't she? Could be fun, eh?"

"Good luck with that, by the way. And don't you have enough to worry about right now without taking on the likes of Sarah Sullivan?"

"Have you ever known me to avoid a good challenge?"

Gunn laughed. "Never."

Bulloch briefed him on the current weather conditions, along with the course and speed made good in the last hour, then gave instructions on taking necessary action to arrive at the mouth of the Savannah River around daybreak. Gunn relieved him, and Bulloch left the quarterdeck and retreated to the wardroom and the comfort of his stateroom for a much-needed rest.

Dawkins, again the helmsman on watch, required little supervision. Despite being a man of many faults and indiscretions, he was a fine able seaman, with years of experience on the helm. He steered straight and true, making small corrections to the helm to sail full and by with no prodding necessary. Gunn was gratified by such competence. It was always welcome and appreciated among shipmates, though often went unacknowledged. Little conversation passed between them as the cutter bounded through the waves toward homeport.

Less than an hour later, after Gunn had settled into the routine of the midwatch, the companionway hatch opened, and a dark form emerged from the cabin, wrapped in a wool blanket, barefoot. It was Sarah. She stumbled at the top of the companionway ladder and nearly fell headlong into Gunn's arms. She looked up at him, her eyes wide with fright. Her right cheek bore two parallel scratches. He put his arms around her and drew her to her feet.

"Help me," she whispered. "Please help me."

"Should I call someone, Mr. Gunn? Maybe send somebody for Doc?" asked Dawkins.

"No, it's all right, Dawkins," said Gunn. "I'll tend to her. Steady as you go."

"Steady, aye, sir." Dawkins eyed the mainsail, then focused on the binnacle.

"Come over here and sit down, Sarah." He offered her a seat on the captain's bench at the stern. She sank to the bench, sobbing quietly, her shoulders shaking. "What is it? Tell me."

She shook her head and continued sobbing, face in her hands. The blanket slipped off one bare shoulder, exposing the dark bruises there, and he adjusted it back into place.

"Sarah?" Her father's voice called out from the cabin. Sullivan poked his head through the open hatch. "Sarah, dear? What on earth—?"

Suspicion and urgent caution flashed through Gunn's mind, now starkly aware of the fresh injuries to Sarah's face and reminded of those on her shoulder and arms. "Stand fast, sir. I'll ask you to stay below for the time being." He placed himself between Sarah and her father.

"I *beg* your pardon, sir!" Sullivan took another step up the ladder.

"I'd ask you again to keep your distance, Mr. Sullivan."

"No, no," said Sarah, gripping Gunn's arm. "Please let him come, Andrew. It's all right."

Gunn took a reluctant step aside. "Very well."

Sullivan emerged from the companionway and rushed to his daughter's side. "What's happened, Sarah?"

"I had another visitation," she muttered, her voice breaking.

Sullivan took a sharp breath. "Like the others?"

She shook her head and lifted her gaze. Tears streaked her face in the starlight, trickling through the raw scratches. "There were two this time, Father. Only, one was . . . different."

"Two what?" Gunn cocked his head.

"Different how?" Sullivan asked.

"He said he wished me no harm. That he wanted to warn me."

The two men spoke in unison. "Warn you of what?"

Gunn pressed, "*Who* wanted to warn you?"

"He said he was the captain."

"The captain of what?" Sullivan asked.

"Of this ship."

Dawkins, within earshot, turned about. "Did she say what I think she said?"

"Mind your helm, Dawkins," Gunn snapped.

Dawkins whipped around and gripped the wheel with both hands. The light of the binnacle revealed the scowl on his face.

Gunn exchanged a long look with Sullivan. He lowered his voice, which did nothing to conceal his incredulity. "What in blazes are you saying, Sarah?"

"He said he was the captain of this ship."

"He? What did he look like, this man?"

"Older man. Tall. Stern-looking. Goatee."

"Did he say anything else?" Sullivan asked.

"He said there were others."

Gunn moved toward her. "Others?"

"We left them behind, Andrew. Survivors. From the *Georgiana*." She gazed at Gunn directly. "He said to tell you that we need to go back and look for them."

"*What*? Wait a minute. Is this a joke? What kind of—"

"Hardly," said Sullivan. "My daughter does not joke about such things."

11

Desmond Bulloch paced at the head of the wardroom table. His long legs covered the width of the space in three strides. The other two officers, seated at the table, watched in silence as he walked back and forth, head down.

It was odd to have all three of them in the same room while the ship was underway since ordinarily one of them was always on watch, but these were odd times, and this certainly was an odd situation. Bulloch had ordered the ship hove to while the officers convened in the wardroom. The entire ship was awake and stirring, although the midwatch had not yet ended and it would be hours yet before sunrise. Word had spread throughout the ship of the strange occurrence involving the young woman once Dawkins had been relieved of his turn at the helm. Gunn had expected nothing less to occur, given the circumstances.

"It's utter nonsense," Bulloch said, stopping mid-stride. "We can't turn back now on the basis of what amounts to a woman's silly nightmare."

"Do you really think Captain Dawes spoke to her?" asked Grant.

Bulloch glared at him. "No, I do not. Get hold of yourself, Mr. Grant."

"She certainly believes he did," said Gunn.

"She . . . she described him perfectly, sir, right down to his goatee," said Grant. "That's what you said, isn't it? How would she know something like that? It made my skin crawl."

"I don't know, for the life of me," said Gunn. "In all other respects, she seems a very rational, intelligent woman, but tonight she seems to have lost her mind. She certainly believed whatever she saw was very real."

"It was a nightmare, Andrew. Nothing more," said Bulloch, cleaving the air with his open hand. "And no wonder, after all she's been through."

"Why in the world would she have dreamed such a thing?"

Grant scratched his balding head and grimaced. "What if she was right, sir?"

"Now, look, you two. We have a decision to make, so we must focus on the facts. *Focus*, now. I freely admit, doubt has been eating at me ever since we called off the search for other survivors, but we had no choice other than to strike for home, given that we were already down by the head. I have the safety of the ship and this crew to think about, weighed against the remote possibility of finding anyone else alive. And I doubt very much that anybody else survived such a catastrophe. These two were very lucky, indeed."

Grant squirmed in his seat. "Still . . . "

"We searched for two full hours until the light faded," said Bulloch. "No sign of life, other than these two."

"You're right, captain," said Gunn. "Those are the facts."

Bulloch sat down at the table. "Yes, well, the question is, should we turn back and search again? What do you think?"

Grant fidgeted while Gunn studied his hands, outstretched on the table.

"I don't doubt the woman's sincerity," said Gunn slowly. "I mean, I think she saw something, though I don't know exactly what. But I also think prudence requires that we head for Savannah, given how close we are. Even though the flooding up forward seems to be under control, we're running short of provisions. Most of what remained went over the side when we lightened ship. And by now, given the amount of time that has passed, the wind and currents have widened the search area to an almost impossible degree. It would be like searching for a pinch of pepper in a pond."

"Mr. Grant?"

"I tend to agree with Andrew, sir."

"Good. Then we're all three in agreement."

"You're the captain, sir," said Grant.

"Yes, Mr. Grant, thanks for reminding me. I just wanted to hear what you two were thinking. As terrible a thought as it might be that someone else might need rescue, we can't afford to risk going back now just because somebody had a bad dream."

"The crew is spooked, Des, even so," said Gunn.

"I know. We'll have to deal with that."

The pocket door to the cabin rasped open. Daniel Sullivan entered the room, turned and slowly slid the door closed.

"She's asleep, gentlemen. She'll need some rest now." He sat at the table, across from Gunn.

"Good. I'm very glad," said Bulloch.

"She's had quite a scare," said Gunn.

"I appreciate your concern over my daughter's welfare, gentlemen. Look, I realize how strange all this must seem to you. No doubt . . . no doubt, you have many questions. I suppose, after all you've been through, an explanation is in order."

"Only so far as you're comfortable explaining," said Bulloch. "We don't wish to intrude. But I have to say, we'd all certainly like to know more."

"Well, we do owe you our lives, after all. It is little intrusion to share with you what I can. What I know, that is."

He sat quietly for a moment, glancing at the half-empty coffee cups scattered on the table. "Is that coffee? Might I have some?"

"Of course, sir," said Grant. He got up to pour a cup from the pot on the sideboard and brought it back to the table.

"I don't quite know where to begin." Sullivan smiled wanly and sipped the coffee, taking his time. When he finally spoke, it was in a deliberate, somber tone. "Since Sarah was a child, she has suffered from what I call spells. Her mother, God rest her, referred to them as her 'second sight.' Over time, these spells have come and gone—not constant, by any means. Lately, however, they've become more frequent and more intense. She endures severe headaches. Sometimes, she'll go into a deep depression, even a trance-like state. Other times, she is lively and apparently very happy, nothing amiss. At the worst times, she has terrible nightmares, like nothing I've ever experienced myself. As she did tonight. Usually, they seem to converge on the notion of her being chased or pursued. Often, during these nightmares, she experiences physical trauma, as though someone has, well, abused her."

"Is there ever any evidence of abuse?" Gunn asked.

Sullivan nodded. "Sometimes, yes."

"Like the scratches on her face?"

"She might have done that herself by accident. I don't know. She doesn't know, either."

"Anything else?"

"Bruising."

"Bruising?" asked Gunn. He recalled the marks on Sarah's arms and neck, as though left by the grip of strong hands.

"Yes, at times. Almost like she's been held down or beaten."

"How terrible," said Bulloch.

"Have you sought treatment for her?" asked Gunn.

"Of course. The best doctors. Chemists. Even priests. We traveled all the way to Ireland to see an exorcist by the name of Father Martin, a Catholic priest from the old country, who assured me that he was quite certain of his ability to help. We were there for nine weeks. Never once did she experience anything like this. Even so, he tried several lengthy exorcisms. In fact, that's where we were returning from when we were shipwrecked." He slowly shook his head. "Apparently, nothing worked. I'm at a complete loss. I don't know what else to do."

Gunn searched the man's expression for any sign of obfuscation or evasion, finding nothing there but sadness and sincerity deeply etched into the lines and creases of his face. He caught Sullivan's gaze and asked the question that was on his mind, but it came out as a statement. "Sarah spoke tonight of having what she called a 'visitation.'"

"Yes, that's right, Andrew. She sees things that others don't see. Knows things that others don't know. Things it might seem impossible for her to know."

"Such as what our dead captain looked like?" Grant asked, stroking his grayed muttonchops, one side, then the other.

Sullivan's glance at Bulloch showed surprise. "I thought *you* were the captain of this ship, Desmond."

Bulloch shook his head and jabbed a thumb aft, toward the cabin. "Captain Dawes died in that very cabin a day before we rescued you," he said. "I am the ship's first lieutenant, acting captain of the *Dobbin*."

"Your daughter described Captain Dawes to a tee, Mr. Sullivan." said Grant, his voice hushed.

"How do you explain that?" Gunn asked.

Sullivan frowned. "I can't, most certainly I cannot. She says she saw him. That's all I know."

"There was a second one," said Gunn. "She said she had two visitations tonight."

"Yes. The other one she has had on previous occasions. Several times, lately. Many times over the years. You might say that he, or it, is a familiar. That visitation was far more terrifying to her than the first one. She is reluctant to talk about it."

"In what way was it terrifying? What happened?"

"She said the apparition—that's my word for it, not hers—the apparition told her that she was not supposed to survive the shipwreck. She was destined to die. He has laid claim to her, and he's angry that she has lived and thus blames this ship. So he has cursed it and everyone aboard."

The silence that followed for a time was broken only by the groan of the ship's timbers as the *Dobbin* lolled in the long ocean swells.

Bulloch gave a nervous chuckle, muttered something unintelligible, then cleared his throat, becoming solemn. "And does this so-called apparition have an identity or a name?"

Sullivan shook his head. "No, sir. She only knows him as the one who follows her."

12

Well before dawn, Tybee Light came into view, shining starkly above the dark western horizon, about twelve miles distant. Gunn made note of the time in the ship's rough log. He had seen the halo on the horizon for nearly half an hour and had altered the ship's heading toward it, but custom and protocol demanded that he wait until the light itself was visible to log the sighting. Bulloch had given orders to heave to offshore from the lighthouse until daybreak, waiting for the flood tide and good light to start the ship's fifteen-mile transit upriver.

The octagonal-sided lighthouse stood sentinel at the mouth of the Savannah River. Rising ten stories above the surrounding lowlands, the tallest lighthouse in Georgia was a prominent and familiar sight to bid hail or farewell whenever the *Dobbin* arrived to or departed from her homeport. A second fixed light, half as tall and about a thousand yards offshore, provided a range on which to steer toward safe water. Gunn sailed the ship to within three miles of the shoreline, in four fathoms of good water by the lead line, then ordered the helmsman to steer head to wind, backed the headsails, and lashed the helm hard over to windward to heave to and wait. He sent word to Bulloch of their arrival.

Overhead, the stars shone undimmed, and the night seemed interminable, though the eastern sky had turned a charcoal gray. It was near the end of his watch. Hands clasped behind his back, Gunn began pacing the quarterdeck from ship's wheel to mainmast. The routine activities of the fraught hours during the remainder of the midwatch had offered only brief, occasional respite from the near-constant disquiet that had occupied his mind since Sarah's eye-opening revelations. The tedium of waiting with the ship hove to did nothing to provide further relief. It occurred to him that his pacing directly above the cabin where she slept might disturb whatever rest Sarah or her father might be able to get. He stopped pacing and walked to the port rail, surveying the shoreline, where the fixed, unblinking eye of the lighthouse glared back at him.

Bulloch came up from the wardroom fully dressed, wiping the sleep from his eyes. "We've arrived sooner than I expected," he said. "Might as well drop the anchor. We'll be here a good hour before the tide changes and another half hour for enough light."

"Aye, aye, sir. Shall we signal for a pilot?"

Bulloch grinned wryly. "Oh, ye of little faith."

Gunn chuckled. "First time, and all, going upriver. As captain, I mean. Just thought I'd ask."

"And I thought we were friends."

Calling for Blake, Gunn gave the order to drop anchor and douse the sails, which the boatswain carried out, directing the movements of the watch section over the next quarter hour or so until all was secure. It was good for the men to have work to keep their minds from speculating about what they had heard from Dawkins, who no doubt by then had embellished beyond measure a story likely to become lore of the sea before long.

"How are the crew?" Bulloch asked.

"As you might expect," said Gunn. "Most seem to be all right, but some are a mite jumpy. I've heard more than one remark that they can't wait to be rid of these passengers. Seems to be a common sentiment."

"Understandable. But I hope you've taken the opportunity to disabuse them of such sentiment as mere superstition."

"Of course. But if they're jumpy about hearing from a ghost captain, just imagine their reaction to believing that the ship is now accursed."

"Which is why we are all three sworn to silence on that score. It never happened. Right, lieutenant?"

"Of course, captain."

Bulloch looked at the sky. "Wind's from the southwest. Hope it holds."

"The glass is steady."

"Good." Bulloch looked him in the eye. "And how are you doing, Andrew?"

"I'm not at all sure how to answer."

"Say what's on your mind."

Gunn focused on the lighthouse, which had grown quite familiar to him over the years, standing firm and real and resolute in the near distance. He thought for a moment, reviewing the incredible events of the past few days. "I mean, have you ever . . . ?"

Bulloch shook his head. "Never."

"It's almost as though we passed through that storm into a different place, a strange new world where things just don't make sense anymore, or at least the same way they used to."

"Don't make it out to be worse than it is."

"No, really, Des. Things are quite different. The reality we left is very different than the reality we're coming home to. Isn't it? At least it seems that way to me."

"It's enough that the crew is spooked, Andrew. Come now, I need you to keep your head about you."

"I understand. You asked me how I'm doing, and I'm trying to tell you. As a friend."

"All right, then. Fair enough. How are things different?"

"Well, the captain is dead, for one thing."

"True. These things do happen from time to time."

"Yes, of course. And in the grand scheme of things, it makes no great difference who captains this ship."

"Well, thanks a lot, friend."

"You know what I mean, Des."

"Yes, I do. Go on."

Gunn struggled to condense the myriad thoughts that had coursed through his mind, speaking slowly, deliberately. "In this case, his death could mean a great deal to you . . . and to me."

"Granted."

"It has the potential to change our lives."

"It probably will."

"Yes, to your advantage, perhaps. Not so much to mine."

"I told you that I will do whatever is in my power to help you."

Gunn detected a note of exasperation in Bulloch's voice. He raised a palm to head it off. "I have no doubt of that, Des, truly. When we left Savannah, however, things were very much in my favor. Things were looking up for me, in no little part due to you, of course. Now, as we're returning, my circumstances have become quite uncertain. You must admit that it's so."

"It is, though perhaps less so than you think."

"I wish I could believe that."

"You could. You might."

"And then we find this woman in the middle of the ocean who gives us a message from our dead captain. A warning to turn back."

"Now, that's where we must differ. What she said and what is real and true are two very different things. *Three* very different things, perhaps."

Gunn hesitated, weighing the next sentence in his mind, wary of its effect. "And then there's the curse."

"Now, Andrew, I'm going to stop you right there."

"You didn't see the fear in her eyes when she talked about it, Des. It was real."

"Of course it was. As was her nightmare, no doubt. But that fact doesn't have any bearing on our lives, Andrew. It is her nightmare, not ours. I won't let you go there. Get hold of yourself. I need you to stand firm, here, now. We are going home to the same reality that we left. We live in the real world, not some fantasy or fable or an imaginary dream-world full of ghosts and goblins. Nothing has changed except time and our material circumstances. Are you with me, man?"

Gunn looked at him and nodded, trying to reassure himself and

Bulloch at once. But he couldn't put to rest the disconcerting nature of the events he had witnessed. Bulloch had not seen and heard them the way he had.

Bulloch gripped his arm. "Are you *with* me?"

"I'm with you."

13

Morning broke over the Atlantic, and the *Dobbin* weighed anchor to wend her way up the river that connected the open sea to the city of Savannah. The wind remained favorable and the tide helpful, so the transit was without event, except for the prudent measures taken with the lead line to plumb the constantly shifting depths of the bends in the river where it meandered through the pied-green marshy lowlands.

Bulloch piloted the vessel with superb skill, anticipating the timely changes in course and sail trim necessary to stay in safe waters. Knowing the river as he did, no other pilot could have done better. Gunn admired his abilities as a seaman as much as he valued him as a friend.

The river, devoid of other traffic at this hour, straightened for a stretch of several miles to the northwest after the cutter passed Cockspur Island and Fort Pulaski. The favorable conditions allowed time for a quick, light breakfast. Daniel Sullivan joined the officers in the wardroom, except Grant, who remained on watch. Sarah did not attend, preferring to remain secluded in the cabin. Gunn inquired about her well-being.

"Sarah is not quite herself this morning, but she is feeling much better, thank you for asking," said Sullivan. "She sends her regards to all and begs your indulgence at her being indisposed."

"Not at all," said Bulloch.

"We are both very grateful to you for saving our lives, gentlemen. I do hope you know that," Sullivan said solemnly.

"We are privileged to do so, Daniel," said Bulloch. "It is our duty, certainly, but we count it as a privilege to be of service."

"Well, sir, duty or no, we both want to show our gratitude to you. We have discussed it and would be most honored if you would be our guests at a soiree to celebrate our safe return, say a week from Saturday evening. Will you come?"

Gunn and Bulloch exchanged glances. "Why, er, certainly," said Bulloch. "If you are up to hosting us, it would be our pleasure."

"Without question," said Sullivan with a broad smile. "We will look forward to seeing you both, I assure you. It's settled, then. We'll send invitations with our address."

Their guests kept to themselves throughout the remainder of the five-hour transit until the cutter arrived in the busy port of Savannah just before noon. Ships of every sort lined the wharves, sometimes two or three abreast, their masts rising like groves of trees all along the riverfront. Others were anchored in the river, awaiting a turn to load or unload in the constant stream of cargo and passengers. Bulloch expertly guided the ship under sail to an open berth at Moore's Wharf, too short for most cargo vessels, adjacent to the gaping maw between the brick-and-stone warehouses at the mouth of Bull Street.

As soon as the lines were secured to the wharf and the gangplank made fast, Sarah and her father appeared on the quarterdeck. She was dressed in her dampened finery, a little worse for wear, though without a bonnet, her hair plaited on top of her head. Her left hand lifted her skirts, and her right shielded her eyes from the high sun as she hurried across the quarterdeck and stepped lightly down to the main deck. She approached Gunn and Bulloch, both waiting at the gangway. Her father followed close behind.

As she lowered the shield from her eyes and extended her hand to Bulloch, she mouthed a few words of farewell, which were drowned out by the din of the waterfront and the incessant clamor of the nearby pumps, still being worked onboard by the sailors. Gunn and Bulloch leaned forward.

Bulloch took her hand gently in his. "I'm sorry, Miss Sarah, but I couldn't hear what you said."

She raised her voice, squinting up at him in the bright sunlight. "I said, thank you for your kind hospitality, captain."

Bulloch bowed his head. "I only regret we could not offer you more comfortable accommodations."

"Nonsense," she said, smiling. "We will always be most grateful to you all for what you did for us."

"Yes, thank you again," said Sullivan. "We are forever in your debt."

She turned to Gunn, again offering her hand. "I am very sorry for all the trouble we put you through. I'm so glad to leave it all behind us."

Gunn took her hand in his. It was warm and soft. "No trouble at all, Sarah."

She lightly pressed his hand, then removed hers. "I do hope you will visit us soon so we can properly thank you." Her tone was polite, reserved, almost demur, in the way a lady of refinement might extend an invitation. Her whole aspect was quite different from the previous night. Gunn tried to catch her eye, but she avoided looking directly at him, again sheltering her eyes from the sun. She turned to the gangplank and made her way across to the wharf.

Sullivan heartily shook both their hands. "I have no card to leave with you, but if I can ever be of service, gentlemen, do not hesitate to ask. Night or day. I trust we will see you both very soon."

"Thank you, Daniel. We will look forward to our next meeting with pleasure," said Bulloch.

Sullivan turned and crossed the gangplank to join his daughter. She put her arm in his, and together they walked across the narrow cobblestone quay and up the short rise, melting into the milling crowd beneath the deep shadows of the landing sheds.

Gunn turned his eyes back to the ship to find that the entire crew of twenty-two stood stock-still along the main deck, watching the pair recede. Even those at the pump handles had stopped to gawk.

"Back to work, men," said Gunn.

"Bos'n!" Bulloch called.

"Aye, sir," replied Blake from the foredeck.

"Get some men over the side to take a look at the bow. Stop the leaks as best you can."

Blake nodded curtly. "Aye, aye, sir."

Turning to Gunn, Bulloch lifted his cap and smoothed the matted blond hair beneath it. "I'd bet a month's pay we'll need a visit to the yards to fix her."

"I'd wager it'll take more than that, sir," said Gunn, peering back into the dusky, featureless shade between the countinghouses and trading rooms of the waterfront into which Sarah Sullivan had disappeared.

14

Elsewhere along the riverfront, many of the factors and warehouses were under construction, their owners and landlords busily adding stories to existing edifices or tearing down old structures to rebuild larger and newer ones to contain their growing businesses. More than a dozen steamers and three times that many tall ships lined the wharves, their masts towering over the muddy river. Longshoremen, a good number of them slaves, shouted and sang sea chanties to accommodate their backbreaking labor of loading and unloading pallets piled high with materials, merchandise, and dry goods.

Along the docks, draymen bellowed warnings and pushed their wagons and two-wheeled carts to and fro, laden with staples and sundries transiting into or out of the city. Passengers streamed up and down the gangplanks, wearily arriving after long voyages or eagerly anticipating imminent departures. Savannah's economy was booming now after years of stagnant cycles of anemic growth and decline, coinciding in part with several previous epidemics of malaria and yellow fevers.

These plagues, one after another, had stunted the growth of the population over the past decade, not to mention the hundreds who fled the city each year for safer climes during the long, hot summers, waiting for the safety of winter to return. When Gunn first arrived in the city in the fall of 1854, Savannah was recovering from a nasty bout of yellow fever that had decimated the population of roughly fifteen thousand. The streets, thoroughfares, and waterfront had lain destitute, almost devoid of commercial or community activity. He had been fortunate, though, to escape any serious illness since his arrival, a blessing for which he remained very thankful. Many others who came down from the North were not so fortunate.

For the past two years, the city had enjoyed a rebound in good health, due in part to efforts by the mayor and city aldermen to improve waterworks and sanitation. Annual deaths had decreased remarkably, a fact upon which Mayor Screven was most careful to remark in his annual reports. And thanks to investments in new railroad extensions westward beyond Macon to the Mississippi River, the port city had been thriving with the export of lumber, cotton, rice, and sugar, which came from all over the Southern states and were at present in high demand throughout the civilized world, especially Britain and France. In short, Savannah was in the midst of a marvelous, rejuvenating springtime.

At Moore's Wharf, where the *Dobbin* lay at her moorings, the new construction was largely complete. There was much to admire about the brick, granite, and limestone structures that had replaced the ramshackle wooden warehouses along the waterfront. The *Dobbin* occupied a prized berth, very close to the foot of Bull Street. The central thorough-fare of the city rose in a steep incline from the wharf. It extended between the buildings of the waterfront, beyond the steepled City Exchange to Bay Street, and from there straight through the middle of town. At the far corner of the intersection of Bull and Bay stood the new United States Customs House in all its splendor.

The Customs House, its massive colonnade and portico facing northward and fronting Bay Street, was one of the newest and grandest buildings in the city. The severe Greek Revival architecture, constructed entirely of gray granite, effectively demonstrated the growing power of the federal government over the state, as well as the city, as it was designed to do. It housed the federal courthouse and various agencies and bureaus, including the post office. Chief among them was the

Collector of Customs, a person of high distinction and importance among the citizens of Savannah, but particularly so to Bulloch and Gunn, who owed their allegiance, not to mention their livelihood, principally to him.

After seeing that the *Dobbin* was secure and shipshape, Bulloch and Gunn set off in the early afternoon to pay a call on the collector, both to report their arrival and to deliver the bad news of the death of Captain Dawes. Bulloch had urged Gunn to accompany him to attest to the circumstances of the captain's death, should there be any detailed questions, since Gunn was the officer on watch when the body was discovered.

In the warmth of the afternoon sun, they passed beneath the dappled shade of two newly planted live oaks along the promenade that lined the north side of Bay Street, or the Bay, as locals called it. As they walked, their light, casual banter noted the many continual changes that were taking place in the city, causing them to see things anew almost every time the ship sailed and returned. In addition to new buildings, the stone retaining walls, made mainly of cast-off ships' ballast, were nearing completion along the forty-foot-high riverbank to hold back constant erosion.

The two men observed other than physical changes, too. The liveliness of the place seemed to have increased just in the last three weeks of their absence. Though they had been home only a few hours, Gunn sensed a difference in the bearing of the people around him, on the wharves, on the promenade, in the entryways of businesses, at the intersection of streets. There was something in the air, an invisible, ineffable energy somewhat like the prelude to a summer lightning storm, when the taste and smell of it were palpable, even in stillness.

"Savannah is becoming more like Boston every day," said Gunn. "I've always enjoyed the slower, more gracious pace of life here. But it won't be long before that's ruined if things keep on booming. You won't be able to tell the difference between Bay Street and State Street in Boston before long, I'm afraid."

"That's because of all the grubby Yankee speculators moving in to take advantage of us poor Southerners," Bulloch joked. "Present company excluded, of course. No offense."

"I might be tempted to take offense if that were not a true statement. Hard to take offense at the truth. Cheer up, though. With any luck, there will soon be one less grubby Yankee around here for you to worry about, if I have anything to say about it."

Bulloch laughed. "One can hope. It's not just the Northern influences, though. There's something else going on here right now. A tension of some sort. Different. Can you feel it?"

They had reached the curb on the north side of Bay Street. In front of them, a dark-skinned elderly man hobbled across the street, leaning on the shoulder of a young boy, who carried a parcel on his back. They had misjudged the speed of a red wheeled piano-box buggy that bore down on them. The driver of the buggy saw them, but instead of slowing down to let them pass, he slapped the buggy whip on the haunches of the horse to urge her on. The mare started and broke into a canter. The old man and the boy barely escaped being run down in the street. They reached the curb just in time, wild-eyed and breathless.

Gunn reached out to steady the old man, whose ragged coat bore a slave's badge. "Are you all right?"

The old man lowered his eyes to the tops of his worn shoes. "Yassah, we's all right, I 'spect," he said quietly.

The man in the buggy guffawed over his shoulder and yelled, "Just like a stray dog. That oughta teach you." The buggy raced on.

Gunn inspected the boy. "How about you, son? Are you all right?"

The boy didn't answer but kept his eyes lowered to the ground like the old man.

"Just on our way back from the post office," said the old man. "Pay us no mind. Thank you, kindly. C'mon, grandson." He leaned on the boy's shoulder, and they shuffled toward the City Exchange.

Gunn faced Bulloch. "You mean tension like that?"

Bulloch nodded, watching the buggy career down the street into traffic. "I despise vulgarity in any man. Somebody should use that whip on him."

They stepped off the curb into the broad, cobbled street, dodging the lively two-way stream of wagons, cabs, and carriages as they crossed to the Customs House. Gunn paused before climbing the steep, immutable granite steps leading up to the massive iron doors of the main entrance.

The view impressed him to think how little their news would matter in the grand scheme of things, despite its significance to their small wooden ship. Their report was extraordinary and no doubt would have consequences, but what those would be he could hardly foretell, though he wished for such ability. The recurring thought ran through his mind that, despite his hopes, the captain was dead, along with his chances of returning home anytime soon. Even so, he was determined that, if given the opportunity, he would ask the man on the seat of power inside this building whether Captain Dawes had pressed his case to seek a transfer back home. Hope demanded no less, though his tread on the stone steps was heavy and slow, due in part to his impaired right leg.

"Coming?" Bulloch asked, turning toward him at the top of the steps.

"Of course," said Gunn, quickening his pace.

"Are you all right?"

"Yes."

"You look worried."

Gunn joined him on the top step. "I'm not."

"Good. Why worry?"

"Right."

"Try smiling."

Gunn forced a wide-eyed grin.

"Oh, Lord. That's worse. Now you look like you've lost your motley mind."

Gunn laughed.

"That's better. Come on, then."

15

They walked together through the center of the three open doors into the spacious gallery, at the far side of which rose a cantilevered double staircase, appearing to climb on thin air, leading to the federal courthouse on the upper floor. The counting-house and the offices of various customs officials, all of whom shared the purpose of sustaining and increasing the revenue of the federal government, lined the right side of the gallery. To the immediate left, two frosted glass doors led to the offices of the Collector and Deputy Collector of Customs. The doors opened to a vestibule. Inside, an officious-looking clerk sat at his desk, his pen poised over a ledger, spectacles lowered on the long, thin bridge of his nose. The clerk glanced up as they entered.

"How may I be of service, gentlemen?" he said, unsmiling.

"We've come to see Mr. Brinkman," said Bulloch, removing his cap. Gunn did likewise.

"Mr. Brinkman has a very busy schedule. Do you gentlemen have an appointment?"

"No, I'm afraid we do not, but I'm sure he'll want to see us," said Bulloch. "Would you please inform him that the commanding officer of the *Dobbin* is here to render a report?"

The clerk raised his brow. "Commanding officer, *indeed*. Where, may I ask, is Captain Dawes?"

Bulloch glanced at the polished nameplate fronting the clerk's rather spacious oak desk. "As it happens, ah, Mr. Tuttle, that is precisely what we've come to talk to Mr. Brinkman about. Now, would you please inform him that we are here?"

"Very well. Please have a seat, gentlemen. You may have to wait a while." Tuttle rose from his desk and scurried down the hallway to the closed door of the inner office. He knocked three times and entered, shutting the tall, eight-paneled oak door swiftly behind him.

Bulloch and Gunn sat in the empty chairs near the door and settled in to wait. In a moment, the clerk reappeared and swung the door wide. Two burly men in work clothes lumbered out, wiping sweat from their brows on their dusty sleeves.

"Mr. Brinkman will see you now," Tuttle said, ushering them to the inner sanctum, his disapproving, watery eyes peering over top his spectacles.

"Thank you, kindly, sir," said Bulloch.

He and Gunn rose from their chairs and entered the capacious, high-ceilinged office with large windows that looked out upon the busy street to the mast-lined port in the distance, beyond the City Exchange and Factors' Row. The grand office, though well-appointed with dauntless, claw-footed hardwood furnishings, appeared at the moment in disarray, the floor littered with crates, packing boxes, and straw. The paneled walls and bookshelves that lined them were stripped nearly bare. In front of the broad windows stood a majestic oak desk, large enough for two, behind which sat Mr. Josiah Brinkman, Collector of Customs, facing them in a swivel chair, where he remained seated.

"That will be all, Mr. Tuttle," he said. Tuttle bowed his head and exited, closing the door behind him without a sound, other than the click of the latch. "Gentlemen, do come in." Brinkman made no offer for them to be seated in the two leather-upholstered chairs in front of his desk. They stood, caps in hand. "Please excuse the mess. As you doubtless know, I am in the midst of vacating the office. We've just taken a well-deserved break from our labors. It is an almost overwhelming task, which I'm sure you can appreciate." Brinkman's gaze landed firmly on Gunn as he spoke, scrutinizing him from head to toe.

Gunn responded. "We were remarking on the walk over here, sir, how many changes in the city seem to be happening so swiftly and all at once. I, for one, did not anticipate this one, however."

"Nor did I," said Bulloch. "Was it the election, Mr. Brinkman?"

Brinkman inhaled sharply, shifting his gaze to Bulloch. "It was, indeed, Mr. Bulloch. At first, I thought President Buchanan would permit me to stay in this position, since we belong to the same party. I certainly hoped he would." He pouted, tilting his head. "However, he has his own people, and they have their own, and so on down the line. After he took office on the fourth of this month, the word came down from Secretary Cobb that I am to vacate the office by the end of this week. So it goes. I'm surprised you have not heard about it before now."

Bulloch's usually confident smile turned bemused. "Sir, the *Dobbin* was on patrol while all this was taking place. We have just now returned, so by what possible presumption should we have known of this change?"

Brinkman's voice turned hard and brittle. "I might ask by what brash presumption should you have presented yourself here today, Lieutenant Bulloch, as the commanding officer of the *Dobbin*? Furthermore, where, may I ask, is my good friend Captain Dawes?"

"Sir, Captain Dawes is dead, I'm dreadfully sorry to say. I am acting captain in his stead."

Stunned to silence, Brinkman furrowed his brow. His eyes narrowed. "Dead?"

"Yes, sir. I have the terrible duty to report his death onboard the *Dobbin* three days ago."

"How did he die, then?"

"Natural causes, best we could tell. He died in his sleep."

Brinkman scoffed. "Impossible. I knew the man like my own brother. Captain Dawes was healthy as a horse."

"We thought so, too. I don't know what else to say, sir."

"Where is the body?"

"We buried him at sea, sir. We had no means of preserving the body."

"Buried him at—" Brinkman's lips twisted into a thin smile. He chuckled softly. "How convenient for you."

Bulloch's jaw dropped. "Mr. Brinkman, I am at a loss—"

"Yes, of course. How convenient." Brinkman turned once again to Gunn. "And you, lieutenant, are doubtless here to back up this—this story, I suppose."

Gunn exchanged glances with Bulloch. "You need not take my word for it, sir. Mr. Bulloch's word should be entirely sufficient—"

"And you are?"

"Gunn, sir. Second Lieutenant Andrew Gunn."

"Gunn. Of course. You're the one who wants a transfer back up north."

"Yes, sir. That's right."

Brinkman laughed outright, curling his lips into a snarl. "Why should I believe the word of a subordinate, and a damned Yankee at that?" He peered down his nose at Gunn. "By the way, request denied, Mr. Gunn. I'll make that my last official act."

Gunn shifted his stance and tightened the grip on his cap.

Bulloch came to his defense. "Sir, that's not—"

"Not what, lieutenant? Not fair? Life isn't fair, is it? I think we all must come to terms with that fact sooner or later." His voice crescendoed. "And the fact is, the captain-commandant left the matter to *my* discretion." He beat his chest to emphasize his authority. "And what I say goes. That's what is fair in this room and on this day." The collector's chair complained as he settled back in it. He wiped the sweat from his upper lip. His voice quieted but still shook with emotion. "You can take it up again with my successor, if you like. You do happen to know, gentlemen, who will replace me as your new superior, do you not?"

Gunn shook his head, bewildered. "I'm sure I do not, sir."

"No idea," said Bulloch.

"His name is John Boston," sneered Brinkman, as though they should have known. "That name should please you no end, Mr. Gunn. Perhaps he will be more sympathetic to your cause."

His inference was obvious nonsense, drawn from the clouded well of the man's distressed mind, evident in his frenzied tone of voice. Gunn steadied himself and simply replied, "I do not know the man."

"Well then, perhaps you know his new deputy. His name is James Bulloch," said Brinkman, eyeing Bulloch. "No doubt you two are somewhat previously acquainted?"

"He is my cousin, sir," said Bulloch.

"And there it is. Our system of patronage is alive and kicking. It will serve you very well, I expect, in your new post, Mr. Bulloch. As I said, how convenient for you both. Although, come to think of it, the inquest will stir quite an interest for inquiring minds, I should imagine. Should be quite entertaining, indeed. I wouldn't miss it, to be sure." He pulled his large frame out of the chair and leaned heavily on the edge of the desk. "Now, I'm a very busy man. If you have a report to file, leave it with my clerk, and he will be sure my successor gets it." He waved his arm as though swatting a pesky gnat. "You are dismissed, *lieutenant*."

16

At the bottom of the steps to the Customs House, Bulloch stopped mid-stride. Gunn nearly ran into him. A perturbed passerby danced back and forth to avoid them, then slipped between the two men and proceeded on his way. Bulloch allowed him to pass out of earshot before speaking.

"Can you believe what just happened?"

"Stunner," said Gunn. "Beyond me to fathom. I don't know what to make of it. Folks around here truly seem to have their teeth on edge."

Bulloch glanced over his shoulder, down the street. "I could use a drink after that meeting. How about you?"

"It's a little early in the day, don't you think?"

"The sun's well over the yardarm, son. Come on."

Bulloch crossed Bull Street at a quickstep, dodging a freight wagon drawn by two mules that lumbered into the lane in a wide turn from Bay Street. The teamster cursed and checked the reins on the frothing mules, halting them in their tracks to avoid an accident.

"That's a damned good way to get killed," the teamster hollered, chucking the butt of his cigar into the street. "Y'all blind or something? Why don'tcha watch where ye'er a-goin'?"

Gunn waved an apology as he trotted in front of the mules to match his friend's pace, chasing Bulloch across the dusty thoroughfare. He heard the driver cluck to the mules and tell them to walk on as he reached the opposite curb.

The two strolled past the Clothing Emporium less than a block west to the City Hotel. There were finer establishments, but the Old Gray Lady boasted one of the most frequented barrooms in town, which served as a meeting place for those with business to do, from ships' captains to wealthy merchants and city aldermen. It was among the best places in Savannah to hear the raw news of the day, unfiltered by newspaper editors or the inhibitions of polite society.

Outside the entrance, several male passengers disembarked from a stagecoach, dusting their clothes before heading inside. One of the drivers eased several large suitcases from the luggage rack on the roof to the outstretched hands of a porter. Bulloch entered the shade of the portico and strode past the travelers to the front door. He grinned and winked as he held the door open for Gunn to enter.

"Things seem a mite strange of a sudden in this town. Now we'll find out what's really been going on since we've been gone."

They entered the hotel's high-ceilinged lobby. Its hardwood parquet underfoot showed wear in places. The reception desk to the left lined two-thirds of the wall, behind which a clerk asked how long the stay might be of the gentleman who stood before him. Comfortable chairs and a couch occupied the area in front of the large window facing the street.

To the right, a room opened to a richly carved mahogany bar trimmed in brass stretching the length of the wall, at the far left end of which rose the stairs to the three upper floors. A dozen round tables with low-backed chairs fronted another large window facing the street and skirted the bar. Around several tables, men drank, smoked, and conversed in low voices, punctuated by occasional laughter. A canopy of cigar and pipe smoke hung overhead. Three men stood at the bar. Bulloch motioned for Gunn to follow him.

Above the bar, a life-sized bust of the Marquis de Lafayette graced the ledge that ran its full length. The bust was a bad copy of a Houdon. The barkeep's name was Herbert, but many regular patrons thought that he resembled the bust above his head, so they called him Duke.

Gunn could never see the resemblance—or the logic, for that matter—except perhaps in the haughty eyes.

"A dram of your finest bourbon, Duke," said Bulloch as they found places at the bar.

"I'll have a beer," said Gunn.

Bulloch peered down at him through hooded eyes. "You'll do nothing of the kind, my friend. Bourbon is the truest solace for the troubled soul." He held up two fingers to the barkeeper.

"Bourbon it is," said Gunn.

Duke poured a finger of the amber liquid into each of two glasses and moved to put the bottle away. Bulloch held up a palm to stop him. "Leave it on the bar, my good man."

"Whatever you say," said Duke.

"Now then, perhaps you can enlighten us." Bulloch sipped his bourbon.

Duke's raised eyebrows furrowed his high forehead. "How so?"

"We've been at sea for almost a month. Something is different about this town since we left. Can't quite put a finger on it. What has happened in the meantime?"

"New president on the fourth," said Duke, wiping down the bar. "Lots of folks excited about that."

Bulloch shook his head. "No, I doubt that's it. We all knew about the election and expected that Buchanan would be taking office. Nobody will miss President Pierce, if you ask me."

"There's something else in the air, Duke," said Gunn. He took a sip of bourbon, which seared his throat so he couldn't say anything more. The warmth of it radiated through his chest.

Duke reached under the bar. "Well, let's see. Other folks is real excited about this here. Come out in all the papers last week, though the word had already spread around town like wildfire." He pulled out a folded copy of the *Savannah Daily News*, dated Thursday, March 12, 1857, dog-eared and well-thumbed. He placed it on the bar between them and tapped his index finger on a front-page headline.

Bulloch read it aloud. "Dred Scott Case Decided."

"It's all most people care to talk about these days," said Duke.

"What was the decision?" Gunn asked.

Duke scoffed. "You fellas really have been out of touch, haven't you?" He waved his hand over the newsprint. "Read it for yourself. Bottom line, the Supreme Court declared that negroes, be they slave or free, ain't citizens of these here United States. Said the Missouri Compromise is unconstitutional, and that Congress don't have the power to outlaw slavery anywheres."

Bulloch gave a low whistle, then took another sip of bourbon as he read through the article. "That's what it says, all right. Well, no wonder, then."

Gunn snatched the newspaper from him and began reading. "I'll be dipped. It can't be so. But I guess it is. I'm looking right at it, aren't I?" His voice rose in astonishment as he spoke.

A man at a nearby table pushed back his chair and stood unsteadily. "Gentlemen!" his voice boomed. "Gentlemen, I give you the honorable Chief Justice of the Supreme Court, Roger Brooke Taney. May God preserve the honorable court."

A general cheer went up in the bar and resounded in the lobby among the travelers. "Hear, hear!" One of the other men at the table jumped to his feet and echoed, "To Chief Justice Taney!"

Gunn looked up from the newspaper into the face of a tall, well-dressed, distinguished-looking man, grinning broadly through a full black beard. The man looked around the room and then straight at him, offering a toast with an outstretched hand, sloshing whiskey from his glass.

"Won't you gentlemen in uniform join us in a toast?"

Gunn offered a placating smile in return. "We don't—"

"Come, now. I insist. To the chief justice."

Bulloch elbowed him and raised his glass. "To Chief Justice Taney."

Gunn straightened his back and raised his glass. "And to the United States of America." He drained the bourbon in a single gulp and gritted his teeth as it went down.

The man lowered himself to his seat, eyeing Gunn warily. He reached for a bottle to refill his glass, spilling half the whiskey on the table as he poured.

Gunn turned his back to the man and whispered to Bulloch, "Who was that man? Do you know him?"

"None other than Charley Lamar. Charles Augustus Lafayette Lamar, to the likes of you and me. Owns a bank and a steamship company, among other things. He's one of the so-called Fire-Eaters." Bulloch refilled both their glasses. "You don't want to tangle with him, Andrew. He has been known to throw down the gauntlet over far less than a refused toast."

Gunn chuckled. "Lamar, eh? Are you saying he would call me out? That's insane. He's obviously in his cups."

"He's called out several men."

"Are you joking?"

"Do I look like I'm joking?" Bulloch's face was solemn. "He's done so in this very bar. Pistols at dawn down by the river. That sort of thing."

A moment later, Lamar was at his elbow, with another man beside him, a short, stoutly built fellow with a flattened nose and a scar above one eye.

Lamar poked Gunn's shoulder. "You didn't like my toast, mister?"

Gunn stood to his full height. "I don't care one way or the other who you drink to. It's a free country."

"That so?"

"Last I checked."

"Maybe you should check again, young fella. Where are you from? Not from around here, I take it."

"I'm from just outside Boston."

Lamar swayed on his feet. "A Yankee. I figured as much."

Bulloch shouldered himself between the two. "He's with me, Mr. Lamar. This man is an officer on my ship."

"Yeah? And what are you doing down here, Yank? You some sort of spy or something? Or just come all this way to tell us poor hicks how to live our lives?"

"I don't want no trouble today, fellas," said Duke.

"Not to worry, Duke," said Bulloch. "We don't want none, either. Believe me, we've had our fill for one day."

"No trouble, Duke. No tr-trouble," belched Lamar. He turned a bleary eye on Gunn. "Don't like Yanks much. Better watch your step. I've got my eye on you, sonny boy."

Gunn smirked. "Which one of me?"

"That's quite enough. Let's leave it there, shall we, Mr. Lamar?" Bulloch placed a hand on each of Lamar's shoulders and pressed him away.

Lamar shook him off. "Get your hands off me. See here, what's your name, Yank?"

"Gunn."

"Gunn, is it? Well now, let me give you a little friendly advice, Mr. Gunn. Me to you."

"What would that be?"

"See to it that you don't let your name be your undoing."

"What is that supposed to mean?"

"You're a bright young lad. Figure it out."

"Why don't you explain it to me, so there's no mistake?"

Lamar turned to his companion. "Mark him down in your book, Donnelly. Remember this one. Don't forget his ugly face." He tottered back to his table and sat down heavily. Donnelly raised an eyebrow, licked his lower lip, and followed close behind.

Bulloch took Gunn by the arm and whispered hoarsely in his ear. "I'm telling you, Andrew, watch your step with him. What will you do if he does call you out?"

"He's bluffing."

"I wouldn't bet deuces on it."

"Are you serious?" said Gunn. "In this day and age? Dueling is against the law, even in Georgia, isn't it?"

"It has been for a long time, but that doesn't mean it doesn't happen every now and then." Bulloch drilled a forefinger into the bar to make his point. "Folks around here still get right peculiar about their honor being offended. Always have. When was it, Duke? Ten, maybe fifteen years ago or so, two lieutenants of our own service, both of the Revenue Cutter *Crawford*, I believe, had their own little skirmish in this very bar. Right over there." Bulloch pointed toward the front door.

Duke nodded. "Forty-one, it was."

"Shot each other point-blank over a stupid argument. Of course, they'd both had a few drinks. One called the other a liar and a drunkard, or some such. Hot words turned to lead. Shipmates, no less. And I'm telling you, it still happens."

Gunn stared at the door, trying to picture the incident.

"Were they killed?"

"No, but the first lieutenant was wounded pretty badly in the chest, so the story goes. A bullet glanced off the second lieutenant's hard head. He was just knocked silly. Or sillier than before. Both lived to tell of it, from what I've heard."

Gunn grinned. "The second lieutenant must have been the more levelheaded, I expect."

"Hardheaded is more likely. Same as you."

"Maybe so. I might be hardheaded, but anybody who can't see that this Dred Scott decision is nothing to celebrate is soft in the head." Gunn nodded toward Lamar. "Like that one."

"I'm hoping it might very well put the whole slavery issue to bed all night and for good."

"Now, I know you're joking, Des. You cannot be serious."

"Dead serious."

"I'm not looking for another argument. But I think you're dead wrong on that one."

"One can hope. You'd better hope so, too, my friend. Otherwise, we'll likely have more than just a bar fight on our hands. And I, for one, wouldn't want to be forced to choose sides in it. Anyhow, I thought you said you didn't want to argue." Bulloch raised his near-empty glass and flashed a winsome smile. "To shipmates."

"Shipmates."

17

Three invitations arrived by courier at the ship two days later, addressed in a bold, elegant hand. Gunn was on duty aboard the *Dobbin* when they arrived. He opened the one addressed to him as soon as the quartermaster delivered them.

Mr. Jay Daniel Sullivan, Esquire
and Miss Sarah Sullivan
request the pleasure of your company
at a soirée to be held in honor of the
officers and men of the Revenue Cutter Service
on Saturday, March 28, 1857 at eight o'clock
at the place of our residence,
in celebration of our safe return home
from the clutches of the sea.

Underneath the formal invitation was a scrawled post-script in the same handwriting. *I do so fervently hope you will come. Sarah.* The back of the envelope was embossed with an address on Jones Street, which Gunn recognized as being among the most desirable in Savannah.

Gunn placed the invitation in an inside pocket and glanced up to see

Bulloch striding down the wharf toward the gangplank. He called to the boatswain. "Blake, the captain's approaching."

Blake nodded and directed four seamen to act as side boys at the gangway. He withdrew his nickel pipe from a breast pocket, placed it to his lips and blew a long trill to announce the captain's arrival. The quartermaster struck the ship's bell four times.

Bulloch mounted the gangplank and saluted the national ensign at the stern as he came aboard. He did not appear to be in the best of moods. His head was bowed and his step lacked its usual bounce. He strode across the quarterdeck, where Gunn snapped a salute.

Bulloch returned it. "Mr. Gunn, I'll see you in the cabin, if you please."

"Aye, aye, sir." Gunn followed him down the ladder.

He handed Bulloch his invitation. "This came for you today."

"Ah. That was quick. Did you get one?"

"Yes, I did. So did Mr. Grant." He displayed the third envelope.

"Well now, one of us will have to stay aboard. And I can tell you it won't be me."

"I'll stay," said Gunn.

"Work it out between you and Grant, but I daresay Sarah Sullivan will be mighty disappointed if you don't show up."

"I doubt it."

Bulloch smirked. "Doubt it all you want to. I know women."

"How did your meeting go with Mr. Boston?"

"Not as well as I had hoped. He was a sight more reasonable than Brinkman, I will say. No nonsense, though. By-the-book sort of fellow. He accepted my report readily enough but with the caveat that there must be a formal inquiry into the death of Captain Dawes. I certainly agree, and that doesn't concern me in the least. However, he received a telegram this morning from the collector in Charleston." He paused and sat at the table, motioning for Gunn to join him. "Apparently, a ship arrived there yesterday, a packet ship from Liverpool, carrying a dozen or so survivors of the *Gloriana* shipwreck. They had been in a lifeboat for several days. Three of their company were dead from exposure. The rest were nearly so."

"There were more survivors. Sarah was right, then."

"That's not the worst of it. The first mate was one of the survivors. He claims they saw a ship on the first day after the shipwreck and tried to signal their attention. Says they were close enough to see the flag, though it was at dusk. No doubt it was an American topsail schooner."

Gunn sat quietly, looking at his lap. "We left them."

"Yes. I told Mr. Boston it was very likely the *Dobbin* they saw."

"What did he say?"

"He was not pleased but said he understood. He asked some very pointed questions about our situation and my decisions."

"I could go talk to him. I'd be happy to."

Bulloch shook his head slowly, staring at the table. "They were my decisions. Mine alone."

A half minute passed before either of them stirred. The bilge pumps squealed and thumped in the distance, as they did every quarter hour or so, to keep up with the leak in the hull. Bulloch crossed his legs, reached inside his tunic, and pulled out a cigar. He offered it to Gunn.

"Want one?"

Gunn took the cigar. "Thanks."

Bulloch retrieved another from his pocket, produced a cutter, and snipped the cap. He handed the cutter to Gunn, who took it and did the same.

"You know, I bought these at the City Exchange on the way to the meeting because I hoped we might have something to celebrate. Best I could afford. Real Havanas." Bulloch struck a match from the box on the table and held it to the end of his cigar, toasting it lightly, watching the flame darken the tobacco. Then he placed the cigar in his mouth and lit it, puffing until the flame leapt and smoke streamed from the glowing tip. He blew out the flame with a breath of smoke and tossed the smoldering matchstick on the table. "But I doubt we will now."

Striking a match, Gunn replicated the ritual. He had only started smoking cigars in the past year at Bulloch's urging. He said it helped him think, especially when he wanted to do anything else but think. Gunn had come to agree. Over time, their moments together over a smoke had somehow deepened the bond between them.

Gunn rolled the lit cigar between his fingertips. "How could she have known?" he muttered.

They smoked in silence for a while. The cigar tasted of cocoa with a hint of pepper. Gunn took a deep draw and let the smoke—rich, lazy, and aromatic—roll from his lips.

"Did you and Mr. Boston happen to talk about anything else?" Gunn asked.

"We didn't discuss your situation, if that's what you're asking," Bulloch said. "Best leave that until my cousin arrives next week. I'm guessing he might be a very good advocate. Can't hurt. Besides, I think I have a plan that might just work."

"A plan?"

"Of sorts. Not perfect, of course. Better than none." He sighed a stream of smoke that curled and climbed toward the skylight overhead. "I mentioned the need to haul the ship to repair the leak up forward."

"You mean put her in drydock?"

Bulloch shook his head. "Marine railway down at Willink's on the east end. Cheaper and faster. Boston approved that idea. Not that we have any choice, mind you." His drawl deepened, and his eyes took on a conspiratorial gleam as he relaxed into his chair. "Anyways, I figure it will take at least three weeks to do the job, the way those fellas work. There wouldn't be much for a second lieutenant to do while we're hitched up. It might be a good time for you to take some leave and head up north for a spell. At least we can do that much."

Gunn sat upright. "Do you mean it?" He felt light-headed, as though from strong drink, unsure whether it was the cigar or the news that caused the sensation.

"Let's see how things play out. Wait for James to get here. We'll work on it together."

"Well, that is something to celebrate. I will be forever grateful, my good captain, if you can manage to bring that about."

"Belay the captain talk, Andrew. I mean it, now. And please instruct the watch accordingly. No more side boys and bells. I would say the prospects for me are fairly dim on that score, under the circumstances. At least for the time being."

18

From time to time, when his duties allowed a brief absence from the ship, Gunn stayed in town at the home of his mother's only living relatives. They were two sisters, whose father had arrived from Wales on the same ship with his grandfather more than half a century earlier. Julia Gryffith, the younger of the sisters by two years, had chosen to remain unmarried all her life after being jilted at the altar by the only man she had ever loved. She lived with her sister Josephine—called Josie by those closest to her—whose wealthy husband, John Moore, had died of heart failure ten years earlier. Josie owned the large three-story townhouse on Perry Street they now shared, just off Chippewa Square. Her two sons were grown with families of their own, living in Charleston and Atlanta.

For the past fifteen years, the two had shared the same roof, though they differed greatly in their dispositions. In fact, they had been known to disagree quite often, at times making it difficult for them to remain in the same room for any length of time more than necessary to exchange pleasantries. They never disagreed, however, about their mutual, abiding love for Gunn's mother and their equal dislike, even animosity, for his father, who had married their dear cousin in Massachusetts almost three decades ago, only to abandon her to raise three children alone.

Other than his friend Bulloch, these two sexagenarian women were the only people in the entire city of Savannah who cared very much at all about Gunn's well-being. They kept a room for him in the townhouse, available whenever he should choose to stay. He was grateful for their hospitality and for the opportunity to save a little money toward the day when he could afford his own place in town, should he not get his wish for a transfer. Above all, he had come to love them dearly over the past two years, especially for their frank honesty about almost everyone and everything of consequence that touched their lives, or his for that matter. He certainly never doubted at any time where he stood with them, which he found most refreshing these days and increasingly rare.

Julia met him with a smile at the door when he arrived on Saturday morning. She held a letter in one hand and spectacles in the other. Gunn greeted her with a light kiss on the cheek.

"Good morning, Cousin Julia."

"I was sitting in my chair, there by the window, and I saw you crossing the street. It's so good to see you, Andrew. Come in, come in. I was just reading a letter from your mother."

Gunn removed his cap. "Oh? Does she yet remember me?" He laid his cap on top of his canvas kit near the staircase, alongside his hand-carved shillelagh, a prized gift from his former crew, which he often used on long walks about town.

"Oh, you. What a silly question. You know she hardly writes of anyone else, other than your sister." She led him into the richly furnished parlor. "Come, sit down on the settee. Make yourself comfortable."

"Is Cousin Josie at home?"

"Yes, I expect she is upstairs. Let me send for her. She will want to know you are here, of course." She reached for a bell on the table beside her and rang it. Presently, Mrs. O'Reilly, the housekeeper, appeared in the doorway.

"Yes, Miss Julia?"

"Would you please let Mrs. Moore know that our cousin is here?"

"Of course. Good morning, Mr. Andrew." Her warm smile welcomed him as one of the family.

"Good morning, Fanny."

"Shall I prepare a room as well?"

Julia eyed the belongings that Gunn had dropped near the staircase. "Are you staying, Andrew? I do hope you will."

"Yes, I'll stay until Monday, if that's all right."

"Why, you know it is. Please do prepare the room for him, Mrs. O'Reilly."

"Of course, Miss Julia." The housekeeper picked up Gunn's cap and bag and climbed the staircase to the second floor.

Gunn settled into the comfort of the settee. "So what news from Concord?"

"Well now, I was just reading this letter for the second time. It came a few days ago, but I just wanted to read it again to make sure I hadn't misunderstood anything. The news is quite unusual, to be sure."

"Is that so? Not bad news, I hope. Is everything all right?"

"Your mother is fine, dear, in very good health. Not to worry. By the way, she sent a letter to you as well, which arrived at the same time, so some of this news may be repeated there. Perhaps in more detail."

"What is it, then?"

Josephine's uneven tread sounded on the stairs, accompanied by the steady thump of her cane. Her voice rang out. "Andrew, is that you?"

"Yes, Cousin Josie. Home from the sea."

"Ah, good. Now, wait just a moment while I join you, won't you? I don't want to miss a word."

"Of course, dear," said Julia, winking at Gunn. "Take your time, no hurry."

Josie descended the stairs slowly. "I daresay if I were to take my time, dear sister, you'd have sung the amen before I could find the right pitch." She wheezed as she took several more stairs, one by one, descending to the main floor. She paused at the bottom of the staircase to adjust her tinted glasses, slipping low on her nose.

Julia's face reddened as she folded the letter and placed it alongside her spectacles on the table. Gunn rose to greet Josie with a kiss on each cheek at the bottom of the staircase. He offered his arm and escorted her to a nearby armchair before resuming his seat.

"Now, then," said Josie, resting her cane against the arm of the chair. "Where in the world have you been these last few weeks, young man?"

"Our ship was on winter patrol, Cousin Josie. We were cruising the shipping lanes, searching for vessels in distress. Last week, we got caught in a major nor'easter, which swept us quite a ways out to sea. At least one ship was lost in the storm, I'm sad to say. We arrived home this past Wednesday. I would have paid a call earlier, but I had to remain on the ship until today, when the captain granted me a few days' leave. So here I am."

"Well, we are very glad to know that you are safe," said Julia. "We do worry so while you are away at sea, especially when weeks go by without word."

"That's very kind. As you can see, I am safe and sound and no worse for wear. Others were not so fortunate, I'm afraid."

"You say a ship was lost at sea," said Josie. "Were there survivors?"

Gunn nodded. "Some. We picked up two, a man and his daughter. Another ship recovered a lifeboat with about a dozen others, apparently from the same vessel, the *Georgiana*, a British steamship out of Liverpool. They were all very fortunate to survive."

"Anyone we might know?"

"Well, I'm not sure. The man we rescued is named Sullivan. Jay Daniel Sullivan. His daughter is in her early twenties, I expect. Her name is Sarah. Sullivan seemed to remember my mother and Aunt May."

Josie sat straight up in her chair. "Daniel Sullivan?"

"Yes. Do you know him?"

"Well, I can't say I know him, but I certainly know of him," said Josie. She waved her hand, then reclined again in her chair, gazing out the front window into the distance.

"Who is he?"

Josie turned her head toward him, eyebrows raised, the emerald-green lenses of her glasses eyeing him squarely. "Only the man your mother should have married instead of that no-account vagabond free-thinker she chose to hitch herself to."

"Oh, come now, Josie," said Julia.

"It's true," said Josie. "And you know it, Sister."

"That's all water under the bridge. They were very good friends at one time, it's true."

"Good friends, my arthritic left foot."

"Wait just a minute," said Gunn. "Are you suggesting they had a relationship? My mother and Daniel Sullivan?"

Both women remained quiet, avoiding his gaze, which alternated between them.

"Well?"

"Perhaps you should ask your mother about that," Julia said presently.

"I'm not suggesting anything," said Josie. "I'm saying it outright."

19

The two women were reluctant to say anything more, asserting that it was his mother's prerogative to tell the story, if she chose to. Julia tried repeatedly to change the subject, taking up his mother's letter to share her latest news, but he insisted the news could wait. Josie threatened twice to leave the room if he did not relent in his attempts to persuade them. His persistence finally paid off, however, when he teased them that he had every mind to leave and go back to the ship without further word, worry or no, only to return when they agreed to share with him what they knew.

"What do you know of your grandfather?" Josie finally said.

"Hardly anything. Mother rarely spoke of him. I met him a few times, but we never spoke of anything important."

"I thought as much. Well, I suppose we should begin there."

Julia nodded in agreement. "As good a place as any."

"By all means," said Gunn. "Begin somewhere."

"Your grandfather, our uncle Alexander, was a hard man," said Josie. "A good man, a resilient man, mind you, but hard. And proud. He started a trading company as a young man but went bankrupt due to a bad investment in railroad stocks. I've forgotten which railroad just now, but if you'll give me a moment, I'll likely remember. Anyway, he had a rocky start, and it hardened him where it mattered. He made and lost more than one fortune in his life. He was good with numbers but bad with money, you might say. Many disappointments."

"Seems to be an inherited trait. Describes my mother fairly well."

"Be that as it may. He and your grandmother married much later than our father, which is why your mother and Aunt May are nigh a decade younger than we are, though we're still more like sisters than cousins."

"I've always thought so," said Julia.

"Julia, if you are going to keep interrupting me, we'll be here until the Resurrection."

"Why don't you let me tell the story, then? I think you're missing the whole point, anyway. Headed down a rabbit hole with a short match, as usual."

"Very well, then, go ahead. Long as you don't mind my correcting you now and then. You always get the facts wrong. Start making things up out of thin air."

"Would it matter if I did mind?"

Josie sniffed. "Go on, Sister."

Just as well. Julia's voice had a pleasant, lyrical quality to it, like gentle waves at sea rising and falling, whereas Josie's was flat calm, without perturbation.

"When she came of age, your mother began keeping the books for your grandfather. He taught her what she needed to know, since he had no sons to take it up. None that lived, anyway. His firstborn was a boy, also named Alexander, but he died at eleven months, which just about crushed him, you know. Well, Eleanor liked the work. Took to it like a June bug on a rosebush. It was unusual—some might say undignified— for a young woman to get involved in such things. She liked that, too. Said she didn't care much for what other people thought, as long as she could do whatever pleased her."

"Are you sure you're talking about my mother?"

"Of course I am. Let me finish, now. By that time, her father had become quite successful again, you know. He hired Daniel Sullivan as one of his attorneys to advise him on expanding some overseas trade. Daniel was a young lawyer back then, just starting out, but he had quickly gained a reputation as a good one. Quite successful, he was. And that's how they met."

Josie sputtered. "There's—well, there's just a whole lot more to it than that, Julia."

Julia sighed. "Of course there is, Josie, but I'm trying to get to the important part."

"Go on," said Gunn.

"Daniel Sullivan had a keen eye for beauty. And your mother had that in spades, which was the least of her good qualities. She always enjoyed the company of men, far more than she did women. Especially older men, who knew what they were about. So there was a mutual attraction from the start. Daniel tried to court her, and she was very happy about that, and you might say she set her cap for him."

"Was she in love with him?" Gunn asked.

"'Course she was," Julia said.

"Pish," said Josie. "They hardly knew each other. Who can say?"

"She told me she did. And that he loved her." Julia nodded once for emphasis. "But she was very young, wasn't she? The heart is deceitful above all things, as the prophet says. Who can know it? Love especially is such a fickle thing. And I should know all about that, shouldn't I? One day he does, next day he doesn't." With a careless shrug, she pretended to pluck a daisy and toss the petals aside. "I've always thought she was just looking for a way to get out from under an overbearing father. Not that I ever would have blamed her." She shook her head and waved an open palm in the air. "But I'm getting ahead of myself. Whether she did or didn't, her father—your grandfather—would have none of it. As far as he was concerned, courting could only lead to one thing, and he said in no uncertain terms that their marriage would happen over his dead body. Daniel had very little means at the time, you see, which made him unacceptable as a suitor. Not only so, but he was a Catholic, and your grandfather came from a long line of dissenters. In no wise was he ever going to think about leaving any part of the fortune that he had worked so hard to build to 'an upstart papist pettifogger,' as he put it." She waved her arms, emphasizing the words as she spoke, as though mimicking his grandfather.

Gunn shrugged. "So nothing ever came of it."

"Well now, here is where the axe meets the apple tree. As I said, your grandfather was a hard man, very strict, and with a temper to boot. The only freedom he ever granted either of his girls was to allow Eleanor to keep the books. And that hadn't worked so well to his advantage, so far as he could see. Eleanor was just as stubborn and hardheaded. She was determined to have her way. Above all, she wanted the freedom to seek her own happiness. At least, that's what she confided to me. After all, their father already had allowed May, who was two years younger, to marry that rake of a sea captain, Billy Bones Mitchell. Had I mentioned that? Now, then, Captain Mitchell owned an admiral's fleet of ships and had money falling out of his pockets, though, didn't he?" She shook an index finger in the air.

"Who is headed down a rabbit hole now?" Josie snipped. She removed her glasses and polished them on a handkerchief. Her clouded eyes, almost as opaque as the tinted lenses of her glasses, revealed nothing of the impatience in her voice.

"I am not. This is the point, after all. As the elder daughter, Eleanor claimed her right to marry and to court whomever and whenever she pleased. So, she and Daniel started sneaking around behind her father's back to see each other. Well, didn't he find out about it, and right soon? He was mad as the dickens, too, don't you doubt it. He told Eleanor that if they didn't stop seeing each other, he would throw her out and cut her off without a bent penny to her name. And he'd do everything in his power to see to it that Daniel Sullivan was ruined. Her mother, bless her soul, tried to intervene, but there would be no *troi rownd*, as far as he was concerned."

Gunn squinted. "*Troi rownd*?"

"About turn. His Welsh mind was set. The die was cast. That was it." She stopped, as though uncertain how to proceed, staring at her hands, folded in her lap.

Josie replaced her glasses and resumed the story. "There was a huge row. Our own father told Uncle Alexander that he was being unreasonable and that Daniel had already proven his worthiness as a man, as worthy as himself had ever been. Alexander said that any man who had the temerity to go behind his back and the impertinence to disregard his wishes was not worthy of anything but scorn. He told our father to mind his own business, and they stopped talking. Didn't speak for years after that. Anyway, Eleanor decided that rather than risk any harm to Daniel, she would leave of her own accord. She booked passage on one of Bill Mitchell's ships and went to live with her sister in Boston. And that's where she met your father."

Julia escaped her reverie. "They'd only known each other for two months before your father asked her to marry him. He claimed he loved her for herself alone, regardless of her worldly possessions. She agreed right away, without a second thought. Married to a minister, of all things, and poor as church mouse. Imagine how that set with your grandfather. True to his word, he cut her off without a penny. Said she'd made her bed of mud and straw and was welcome to lie in it with whomever she chose. Just as she wished."

Gunn sat quietly, picking at some lint on his uniform trousers, trying to imagine the young woman, headstrong, defiant, full of vim and vigor, who eventually was to become his mother and none of those things. No wonder. He had seen with his own eyes and didn't need to imagine what marriage to an unfaithful, lying, double-minded, degenerate man could do to a woman and her children over time. The consequent heartaches and hardships for them all had proven hard, perhaps impossible, to forgive. He was still trying to forgive what he could not forget. He could only utter a short phrase in response to the sad story, one that he'd never heard told until now.

"Two months?"

20

Whether his mother and Jay Daniel Sullivan had once loved each other held less importance to him than the fact that whatever relationship they had shared was the cause of her leaving home and family to seek happiness elsewhere. It so happened that happiness had eluded her, even so. He could not help thinking about what might have happened if she had stayed in Savannah all those years ago. Would she have been any happier? Of course, he would not be here if that were the case. It was a lot to take in all at once.

Josie and Julia implored him to join them for something to eat. Despite their Welsh ancestry, they had adopted the Southern custom of serving the main meal of the day just after noon, calling it dinner. Gunn had no appetite for a large meal, however. He elected instead to take a walk to sort things out and asked to be excused. They both said they understood and encouraged him to go.

He changed into a comfortable suit of clothes that he kept for convenience in his room on the third floor, tucking into his breast pocket the letter from his mother, along with two others awaiting him at the townhouse. One was from his sister, Marguerite, and the other from Elizabeth. No doubt all three contained tidings that would help entertain and distract his troubled thoughts.

Taking his shillelagh in hand, he donned a soft cap and headed out the door and down the steps of the town-house. In the splendor of the warm spring sunshine, he walked half a block east along Perry Street to Chippewa Square, where newly planted live oaks offered stippled shade to shrubs of azaleas in bloom. The gnarled evergreen live oaks were a welcome change to the dense groves of chinaberry trees they recently had displaced, many of which had been damaged in a hurricane several years earlier. It was no great loss since chinaberry trees dropped their leaves in fall and winter months and littered the ground with remnants of foraging by huge flocks of birds, gorging themselves on the berries, sometimes to the point of drunkenness. It was easy to imagine that the oaks, planted by attentive neighbors to beautify the grounds, would one day grow to a stately height, bringing greater charm to an already charming city. They beckoned him to rest a while on the grass beneath their outstretched boughs, but he pressed on, turning south on Bull Street.

The layout of the streets appealed to Gunn, though very different from the familiar narrow, winding streets of Boston that followed the routes of old cow paths and worn indigenous traces. From the beginning, the streets and avenues of Savannah had been designed in grids and open squares, carving order and purpose out of what once had been rambling lowland scrub and swamps. A few of the main thoroughfares were paved, either with macadam or wood planks, but most were of sand, which slowed the travel of coaches and wagons to an easy pace. Likewise, most of the people Gunn met on his frequent strolls away from Bay Street through the more tranquil parts of town seemed to be in no hurry, though not without purpose, especially in the hot summer months, when they walked only where and when necessary.

The activity in the alluring treelined lanes, fronting tidy row houses and elegant brick, stucco, or wood frame dwellings of two and three stories, along with the occasional shops or restaurants, spoke at once of ambition and resolve on one hand, grace and indolence on the other—a strange, even exotic combination, to be sure. Of course, like any thriving city, it had seedy, undesirable areas, too, with numerous liquor shops, brothels, and rough boardinghouses, where it was not safe to walk, even in daylight. However, those areas were isolated to the northwest and northeast quadrants, especially east of Habersham Street, and easily avoided unless one had a mind to go looking for trouble or lacked the means to escape it.

He hadn't walked but a few minutes when he came upon one of his favorite spots on Bull Street, the Boar's Head, a replica of a British public house, where he often liked to eat and enjoy a pint of ale. Curious to read the news contained in the letters in his pocket, he sat at one of the empty tables outside.

The street was busy with merchants and shopkeepers going about their labors. Women with bright parasols strolled by, stopping to point into the nearby shop windows and marvel at the wares. Gunn leaned his walking stick against an empty chair, stretched his legs beneath the table, and leaned back in his seat to enjoy the warmth of the afternoon sunshine. Occasionally, a passerby nodded or offered a polite greeting and a smile, as if to acknowledge his pleasant state of leisure. After a moment, a stout, beefy waiter appeared to take his order. Gunn intended to continue his walk, so he limited himself to a half-pint pour and a plate of fruit and cheese. The fare promptly arrived, not long after he opened the first of the letters, the one from his mother.

The news from home, which Cousin Julia had never gotten around to sharing, was not as shocking as she had led him to believe, at least not to him, but it was unusual and unexpected. It was not shocking because it involved his sister, Marguerite, whose high-spirited antics had long since ceased to surprise him. In many ways, she reminded him of the young woman that his mother apparently once had been—headstrong, full of life and vitality, defying convention. He was finally beginning to understand the source of his sister's most defining qualities.

His mother wrote that Marguerite had decided without fanfare or fuss to leave the comforts of home with their mother in Concord and move to New York City, where she might more effectively pursue her passion to become a widely published, renowned writer. She intended to live with their father, who had recently moved there. Unlike Gunn, Marguerite had remained in contact over the years with their father, who continued to dote on his only daughter, as he always had. His mother expressed a degree of measured understanding and support about her decision but was mainly concerned for the safety and well-being of her young daughter in a city notorious for ruinous behavior. Not to mention the fact that her former husband was not the best of influences. Gunn knew that, if nothing else, living with their father would afford some measure of security while allowing ease and near-absolute freedom of movement, which was what his sister truly wanted above anything else.

Gunn paused to take in the news. A small black-and-tan terrier trotted by, stopping to beg a morsel. He tossed the dog a piece of cheese, caught in midair before it hit the ground. The dog stood on hind legs and placed two paws on Gunn's thigh. He offered another slice of cheese, which was accepted gratefully. The waiter happened by.

The waiter frowned. "Sir, the proprietor would not look kindly on feeding strays from the table."

Gunn grinned. "My apologies. The poor fella looked hungry." He gently removed the dog's paws from his leg and sent him on his way. "That's all, friend. Go on now. Be off with you." The dog looked back once, tongue lolling, and scampered on down the sidewalk.

He resumed reading, skimming the remainder of the letter, which offered tidbits of news from Concord as well as tender sentiments of her love and concern for him, followed by an inquiry about when he might possibly be able to come home for a visit, of course.

Turning quickly to the second envelope, addressed in his sister's scrawling hand, he turned it over to open and noticed the return address was not their home in Concord, but in care of an unfamiliar address on Second Avenue, Manhattan.

Marguerite's letter began in nonchalance, as though her decision to leave home and move to New York were an everyday accommodation, like deciding which frock to wear on a Wednesday. Gradually, it crescendoed into all-out exuberance, which he had learned long ago usually meant that she was trying hard to mask something. She marveled at how expensive everything was, how crowded the city, and how hard it would have been to find suitable lodgings if their father had not so generously offered that she should stay with him. She had hoped to live on her own, but the affordability of doing so had proven impossible, though she had considered a boarding house on Mulberry Street, which would have been fine, she supposed, except for the neighborhood. And the drunkards who inhabited it. Anyway, she hoped that soon enough her situation would change, and she could finally be her own person, secure and comfortable by her own two hands.

No matter, she was happy and excited about her prospects, although the daily attempts to find work so far had all failed. She went on to say how pleased she was at meeting so many diverse and interesting people. New York was so very much alive and there were so many distractions and an endless number of things to do, day and night. It was impossible to be lonely. Although wouldn't it be wonderful if he could manage to take a steamboat and visit someday very, very soon, even for just a few days? It wasn't so awfully far, was it?

He pursed his lips and blew through them in a near whistle, then shook his head as he folded the letter and placed it along with his mother's back inside his jacket. Leave it to Meg to leap and then look. He knew deep down that she would be all right—at least he hoped so. If anyone could make it in New York City, she could. A little time in the big city might even bestow some much-needed humility, of which she lacked a great deal, though he had to admit his longstanding, constant admiration of her boldness and confidence in herself. They were enviable qualities of which most people had too little, himself included. Of course, he didn't envy the fact that she had chosen, apparently without much reluctance, to live with their estranged father after so many years and despite the circumstances of his estrangement. He wasn't at all sure that her boldness and confidence would serve her well in that regard.

Before opening the letter from Elizabeth, he took a few sips of ale and finished the plate of cheese. With every letter from her, he faced a mild, fleeting trepidation she might one day come to conclude that their long separation had become too much for her to bear any longer. Not that he doubted her love for him, but they had been apart for over two and a half years without seeing each other. How long could any love survive not being tended and nourished? She was young and beautiful, the desire of any virile man's heart, especially his own. Plenty of others, he knew, were far better able to support a wife and future family. Others were not scarce, particularly in such a large, wealthy city as Boston.

He broke the seal and peeled open the envelope, unfolded its contents, and laid the single page on the table, smoothing it open.

Leaning over, he focused on her handwriting, a neat, flowing cursive that had become so intimate and dear to him, the way notes to a favorite sonata might appear on a sheet of music. The ink was smudged in places. He took in a deep breath and with it the slightest hint of lavender.

My dearest Andrew,

This letter will be very brief. Oh, if only I had better news to share. I do not wish to burden you, but I cannot help myself.

I'm overwhelmed with grief at the passing of my dear mother, just yesterday. She had been ill for several weeks, but we thought she was improving. Then, suddenly, her health declined again, and the doctor could do nothing more for her. She slipped away in her sleep yesterday afternoon.

My father is distraught and inconsolable, as you might imagine. I don't know how he will ever recover. They were very close, as you know, as close as any man and wife should ever hope to be. His grief makes mine seem paltry in comparison.

Yet, I miss her terribly. Words fail me. I cannot express the sense of loss entirely, except in tears, which have not as yet ceased. My father's grief at her passing and my own remind me at every breath how dear you are to me. Please come to me soonest, my love, if you are able.

Robert and Marianne send their love along with mine.

Your dearest,

Elizabeth

The letter was dated the eighth of March. Nearly two weeks had passed without his being even remotely aware of Elizabeth's grief and misery. He had never felt so isolated in his life. If he'd been shipwrecked on a desert island, he doubted whether he could have considered himself more alone.

21

He wandered aimlessly, unaware of how many blocks his walk had covered. All he could think about was his need to get home, heightened now by Elizabeth's desperate plea to come to her. He had to find a way, somehow, to make that happen.

At the nearest corner, he stopped to get his bearings. He stood at the intersection of Whitaker and West Gordon streets. A block away, the familiar white column of the Pulaski monument in Monterey Square rose above the surrounding rooftops.

Something pressed against the back of his left leg. He looked down to see the little terrier panting and begging to be picked up. Gunn reached down, but the dog shied away, stopping short a few feet from him, then turned about-face, front paws spread.

"Hello, friend. Have you been following me?"

He moved toward the dog, which sidestepped away. The terrier's small, merry eyes gleamed in his tufted face.

Gunn laughed. "Do you want to be picked up or not?"

The dog held his ground, still panting.

"Well, suit yourself. I'm just taking an afternoon walk. You're welcome to join me or not."

Drawn to the distant monument, Gunn crossed West Gordon

Street and headed east toward the square. The dog followed a few paces behind. His nails ticked a quick, syncopated rhythm on the brick sidewalk.

Across the street, a whitewashed post-and-rail fence skirted the square, protecting it from the occasional stray cows or goats. They crossed the sandy street and entered the square through an opening in the fence on a gravel walkway that crunched beneath Gunn's boots.

The marble column, topped with a bronze statue of Liberty, towered fifty feet above him in the center of the square, surrounded by a wrought-iron fence. Erected a few years earlier, the monument commemorated the brave sacrifice of Casimir Pulaski, a Polish count who commanded Continental cavalry against the British in the American Revolution. He was killed in a daring charge against superior forces during the siege of Savannah in 1779.

Gunn was frequently reminded of this heroic figure every time the *Dobbin* passed by the huge brick fort near the mouth of the river, named in the general's honor. These were fitting tributes. He admired the selfless devotion that had moved this man to die defending the cause of freedom for a people not his own. He often came to this spot where the paladin known as "the soldier of Liberty," who had laid down his life for his friends, was buried at the foot of the monument to his name. Somehow, among other benefits, it helped to clear his mind and bolster his resolve, especially when he was uncertain about whatever lay ahead.

He sat in view of the monument in the dense shade of a tall magnolia not yet in bloom, with his back against the trunk of the tree. He laid his shillelagh across his knees. Watching him intently, the little dog sat in the grass a short distance away, just out of reach.

"Well now. You've followed me here. What is it you want? I have no food." Gunn splayed his palms. "See?" The dog looked from one to the other and back again. "Look here, what shall I call you? Do you have a name?" The dog glanced away, as though indifferent. "So, that's how it is. All right, then, maybe you won't mind if I give you one. Let's see." A moment's reflection was all it took. "I know. How about Casimir?" The dog yawned and scratched himself. Gunn reached out to him. This time, the dog did not move away. "It has a nice ring to it. Come here, Casimir." The dog warily eyed his outstretched hand and darted a glance toward the shillelagh balanced on his knees. Gunn moved the shillelagh with his free hand, hiding it in the grass against his right leg. "Not afraid of this old thing, are you? Come on, now." No movement. "Stubborn, eh? Or is it that you don't trust anyone?" Gunn withdrew his hand. "I don't blame you. I don't trust most people, either."

The dog lay in the grass, resting his head on extended paws, eyes fixed on Gunn's near hand. A quiet moment passed as they sat watching each other. A breeze stirred the grass between them, and upon it wafted the scent of nearby lilacs.

"Do you have a home, Casimir? I take it you don't, or at least you don't spend much time there. So we have that in common. Not that I wouldn't like to, mind you. Go home, that is. Matter of fact, I'd much rather be there than here right now. No offense."

The dog's brow twitched as his bright eyes fixed on Gunn's face. Gunn sighed. "The question is how? I'm looking for a surefire way. Any ideas?" Casimir blinked and smacked his lips. "Just go, eh? That's what you'd do, is it? If only it were that simple, my friend. Not that it hasn't crossed my mind once or twice, truth be told. It's really not a good idea, though, unless I want to end up like you, wandering the streets and begging for something to eat. No offense. Besides, do you have any idea what a steamship ticket costs these days? No, I didn't think so."

Casimir got up, stretched, and stepped hesitantly toward Gunn. He stopped and sat again about half a foot away. Gunn reached out to pet him. The dog's wet nose touched his hand and sniffed. Gunn stroked his chin.

"There we go. That's better, isn't it?" Gunn moved his hand along the dog's back. The silky hair was matted and dirty in places but still soft to the touch. The dog moved closer to him and yielded to his caress. The protrusion of tiny, flimsy ribs attested to a poor diet. Otherwise, the dog seemed healthy enough and lively.

He had intended to continue his walk on one of the new paths carved through the tall pine forests in Forsyth Park, but in that moment decided otherwise.

"Say, I'll bet you could use a good meal, couldn't you? I have an idea. Why not come on to Cousin Julia's with me? She won't mind, I'm sure. You'll need a bath, of course, but we can manage that. What say you?"

He raised himself to his knees and leaned on the shillelagh to get to his feet. The dog leapt up expectantly and darted away to a safe distance. Gunn brushed himself off with his hat and reset it on his head. They started off together out of the square and across the street. The dog trotted along in front of him this time, occasionally glancing back to see if Gunn was following.

They headed north along Bull Street through the center of town. After two blocks, they came to the corner of Jones Street. Realizing that the Sullivans lived somewhere in this neighborhood, Gunn stopped to recall the address he'd seen printed on the invitation. Casimir halted in the middle of the street and turned back, waiting expectantly.

"Let's take a slight detour, shall we? I promise it won't take a minute."

He turned east on Jones Street, and the dog followed without complaint. The house was three doors down on the south side of the tree-lined street. One of the newest houses in town, the raised two-story made of Savannah grey brick stood apart from the surrounding homes in size and elegance. Stately and symmetrical, its classic architecture spoke of established wealth. A double staircase guarded by wrought-iron railings rose to a broad door painted black to match the shutters.

To the left, an iron gate gave entrance to a walled garden. The heavy gate stood ajar. Curious, Gunn stood outside, peering in. The lush parterre garden, shaded with trees, bounded by boxwood, and accented in vibrant spring flowers, surrounded a raised fountain in its center. The music of falling water sang of serenity and concord. The garden extended the full length of the house, expanding beyond it all the way to a carriage house in the rear of the property. It was a splendid sight, even in a city that prided itself on the beauty of its gardens.

A gray-bearded man, bent like a twig and carrying a shovel, ambled around the back corner of the house. Gunn hid himself behind the open gate. The man, apparently a gardener of sorts, turned to address someone out of view, nodding and pointing to an area where the soil had recently been turned.

Casimir trotted boldly through the door and into the garden.

Gunn called to him in a hoarse whisper. "Casimir, come back here."

The dog paid no attention, following the path deeper into the garden. He stopped at a nearby azalea, alive with pink blossoms, and lifted his leg.

"Casimir, no!"

At that moment, the bright blue skirts of a young woman rounded the back corner of the house. As she came into view, Gunn immediately recognized her as Sarah Sullivan. She passed the man, pointing and talking as she walked, and then gestured toward the front gate. They both looked in Gunn's direction.

"Oh, look, Clarence," Sarah said. "A little dog. You must have left the gate open again."

"I'll take care of it, Miss Sarah."

"Don't bother. Keep on with your planting. I'll see to it."

Casimir lowered his leg. Beneath him on the brick pathway spread a small, dark pool. He began sniffing the ground among the flowers and shrubs.

As Sarah approached, she called to the dog, but he ignored her. She spotted the puddle on the path and chuckled.

"Just like a little man," she said. "Come on, then, time to go home. You've had your fun."

Gunn stepped from behind the gate and tipped his hat. "Hello, there."

Sarah started. "Oh, hello. I didn't—"

"I'm sorry to startle you. I should have—"

"No, not at all. What a pleasant surprise."

He smiled and cleared his throat. "It's nice to see you. How have you been?"

She nodded. "Very well, thank you. Much better. I am much more myself, these days."

Her face glowed in the late afternoon light. It shouldn't have been possible, but she was even more lovely than the last time he'd seen her. He swallowed hard.

"I am very glad to know it."

"And you?"

"Oh, fine. Just fine."

She turned and pointed at Casimir. "Is this your little dog?"

"Not really. We've just become acquainted."

She removed her broad-brimmed straw hat, uncovering her dark, lustrous hair. "Does he listen to you?"

"Hardly, but I'll try. Come here, Casimir."

The dog continued to sniff.

"Casimir?" She smiled, touching the tip of her tongue to her upper lip, as if to keep from laughing. "What a funny name for a dog."

"Well, it's just on trial."

"No wonder he won't come to you."

"Do you think that's why?"

"I do not doubt it. He's a cute dog. I wonder if he answers to someone."

"I don't think so. He has no collar. He seems to do whatever he pleases."

She laughed. "That's rather obvious. Well, let's see if we can change that." Sarah handed her hat to Gunn, gathered her skirts about her, and knelt to the ground. The dog watched alertly as she reached into the pocket of her skirt, then removed her hand and held it out, fingers pinched together.

"Come on, Casimir. Come on, boy."

The dog hesitated for a moment, then trotted up to her, stopping just out of reach.

"Come on," she said, pulling her hand back.

Casimir edged toward her. She eased her hand back farther.

"You know you want it," she said softly. She opened her empty hand. Casimir took another step and leaned forward to sniff. She fondled the beard beneath his chin. "There you go," she whispered. She reached over with her free hand and picked him up, pulling him close to her. She stood and held him out to Gunn.

"Your hand was empty," he said.

"Of course."

He exchanged her hat for the dog, cradled Casimir in one arm, and tousled his ears. "You made it look so easy."

She shrugged. "Dogs are not so different from people, are they? They want what they don't have. Or what they can't have."

"Not always."

"Mostly."

"I suppose so."

"He's a cute little thing. He looks half-starved, though. Would you mind very much if I keep him? I've always wanted a little dog just like this."

"I'm thinking he'd prefer that." He handed the dog back to her and she took him in her arms, stroking his soft coat.

Her eyes narrowed. "What is it that you want, Andrew?"

"I beg your pardon?"

She smiled again, more broadly this time. Her eyes were laughing, though she was not. Evidently, her former confidence and sense of self had returned, undiminished. "I mean, were you here for a reason?"

"I was just taking a walk. Happened by."

"Happened by. I see. Tell me, did you receive our invitation?"

He felt drawn to her by an ineffable connection, a vague affinity that had something to do with his new knowledge of the long-past relationship between her father and his mother. "I—I did. We did. That's how I came to know where you live. Just thought I'd, you know, take a look."

"Ah. You came. You saw." She arched her eyebrows. "I'd invite you in—"

"No, no. I wouldn't want to impose, and I really should be going. Give your father my respects, if you will."

"Will we see you at the party? You will come, won't you? You are a guest of honor, after all."

"Yes, of course. I wouldn't miss it."

22

On Tuesday morning at high tide, the ship took a steam tow alongside, making the short transit from her berth at Moore's to a shipyard known as Willink's at the far eastern end of the riverfront. Gunn had the watch. As they approached, he noted that Willink's was a sprawling compound of one sizable building with open barn doors among several ramshackle sheds. A dedicated slip with an inclined railway led up to it all from the water.

Next door to the shipyard, separated by a narrow canal, stood a large cotton press, covered by a long shed and fronted by a broad wooden wharf, behind which a two-story warehouse stretched away from the waterfront farther than he could see. A barge was tied up at the wharf, and workmen, badgered by a red-faced foreman, loaded bales of cotton onto the barge in stacks with the aid of a boom. More stacks of bales occupied every open space under the shed and along the wharf. Above the press, a sign in bright red block letters declared its ownership: LAMAR.

Gunn drew Bulloch's attention and chucked his chin at the sign. "That who I think it is?"

Bulloch nodded. "The very same. It's a big operation, one of several enterprises that he took over from his father. Charley's got a big head about it, too. He turns out over a hundred and fifty thousand bales a year, from what I hear. The whole operation burned to the ground about five years ago. Lost everything, but he built it back grander than ever."

A few minutes later, the tug nudged the *Dobbin* bow-first into the slip at Willink's and then released the tow, backing nimbly away from the wharf in a puff of black smoke. Line-handlers onshore caught the ship's mooring lines and harnessed them to a team of mules on either side of the slip, which then pulled on the lines to warp the cutter neatly into place. They secured the lines and then began mooring the ship to a cradle submerged in the water beneath her hull.

A broad-shouldered man with long chin whiskers sauntered down to the slip from one of the outbuildings. He waited while the crew put over a gangplank and then came aboard. Gunn and Bulloch met him at the gangway.

"Henry Willink's the name."

Gunn and Bulloch introduced themselves and exchanged pleas-antries. "Thanks for taking us in so quickly," said Bulloch.

"Glad to oblige. We've just finished up work early on that brigantine out there," Willink gestured with his head at a ship swinging at anchor, "so it worked out just fine. I hear tell you've sprung a leak."

Bulloch nodded. "Hit a bad storm last time out. I think we busted a seam."

Willink surveyed the ship with a critical eye, finishing on the men who labored at the creaking bilge pumps. "Love the lines of a Baltimore clipper. She's a beauty, I must say. Fairly new ship, I see. Well, it happens, 'specially if the planks ain't seasoned proper. Folks is in too much of a hurry these days. We do things the right way around here, though, don't you worry about that. Soon as we get your ship secured, we'll haul her out. Then, those fellas can rest easy." He jerked a thumb toward the men on the pumps. "Already got a head of steam on the winch, so we should be ready to go shortly."

"We appreciate that, Mr. Willink."

"Let me introduce y'all to the man who'll be working with you. Best shipwright in these parts." He turned and hollered through cupped hands. "Hey, Jayjay!"

"Suh!" came the immediate reply from a short black man, at work with a spokeshave, paring the end of a long spar.

"C'mere a minute."

"Right there, yes, suh, Mistuh Henry." The man took three more strokes, the wood shavings in curls at his feet, then placed his tool on a nearby bench. He ambled toward the *Dobbin* on bowed legs, taking his sweet time as though it were his to spare. He wiped his broad brow with a red bandana pulled from the back pocket of his overalls as he crossed the gangplank.

"This here is Jesus Johnson, but folk round here calls him Jayjay."

Jayjay's face glistened with sweat. He wiped his eyes, squeezed them shut, and blinked twice. "Pleased to meet you, gentlemen," he said in a raspy voice.

Gunn stuck out his hand. "Pleasure, Jayjay."

Willink cleared his throat and looked away. Jayjay refused the handshake with a toss of his bandana. "Oh no, suh. I won't shake your hands, if it's all the same, since mine's all drippin' wet, you see." His eyes widened, avoiding direct contact with the others. "Beg pardon."

"Of course," said Gunn, withdrawing his hand. "I'm Lieutenant Gunn, and this is Lieutenant Bulloch, our, uh, acting captain."

"Pleasure, I'm sure. What can we do for you, suh?" His eyes took in the entire ship, not lighting anywhere for long.

"They've sprung a seam. Likely, more'n one," said Willink.

"You've come to the right place, then," said Jayjay. "We'll fix 'er right up. Might take some time, but we'll git 'er done."

"That's all we ask," said Bulloch.

"Well, I guess I best be gettin' back to it," said Jayjay, gazing at the abandoned spar. "Unless you be needin' something else, Mistuh Henry."

"No, Jayjay. We'll talk later."

Jayjay nodded curtly and made his way back over the gangplank to resume his labor.

"He's a good sort," said Willink. "Kinda keeps to himself these days, though. Doesn't have much to say to anyone of late. I suspect he's still a little touchy about the news, ya know, on the Dred Scott case. Most blacks are. It affects him, too, you see, even though he's a freeman. Shame."

"He's on your payroll, then?" Bulloch asked.

"Not as an employee. I pay him by the job. And that boy can bargain, let me tell ya. He has his own crew of three workers. One of them's his old man and another's a slave—his own, mind you. Odd situation, but as I said, he's the best around. I hire him for the jobs where I need a real craftsman. And they're a sight cheaper to hire, too, than any whites. Bet on that. Bottom line, I trust him to get the job done right. You can, too."

The yard workmen finished securing the *Dobbin* to the cradle beneath her. They led a four-inch cable tethered to a bridle and fastened it to the ship as a hawse. At the other end, inside the massive machine shop, the cable wound around a huge drum, driven by a steam engine that looked like a locomotive without wheels.

Bulloch ordered Grant to disembark most of the crew, save the boatswain and two other seamen, who would remain aboard with him and Gunn in case something should go wrong. They assembled and went ashore, standing off a distance to watch what was about to happen.

When all was ready, the yard foreman whistled and gave a hand signal. The engineer eased the throttle open, and the drum slowly began to turn, tightening the slack in the cable.

The deck jolted under Gunn's feet. He grabbed the rail to steady himself. The ship began moving, haltingly at first, then gaining momentum as the cradle groaned beneath her weight. The deck inclined as the ship was pulled steadily up the marine railway and out of the water. Gunn leaned forward to keep his balance, as did Bulloch and the others. It was an odd, unfamiliar sensation, very unlike the constant rolling of the deck at sea.

The engine chuffed and billowed smoke and steam from the stack above the roof of the machine shop. A foot at a time, the ship rose out of the water, rocking slightly as she settled onto the cradle. Workmen hammered chocks into place with large wooden mallets where the ship's hull touched the cradle to make her more secure.

At last, the cutter reached the top of the ways. The engineer wrenched the throttle shut, and the winch stopped turning. Workers chocked the wheels of the cradle. Someone placed a ladder against the starboard side of the ship with a clatter. Gunn climbed to the ground. He stepped away from the ladder and looked back to take in the sight that few ever had the opportunity to see.

He beheld from bow to stern the ship's graceful lines and long, sleek, sensuous curves, usually hidden from view beneath the waves. The *Dobbin*, like a sea nymph mounted on a dolphin, her undersides glistening and shedding rivulets of water, emerged from the depths naked, helpless, and exposed for all to see, yet brazen and unabashed.

23

Standing on a stepladder, the master carpenter ran his rough, chafed hands over the planking beneath the ship's waterline on the starboard side. He stopped at the place of the worst damage, an obvious concave feature where there shouldn't be one, on a split joint between two planks. He shook his head.

"Not just a sprung seam or two," he said, bobbing his head and sighting one-eyed along a strake down the length of the hull. "Mebbe more. There's most likely some damage to the framing inside. Musta took a helluva beating."

"She did. We did," said Gunn. "What do you think the damage might be?"

"Could be a busted rib or bilge stringer. Broken fasteners. Split sister, mebbe. Happens if they used wood that ain't seasoned proper, 'specially if it be overheated or bent too quick. Won't know for sure what all, till we strip 'er down."

"If that's the case, how long will it take to repair?" Bulloch asked.

"That being the only thing," Jayjay shrugged, "about two, three weeks before she back in the water. Don't want to hurry it. Need to mill the lumber. Shape and bend it proper. Takes time."

"And if we offered our men to help?"

Jayjay shook his head as he climbed down the ladder. "Won't help none, cap'n. They jes get in the way. I got the best crew there is."

"Mmmm. All right, then. Best get to it."

"We'll do that, suh, yes, indeedy."

Bulloch turned to Gunn. "Fetch Mr. Grant, will you? We'll need to discuss how to keep our men busy in the meantime. Idleness will draw a losing hand every time."

"Aye, aye, sir."

The three assembled near the stern.

"So we must keep the men busy, gents," said Bulloch. "No time to slack off. No lallygagging. As we've discussed, while the ship is on the hard, the men who don't have homes to go to will be quartered at the Customs barracks down the way a bit." He chucked his chin westward. "But I don't want anybody thinking that they've suddenly arrived on pleasant street. First, we'll hold muster here every morning at eight o'clock sharp, just like we're living aboard. That means everybody. We'll be able to do some work, even with the ship on a slant like she is. Feed the men out of the rations. We'll keep a fire watch on board every night, no fewer than four men, just in case that cotton press next door goes up in flames. Rotate the watch sections. Right. Marcus, I want you to take some men to retrieve the old dinghy from our spares down at the Customs dock. It has a rotten transom and might need some patching up, but otherwise it should be a serviceable replacement for the one we lost. Make the necessary repairs. Scrape it down to bare wood and repaint it. Put a good three coats on her. Tell the men I want to be able to shave in my reflection."

Grant nodded.

"That's just for starters. We'll need to replace all the gear we tossed overboard. Tell the bos'n to start making a list. Let me know what we need to purchase. Next, I want a thorough inspection of the spars and rigging from stem to stern. Replace anything that's damaged or worn. All right? Once that's done, we'll tar the rigging. Whoever's not tarring can chip and paint the hull and whatever else doesn't move. Point is, I want these men working all day, every day. Got it?"

"Aye, aye, sir," they said in unison.

"Andrew, get with Jayjay and set up a schedule of sorts. I don't want him to think he's driving this mule train. Let him know that he can't just take his sweet old time on this job."

"Aye, sir. Will do."

"I'm going up to the Customs House to let the deputy know what's what. Be back in a couple hours, no more. When I get back, I expect to see every man Jack turning to. Any questions?"

"No, sir," said Grant.

"All right, then."

As Grant moved off toward the crew, Gunn raised an index finger. "Sir, may I have a word?"

"What's on your mind, Andrew?"

"I've received a letter from Elizabeth."

"Oh? I hope she's well."

"Well, that's just it. Her mother has died. Her father is in a bad way. She's asking for me to come home, if it's at all possible. Seems desperate."

"I see. Sorry to hear that."

"If the situation allows, would you mind broaching the subject of my leave with Mr. Bulloch? Your cousin, I mean. Seeing as how it appears we're going to be on the hard for a few weeks and all. Like you said."

"Of course, Andrew. I haven't forgotten. I'll see what I can do. No promises, though."

"Thanks very much."

"See to it that you nail down a schedule with that Jayjay. Don't let him get the upper hand. We can't afford to let the work go on any longer than absolutely necessary. And in any case, you'll need to return by the time we put back into the water. No delays. That won't give you much time."

"Understood."

Bulloch winked and strode away.

Jayjay was instructing one of his crew to start removing one of the damaged planks. The young man appeared to be in his early twenties, whose shirtless, dark chest and sinewy arms shimmered with sweat. He picked up a mallet and a crowbar and started to work.

Gunn approached Jayjay and cleared his throat.

"Yessuh?" Jayjay said. "How can I help you?"

"Jayjay, I wanted to discuss with you a work schedule for this job. Just trying to get a better grip on what's going to happen and when."

The weathered face took on a bemused, somewhat disappointed look. He sighed through his nose, avoiding eye contact with Gunn.

"I mean, if you don't mind," Gunn added.

"Well, suh, I expect by the end of the day, we know better what we's lookin' at. What's broke and what ain't, see. By the end of tomorrow, we'll likely have took this part of the bow down to bare bones, I expect. We also gwine have to strip them two strakes." He pointed along the hull. "All the way back to 'midships. That be how far the sprung seams goes, see. Then we can know for sure whether it be a week or three weeks. Depends what we find. If we need to replace framing, that's what will take most of the time, cuttin' and planin' and shapin'. That's 'bout the best I can do, other than to say, unless I miss my guess, shouldn't be no longer'n a month."

"Can you guarantee that, Jayjay?"

Jayjay snorted. "Gwar'ntee? Ain't nothin' in life gwar'nteed, lieutenant. "What'd you say your name is?"

"Gunn. Andrew Gunn."

"Well, Mistah Gunn." His hooded eyes looked into Gunn's for the first time, the gaze direct yet unassuming. "What I can say is that y'all can depend upon my word. Been doin' this work a lotta years, see. I've found the closest thing to a gwar'ntee is to know who you're workin' with. Now, this here young fella with the mallet is my nephew, Onemo."

"On-ee-mo?"

"That's right." He spelled out the name, then repeated it. "On-ee-mo. He called that 'cause when he's borned, he be the seventh child what come out of his mama, my sistuh. She borned so many, she didn't know what to call him, so she jes' say here's one mo'. Dat's how he come to be Onemo. He live with me now, see. Love him like he be my own son. Taught him everything he know. Say hey to the man, Onemo."

Onemo stopped working and turned sideways on his ladder. "Massah."

"Hello," said Gunn. "Don't let me stop you."

The young man resumed his labor.

Jayjay pointed to an older man with gray hair hunched over a bench, sawing a piece of lumber. "That old coot over there be my father. His name's George, but most folks call him Deacon. He taught me everything I know—not 'bout carpentry, but 'bout keepin' my word and such. He still a slave, hired out to me. But we doin' something 'bout that."

Another black man, full-bearded and nearly large enough to make two of Jayjay, walked up to them, shouldering a huge wooden toolbox as though it were a stick of firewood. He carried a brace and bit in his right hand. On his ragged, sweat-stained shirt, he wore a blue badge, indicating a slave for hire.

Jayjay lifted his brow, almost smiling. "This here Esau. He belong to me. Ain't that right, Esau?"

Esau grinned through his beard. "For now, massah."

"Belongs to you? Do you mean as a slave?"

"I do. Bought him from a white man was gwine sell him someplace in Miz'sippi. He sweet on a young thing, and she don't want him to leave 'er. They gwine get married someday. So, I bought him, see. Cain't set him free 'cause he'd have to leave Georgia. That's what the law say now. But we got us a deal. Ain't that so, Esau?"

Esau set his toolbox down in the dust with a thud and a jangle of tools. "'Sright."

"So, Mr. Gunn. That be the lot of us. That be who y'all dealin' with. We a tight bunch, see. Ain't a man here won't do the bes' he can. We works hard and takes pride in everything we do. We men, jes like anybody else." He spat on the ground, the spittle pocking the dust at his feet. His hooded eyes gleamed. "'Spite what any white man court got to say. No offense."

"None taken, I assure you."

"Is that good 'nough for y'all?"

"I should say so."

"One mo' thing. My eyes ain't what they used to be, but my ears jes' fine. Like a old fox been hunted a few time. You can tell your cap'n that we do this however which way he want do it. He the bossman."

Gunn grinned. "All right, Jayjay. That's all I needed to know. I'll be sure to tell him."

24

When Bulloch returned, he brought with him a short, stout man of about the same age, their only point of similarity. His straight black beard matched the tufts of hair that peeked out from beneath his top hat. His buoyant gait expressed energy and enthusiasm. They bantered and laughed as they approached. Bulloch spotted Gunn talking to Blake, the boatswain, and steered the man toward him.

"Aye, sir. I'll see to it right away, sir." Blake saluted and moved away as the two men approached.

"James, meet Second Lieutenant Andrew Gunn. Andrew, this is my cousin, James Bulloch, our new deputy collector. He's come to see for himself what we're up against."

Gunn stretched out his hand. "Pleased to meet you, Mr. Bulloch."

The two exchanged a vigorous handshake. "James, please. No need to be so formal. Desmond's told me so much about you. I feel as though we've known each other forever. You should know that he speaks very highly of you. Glad to finally meet you in person."

"Your cousin's obviously overlooked my more serious flaws. No surprise there. Des has always been most generous and kind to me. I have never known a truer friend."

Desmond chuckled. "Not overlooked. Downplayed is more the case. Besides, your flaws are so obvious they hardly need a mention."

Gunn laughed. "As I said, no truer friend."

James nodded toward the ship's bow. "Well, let's see the damage, shall we?"

They walked forward to where Jayjay's crew was busy removing planks from the hull, exposing the interior of the forecastle. Foster peered in wonderment through the enlarged opening from inside the crew's quarters, where a work party scrambled to secure and stow their belongings.

Jayjay wiped his brow with the red bandana and tied it around his head. "Jes' in time, gentlemen. Let me show you something." He climbed the ladder and pointed to one of the exposed ribs, running his finger along a crack in the bowed wood to where it splintered on the backside. "See there? Busted clean through. And down lower there." He picked at some cracked wood that flaked and crumbled in his strong fingers. "That there be dry rot. Won't hold a nail. Come from water gettin' in and dryin' out. Been gwine on a while, I'd say. Seams warnt holdin'. Likely, there be more, and some wet rot down below, too, unless I be mistook. Won't know till we peel 'er down."

James Bulloch sucked his teeth. "Looks serious."

"Seen a lot worse, suh," said Jayjay. "Likely started small. Been gettin' worser over time. Storm jes' busted things loose."

Willink walked up to join them. After introductions and polite chatter, he surveyed the exposed ribs. "So what's the damage?"

"Looks like we'll be your guests for a little while," said Bulloch.

"How long, Jayjay?"

"Most likely a month, Mistah Henry, like I jes' told Mistah Gunn, there. No mo', leastwise I reckon."

Willink winced and rubbed the back of his neck. "Ah, it can't take any longer than that, or we'll start backing things up to a fare-thee-well."

"We do our best, suh," said Jayjay.

"I know you will," said Willink. "Best go over the rest of the hull, too. See if there might be other spots, just in case."

Jayjay nodded.

"Let's hope not," said Gunn.

"How much?" James asked.

"Why don't you join me in my office in about thirty minutes? Jayjay and I will work up a rough estimate. Of course, we won't know for sure until we strip her down completely."

"That'll do," said James.

"I guess that does it. Best get to it, then, Jayjay. Gentlemen." Willink touched his cap before he and Jayjay strode away together toward the office.

The deputy collector turned to Gunn and Bulloch. "Shall I assume you've made arrangements for the crew?"

"Yes, certainly," said Bulloch. "Those who have no homes in town will be at the barracks down the way."

"Good. Now, I know that Desmond has accepted my offer to stay at our place on West Gordon. Andrew, what about you?"

"I have some relatives in town. I'll be staying with them."

"And Mr. Grant, is it?"

"He's taken a boardinghouse in town."

"And you'll all report here to work everyday?"

"That's right," said Bulloch. "Well, except for . . ."

"Ah, yes, yes." James turned to Gunn. "Andrew—may I call you Andrew?"

"I'd prefer it."

"We should talk about your situation. Desmond has explained it to me, but let's discuss it between us, shall we?"

"Glad to."

"That's fine. Let's find a quieter place. How about my office in an hour?"

An hour or so later, Gunn sat with James Bulloch in his office at the Customs House, which was very similar in grandeur to that of the collector, though situated away from the street at the rear of the building and not quite as well furnished. After additional pleasantries, which continued from their walk together, James cocked his head, regarding Gunn with a look of curiosity.

"So tell me, how did you come to be stationed here in Savannah?"

Gunn outlined the story, as he had told it to Sarah and her father.

"I see. So if I take your meaning, this assignment was some sort of punishment for taking matters into your own hands."

"That's right."

"And do you think you deserved such punishment?"

"I certainly understand why Captain Whitcomb could not allow me to remain onboard the *Morris*.

A thin smile crossed James' lips. "That's not the question I put to you."

Gunn shifted in his seat. "I think his decision was fair."

"Do you regret what you did?"

"I do regret my actions and always will. Although I do not regret my reasons for doing so and never will."

"Very well. Now, Desmond tells me that Captain Dawes had been working toward some sort of arrangement by which you should be transferred somewhere up north, closer to home, perhaps."

"That was my understanding, yes. Mr. Brinkman was aware of his efforts. He apparently decided to nullify any plans after the death of Captain Dawes. At least, so he told me. He said I could appeal to his replacement, if I so wished. I do so wish."

"Well, that will be up to Mr. Boston to decide, of course. He has taken a quick trip to Charleston to confer with the collector there. You can take it up with him when he returns. Be back in a day or so. Meanwhile, I'll be glad to do what I can to support you. I will say it is likely to be tough going. There isn't likely to be much movement in the ranks, to my understanding. Budgets are tight. Billets are not grown on trees, you know.

"I understand. Thank you, sir."

"James, please." He flashed a smile. "We are friends, Andrew, are we not?"

"I hope so."

"Good. Now, let's talk about your plans for leave. If I understand correctly, you haven't been home since you arrived, is that so?"

"That's right. We've been stretched fairly thin, not having another cutter this far south. Winter patrols have kept me here every Christmas so far."

"We should do something about that, I think." He drew a leaf of paper from the top right-hand drawer of his desk and took up his pen, dipping and tapping it in the inkwell. "I'm hereby granting you twenty-one days of leave, starting next week."

Gunn sat upright. "What's that?"

James' brow lifted as he wrote. "Beg pardon. Did I speak another tongue? I am prone to mutter in Spanish now and then. Old habits."

"I thought I heard you say that you're granting me twenty-one days of leave."

"You did. Now, I want you to stay this week to help oversee the start of this project. But go ahead and make your travel arrangements as soon thereafter as possible." He scribbled a few lines. "I am only authorized to grant two weeks, but I will cable Secretary Cobb, who I'm certain will have no problem extending it. Just a formality. He has much greater worries right now, I'm quite sure. Unless you hear from me, I want you to go ahead and buy your tickets."

Unused to the tide of good fortune turning so abruptly in his favor, Gunn was taken aback. "I don't quite know what to say. But what about Mr. Boston? Won't he have something to say about it?"

James waved a hand. "He has delegated minor administrative matters to me. Besides, he's far too busy rubbing elbows and hobnob-bing with Savannah's finest. Not to worry. I'm sure he'll agree with my decision. Go ahead with your plans."

"I am most grateful, James. Thank you very much."

"Not at all. Desmond tells me you're a good man, well deserving of some time off. Says he can do without you for a short while. I agree. Of course, it means he's going to have to work for a change, won't he? But I'll be sure to hold his feet to the fire. Got some old accounts to square with him, now that I finally have the upper hand. Should be fun. *Lo pasaremos bien*." His merry brown eyes twinkled.

"This is a very welcome surprise. I'll make arrangements right away." Gunn rose from his chair and pushed it back.

"One thing before you go."

"Of course. Anything."

James finished writing, placed his pen on the desk, and paused, sitting back in his chair.

"There will be an inquiry into the death of Captain Dawes, rest his soul. No doubt you've anticipated that event. Likely, it will take place while you're gone. I don't think it will raise much of an issue, based on what I know so far. However, I will need for you to provide written testimony, by formal inquiry, and sworn before the federal magistrate. No court today, so you'll likely find Judge Nicoll in his chambers upstairs, second floor, unless he's out at Ten Broeck."

"What's Ten Broeck?"

"Where've you been living? Under a rock?"

"Or out to sea."

James Bulloch's staccato laugh filled the room. "Ten Broeck is the old Jencks racetrack, about three miles west of town. Charley Lamar renamed it when he bought the grounds back in January. From what I hear, Judge Nicoll just acquired a new filly thoroughbred. Thinks she stands a chance against Lamar's stallion, Black Cloud."

"Why does Lamar appear everywhere I look lately? Like a bad penny."

"Gets around, doesn't he? Anyway, you'd better hurry if you're going to catch Judge Nicoll."

"Of course. I've already written a statement, as have the crew who were witnesses."

"Not good enough. Needs to be sworn testimony, signed and sealed before the judge."

"I'll take care of it."

Bulloch handed him the written orders. "Good man. Take time by the forelock, eh, sailor? Now, off with you."

25

Bounding up the curved staircase two steps at a time, Gunn reached the landing on the second floor breathless, but not from the climb. He could not believe his good fortune at last. He found Judge Nicoll exiting his chambers, fumbling with a set of keys, preparing to lock the door. Gunn explained his situation in halting sentences between excited gulps of breath.

After hearing the exigency of the issue, the judge agreed with some reluctance to take his testimony and summoned the Assistant U.S. Attorney Joseph Ganahl and a court reporter to take his deposition—and to be quick about it. They all assembled in the judge's chambers, seated around his desk. Listening with a preoccupied look in his baggy eyes, Judge Nicoll pared his fingernails with a pocketknife as Ganahl asked a series of pointed questions related to the circumstances surrounding the death of Captain Dawes.

"So you saw nothing suspicious in the events surrounding his death?" Ganahl asked.

"No, sir, nothing. I was on watch when the captain entered his cabin. And I was still on watch when he was found dead in his bunk. Nobody entered the cabin in the meantime."

"How long was the period between the captain's entry to the cabin and the discovery of his body?"

"About two hours, I suppose, more or less."

"Was there no other access to the cabin that you could not observe?"

"Only the door to the wardroom, where the other officers were quartered."

"How can you be sure, then, that nobody entered the cabin?"

Gunn hesitated. "Well, I can't be absolutely certain. But the only persons who could possibly have entered were the first and third lieutenants. Both were asleep at the time."

"How do you know this to be true?"

"I presume it to be true."

"You presume it so?"

"Well, yes, of course. Both had to be awakened after the discovery of the body."

"Who awakened them?"

"The captain's steward, Seaman Walters."

"I see. So you can't swear that both were asleep at the time of death?"

"No, sir. I can't swear it."

Ganahl pursed his lips. "I see."

"Look here, Mr. Ganahl. I know both men very well, and neither of them had any desire for any sort of harm to come to Captain Dawes. Nobody on the *Dobbin* did. Everyone liked him—admired him, in fact."

"That so?"

"Most certainly, sir."

"The first lieutenant, Mr. Bulloch, is it?"

"Yes, sir."

"Would he stand to benefit in any way from the captain's untimely death?"

Gunn raised his voice. "That's absolute rubbish, sir."

"And why so?"

"Because I know Lieutenant Bulloch to be a gentleman of the highest integrity, honor, and devotion to duty. He would never even contemplate such a thing."

"So say you."

"So say I."

"Very well, then. I have no further questions."

"Excellent," said Judge Nicoll. A puff of breath flared the ends of his long, drooping mustache. "Mr. Gunn, do you swear that your testimony given today is the truth and nothing but the truth, so help you God?"

"I do, Your Honor."

"Very well, then. Mr. Ganahl will have your deposition written out and then you'll sign your name to that effect. All right?"

"Certainly, sir."

"And I charge you not to share or discuss your testimony with anyone outside these chambers. Is that clear?"

"Of course, Your Honor."

"All right, gentlemen. I must go see a man about a horse, and I'll be late as it is getting out to Ten Broeck. You'll excuse me."

The judge ushered them out of his chambers and departed without waiting for a reply. Ganahl instructed the reporter to draw up a verbatim transcript of the proceedings, to which Gunn signed his name and Ganahl attested about three-quarters of an hour later.

"Well, Mr. Gunn, I must say you seem rather sure of yourself and your first lieutenant," said Ganahl after signing the document.

"I am, sir. I've never been so certain of anything in my life."

"Glad to see it. I hope your testimony bears up. For both your sakes."

Gunn scrutinized the intelligent, rather good-looking face of the young officer of the court, who appeared to be not much older than himself. Standing tall, slim and straight-backed, Ganahl had a certain arrogance and intensity about him, not uncommon to his profession, but seemed otherwise sincere and without malice. Gunn hoped that was the case and could not help thinking that he wouldn't ever want to be prosecuted by such a man.

"I have no doubt of it, Mr. Ganahl."

After leaving the Customs House, Gunn rushed across the Bay and the Strand, down the steps of the Exchange to the steep incline of the cobblestones of Bull Street to arrive at the busy waterfront. It was hard to believe the sudden and rapid changes in his circumstances during the last few hours. His pace quickened. A short walk eastward on River Street, dodging drays and wagons, took him to the steamship piers.

For months, he had perused the local advertisements for steamship lines offering regular passage to the North. Since Meg's letter, he had planned, if he ever got the chance to go home, to stop in New York on the way for a brief visit with her. Then catch a train on to Boston to save money and time.

He passed the long, sleek hull of the *Lyoness,* a modern, luxurious side-paddle steamer, which was a favorite of the well-heeled travelers to and from New York. A ticket aboard her would cost more than a month's wages, which was far more than he could afford. His best bet would be one of the old two-masted coastal schooners, which would take a day or two longer, under favorable weather conditions, and make more stops along the way, but they cost less than half the fare.

The fare. The fact dawned on him that he had very little cash in his pocket. He turned on his heel and dashed back up River Street, hastily retracing his steps across the Strand to the Bay and the Bank of Savannah, where he withdrew the cash he needed.

Twenty minutes later, he stood at the ticket window for the Cromwell Line and bought passage on a coastal packet ship, the *Memphis,* departing the following Tuesday. The ticket, which cost him eight dollars, was for steerage class. He could not spare the extra for cabin fare, even at thirteen dollars. He was saving his money for a future life with Elizabeth. It would have to do.

Walking away from the booth, he held the ticket in his hands, staring as though it were stamped in precious metal. Someone bumped his shoulder and offered an apology, but he scarcely noticed. It was hard to believe, but there it was, the tangible evidence that he was at last going home. He tucked it carefully away in an inside pocket.

He decided to press his luck and send a telegram right away to Elizabeth and his mother to tell them that he'd be home—in about a week or so from Tuesday, he figured. Marguerite he would surprise, just show up out of the clear blue sky. She'd like that, wouldn't she? Of course she would. She'd be thrilled to see him.

The nearest telegraph office was in the Exchange, so he headed there next, stepping lively up the inclined cobblestone of Bull Street to the stairs leading to the side entrance of the building. He found the crowded offices of the Washington and New Orleans Telegraph Company on the ground floor and pressed his way inside the door. The air was heavy with cigar and pipe smoke, which served to mask somewhat the pungent aroma of body odor.

While he awaited his turn at the counter, he calculated the travel time in his head. Three or four days to New York. A day or so to visit Meg. Then maybe two days by train to Boston. Better figure arriving sometime between the sixth and the eighth of April. Sooner, if possible. The excitement began to build. He had broken a sweat in his rush to buy the ticket, and his quickened heartbeat pulsed in his ears. He tried to settle himself, pulling out a handkerchief to daub his damp neck and forehead.

The sign above the clerk's head declared that it would cost fifteen cents a word to send a telegram to Boston. Gunn winced. Even so, it was an expense that must be borne. A letter simply wouldn't do in the circumstances. When he arrived at the counter, he composed two messages announcing in the briefest of terms that he was coming home and when to expect him. He paid the clerk two and a quarter.

"Highway robbery," he muttered.

The beleaguered clerk shrugged and sniffed. "You want I should send these, or would you rather take 'em there yourself?"

"Yes, by all means send them. It's just the Scotsman in me talking."

"Maybe you shouldn't let him talk so much."

"Yes, all right, then. Thanks, anyway. Isn't it a great day, though?"

"Next."

Nothing could spoil his mood. Not today.

Clouds had been gathering and conspiring all afternoon. By the time Gunn exited the Exchange, they had turned dark, and thunder rolled a dismal warning somewhere close in the western sky. Before he reached the shipyard fifteen minutes later, the firmament opened and rain poured down in a deluge, drenching him from top to toe.

26

The rain continued off and on for the next three days. Work on the ship slowed to a crawl. The crew set up a tarpaulin lean-to against the breach in the hull, which allowed the work to continue, but on the occasions when the wind whipped rain sideways through the shelter, everything ceased until the wind or rain subsided. Nothing much got done onboard the ship, except whatever could be accomplished below decks, such as mending sails or making small stuff.

Gunn took turns with Grant to stand overnight fire watches, along with a skeleton crew. Sleeping was difficult due to the ship's cant on the ways. No matter who had the watch, the officers would keep each other company in the wardroom well into the evening before they retired, playing cards or cribbage, smoking and talking until weariness overtook them.

On Thursday evening, around midnight, they finished a round of hearts. Grant yawned and rubbed his bald spot.

"Guess I'm about ready to turn in," he said.

"I'm done for, too. Time to head back to my place. Before I go, let me ask you something, Marcus."

"What's that?"

"The party at the Sullivans' on Saturday night."

"Oh yes. I received an invitation, Andrew. But I am not much for parties, you know."

"So you don't intend to go?"

"No, I figured on spending a quiet evening on the old *Dobbin*. She's my best gal these days. Besides, it will be my night for fire watch. You go, and enjoy yourself."

"If you're sure. I thought I'd have to flip you for it."

Grant waved his arm. "Absolutely."

"All right, then. I suppose that's settled."

"Don't give it another thought."

Rain had begun to fall again, though it was just a cool drizzle. The wind had subsided. At least it wasn't snow. On his walk to Perry Street, Gunn thought about what the weather might be like in Boston. Most likely it was still cold, gray, and damp. The ground was just beginning to thaw after a long winter, but snow would be possible well into April, sometimes after the first of May. He didn't miss that, not one bit, although he wouldn't mind any weather at all if it meant he'd be able to go home.

It still seemed a bit dreamlike to think of seeing Elizabeth and his other loved ones after so much time. He had shared the news with his cousins the day he'd learned of his good fortune. Of course, they were thrilled that he would finally have the opportunity to go home.

"What an absolute joy, Andrew!" Julia had cried.

Josie had sniffed, "It's about time. Tell me, when you see your mother, are you going to ask her about Daniel Sullivan?"

Even now, as he trudged through the muddy, gaslit streets across town on his way back to the shelter of his room, he thought about the shocking circumstances of the relationship between his mother and Daniel Sullivan. The rain began to fall harder. Of course, there weren't any cabs to be found this time of night on the east side. They were as scarce and elusive on a rainy night as a good answer to Cousin Josie's question.

～

The next day dawned with a cool, clear sky and bright sunshine. Gunn returned to the ship just before seven. Work began again in earnest not long after he arrived and continued apace until the end of the day, with an hour-long break for the noon meal.

After a careful inspection of the rest of the ship's hull, Jayjay was satisfied that the damage was limited to the areas already discovered, and he assured Bulloch and Gunn that they had nothing more to worry about. The ship was otherwise sound. He and his crew continued work, removing two strakes back to amidships, exposing the bilge beneath the galley and a portion of the hold.

That evening, as the workday drew to a close, Gunn sat to rest on a three-legged stool on the port side in the shade of the ship's hull, sipping a beaker of water. Across the way, he saw the workers at Lamar's cotton press loading bales onto the deck of a three-masted ship moored alongside the wharf. Off to the side sat a lone bearded figure, dressed in black, inclined on a cotton bale, puffing on a cigar. The man rose suddenly, obviously agitated, and threw down his cigar, swearing and shouting to the men that if they worked any slower, the next crop would be in before they got this one loaded. He recognized the man as none other than Charley Lamar himself.

Jayjay appeared at Gunn's shoulder. "We all done for today, Mr. Gunn," he said.

"Good. Thanks for letting me know, Jayjay."

Jayjay wiped the sweat from his brow. "Be back at it tomorrow, bright and early."

Gunn went back to watching the man in black wave his arms and shout. He nodded. "All right."

"You know that man?"

"We have met. I do not care to know him."

"He is bad news."

"So I hear. Looks like he's a bit upset."

"He might be, but it'll do no good. Those men is mostly slaves. They ain't gwine work no harder than they have to, lessen he whup 'em. He ain't got the guts to do that. Even if he did, 'fore long they jes' go right back to doin' as little as they can to get by."

"I think you're right about that."

"I know I'm right. That's how it be. They got no reason to be no other way."

Gunn looked up at him. "But you own slaves. And from what I've seen, they've been working pretty hard."

"They be slaves, Mistah Gunn, that's true, but I don' own nobody. Not really, see. I buys 'em, but nobody owns 'em."

"Is that how they see it?"

Jayjay's eyes blinked slowly. He lowered his chin. "They see it same way as I do."

"I see. So why don't you just set them free?"

"Law say it must be this way. Too many free black men in this here town."

"Are there others with the same, ah, arrangement, then?"

"Some. But they some niggahs own slaves, they worser'n that man, dere." He nodded toward Lamar. "Much worser. Don' aks me why. I don' know. Sho' as hellfire, I don' know. Jes' the way it be."

Gunn shook his head. "I just don't understand it all. Never will."

"You ain't from round here, is you, Mistah Gunn?"

"No, I'm not, Jayjay. How can you tell?"

"You still tryin' to make sense of things that jes' be."

"Don't you try to make sense of things?"

"Vanity of vanities, say the preacher."

"I suppose you're right about that, too."

"Know I'm right."

"Well, let me ask you this, then. I'd appreciate an honest answer."

"Ain't got no reason to be dishones' with you, Mistah Gunn. Leastwise, not yet."

"Do you think things here will ever change?"

"Change how?"

"You know. Will slavery ever come to an end?"

"In Georgia?"

"And everywhere else."

"Hones' answer?"

"Yes, if you will."

Jayjay surveyed the scuffed toes of his boots. "Not without bloodshed, Mistah Gunn. Rivers of it. 'Night, now."

27

Gunn hurried across the wharf to where Reynolds Street sloped to the waterfront. Laboring up the steep incline of the river bluff, he reached street level in a very seedy, industrial part of town among millworks and warehouses, across the Bay from the new gasworks, all of which now stood upon the sites of several previous fortifications dating from the earliest days of the city. The gasworks promised to bring energy to the entire city, starting with the replacement of the old whale-oil street lamps, a project the newspapers hailed as lighting the way for a new era of progress and prosperity for Savannah.

He turned the corner on East Broad, walking past the Trustees' Garden, long untended and overgrown, where colonial experiments with the first cotton plants had taken place, along with failed attempts at silk production by cultivating mulberry trees. On the grounds now stood the old Seafarer's Tavern, which had been built around the walls of the former gardener's cottage.

For years, many tall tales had circulated about that decrepit place, the stuff of penny dreadfuls, sensational stories of the days when Blackbeard terrorized the coastline aboard the *Queen Anne's Revenge*, the bane of the colonies from Georgia to Virginia. The yarns often told of the hapless sailor, fallen into a drunken stupor, carried away unconscious through a hidden tunnel in the cellar that led to the river, only to awaken and find himself at sea on a strange ship, forced into piracy or impressed to sail to an exotic port beyond the Spanish Main, perhaps never to return. Some even claimed the inn was haunted by the ghosts of the pirates and their victims or others who had suffered misfortunes there.

Gunn smiled to himself. It made for good storytelling, and he had always loved a good, even fantastic story from the time he was a young boy, but he avoided the inn just the same in case the tales were anywhere close to being true. Besides, he'd been told the fare served there was not much better than galley tripe and far more dear, though the drink was decidedly more favorable by any sailor's standards.

This was not the fairest part of town, and he wondered why he had chosen to come this way in his rush to get back to his room on Perry Street, but it was the quickest route, allowing him to pass through the large open space of the Colonial Park Cemetery on the way. Of course, it meant he also had to pass the noisy, sooty rail yards of the Savannah and Albany Railroad, which brought cotton, timber, and other commodities into the seaport from all over south Georgia to be shipped around the world. The brisk traffic of commerce and industry also brought with it less desirable elements of human endeavor, which sometimes made it difficult or even dangerous to walk the nearby streets. Consequently, most everyone on this side of town likely was armed with a blade or a firearm—or both—as they went about their business. He carried a pocket rigging knife with him wherever he went, along with his shillelagh, which he hoped would prove sufficient, if necessary.

He quickened his step while realizing that it wasn't the prospect of danger or harm that made him anxious to get where he was going so much as it was the anticipation of the Sullivans' party, which was to take place later that evening. He needed to knock the dust off and get ready for the event with little time to do it, of course, but more than that, he found himself looking forward to it with a good deal of excitement and expectation, especially since his brief meeting with Sarah outside her garden.

Block by block, the streets became more residential as he walked farther south. Large and small wood frame homes were interspersed with vacant lots in places. This section of town, less affected by the many fires that had blazed through the city from time to time, boasted some of the oldest homes, where the wealthy once resided, now inhabited by those who couldn't afford to live elsewhere.

Gunn decided to cut through the streets on a diagonal to shorten his walk. Turning the corner on State Street, he soon crossed Greene Square, on the west side of which stood a one-story wooden church whose modest sign indicated its name as the Second African Baptist Church. Curious about its name, Gunn had learned the history of the church, which was established early in the century by former slaves, under the auspices of the white Baptist Church of Savannah. The first minister of the church was a freeman by the name of Henry Cunningham, a former slave and successful businessman, a hauler and cooper by trade, well respected by both blacks and whites. The unsettling fact that Cunningham himself owned no less than five slaves had astonished Gunn, so much so that it was etched in his mind.

As much as he had learned to love this city and appreciate its venerable history, Savannah's many unresolved contradictions still baffled him, though they seemed to go unnoticed—or at least unmentioned—by most of her proud citizens. But that uncomfortable fact was not so unusual, was it? To be sure, his beloved city of Boston had her own unsightly flaws in ticklish places, scarcely, if ever, mentioned in polite company.

At the far side of the square, two constables attempted to rouse a man, poorly dressed in dirty rags, asleep on the grass under a chinaberry tree. The bearded man, apparently drunk, responded slowly to their urgings.

"Do you know who I am?" the man slurred, waving them off.

"Likely a former congressman, I'd wager," one of the constables said, laughing.

The other grabbed him by the collar and hoisted him to his unsteady feet. "Why, if it ain't President Pierce hisself. You old lush, you. I knew you'd come to this one day."

In the past year, the aldermen finally had decided to crack down on vagrancy and other lawlessness, which had increased recently, despite the otherwise burgeoning wealth of the city. Consequently, they had doubled the number of constables on patrol. Gunn gave them a wide berth as he stepped into Houston Street, headed south.

He looked back over his shoulder to watch as the constables carted the man away by the arms. As he did, he noticed someone walking behind him, about thirty paces back, wearing a soft cap pulled low over his eyes. When he did so, the man stopped and turned, bending over as though to retrieve something dropped. He looked somewhat familiar. Not quite sure whether his concern about taking this route had excited his imagination, Gunn walked on.

Several blocks later, he turned west on South Broad Street, once the southern boundary of the city, but the sustained growth of the past century had since more than doubled the area extending now beyond to the south. He soon came to the north gate of the cemetery, which was open to the public.

Since its closing to burials four years earlier, the six-acre cemetery had become more of a park, where it was common to see people enjoying a quiet stroll or an afternoon picnic. It was a noble, peaceful site in the very heart of Savannah, a place of last repose for many of her finest citizens, including patriots, soldiers, and statesmen, as well as more than nine thousand other mere common folk. Many of the tombstones dated from colonial times, their epitaphs worn smooth and hardly legible.

Gunn passed the square-sided white marble monument to Archibald Stobo Bulloch, a revered hero of the Revolutionary War, a member of the Continental Congress, and the first governor of Georgia. The accomplished man, who had done great service to his country over many decades, also happened to be the great-uncle of his good friend, Desmond. Among other notable qualities, Gunn appreciated that one most of all. It was amazing what one man of courage and determination could accomplish in a lifetime. A hope resided in the depths of his mind that his own life might account for as much someday.

Peering over his shoulder, he noticed the same man as before trailing behind him, feigning nonchalance. It was beginning to worry him.

Gunn exited the west gate and crossed Abercorn Street. It was a short walk down McDonough to Chippewa Square and then to Perry Street, which he covered in the last five of his roughly twenty-minute walk. He had worked up a good sweat, and after spending a full day and night on the ship, he was in dire need of a hot bath.

Pulling his watch from its pocket, he noted that he had about two hours to prepare for his arrival at the Sullivans' residence, which included the time to walk there at a leisurely pace, so as not to ruin the effects of his preparations. He hoped Mrs. O'Reilly would have some hot water available, but he'd settle for a cold bath if necessary.

As he bounded up the front steps of the house on Perry Street, he tried to imagine what the evening would be like. More than anything else to be enjoyed, all of Savannah loved a good party. Over the course of the time he'd lived there, Gunn had attended half a dozen or so, including several military dinings-in, some of them quite lavish. None of the hosts, however, had ever invited him as a guest of honor. This occasion would be unusual, to say the least.

Before opening the door, he looked back one last time. There was the man again, a little nearer this time, close enough to recognize. It was Donnelly, the short, stocky man who had been with Charley Lamar at the City Hotel that day a week or so ago.

Gunn turned to descend the steps. The man reversed direction and walked briskly the opposite way. Gunn called after him. "Hey, Donnelly! What's your hurry?"

The man ignored him, turned the corner on Bull Street, and strode out of sight.

28

At a minute past eight o'clock, Gunn arrived at the Sullivan residence, just as Desmond Bulloch alighted from a carriage in front of the house. Although Gunn preferred to walk whenever the weather was fine, as it certainly was that evening, Cousin Josie had warned that the best way to ruin a good party was to show up late in dirty shoes. She'd offered the use of her own gig, which was not by any means ornate or luxurious, but it served the purpose. He asked Tobias, her driver, to drop him off at the curb, and informed him not to return since he would be very pleased to walk back to the house after the party. Tobias acknowledged with a tip of his hat, spoke softly to the horse as he pulled expertly on the reins, did as Gunn requested, and drove on.

Bulloch presented a gallant appearance in his finest dress uniform. Although they both wore the same double-breasted swallowtail coats replete with epaulettes and gold buttons on the sleeves, and a cocked hat pinned with a cockade of gold bullion, somehow Bulloch seemed to wear it better. Maybe it was the tailoring or the better quality of cloth. In any case, Gunn forced a smile, hoping that his appearance measured up.

The first lieutenant clapped him on the shoulder. "Well now, aren't we the cock's crow? You clean up nicely, Andrew. Don't let anyone tell you otherwise."

Gunn grinned. "This old cast-off? Why, I only wear these duds when it just doesn't matter."

"It's been a month of Sundays since I last wore this rig. Can't remember when."

"Fidgety at all?"

Bulloch snorted. "Like a hog in a smokehouse. But I don't know why I should be."

"Same. Never been a guest of honor before."

"Maybe that's it. Let's go in before they change their minds."

Other guests were arriving as they walked up the broad steps to the front door of the three-story brick house, open to the cool evening air. An Irish waiter in livery, one of several who attended the arriving guests, met them at the door and ushered them through a spacious, brightly lit hall into the parlor. Gunn noted with interest that all the servants visible in the house were white.

At the center of the resplendent, tastefully decorated room stood Sarah Sullivan, their hostess, wearing a confident smile and dressed splendidly in a low-cut burgundy silk gown. Around her neck shone a stunning diamond-shaped pendant, finely crafted in gold, studded with white diamonds in delicate floral settings, with a ruby in its center. She appeared more beautiful than ever, elegant and refined, much different than the last few times he had seen her, standing with her distinguished-looking father in evening dress. Both were surrounded by a group of men all in military full dress, except one. As they approached, the group opened into a semicircle.

"Ah, gentlemen," said Sarah. "Here come our saviors. Good evening to you both. I'm so glad you've come. I've asked some friends to join me in welcoming you. Shall I introduce you, or have you already become acquainted?"

"We know each other quite well, Miss Sullivan," said Bulloch, bowing to acknowledge them all. Gunn followed suit, a courtesy the others returned.

The circle of friends were all familiar faces whom they'd met on a number of occasions, both formal and informal. Mayor James Screven, also Captain of the Savannah Volunteer Guards, was chief among them, though not in uniform. The others flanking him were Francis Bartow, captain of the Oglethorpe Light Infantry, Joseph Claghorn, captain of the Chatham Artillery, and John Flannery, captain of the Irish Jasper Greens, the only company chosen to represent Georgia in the war with Mexico.

"I'm so sorry that Colonel Wright was unable to attend this evening," said Daniel Sullivan. "He sends his regrets."

"We're both honored to be in such distinguished company," said Bulloch.

"And is Mr. Grant not with you?" Sarah asked. "He was so kind in helping me."

"Regrettably, someone had to stay behind to attend to duty aboard our ship."

"Please do remember me to him," she said.

"Of course," said Bulloch.

Mayor Screven cleared his throat. "May we offer our condolences on the loss of Captain Dawes, gentlemen? He was a fine man, the best of his kind. I'm sure I speak for others here in saying that he was a good friend as well."

"Hear, hear," said the others.

Sarah glanced furtively at the floor, and the color drained from her cheeks.

"I apologize, Miss Sarah, I sincerely do. I had no desire to upset you or to bring a pall upon your lovely festivities. Do forgive me."

Gunn wondered if she were recalling her terrifying visitation on the ship.

"Of course, Mayor Screven, but there is nothing to forgive. I did not actually know the poor captain, but I do grieve his loss with you. And with all of you."

"Perhaps we will have an opportunity to raise a glass in his memory at some point in the evening," said Bulloch.

"I should like nothing better than to accommodate your suggestion, Mr. Bulloch," said Sullivan.

"My, my, aren't we all being so terribly formal this evening?" Sarah teased. "I think it's time we lighten the mood, don't you? This is a party, after all."

"Never you mind. It happens that I have some of the finest aged bourbon in the South. You gentlemen are all welcome to join me a little bit later to enjoy it. We'll pay our respects and lighten the mood all at once."

"I meant right now, Daniel," Sarah said. "Would you be so kind as to go and tell the conductor to start the music, if he is ready? Insist on something light and airy, please. Oh, and please remind him of my request for the first waltz."

"Of course, my dear."

"And as soon as the last guest has arrived, we'll begin dancing. Desmond, I have reserved the first dance for you, if you'll but ask me."

"Nothing would please me more, Miss Sullivan."

"Nothing would please me more than if you would refer to me by my given name."

"Sarah."

"There now, isn't that so much better? Come, gentlemen, we must revive the evening. This is to be a party, not a wake."

Situated in a corner of the room, a string quartet began playing a familiar Liszt nocturne, *"Liebestraume,"* heard frequently in parlors around the country. Sarah rolled her eyes.

The next guest to arrive was Dr. Richard Arnold, a widely known figure in town. As a physician, former state senator, two-term mayor, and current alderman, he had done as much or more than anyone else in Savannah to improve the habitability of the city over the years by addressing improper sanitation and drainage, which caused the various fevers that had plagued the entire population, rich and poor. Although they spoke only briefly to exchange pleasantries, Arnold impressed Gunn as direct and straightforward, with none of the affectations or pretensions one might expect of a former politician. Despite his thin, austere, somewhat aloof outward appearance, he offered Gunn a warm, hearty handshake and genuine appreciation for the rescue of his friends.

When Judge Nicoll and his wife walked in a few minutes later, Gunn greeted them right away and shook the judge's hand. A flummoxed look came across the man's lined face. He puffed through his mustache.

"Eliza, may I present . . . I'm sorry, young man, what is your name again?"

"Second Lieutenant Andrew Gunn, at your service. I gave a deposition in your chambers the other day about Captain Dawes."

"Ah, yes, yes. Now I remember."

"I am curious, judge. How did the horse race turn out? Did your mare win?"

Eliza turned on her husband. "John Nicoll, what horse race? Why, have you been at the track again?"

"Oh, now you've gone and done it, young man," Nicoll said with a mischievous gleam in his eye.

"I'm going to have another talk with that son-in-law of ours. He's incorrigible. Charley Lamar knows better than to tempt you against that stallion of his. I just hope you didn't bet anything this time."

Gunn did a double take, thinking that he surely must have misheard. "Excuse me, but did you say that your son-in-law is Charles Lamar?"

"Why, yes, of course, lieutenant," Eliza said. "He is married to our daughter, Caroline, though I never have understood what she sees in him. If it weren't for our grandchildren . . . why, do you know him?"

"Yes, I do. Though not very well."

"Do you consider yourself a friend of his? If you are, perhaps you could be a better influence on him. Try to get him to mend his ways. Lord knows I have."

"I can't say that we're on friendly terms."

"Well then, save yourself the trouble of trying. I swear, I can't wait until he gets here and then see if I don't give him a good piece of my mind."

"Now, Eliza—"

"Don't you *Eliza* me, John Nicoll."

As she led him away, the judge held up a thumb and forefinger spaced an inch apart and whispered, "Lost by a nose."

Someone placed a hand on Gunn's arm. He turned to find Bulloch at his elbow, along with a tall, distinguished, very somber-looking fellow.

"Mr. John Boston, allow me to introduce you to Second Lieutenant Andrew Gunn. Andrew, this is our new Collector of Customs, John Boston."

"I'm very pleased to meet you, Mr. Boston."

"Likewise. Mr. Bulloch here has told me much about you." Boston spoke in a genteel drawl.

"In that case, I should like a chance to defend myself."

Boston almost smiled. "All good, I assure you. He's informed me of your plight. Both he and my deputy have told me that you will be traveling home to New England shortly on leave while the ship is under repair. I must say that I heartily agree. I hope you will have safe travels and return to us well refreshed."

"I'm very grateful, sir. It's been a long two and a half years."

"No doubt. And let me say that I'm very sorry to hear about the death of Captain Dawes. He had a distinguished record and will be sorely missed."

"Yes, sir. Thank you. We all admired him."

"We will be hard-pressed to find someone to replace him, I'm sure."

"Well, sir, if you are seeking recommendations, there is no finer candidate than Desmond Bulloch."

"Andrew, there is no need—"

Boston raised an eyebrow. "Indeed? It is good to know that he is so well-regarded by a subordinate. But you will indulge me, I hope, in conducting a thorough search to my own satisfaction."

"Of course, Mr. Boston. I didn't mean to presume—"

"Nonsense, Mr. Gunn. I encourage any man to speak up and say his piece, if he's a mind to. I simply bear no obligation to pay any more heed than to give an opinion its due. Most every man has one, you know, just as he has a wallet. Some are of far greater worth than others, of course. Some have no value at all. I'm sure you'll agree."

"Some pretend wealth and have none."

"I often think it a pity that more do not pretend poverty. Don't you? Well, Mr. Bulloch, I see what you mean. Mr. Gunn here strikes me as a man of uncommon sense and sensibility. I'm sure you two will serve your fine ship very adequately, once she is again fit to sail, that is. And I wish you both very well in that endeavor."

"Thank you, sir," they said in unison.

"Now, will you excuse me? I must find Mr. Lamar, if he has arrived. Have you seen him? We have a matter to resolve between us." He did not wait for a reply.

"Of course, sir."

As Boston left, Bulloch caught Gunn's eye and shook his head without speaking.

Several other aldermen soon arrived, as well as attorneys, bankers, wealthy merchants and planters, along with wives or daughters who accompanied them, whose names Gunn could not keep straight, though he tried every trick of mnemonics he knew to remember them. Soon, the room overflowed with guests, who spilled into the adjoining drawing room, chatting animatedly in small groups. One name, however, he would not forget that evening. He couldn't, it seemed, even if he tried.

Charley Lamar was the last arrival of the evening. He breezed in twenty minutes late in a squall of jovial banter and laughter, his thunderous voice overpowering the polite chatter of the rest of the thirty or so guests. His wife, Caroline, followed him into the room, nodding apologetically to everyone who met her eye. Sarah immediately went across the room to her.

"Oh, Caroline, I'm so glad you could come. Please join us in welcoming our special guests." She linked arms with Caroline, whispered in her ear, and led her over to where Gunn and Bulloch were standing. "Allow me to introduce you. Caroline Lamar, may I present Lieutenants Bulloch and Gunn of the Revenue Cutter *Dobbin*. Gentlemen, this is my good friend Caroline Lamar."

They exchanged pleasant greetings. Caroline's gaze settled on Gunn. "Ah, and here is the young man we've been hearing so much about. It is a pleasure to finally put a face with such an illustrious name."

"Now, Caroline. Don't embarrass him," said Sarah.

Charley Lamar approached behind them. The air around them was charged with the odor of bourbon and stale cigars.

"And this is Caroline's good husband, Mr. Charles Lamar."

Lamar's magnanimous grin faded from his face. "Yes, of course, we've met."

"We have, indeed," said Gunn.

"Good evening, Mr. Lamar. How do you do?" Bulloch said.

"Splendid. Just splendid, thanks for asking. Never better. Always in favor of a good party, and the Sullivans are known for hosting the best ones, eh, Caro?"

"The very best," said Caroline. "And we're so glad you've returned to us safe and sound, Sarah. You and your father."

"You're too kind," said Sarah. She turned to address the crowd, raising her voice. "Ladies and gentlemen, if I may have your kind attention, please." The voices quieted. "Now that we're all here, I welcome you to our humble home, to which we are most gratified to have been restored by these two marvelous gentlemen and their heroic ship's crew, who saved us from certain death upon the high seas. We are greatly indebted to them all and deeply grateful. I give you Lieutenant Desmond Bulloch, of the Revenue Cutter *Dobbin*, and his second, Lieutenant Andrew Gunn."

A long round of applause erupted among the crowd, accompanied by shouts of acclamation.

Sullivan broke in. "Lieutenant Bulloch, won't you say a few words?"

Bulloch paused a moment, composing his thoughts. "On behalf of the officers and men of the Revenue Cutter *Dobbin*, let me just say how gratified we are that both Mr. Sullivan and his lovely daughter, Sarah, survived their ordeal at sea and that we were able to offer them shelter from the terrible storm. I only wish we could have saved more. We are deeply humbled to be honored as your guests this evening. Thank you all."

Another round of applause.

"How splendid," Sarah said. "Thank you, Captain Bulloch, for those kind words. It is a great comfort to know that we can rely on brave men such as yourselves to guard our coasts, our property, and our lives. And now, to celebrate our homecoming, we'll enjoy some wonderful music and dancing for those so inclined. Refreshments will be served afterwards, in the dining room, which you may enjoy throughout the house. Make yourselves at home, won't you? And if I may ask your indulgence, later this evening we have a special treat in store. We will have the distinct honor of being entertained by none other than two accomplished Shakespearean actors, the handsome and rakish John Wilkes Booth and the lovely Miss Claudia Connell, who have graciously agreed to join us after this evening's appearance at our own Athenaeum, to perform a few scenes from some of the finest plays ever written by human hand."

The crowd murmured their approval as they moved toward the walls to form an open circle while Sarah took Bulloch's arm and led him to the center of the room. The quartet struck up a delightful waltz that Gunn had never heard before. The two took a position in the middle of the circle and stepped without hesitation into an elegant dance. Sarah motioned for others to join in, and soon the Lamars and four or five other couples glided around the floor. Between sweeping turns, Sarah caught Gunn's eye and smiled.

After the third change in melody, about two minutes into the dance, Gunn acted on a whim to dance with her, a blithe impulse that he could no longer resist. He waited until Sarah and Bulloch passed his way, reached out, and tapped Bulloch on the shoulder. Bulloch turned and, seeing who it was, stopped and bent at the waist in a deep bow, releasing Sarah's hand. Gunn stepped in and continued the dance.

Sarah glanced up at him, her bright eyes smiling, her face glistening. "Do you like the music? I just love it."

"Yes, I do. I've not heard it before."

Her light perfume, the faint aroma of jasmine, tantalized him in the same way as her lovely smile. Her long dark hair, parted in the middle and gathered at the nape of her neck with a pearl-studded comb, cascaded in ringlet curls over her right shoulder and down her back, in what the common sailor would refer to as "follow-me-lads." Each time she moved her head, her hair brushed the back of his left hand.

"It's a new Strauss waltz with a German title that I find hard to pronounce."

"What is it in English?"

"You only live once!"

Her teasing laugh made him wonder for an instant if she had made it all up, but with Sarah in his arms, he decided in the moment that the title must indeed be true.

29

Their delightful waltz, which lasted all of four minutes and was over before Gunn could convince himself it had happened, was their only one of the evening, given that every other man present asked Sarah to dance, even her father. He was glad that he had decided to cut in on Bulloch. Throughout the evening, he danced with several other ladies, including Eliza Nicoll, who more than willingly conceded to dance with one of the guests of honor.

After more than an hour of merriment, refreshments were served, which included several layered cakes and a choice of vanilla bean or pistachio nut ice creams. Champagne flowed throughout, and many guests, including Charley Lamar, imbibed more than their share.

Later on, the men retired to the comfort of the library to smoke cigars and sip Daniel Sullivan's good bourbon and brandy, while the ladies gathered in the drawing room, drinking tea or coffee.

In the library, Bulloch and several of the military officers sat around a table playing three-card brag. Others lounged in the overstuffed leather chairs and settee. Mayor Screven, Judge Nicoll, and John Boston leaned against the fireplace mantel, chatting. Cigar smoke wafted to the high ceilings and hung there like mist over a moor.

Gunn stood near the far wall with Dr. Arnold, examining a brightly colored painting that had caught their mutual interest.

Lamar wavered with a drink in his hand, admiring a brace of dueling pistols in a velvet-lined case affixed to the wall behind Sullivan's desk. Sullivan poured himself a drink and joined him.

"Beautiful set, Sullivan. I've always admired them."

"Thanks. I'm told they belonged to Andrew Jackson himself—before he was president, of course. He apparently never used them."

"Balderdash."

"No, it's true. I bought them from a collector in Memphis. He got them from an estate sale at the Hermitage, or so he said."

Lamar raised an eyebrow. "Got balls?"

"Pardon me?"

"Bullets, man. Have you fired 'em?"

"Many times, and recently, I might add. They're very much in working order. Pretty accurate, too."

"Huh. I'd bet a thousand dollars they're not genuine. You want to sell them? Give you a hundred." Lamar drew out his wallet.

Sullivan laughed. "Put your money away, Charley. They're not for sale."

Gunn tried to bail him out. "Daniel, come tell us about this curious painting."

It was a provocative scene depicting a young couple seated at a piano in a parlor, with the woman, her clothing and hair somewhat disheveled, just rising out of the man's lap with a look of sudden revelation on her face. On the floor at their feet lay a discarded glove, and in the background a cat toyed with a broken-winged bird. Light flooded the room through a window from a garden outside, reflected in a looking-glass behind the couple.

Sullivan walked toward them. "It's called 'The Awakening Conscience.' To my understanding, it was painted several years ago by an Englishman by the name of William Holman Hunt. It's a copy, really. This one was painted by someone named Rossi, apparently a young art student somewhere. In fact, none of my paintings are originals. I simply can't justify the expense. I don't know much about art, anyway. I only know what I like. One of my clients bought this painting in London, but his wife decided she didn't like it very much, so he sold it to me. My daughter hates it. I don't know why. She won't say. So it hangs here in the library. But I find it intriguing. I think it says something about the condition of society today, don't you?"

"The details are incredible," said Dr. Arnold. "Quite realistic, I must say."

Gunn stared quietly at the painting. He looked at the face of the man, an expression of amusement in his eyes, pleading with the woman not to get up. "One wonders where the inspiration comes from."

"I certainly don't pretend to know," said Sullivan. "Although it is reported that the girl in the painting resembles Hunt's former girlfriend, an uneducated barmaid whom he met when she was just fifteen."

"Shocking," said Dr. Arnold.

"Very intimate," said Gunn. "And human, I suppose. Perhaps more human than the paintings of the past, which always seemed to be inspired mainly by virtuous or heroic themes. Don't you agree? Perhaps it tends toward a more honest depiction of the human condition."

"A more vulgar depiction, perhaps," said Dr. Arnold. "On that I would agree."

"Or more realistic," said Sullivan. "I think that's what I like most about it—its realism. I think we can be too idealistic at times. And we can forget who we really are. Sometimes, we need to be reminded."

Lamar poured himself another bourbon from the decanter on the desk.

"Who we really are," Lamar repeated. "Yes, I'll drink to that." He raised his glass, sloshing some of its contents. "A toast, gentlemen, to who we really are." He paused, as if to think. "And who are we? I mean really."

"Charley," said Judge Nicoll. "Haven't you had quite enough to drink?"

"No, no, dear papa-in-law. I'm as clear-eyed as I can be. In fact, I can see so clearly it's as though everything has become transparent to me. All at once, of a sudden."

"Why don't you sit down, Charley?" said Dr. Arnold. "Before you fall down and hurt yourself."

Sullivan changed the subject. "Perhaps it is time for us all to toast the memory of Captain Dawes, who sadly is no longer with us."

"Oh yes," said Lamar. "Let's toast the memory of all who are no longer with us, including, shall we say, my good friend Albert Jacobson's entire family, along with another hundred or so unfortunate souls, who perished in the unlucky sinking of the good old *Georgiana*, may they rest in peace. Happily, Albert survived, along with a dozen or so others just as lucky, no thanks to these two so-called gentlemen." He raised his glass, first to Bulloch and then to Gunn. "Are they gentlemen? I ask again, who are we really?"

"Charley, that's quite enough," said Judge Nicoll. "Go home now. You're obviously drunk."

"I am nothing of the kind," Lamar slurred.

"We are very sorry for your friend and his family," said Bulloch. "I assure you, Mr. Lamar, we did everything in our power to search for other survivors. We were blessed with good fortune to find Mr. Sullivan and his daughter."

Lamar raised his brow. "Did you do everything? Did you really? Well, how is it that another ship did find others? Answer me that. Let me tell you something. Let me tell you all what it's like to be stranded at sea on a piece of wreckage no larger than a dining table, or in an open boat, for days on end, waiting, just waiting for somebody to come along to save you. What it's like to lose hope, thinking that nobody will come and you'll die out there, alone, and your body will be picked apart by fishes and crabs." He thumped his chest. "I know. Yes, I know. I've been there, you see. And I've lost friends and family members to the sea. But you, Mr. Bulloch, so high and mighty, and *you,* Mr. Andrew Yankee Gunn, you don't know, do you? You have no idea."

"Charley, go home." Judge Nicoll left his place by the fireplace, took Lamar by the arm and forced him toward the door.

Lamar wrenched his arm free and spun around to glare at Gunn. "And I know just who you are, Gunn. Yes, I do. You've been sent down here to spy on me. Why, I'd bet Howell Cobb himself, Secretary of the Treasury of these so-called United States, your superior, sent you down here to spy on good old Charley." He thumbed his chest. "See what I've been up to. Well, I'm wise to you. Don't you think I'm not. And I've got my eye on you."

"That's simply not true," said Gunn. "It's preposterous. I have never met the man. And I have been assigned to the *Dobbin* for the better part of three years, long before Secretary Cobb came to office."

"A likely story."

"Well, I'm sure your man Donnelly will bear it out, once he's finished his snooping," said Gunn. "Ask him."

Lamar's face reddened. He seemed taken aback for a moment. "We'll see. We'll just see about that."

"And while you're at it, you can tell him to quit following me around town."

"Come on, Charley," Judge Nicoll urged quietly. He tugged at Lamar's arm. "Let's get Caroline and go home. My apologies to our host and to you all. We bid you good night."

"Don't apologize for me, judge," said Lamar. "I have nothing to apologize for. I'm proud of who I am, who I *really* am. And one of these days you'll find out who that is. Big changes are coming, believe you me. You'll see, all of you. And then, mark my words, you'll be apologizing to me."

Judge Nicoll led Lamar out of the room, and Sullivan shut the door behind them. The others sat or stood in silence. Boston put down his drink and made his way over to Gunn.

Sullivan turned to Gunn and waved his hand. "Pay him no mind, Andrew. You'll have to excuse Charley. He did lose his mother, two brothers, and three sisters when the steamship *Pulaski* went down back in thirty-eight. He and his father and his Aunt Rebecca were the only members of the family who survived. They were rescued after five days and nights, clinging to a bit of wreckage. Pretty harrowing. And he's had a run of what might be called bad luck, lately. He's obviously in poor spirits."

"What's this about Howell Cobb?" Boston asked.

"I have no idea, Mr. Boston," said Gunn. "I assure you that I don't know what he was talking about. I've never met Mr. Cobb, even when he was a congressman."

Bulloch rose and joined them. "Did you say something about being followed?"

Gunn waved him off. "It's nothing. Just trying to intimidate me."

"Maybe it's a good thing you are leaving town for a few weeks. Give things time to cool off."

"Oh, don't worry about Charley," said Sullivan. "He's all bark and no bite. He'll likely wake up tomorrow and not remember a thing about what happened tonight."

"I wish I could be so lucky," said Gunn.

"Say, what's this about your leaving town?" Sullivan asked.

"I am taking some leave to travel home for a few weeks."

"Ah, splendid. When are you leaving?"

"Tuesday, on the packet boat."

"The packet boat? Why, that will take forever. No, that won't do. Listen, I have an idea. Why don't you travel with me and Sarah up to New York on the *Lyoness*? We're leaving Monday. I have urgent business there with Charley's father, as it happens. He's one of my oldest clients. He needs to discuss a matter that won't wait. Sarah is feeling a bit restless, too, so off we go. Come with us. I'll pay your fare to New York in a nice, comfortable stateroom. A lot nicer than an old, cramped packet ship, I'd wager. One stop in Charleston, then two days to South Street. And you can take the express train to Boston from there. It will be much faster."

"I could never presume—"

"Nonsense. We'd love the company, Sarah especially. Someone her own age. I insist. You can turn your ticket back. What do you say?"

Bulloch chuckled. "Sounds a lot better than steerage, Andrew."

"Steerage? Oh, heavens no. We can't have that. No, no. I insist. You must come with us. It's the very least we can do to repay you for saving our lives, not to mention putting up with abuse from obnoxious party guests. Let us make it up to you."

"I can't—"

"I won't hear any objections, unless Mr. Boston has any reservations."

Boston shook his head. "I see no improprieties. I don't reckon that it would involve payment or *quid pro quo* of any kind. And it would allow you to spend more time with your family. Better take him up on it, Mr. Gunn. I would. It's the sensible thing to do. The *Lyoness* is about the best there is."

Gunn thought a moment. "Well, I guess it's settled, then. I'm very grateful, Daniel."

"Good man." He looked at his watch. "Now, unless I miss my guess, it's time for our entertainment. Sarah will be waiting for us. Gentlemen, if you please."

The men took a last sip of their drinks, then rose to accompany Sullivan back to the parlor.

Gunn touched Bulloch's sleeve. "I'm not feeling much like entertainment, Des. Not after all that."

"Don't go home, not yet. The night is young."

"I won't. I think I'll just sit a spell out back in the garden. Get some fresh air. It's a nice evening."

"All right. I'll let Sarah know."

"Thanks."

Gunn left the library and went down the center hall to the back door, which was louvered to allow air to circulate through the house. He unlatched the door and walked out onto the veranda. A set of stone steps led down to the garden, part of which was sunken below grade, lined with brick. Several benches offered seating there. He descended slowly, coming to rest on one of the benches.

Unbuttoning his uniform coat, he realized that he was drenched in sweat. The coolness of a slight breeze felt good on his skin. He took several deep breaths, which calmed his nerves. He felt his heartbeat slow as the rushing in his ears subsided.

Casimir trotted up and placed his forelegs on Gunn's knee.

"Well, there you are," said Gunn, scratching the dog's ears. "I was wondering why you weren't at the party. Couldn't take it anymore, either, eh?"

He wondered at his several encounters with Charley Lamar. Why was it that some people took an immediate disliking to a mere acquaintance? At this point, he felt the same way toward Lamar. He was starting to develop a resentment toward the man, despite knowing little about him, other than that he was arrogant, rude, and obviously well connected and influential in this town. And why should he not? Lamar had antagonized him from the first time they'd met, for little reason. And then sent his henchman to follow him around town to investigate or harass him. Why?

After a few moments, he heard the back door open and a light tread on the steps. He looked up to see Sarah, backlit from the lamp glow streaming through the windows of the house.

"Here you are," she said.

"Here I am."

"You don't want to come in?"

He shook his head. "Not in the mood. But you should. You'll miss Shakespeare."

"As it turns out, Booth isn't really my cup of tea. Oh, he's handsome enough, that's certain. But too dramatic. Too much waving of the hands." She mimicked him, and they both laughed. "Takes himself way too seriously."

"Like someone else I know."

"I heard what happened. I'm terribly sorry."

Gunn brushed the matter away with his hand.

She sat next to him on the bench. Casimir jumped into her lap and settled there. She stroked the little dog's head. "You mustn't let him get to you, Andrew. He can be a real brute sometimes. I often feel sorry for Caroline and what she's had to put up with. I wouldn't even have invited him if not for her, and for the sake of Charley's father, who has been one of Daniel's most steadfast friends, not to mention one of his best clients."

"I understand. I shouldn't let him get to me. I don't know why I do. He just rubs me the wrong way."

They sat quietly for a moment. The hint of jasmine scented the night air.

"Daniel tells me you're going with us to New York."

"Yes, he made a very kind offer that was nigh impossible to refuse."

"I'm very glad you accepted."

She took his hand in hers.

30

It was an innocent gesture, one of sisterly affection, nothing more, or so Gunn told himself the rest of that night and into the next day. She had taken his hand in hers, stroking it tenderly with the other, then looked into his face, as though about to say something.

"What is it?" he had asked.

"Nothing." She shook her head and smiled. "Never mind."

He should have reminded her that he was engaged to be married, but doing so might have imputed something to her gesture of kindness that wasn't intended. It was an awkward moment, to be sure, and there was nothing to be said for making it more awkward.

Sunday was of little consequence, other than that morning Gunn noticed some of his personal items—books, letters, his journal, and notes to himself—seemed to have been rifled through and shuffled, though he wasn't certain of it. When asked about the matter, Grant asserted that, to his knowledge, nobody other than he had been in the wardroom or anywhere near officers' country. None of his belongings appeared to have been disturbed, though he couldn't really say because his gear was always in disarray. He asked Bulloch as well, who said that nothing of his seemed disordered, but if anything was missing from their belongings, he would order a full investigation.

As far as Gunn could tell, everything appeared to be present except for his last letter from Elizabeth, which he thought he recalled leaving at the house. After some discussion, the three of them decided not to make a further issue of the matter among the crew, though they agreed to keep a closer eye on things. The greater disturbance in the entire incident, as far as Gunn was concerned, was not to his belongings, but to his peace of mind.

Monday dawned cool and overcast. After returning to the house to pack his valise and say his goodbyes to Josie and Julia, Gunn made his way to the waterfront, again accepting Josie's offer to have Tobias drive him in time to meet the Sullivans for a ten-o'clock departure on the outgoing tide.

His first concern was to return his unused ticket. The same clerk who'd sold it to him attended to his request for a refund, this time with the surly reply that he could only get back half what he paid. It was better than nothing, and four dollars was little enough to surrender for the opportunity of obtaining passage on a luxury steamer.

When he arrived at the *Lyoness*, Daniel and Sarah were already at the foot of the gangway. They both offered a warm greeting, Sarah with a kiss on the cheek.

"Ah, there you are," said Sullivan. "We were beginning to think you'd changed your mind."

"Not at all. I just had to wait for the change of watch this morning."

Sullivan handed him an envelope. "Good. Here is your ticket and stateroom assignment."

Gunn thanked him again for his generosity. "How did you ever manage to get a ticket at such a late date?"

"Oh, it was no problem, really. They were practically giving the staterooms away. Seems hardly anyone is traveling these days. You'd think we were headed into hard times, or something."

As they prepared to board the ship, Sarah turned to address a woman, tall and dark, who stood nearby. Gunn was a bit taken aback by her unexpected presence.

"Come along, Odah," Sarah said.

Odah followed a few steps behind, avoiding eye contact and fiddling with a small parcel in her hands, as they boarded the steamship together.

Gunn removed his ticket from its envelope, unfolded and handed it to the purser, who met them onboard. The purser assigned them each a porter to attend to their luggage and escort them to their staterooms.

"Meet us on deck when we depart," called Sullivan. "I always enjoy watching as a ship gets underway. Never tire of it."

Gunn nodded his agreement. He, too, liked to observe a ship of any size maneuver, to admire the skills of other mariners as they went about their work—or to otherwise criticize them, if the circumstances warranted.

The porter led him aft along the main deck to stateroom number eight on the port side. He noted that Sullivan entered number ten, adjacent to his, and Sarah the next one farther aft, which was number twelve. Odah waited outside. He had no idea where she might be staying, but that was of little concern to him.

Standing aside, the porter held the door open, and Gunn entered the roughly ten-by-twelve compartment, furnished with two bunks, both fitted with green damask curtains for privacy, a mahogany commode with two sinks, a comfortable-looking settee, and a steamer trunk beneath the lower bunk. A porthole on the outer bulkhead near to one side of the door shed light into the room. The porter lit a gimbaled oil lamp and indicated that the door on the far side opened into the main saloon. Compared to what he had anticipated in steerage on a mail packet, and what he had been used to aboard the *Dobbin*, the accommodations were nothing short of luxurious.

"May I suggest, sir, that you place any valuables or clothing into the sea chest? Should the compartment become flooded, it will serve you well."

"Does that happen often?"

"It has been known to, from time to time, especially in stormy weather, if we happen to take a wave over the stern."

After placing Gunn's valise next to the lower bunk, the porter stood by the open door expectantly. Gunn reached into his pocket and retrieved several coins. He gave the porter two bits, hoping that would be enough. Without batting an eye, the porter thanked him and exited, closing the door behind him and leaving Gunn to unpack his valise.

Gunn removed his hat and placed it with his shillelagh on the upper bunk, then pulled the steamer trunk from its place. He had packed lightly, mainly because he didn't own many clothes to speak of, other than his uniforms and two good suits, one of which he was wearing. He took the other from the valise, shook it out, and folded it neatly in the steamer trunk, along with three shirts and various other items of clothing.

Unpacking and stowing his things had taken less than five minutes. Certain that he had plenty of time before departure, he decided to explore.

He opened the door to the main saloon and stepped into what looked very much like the spacious lobby of an elegant grand hotel. The wood-paneled walls shone with a soft luster. Plush carpeting of burgundy and gold covered the entire floor. Polished brass oil lamps hung from the ceiling, spaced between two large skylights, one on either end. In the middle of the room, the great oaken trunk of the mizzen mast extended from the overhead of the spar deck down through the floor, around which was built a cushioned settee. Groupings of over-stuffed chairs and several gaming tables occupied the length of the saloon, along with three other elegant settees and a chaise-longue here and there. At the far end, an upright piano stood against the after bulk-head, with several chairs surrounding it. Across the way, a dozen doors led to staterooms on the starboard side. The forward end of the saloon opened into the dining room, the tables covered in white linen and set with fine china.

A ready waiter approached and asked if the gentleman desired anything at all. Gunn thanked him but declined and returned to his stateroom.

He exited to the main deck and walked forward along the cabins to the center of the ship, the length of which appeared to be well more than twice that of the *Dobbin*. He stopped to take it all in. It was the largest vessel he'd ever sailed in, capable of both wind and steam propulsion, with three tall masts, two side paddlewheels, and a large red funnel rising high amidships, belching coal smoke and steam. The gear and equipment were both familiar and foreign to him. Four covered lifeboats, two on the port side and two on the starboard, were snugged to their cradles. Everything seemed larger and more substantial than what he was used to.

It was a beautiful ship, majestic in size and proportion, though not as sleek and graceful as most sailing vessels, and certainly not anywhere near as nimble and handy as the *Dobbin*, or any other Baltimore clipper, for that matter. It was clearly built for comfort and ease of passage. He had been told that the *Lyoness* was a veteran of the transatlantic trade, but her owners had fallen on difficult times and sold her at a loss to a coastal line.

An officer, presumably the ship's first mate, blew a whistle, prompting crewmen to close the gangway and take the gangplank aboard. Line-handlers prepared to take in the mooring lines. Behind and above him, atop the pilot house, stood the full-bearded captain, hands clasped behind his back. With him, the pilot, speaking trumpet in hand, began barking orders.

A steam tug came alongside with the aid of hand signals from the boatswain and made fast to a hawser at the bow. The pilot ordered the mooring lines released, one by one, and when the last was aboard, the ship's steam whistle sounded one long blast. A moment later, the deck beneath his feet began to rumble, and the stack above coughed black smoke and sparks skyward as the starboard paddlewheel turned slowly in reverse. Cinders drifted to the deck and out over the water. The great ship's bow crept away from the wharf, coaxed by the backing tug.

Other passengers, though not as many as Gunn expected to see, gathered along the port rail to wave their goodbyes to family and friends ashore. Sullivan and Sarah hurried to join him in the waist of the ship.

"And we're off," Sullivan said.

"I hope they don't blast that whistle again," Sarah said, uncovering her ears. "I've gone half-deaf, I think."

"How are your accommodations?" Sullivan asked.

"First rate, thank you," said Gunn. "Quite a privilege, I assure you. It will spoil me, I'm afraid."

"Nonsense. Well deserved is as well done, I say."

"Where is, ah, Onah?" Gunn asked. "Did she go ashore?"

A bemused look came over Sullivan's face, as might a schoolboy's on his being quizzed with an algebra problem during a history lesson. "Odah has been made quite comfortable in quarters below decks."

"So forgive my forgetfulness on names and my curiosity, but is she traveling with you?"

"Yes, of course. Odah will keep Sarah company in New York, while I attend to business."

"Is she a . . . servant?"

Sarah laughed. "You mean, is she a slave?"

"Well, I—"

"Odah is a slave, Andrew," Sullivan said. His cheek twitched. "She is the only slave I own or ever will."

"I apologize, Daniel. I did not mean to offend."

"I hesitate to even think of her as a servant. She has been with us many years, more or less as part of the family. She was born a slave on a rice plantation out on the sea islands, once owned by my late wife's family. My wife inherited her as a wedding gift. Though I tried to free her after my wife's death, the laws of Georgia would not allow manumission without sending her to Liberia. She did not wish to go there. She stayed with us as a nanny, to tend to Sarah when she was still a girl. Now, she tends to her as a lady's maid, of sorts."

"Odah always has been more like a second mother to me," Sarah said. "She has cared for me like her own child."

"I see. Why wasn't she with you on the trip to Ireland?"

"She was terribly reluctant to go," said Sarah. "She feared something awful would happen. I allowed her to stay home."

"Said she saw it all in a dream," said Sullivan. "I guess I should have listened to her, eh?"

"I wish we both had," Sarah said. "But I thought she was just making excuses. She has always feared travel over water, especially across an ocean. It was hard enough to convince her to come to New York with us."

Tempted to ask the next obvious question about Odah's disparate quarters, as one avowedly so dear to them, Gunn nevertheless decided against it. No sense stirring a hornets' nest, when there was nowhere to escape and nothing of any benefit to be gained. Besides, as a ship's officer who had once sailed before the mast and experienced firsthand the disparities of class and station, he knew the answer quite well. There was nothing at present to be done for it.

31

The transit downriver was largely uneventful, other than the observation that it was far more appealing to Gunn as a passenger rather than a ship's officer, not constantly worried about where the next shoal might be or what ship or stray fishing boat they might meet in the river that would require a tight maneuver.

He spent a good deal of time on deck at the rail, taking in the landscape and enjoying the sights and sounds of the pelicans, herons, and white egrets along the way. He was delighted to see the familiar kingfisher, common as well to the marshes of New England, diving in flashes of blue and white from the branches of nearby bushes and trees into the black water to capture unwary prey in their beaks.

Even with the overcast sky, the lush beauty of the Georgia lowlands, with its tidal blackwater streams, teeming with wildlife, such as the occasional alligator sunning on the banks of the river, had never been more apparent to him. He marveled at the contrasts of the vibrant, variegated green of the expansive salt marshes, consisting of smooth cord grasses bounded by forests of hardwoods, cedar and cypress trees, some more than a thousand years old. They stood tall against the dark mudflats, or slobs, as his grandfather called them, where deposits of ancient upland soil flowed downriver, formed by the constant movement of current and tide into the rich bottomland of the estuary.

Some of the forests and swampland had been converted to large rice plantations, and several were quite evident along the banks of the river. Scores of slaves and indentured workers, mostly women, labored in the fields. Some were planting new checks, digging holes with their heels in the muddy clay, while others bent over in calf-deep water, cutting weeds with their hoes and chanting as they chopped.

Gunn glanced to his right to see Odah standing alone at the rail near the stern, looking out over the rice fields. She was wrapped in a white shawl, which also covered her head. Her face, fine-featured with high cheekbones, was solemn and stoic, her slender body erect and stiff. On an impulse, he approached her, mainly out of curiosity, though he had no idea whether to speak to her or what he might say.

"Good day, Odah."

She stood motionless, transfixed, silent, her eyes narrowed.

"I understand you have a long history with the Sullivans. They speak very highly of you."

She turned her head and measured him with her eyes. The wind played with the edges of her shawl, and it fell away from her face down to her shoulders, revealing dark wavy hair streaked with gray.

"Sarah, especially. She says you are like a second mother to her."

Odah reached up with a slim hand to clutch a sort of diamond-shaped talisman, made of bone and feathers, tied around her neck with a leather thong.

"I think it is good and very needful to feel so loved and cared for, especially for a child who has lost her mother at such a young age. It takes a special person to provide that, I think."

Her eyes fixed on his. They were the color and luster of pale blue sea glass, unlike any he had ever seen. They mesmerized him.

"You must have had someone in your life who did that for you. Your own mother, perhaps? A grandmother? Another of your people?"

"Meh peoples. You wan' savvy 'bout meh peoples."

"Yes, I do. I'm very curious. Won't you tell me?"

"What for you wan' savvy?"

"I don't know. I guess I'd just like to know something about you. Just curious. Where you come from. That sort of thing."

She turned her face back toward the bank of the river and reflected a moment on what she saw there. "You savvy how come de gator nebber sleep far from de ribberbank, massah?"

Gunn followed her gaze, where he spotted the alligator that she referred to, barely visible in the tall grass, its tail curled down the bank toward the water.

"No, I don't guess I do. I suppose it's to be ready to slip away quickly from any danger that might be at hand."

A wan smile crossed her lips, then disappeared. She nodded. "Das right. Eh done learn de hard way. An' eh ain't got no peoples. 'Scuse me, massah. Got to go tend to Miss Sarah."

She lowered her eyes, pushed herself away from the rail, strode to the nearest ladder, and made a rapid descent to the decks below.

It was an odd exchange, at once evasive and revealing, and Gunn couldn't help but feel Odah's disdain for him, hardly overt yet scarcely hidden. Her attitude troubled him, and he wondered whether he had unwittingly caused offense simply by talking to her.

In a little less than two hours, the ship steamed out of the mouth of the river and left the lighthouse at Tybee Island astern. The weather by that time had cleared, and as the rays of the afternoon sun slanted through the skylights of the dining room, Gunn sat with Sarah and her father at the table eating a sumptuous dinner.

"You know," said Gunn while cutting a morsel from the thick slice of prime roast beef on his plate, "I had a chance to meet Odah this morning as we came downriver."

Sullivan looked surprised. "Oh? And what brought that about?"

"She was up on deck, looking out on the rice fields. She was alone. I just thought I'd take the opportunity to speak to her. Get to know her a bit."

Sarah smiled in amusement. "Odah isn't the kind of person you just get to know a bit."

"I gathered that. She didn't have much to say."

"Not surprising. She usually doesn't. I am surprised she said anything at all to a total stranger."

"I was trying not to be a total stranger since she means so much to the lives of two people who I've come to consider good friends."

Sullivan took a sip of his wine. "Well, what did she say?"

"She was a little difficult to understand, but from what I gather—"

"Her people have their own language, a sort of Creole."

"Yes, well, when I asked about her people, her family, she said something odd about an alligator staying close to the water and that it doesn't have any people."

Sarah laughed. "She was telling you that she doesn't trust you enough to tell you anything."

"She called me 'massah.' I still find it impossible to get used to that form of address, no matter how long I live here."

"You are a stranger to her in a world that does not accept her as fully human. A world that has the power to make her life utterly miserable, if it so chooses. How else is she to refer to you?" Sarah said.

"I do not consider myself anyone's 'massah.'"

"But how would she know that?" she said. "You are a white man in the South, Andrew. That is the way of things. Surely, surely you understand that by now."

"That doesn't mean I have to like it."

"It doesn't mean she likes it, either, any more than you do. Likely less."

"Point taken." He put down his fork. "But am I to infer, then, that she really has no people, no family? Or was she just keeping me at arm's length?"

"Why should it interest you so much?" Sarah asked. "What difference does it make?"

Her challenge to him made him question his own motives. Though he had learned long ago not to ask too many unwelcome questions, some inquiries simply could not be avoided for the sake of prudence and sometimes even well-being, especially when he felt uneasy about the circumstances. "No great difference, really. Just curiosity." He shrugged. "One cares, you know."

Her eyes teased him. "One cares, does one? Care'll kill a cat."

"I don't think she does have any close relatives, if that's what you're asking about," said Sullivan. "As I understand it, she never knew her father, who was sold to a plantation in Mississippi before she was born, and her mother died when she was very young. Her people are the Gullah. Some call them the Gullah-Geechee. They are a very close, tightly knit community, mainly of the coastal islands. But she would not likely tell you anything about them."

"Her mother told her that she was descended from African nobility," said Sarah. "At least that's what she told me. She's from a long line of priestesses going back generations, that began over two hundred years ago in the land of her ancestors, the Dyula people, in what the French refer to as the Ivory Coast. Her people were conquered and sold into slavery by a warring Mohammadan tribe. She also has told me that she still maintains contact with her dead mother, who tells her things that others do not know. Things about the past and the future. She has dreams."

"Yes, you said so earlier."

"Yes, I did."

"And you have dreams."

"Yes, I do."

"Sarah," said Sullivan.

"Daniel," she said. She put a wineglass to her lips and peered over the brim.

"We agreed to avoid that subject for a while."

"It has been a while."

"Longer. A while longer."

"I haven't had one for a while."

"Good. I'm glad to know it. Now, can we please change the subject? Certainly, we can find other things to talk about than the history of the African slave trade and supernatural visitations."

Gunn cleared his throat. "I'm sorry to have raised it, Daniel. I seem to be stepping all over my own beard lately. Again, I do apologize."

"But your face is always so clean-shaven, Andrew," said Sarah. "And such a nice, handsome face it is. How is that for a change of subject?"

"Never mind, Andrew. I know you don't mean any harm." Sullivan downed his glass of wine. "Now, if you'll excuse me, the captain has kindly offered me a tour of the engine spaces after dinner. You're welcome to join me, if you like."

Sarah shook her head. "No, thank you, Daniel. You go enjoy yourself."

"I'll pass, thanks, if it's all the same," said Gunn. "It takes all the mystery out of it for me." Nothing could interest him less than the ugly, oily machinery of a steamship, given his preference for the grace and wonder of a ship sailing on the wind. Besides, he had a few more pressing questions for Sarah.

Sullivan laughed as he rose from the table. "Suit yourselves. But if you truly want to see into the future, and what dreams are made of, I can't think of a better way."

After Sullivan left, the two of them sat silently for a moment.

"You must forgive Daniel. He has a great deal of sensitivity about certain subjects."

"It's entirely understandable. I must try harder to steer away from the more obvious shoal waters. I just can't seem to help myself, especially when it comes to the topic of slavery. It's just all around us. You can't escape it, no matter how hard you try."

"If Daniel had his way, the topic and the practice of it would die a very quick and unwept death."

"As it should."

"Good. We all agree. That's settled, then, isn't it?"

"Yes, but now that your father is not here, I must ask you something else about Odah."

"And what might that be?"

"Do your dreams have anything to do with Odah's influence, do you think? I mean, you referred to her as some sort of spiritualist. A priestess, I think you said. What sort of priestess, may I ask?"

Sarah folded her napkin and placed it neatly on the table. "Now, young sir, you are at risk of offending me."

"Forgive me. I'm very sorry. I'm just asking. Where do your dreams come from? What causes them? It's a question worth asking, isn't it? I'm interested, even if your father isn't." Her visitations while on the *Dobbin* had astounded, troubled, even frightened him. He had thought about them ever since, and he could no longer keep from asking these questions. He had wanted to ask them several times before. The lesson that he had learned years ago about asking needful questions was not lost on him. This was his chance.

"Oh, he's interested, Daniel is. Interested in getting rid of them once and for all." She took a deep breath and exhaled. Her gaze fixed on his chest. "This is all so deeply personal." She hesitated, brushing a wisp of hair from around her face, her hand trembling for a split second. "My own mother had dreams. Have I told you that?"

He shook his head, keeping silent on the disclosures that her father had made to him.

"She used to tell me that I have the gift of second sight. Odah saw it in me, too, and has always encouraged it, taught me to use it for the sake of others, as my mother did. They were kindred spirits, the two of them. They were of the same age, you know, and they grew up together, virtually inseparable. So close. Odah was heartbroken when she died."

"I see."

"Do you? I doubt it. I'm not sure I do, at least not entirely. I'm trying to describe something that defies description."

He sipped the last of his wine. "I understand how difficult it must be. Go on."

A sudden, mischievous smile parted her lips. She chuckled. "Certainly, no more difficult than to be seen naked in public view, now is it? You seem to have a penchant, dare one say a proclivity, for having me bare my soul, so to speak, don't you?" she teased.

He glanced over his shoulder at a nearby table. "Stop joking. Someone will hear you."

She put on airs of false modesty, crossing both arms over her bodice. "Why, you, sir, methinks are no gentleman."

His face grew warm. "Stop it now. Be sensible and serious."

"I am being sensible. And most serious." She laughed out loud, attracting the attention of the foursome at the next table. She waved her fingers at them, and they nodded a polite greeting with feigned smiles. "You know, you reminded me very much of my father just now. You're the one being silly, Andrew."

"Hardly my intention, I assure you."

"Ye gods!" she said under her breath so only he could hear. "Are you always so easily set upon? Do all your friends have such an easy time of it?"

"I have but few friends. For the most part, I find they in general seem to have an easy time of being *friendly* to me, more often than not. Hence why I call them friends."

She laughed again but not at his expense this time. Her eyes held an acceptance, an affirmation in them that he hadn't seen before, and she seemed genuinely amused. She regained her composure and settled into a more serious demeanor. Her head tilted to one side. She leaned forward and her voice lowered into a near whisper.

"All right, then. I choose to be serious. And I'll be straightforward with you. Perhaps it is an inherited trait, this second sight, or whatever you want to call it. Or maybe it is acquired. I don't know. It's like the wind. You don't know where it comes from, you don't know how long it will blow, and you don't know where it's going. I don't question it anymore." She raised her voice. "But whatever the cause or the circumstances, I don't blame Odah, nor do I suggest that she is somehow a negative influence, and I would never do so. How could I? And I resent the fact that you would ever suggest such a thing."

"Sarah, believe me when I say—"

"It is a gift, Andrew. That's how I see it. A gift to me. You must understand this. Sometimes, I view this gift of mine as a curse as much as a blessing, admittedly, and there are times, many times, I wish I didn't have it, that it would just go away, but there it is." Her eyes, widened, met his. "It hasn't gone away, and it might never go away, Andrew, no matter how hard my father and others, including you, might wish it gone."

It occurred to him, though he did not say it aloud, that what she described as her gift was not so very different from slavery of another kind.

32

With a favorable wind and following sea, the *Lyoness* made Charleston by six o'clock in the evening to take on additional passengers and cargo for the trip to New York and to discharge those whose business took them no farther. Gunn calculated that, if he made the same trip on the *Dobbin*, even in ideal conditions, he probably would not have arrived until well after midnight. As much as he preferred the cut and carry of a sailing vessel, there was no denying that, in terms of comfort and speed, steamship travel was far more desirable. And the accommodations were certainly preferable to the berthing deck on a lumbering packet ship.

As the steamship left Charleston harbor about two hours later, off her starboard side the dark outline of Fort Sumter towered against the evening sky. The newly constructed brick-and-stone ramparts, facing seaward, away from the city, were complete, and work on the interior continued apace. It would not be long now until the imposing fortification could perform the duty of the federal government to defend the coastline of South Carolina and the city of Charleston against even the remote possibility of foreign invasion.

Gunn took a good deal of pride in sharing part of that same duty to protect and defend the United States, even in the midst of past and current threats by hotheads in South Carolina and elsewhere among the Southern states to secede from the Union over the issues of states' rights and slavery. Forces had been at work for decades to break the fragile Union into pieces, and he hated even the idea of it happening.

Several squalls passed through as they reached the open sea, and the heightened waves and offshore swells caused many passengers to get seasick. Supper onboard that evening in the dining room was not well attended. Those who could eat enjoyed a light meal of soup, cold meats, cheeses, and loaves of fresh-baked sourdough bread, which Gunn found delightful, as did the Sullivans.

That evening, after the weather cleared, Gunn and Sarah took a stroll around the main deck together. Clouds hovered on the horizon in the distance, but above them shone brilliant starlight. She took his arm, and they walked for an hour and spoke of hopes and dreams, laughed about what-if schemes, and shared thoughts on other things that pleased or vexed them both before saying good night.

Back in his stateroom, Gunn undressed by the dim light of the oil lamp. He stripped until naked, his preferred state of sleeping since coming south and having to endure the heat and humidity of the sultry summer nights. He doused the lamp and crawled into the lower bunk. The fine linen sheets felt cool to his skin. When he at last drifted off, the dream that had troubled his sleep many times in the past several years visited him yet again. It was the familiar nightmare of standing alone on the high banks of a windswept coast, and losing his footing to fall head-long to the surf, crashing against the rocks below. He awoke in a cold sweat just before dawn.

Sarah did not appear at breakfast that morning. When Gunn inquired about her, Sullivan said she'd had a bad night but didn't specify any details. Her father assured him that she soon would be fine, however.

As they sat eating breakfast together, Gunn thought about something that had been on his mind for some time since his discussion with Josie and Julia about the history that his mother shared with Daniel. He debated whether to broach the subject with Sullivan, concerned that he had already caused some consternation with his previous questions and observations, but he came to the conclusion that there was no time like the present. He simply had to know.

"I hope that you won't find it disturbing, Daniel, but I must ask you about something very curious to me that I learned recently about my mother and . . . well, you."

Sullivan put down his knife and fork, picked up his cup and took a tentative sip of coffee, testing the heat of it.

"Oh?"

"We spoke previously about my cousins, Josie and Julia, and you said you didn't know them. But you did remember my grandparents. And my mother, Eleanor, and her sister, May Gryffith. Do you recall?"

"Certainly."

"Well, I mentioned your name to my cousins, and they told me something very interesting."

Sullivan's cup rattled as he placed it in its saucer. A slight frown appeared on his lips, which he brushed with his napkin. "And?"

"They told me that they remember you very well. And that you knew my mother very well. In fact, you were once engaged to be married. Is that true?"

Sullivan bit his lower lip and shook his head. "We were never engaged."

"You weren't?"

"We had an understanding. That's very true. Your grandfather would not permit our engagement."

"Why didn't you tell me that?"

"Well now, Andrew, it's not exactly relevant anymore, is it? What happened so many years ago between your mother and me is just that— between us. But it has no bearing on the present, which is . . . now." He glanced up at the skylight for a moment. "'Things without all remedy should be without regard. What's done is done.' Shakespeare." He looked back at Gunn. "Very appropriate, I think. And true."

"'What's past is prologue.' Also Shakespeare, I think. Also true."

"What's your point?"

"It's fascinating, don't you agree? What happened then does affect us today, certainly in ways that are plain and unmistakable, and perhaps in ways that neither of us are even aware of."

"How so?"

"I don't know. Decisions we've made. Memories we carry with us. Thoughts we can't shake. They all affect our lives, don't they? Even unconsciously. Sometimes materially."

"I suppose they do."

"Take my mother, for instance. Things that've happened in her life have had a profound impact on her. According to my cousins, she was a very different person back then, full of life and vigor. A strong, beautiful woman who knew her own mind, who lived in the present and longed for the future, though maybe a bit naive about what it might bring."

"Yes, that was the Eleanor I remember."

"What else do you remember about her?"

"Really, Andrew."

"I'd truly like to know."

"Well, the one thing I'd add to what you've already said is that she had a way of making me feel that her love would never fail. I once thought that she would never forsake anyone she truly loved."

"That is still true."

"Is it?"

"I believe so. Have you come to doubt it?"

Sullivan put off the question with a backward wave of his hand. "The other things you said, are they no longer true of her?"

"My father stripped them away, one by one."

"I am sorry to hear that."

"So am I. He betrayed her and our entire family. I won't tell you how, because it is too humiliating even to mention. Let's just say he went his own way. I've tried to forgive him because my mother asked me to, for my own good. But I have found it very hard to do. I still can't stand the thought of him for more than a moment."

"That's too bad, truly. A son should never have to think ill of his own father."

Gunn winced. "I am not looking forward to seeing him in New York, where he now lives. The only reason I'm even considering it is that my sister lives with him. She recently moved to New York from our home in Concord to live there. I want to visit her and make sure she's all right. So I may have no choice."

"I see."

"Enough about me. My first question was about you and my mother. What happened? I mean, from your point of view."

Sullivan paused a moment and breathed a slow sigh. "I guess in the simplest terms, I'd have to say that her love failed me. Failed us."

"What do you mean?"

"She left Savannah, left me, without even a goodbye or a fare-thee-well. Didn't write. No address. Nothing."

"Do you know why?"

"I can only assume she changed her mind. Her heart."

"No. I doubt that very much. You see, my grandfather threatened that if she didn't give you up, he would disown her and do everything he could to destroy you."

"Well, he told me the same thing. But I didn't care. We loved each other. That fact was all that mattered. At least, to me. I begged her to stay. We could have done something to make it work."

"Maybe she couldn't stand the thought of you left with nothing."

"If I'd had her love, I would have had everything."

"Did you really feel that way?"

Sullivan leaned back. "I always have. Still do. But I guess in truth I've also admired the strength that it took for her to do what she did. And she did it for me, or at least that's what I've managed to convince myself. But in the end, I can't help believing that there was some other reason. Something she wasn't telling me, more compelling than anything else."

"What would that have been?"

"Don't know. One can only imagine."

"You must have hated my grandfather."

"I did, for a time. When I later married and had my own daughter, I understood a bit more how a loving father will do anything that he thinks is in the best interest of his child."

Stunner. He had never known that kind of love from his father. How different their lives would have been if his own father had felt the same way about him and his siblings. A sudden yearning stirred deep within his gut.

"That's fascinating to me."

"Now, don't get me wrong. I've had a good life, despite what happened early on. I loved my wife, Miranda, bless her soul. She was a good person and the mother of my only child. Though we may have quarreled a great deal about how to raise her, we managed to make a decent life for ourselves. But it was very different from the one I imagined with Eleanor. The two of us shared a passion for life, and we knew where we wanted it to go. It promised to be a great adventure."

"I wish you'd had the chance, Daniel. As God is my witness, I truly do."

Sullivan rested an elbow on the arm of the chair, his chin in his hand. "Does it occur to you that if we had, things would have been very different? You might not even be here right now."

Gunn grinned. "It has crossed my mind. But I think that illustrates the point I was trying to make very well. Don't you?"

Sullivan leaned forward again. "You ask some hard questions, Andrew. Now, let me turn the tables and ask you one."

"Fair enough."

Sullivan took a deep breath. "Just what are your intentions toward my daughter?"

Gunn blinked twice. "Beg your pardon?"

"You heard me."

"In what way, exactly?"

"In the only way that matters."

"Perhaps she has told you that I am engaged to be married."

"She has. That's why I asked the question."

"Well, I—"

"Sarah has become very fond of you."

"As I have become of her. She's a fascinating woman."

"There's that word again. *Fascinating*. You use it a lot. I think you like that word."

"I suppose I do. It's a good word. I find it fascinating. Don't you?"

Sullivan chuckled. "You're avoiding the subject."

"Yes, I am. Because I don't know how to answer you, altogether."

"Simple. Just say it. Answer me. What are your intentions?"

Gunn pulled at his ear. "My intentions are entirely honorable, Daniel. I can't believe that you would imagine otherwise. Your daughter is a delightful young woman. And I take delight in knowing her. She has become my friend, and I'm glad to call her my friend. I hope she feels the same toward me. That is all."

"Things can happen between two people, a man and a woman. Things we don't anticipate, or even comprehend sometimes."

"I know. I understand that. But I assure you that I have no intention of anything beyond being a good and decent friend to Sarah."

"I've seen the two of you together. I've watched you closely. I see the way she looks at you and laughs and jokes with you. I hear the way she talks about you. There is a closeness growing between you two. A bond that goes beyond mere friendship."

What he asserted was true, though it made Gunn uncomfortable to admit it. "Well, I suppose it might appear that way."

"Part of the reason I asked you to come with us on this trip was to have this little talk and to nip things in the bud, so to speak, before things go too far. But I fear it may have worked against my purposes."

"There is no bud to nip, Daniel."

"Really? If that's true, then I leave it to you to tell her so."

"By all means."

"Good. The sooner the better. Andrew, I like you very much. You have many fine qualities that are lacking in many men these days. In fact, I wish to God that I'd had a son like you."

Gunn started to speak, but Sullivan held up his palm.

"Nothing would please me more, if things had taken a different path, than to have you as my only son-in-law. And I would never stand in the way of Sarah and her happiness with someone she truly loves. I know better than that, believe me. As a result, at times, I have perhaps erred in being too permissive with her, and she is a very willful woman, as you very well may know by now. She has a mind and heart of her own. But here is the crux of the matter. You are betrothed to another, whom I presume you love above all others. And as a father, I must warn you, if you mislead Sarah, misplace her affections, or do anything else to hurt or dishonor her, I will do everything, and I mean everything, that is in my power to destroy you. Just so we understand each other."

The words had the effect of a door slammed in his face. "Sir, I am speechless."

"I'll settle for that. I was aiming for fascinated."

33

After supper that evening, Gunn sat alone in a comfortable chair at the far end of the saloon near the piano. Although Sarah had joined their table for supper, she seemed withdrawn and tired, not at all her vibrant self. Their conversation had been subdued, and she'd excused herself abruptly, saying with apologies that she still was not feeling well and wished to retire early.

Gunn wondered what might be the matter, surmising that perhaps she and her father had spoken previously about his concerns, although neither of them had said anything to indicate such. No doubt, *no doubt*, it would have been a lively confrontation between them, if so. He also tried to compose the words to say what must be said to Sarah, though he was not at all sure when he might have the chance, given the ship would arrive in New York the next day. He could have kicked himself for not taking the opportunity sooner to make himself plain to her. Though he could not deny his nascent feelings for her, his betrothal to Elizabeth meant that those feelings could go no further than friendship.

The door to her stateroom opened, and Sarah stepped into the saloon wearing fashionable evening dress, along with her ruby pendant. Her face seemed refreshed and rejuvenated, and her hair was styled in the same lovely way it had been at the soirée. She surveyed the room as she walked through, smiling as she spied him.

"I was hoping to find you here," she said brightly as she approached. "Sitting with all your friends, I see."

He rose to greet her and returned her smile. "Yes, and they are all being unfailingly nice to me, though I'm being rather hard on myself. You may join us, if you are inclined to do the same."

"Why, of course. And why wouldn't I? Be hard on you, too, that is."

They both laughed. He offered her a seat next to his.

Instead, she took a seat at the piano. "Oh, look. What a lovely piano," she said. "It looks as though it wants desperately to be played. Shall I?"

"By all means." He sat back in his chair to listen.

She placed her hands gently on the keys and began playing with a delicate touch one of Gunn's favorite pieces, a nocturne by Chopin. It had an ethereal, dreamlike quality and she played it from memory as though she had composed it herself. Her eyes closed and her head inclined toward the keyboard. She played the piece so softly, at times he could scarcely hear above the steady thrum of the engines, especially at the closing notes.

"That was lovely," he said as she finished. "Dreamlike."

She opened her eyes and smiled at him. "I'm so glad you enjoyed it."

"You're quite talented. I had no idea."

"Oh yes, of course. Daniel insisted that I become nothing if not quite accomplished in all the womanly arts. And I live to please my father. I can sew, too, you know. Exceedingly well. And cook and garden and hold a conversation on all the important topics, like the vagaries of the weather, how perfectly marvelous the homily was last week, and what a simply wonderful event the ladies' aid society has planned for next month. I'll make such a good wife, one day, don't you think?"

"I expect so."

"Yes, well, except that's not necessarily what I want. At least not right now."

"What do you want?"

"What do I want? Let's see, now." The fingertips of her right hand tapped lightly on the keys, then she reached out to take his hand, which he withdrew. "Come sit with me at the piano."

"What?"

"Come here and sit with me. I'll sit in your lap, like the painting in our library. Have you seen it? I'm sure you have. Daniel shows it off to everybody. Come on." She waggled her fingers. "Come."

"You know I can't do that, Sarah."

"Why not?"

"Well, it wouldn't be a proper thing for an unmarried couple to do, especially in public, for one thing. And for another, I am engaged to be married soon. You know this."

"Why should that matter? We're here now. Together. In this moment."

"It does matter. And you know why."

"Oh, the conscience thing. Yes, of course. Of course. I hate that painting, you know."

"Why do you hate it?"

"Because of the pathetic, insipid look on that silly girl's face. A stupefied stare of sudden revelation, as though an unseen angel whispered in her ear at just the right moment. In the nick of time. It makes me want to scratch her eyes out."

"Don't hold back."

"As I said, I hate it."

"What else do you want?"

"I want what I cannot have, and I cannot have what I want. It's all in the yearning, not the getting. Yearning is sublime. Getting is so mundane, blasé."

"That is a very romantic notion."

"I love the romantics, don't you? Madame de Staël, Schlegel, Byron, Keats, Shelley, Wordsworth. They all wished to turn the world upside down, even to create a new one, where all the old order is tossed aside. They write of a new genesis, by which we can reconcile and rebalance opposite and discordant qualities by elevating the common over the noble, the savage over society, chaos over order, darkness over light, sensibility over sense, emotion over logic, sensuality over the spiritual. Only then will we all be truly free. Free of ancient social mores and outdated, silly rules about how we all must live."

"That would indeed be a new world. I'm not sure we would survive in it. Any of us."

"Nonsense. Only then will we thrive. I likely will not live to see it. Maybe it will take a hundred years or so to bring it about, but I desire that world in which we all, especially women, are free to do as we wish, as someone once said—I've forgotten who—'to enjoy what pleases us, to be moved by what moves us, to admire what seems to us admirable, even when it can be proved to us that we ought not to admire it or be moved by it or enjoy it.' Something like that."

"I've heard that wind blow before."

"Now you're mocking me."

"No, truly, I have heard it all before. Or something very similar. My sister feels very much the same way."

"I think I'd like your sister."

"I'm sure you would. I think she'd like you, too."

"What is her name?"

"Marguerite. We call her Meg for short. Or at least I do. She hates it when I do."

"Then you shouldn't."

"I suppose you're right."

"And I'm right about the world I want to see. Just imagine it."

"I'm trying to. It would seem to me, and I've told Meg—um, Marguerite—the same thing, that the entire world likely would end up fighting ourselves. We all want different things, don't we? People are selfish by nature. We'd very likely be constantly at war with each other, at each others' throats, to get what we want. Don't you think?"

"No, I don't. We'd be a lively coalition of diverse interests, united in a common goal. We'd be at war with the rules, not each other. The rules of convention. Ludovic Vitet said that."

"Your father must have quite the library."

"Maybe you should ask him to use it sometime. You'd likely benefit from it."

"Oh, ho. Say what you truly think. All right, then. Maybe I will sometime."

"I'm sure he wouldn't mind, although he says that sometimes he wishes I'd never learned to read."

He shook his head. "Look, I don't know who Vitet is, but what he said, that tripe about being at war with the rules, sounds a little absurd to me."

She scowled at him for the first time since they'd met. "How so?"

"Well, I don't mean to offend, but think about what you just said. 'Diverse interests united in a common goal.' Diversity is the exact opposite of unity. Their meanings are in direct contradiction. You can't have both. You can have a coalition of *common* interests in a common goal, but people with diverging interests will never achieve unity in a common goal. It is an ideal that can't be reached."

"'Do I contradict myself? Very well then, I contradict myself.'"

"Ah, there's our friend Whitman again."

She closed her eyes, and they fluttered for a moment. "You don't seem to understand. And you're missing the point. That's the exact idea I'm expressing. The reconciliation of opposing values." She opened her eyes and glared at him. "I was hoping for better from you, Andrew."

"If you were hoping for some sort of romantic philosopher, I'm sorry to disappoint."

"That's not it. You simply can't see past what is. That's your trouble."

"That's not true. I can see what could be, what might be, what should be. I want those things, too, very much. I value and want freedom as much as the next person, for instance. We just disagree on what it is or how to attain it."

She held out her hand again. "All right then, prove it."

"I am not going to let you sit on my lap, Sarah. That's not a freedom I choose to attain."

She laughed. "That's not what I meant, silly. Come with me. I need to show you something."

"What is it?"

"An illustration. One that even you will understand."

34

Sarah took his hand and led him through the aft door of the saloon to the main deck, where they were windswept as soon as they stepped outside. The door slammed shut behind them.

The breeze had veered to the northwest, and the ship was headed almost directly into the eye of it, amplifying its force and effect. Above them, the wind sang in the rigging of the mizzenmast, and a thousand stars danced around the mizzen top and among the empty spars.

She stopped near the rail and drew him close to her. Reaching up to the nape of her neck, she removed the comb in her hair, then shook her head, allowing her long tresses to blow freely in the wind.

"Isn't it wild?" she shouted, twirling around, her arms held wide. "Do you hear that? Can you hear the voice of the wind singing the song of freedom? I just love being at sea, with nothing else around but the wide-open ocean and the wind in my hair. Nothing at all to hinder or bind. Anything is possible. This, *this* is what I want."

"It can also be a very dangerous place to be, as you well know."

Her wide smile gleamed in the starlight. She spoke above the wind. "Freedom is always dangerous."

"Is that so?"

She nodded. "Think about it. Those who desire safety and security above all else end up enslaved to someone or something. Not me. I'd rather die by my own hand than be a slave to anyone or anything."

He thought about his friend Anthony Burns, who had endured the heavy chains of slavery, choosing to persevere and live in hopes of regaining his freedom rather than lay down and die, as some had urged him to do. He said nothing.

She began to shiver. He removed his jacket and wrapped it around her shoulders.

"It can also get pretty darned cold, too, sometimes, this freedom you seek."

She nestled against him beneath his arm, placing her head on his chest. The warmth of her body radiated through his shirt.

"I think it's time we turned in, don't you?"

"I suppose you're right." She looked up at him, her eyes glistening. "I know what you're supposed to tell me."

"I thought as much."

"Are we still friends?"

"Just that."

"All right, then."

He walked her to the door of her stateroom and said goodnight. She entered and shut the door without glancing back.

As he opened his stateroom door, he saw movement in the shadows beyond the last stateroom at the aft end of the cabin. He peered into the shadows to make out a dark form dimly outlined in the starlight. Just then, Odah stepped out of the shadows and held up the back of her right hand with forefinger and middle finger forked in a V-shape. The features of her face were hidden in darkness. She hissed at him like a mad cat and disappeared again into the shadows.

Startled, he stopped short. Sudden, irrational fear flooded his mind, but he took a deep breath, trying to calm his racing heart. He told himself that she was powerless to do him any real harm, then decided not to give it another thought. "Stunner," he muttered.

He prepared himself, undressed, and settled into bed. Tomorrow, he would be in New York at last. It was a comforting notion that he'd be able to see Meg again, and he was looking forward to it, although he dreaded the coming confrontation with his father after so many years.

He imagined them both living out impoverished lives for the sake of their own heroic independence, the kind that depended almost entirely on the charity of others, like their friend Thoreau had done. But he really had no idea what to expect.

At the moment, he was very tired and relieved that his conversation with Sarah had gone as well as it did. As far as he was concerned, the matter between them was settled, and at least all would be well with Sarah and her father. One less thing to worry about. With that satisfied thought, and the gentle rise and fall of the ship's motion, accompanied by the deep hum of her engines, in a few minutes he was lulled sound asleep.

He awoke to the sound of the latch on his stateroom door.

"Who's there?"

The room was quiet except for the rustle of clothing falling to the floor. The scent of jasmine filled the room.

"Sarah?"

"I was afraid you might have locked your door," she whispered.

"What are you doing here?"

She padded over to his bunk and slipped beneath the covers. He felt her warm, smooth skin against his.

He threw off the top sheet and scrambled out of the bunk. Hurrying to find his trousers, he hopped on one leg, nearly tripping against the bed as he hastily pulled them on.

"Sarah, you can't be in here. What on earth has possessed you?"

"I was afraid," she said in the darkness. His eyes adjusted in the dim light of the porthole to the outline of her face on his pillow. Her ruby pendant gleamed faintly around her neck.

"Afraid of what?"

"I had another visitation."

"When? Tonight?"

"Yes. Just now."

"There is nothing to fear, I assure you. You're perfectly safe from harm. Now, go back to your stateroom."

"Don't you want me here?"

The allure of her perfume and the memory of her warm body aroused every sense in him.

"You cannot be here, Sarah. It is wrong. Your father would skin us both alive."

She laughed gleefully, and her eyes flashed in the darkness. "Don't be such a ninny. Daniel wouldn't dare. Besides, he doesn't have to know. This is just between us. Now, come back to bed." She held out her hand. "You want me. You know you do. I am yours for the taking. Just this once, if that's what you want."

"That is not going to happen." He picked up her nightgown from the floor and placed it in her outstretched hand. "What I want is for you to put this back on and go back to your room."

She took the nightgown and laid it on the bed next to her. "I can't."

"Of course you can. What's keeping you?"

She inclined on an elbow and drew the tousled sheets around her. "I told you, I'm afraid."

"As I said, there is nothing you need fear."

"I'm not afraid for myself. This visitation was not terribly frightful to me. In fact, it seemed very, I don't know, benign."

"What, then?"

"I'm afraid for you, Andrew."

"And why should that be?"

"Because the visitation was a warning for you."

"For me? What sort of warning? From whom? And about what? Oh, never mind. We can talk about this in the morning, in the light of day. Now, put on your nightgown and go back to your stateroom, before . . . I mean it."

"Don't you want to know? I think you should. You see, this time it was a warning from your brother, Thomas."

"Wh—what are you talking about? How do you even know that I have a brother? *Had* a brother?"

"He told me his name and who he was. He said he died at sea some years ago."

"I don't believe you."

"It's true. He was very kind and reassuring—and quite handsome, I must say, but not nearly as handsome as you. Believe me, Andrew, I know how troubling this must be for you. Now, come to bed and we can hold each other and talk about it. I will comfort you. All night, if you like." She held the sheet up as an invitation to him.

"This is just not right. None of it is right. You need to get out of that bed, Sarah. Now."

"Suit yourself." She rose from the bed and stood before him, close enough to feel her sweet breath caress his neck and shoulder.

The nearness of her made him dizzy. His knees trembled. He reached around her and plucked the nightgown from the bed. "Put this on. And get out. Please."

"Oh, very well, then. Have it your way. It's really too bad. I had such high hopes for us." The last part was muffled as she took the nightgown and shrugged it on over her head and shoulders. It draped down over her lithe body. "But I think we should talk, Andrew."

"We will talk tomorrow. I can't right now. I need time to think."

She sighed. "If that's really what you want, so be it." She turned and left the room as quietly as she had come, with a click of the door latch.

He did not sleep, but stayed wide awake on his bunk with his knees drawn to his chest, staring into the darkness until dawn.

35

It was some sort of trick. It had to be a ploy to get him into bed with her. But how had she known about his brother? How could she possibly have known? Where would she get such information? Without answers, Gunn didn't know whether or how to believe anything Sarah said, warning or no warning.

Sarah herself was dangerous to him, a reality that he had come to know full well. Her freethinking ideas were perilous, indeed. He hoped, even prayed that the society she imagined—one without fear of the consequences of pursuing unfettered desires while abandoning restraint on even the basest primal urges—should never come about. He believed those ideas would lead to the utter disintegration of any society that welcomed them. They were, after all, the same ideas that had caused so much destruction and disunity in his own family.

But he didn't fear Sarah. Rather, he feared for her—and for his own sister. Their passion for freedom without boundaries would likely be their undoing, just as it had been for his father.

Many other thoughts had crossed his mind during the previous sleepless night. He thought about Elizabeth and how cross and hurt she would be, rightfully so, if she knew what had happened. He hoped she'd never find out.

He also reflected on a sermon delivered by the new minister of the Independent Presbyterian Church of Savannah, Reverend Isaac Axson, one previous Sunday when Gunn had attended services with Cousin Julia. The gist of the sermon had been about the holiness of God, who also demanded the same from his beloved children, admonishing them to, "Be ye holy, for I am holy." The sermon, delivered with urgency and verve, had made an impact on him then, and it came back to him now.

The unholy temptation that he had experienced with Sarah was unlike any that he had ever known before. He should have known better, should have seen it all coming, and he was ashamed that he hadn't. Though he had resisted it, he was very distraught that he had allowed himself to get into such a predicament, and he was determined never to let it happen again.

In the early morning hours, he spent time in fervent prayer over that resolution.

By the time Gunn dressed for breakfast and entered the dining room, Sullivan was already seated at their usual table. He sat down heavily.

"You look terrible," Sullivan said.

"I feel terrible," said Gunn. "Didn't sleep a wink last night."

"Bad night, eh? That's too bad. Too much rich food, perhaps."

For a brief instant, Gunn thought of confessing what had happened the night before. "Yes, I suppose that must be it."

"Sarah does not appear to be up yet. Maybe she is suffering from the same thing."

"Perhaps."

Sullivan raised an eyebrow. "Or maybe it's something else."

"Such as?"

"Did you by any chance have your little discussion with her last night? I saw you two in the saloon before I retired for the evening. You seemed to be having quite the tête-à-tête."

"As a matter of fact, we did."

"And what was her response, may I ask?"

Gunn paused. "Not what I expected."

"How so?"

He moved the sausage links around on his plate. "Well, I thought she took it quite well. Seemed to be in agreement."

"Seemed to be?"

"Was."

"Something happen to cause you any doubt?"

Gunn shook his head. The image of Sarah lying in his bed flashed through his mind. "Nothing that I'd care to mention." He cleared his throat. "Just a feeling, I guess."

"Well then, I'm of the mind that it is best that you two won't see each other for a while after today. A few weeks' interlude may be just the ticket. In fact, a month or two without any correspondence would be even better. Let's keep it that way, shall we?"

"Of course, Daniel. I am in complete agreement."

"Good. I wouldn't want anything to stand in the way of our friendship, Andrew. As I said earlier, I admire you and I want us to remain fast friends. Now then, I'm in the mood for a morning smoke after such a fine breakfast. Will you join me outside?"

"I'd be pleased to."

They exited the dining room through a door on the port side. Gunn followed as Sullivan chose a spot farther aft, close to their staterooms, and reclined against the rail. He pulled a case of fine leather from his inside jacket pocket and extracted two cigars. He handed one to Gunn and, shielding them with his cupped hand, lit both with a single long match taken from the same case.

They each took a deep puff, and the smoke streamed aft, dissipating rapidly in the wind.

"I want to thank you again, Daniel, for your generosity in providing my transportation to New York."

"It was my pleasure. Think nothing of it. Least I could do. I hope the remainder of your journey is safe and pleasant and you'll find your family in good health."

"And I trust your business in New York will be profitable as well," said Gunn.

"No doubt. I have never known Gazaway Lamar to waste time, either mine or anyone else's."

"Has he been your client for very long?"

"Since early in my career. I have handled most of his business affairs. His personal affairs belong to others."

"What's he like? Very much like his son?"

"Not at all. Night and day. Gazaway Lamar is sober-minded, dedicated, and honest as the day is long. His son is nothing like him."

"That's too bad. Must be a great disappointment to him."

"Charley hasn't always been the way he is now. As a boy, he wanted nothing more than to be just like his father. Cute kid."

"What happened to him?"

"I don't know, really. Losing his mother and the rest of his family at such a young age was hard on him, I'm sure. But lately, he just seems to be keeping the wrong company, for whatever reason. Men who want to have their own way in the world at all costs, often at the expense of others."

"Is there any other kind?"

Sullivan chuckled and took another draw on his cigar. "I suppose not. But with Charley, it seems to be him against the world."

"Why does Gazaway live in New York rather than Savannah? That's his home, isn't it?"

"Yes, but he moved to New York after remarrying. Charley wasn't happy about that, either. New York is where most of Gazaway's financial ties are, though he still has investments and owns a variety of businesses in Savannah, most of which he has turned over to Charley. Over the last few years, however, Charley has been running them into the ground. He lost a fortune when their cotton press burned down. Unfortunately, Charley had canceled the insurance on the grounds that the cost was eating into his profit."

"Big mistake."

"Yes, among others. I believe Gazaway is thinking about recovering what's left from Charley before it's too late. I think that may be what he wants to talk about." He squinted at Gunn. "I really shouldn't be telling you all this. I trust you'll keep it to yourself."

"My lips are sealed."

"Good. Well, I suppose we'll be heading into the harbor soon. Best get packing."

They finished their cigars and tossed them to the wind. Sullivan went to his stateroom while Gunn remained outside, watching seabirds trail in the ship's wake. He had very little packing to do.

Presently, the door to Sarah's stateroom opened, and he watched expectantly for her to emerge. Odah stepped into the bright sunlight. She shut the door behind her and stood still for a moment, shielding her eyes from the sun. She saw Gunn and walked over to him, grasping the diamond-shaped amulet around her neck. Her face was as stoic as ever, with no indication whatsoever of what had transpired between them the previous night.

"Miss Sarah, eh say to gem you dis message."

"Oh? What's that?"

"Eh say, tell Massah Gunn dat dere be dose wut seek to do you harm. Eh say, beware dose dat follows."

"Who are those that follow?"

"Dunno. Das all. Eh say you wud know."

"That doesn't make any sense. May I speak with her? Is she coming out?"

She again shook her head, and her eyes narrowed. "Eh say eh stay where eh is. Eh done said nuff."

"That's ridiculous. I must speak with her. Ask her to come out. Please."

Odah pursed her lips and shook her head a third time. "Eh say no. Das all." She turned and walked back to the stateroom, entered, and shut the door.

He walked over and knocked on the door of her stateroom. "Sarah?"

No answer.

He knocked again. "Sarah? Are you there? Please come out and talk to me."

"Go away, Andrew," came her muffled reply.

"Sarah, I need to speak with you. I need you to tell me more."

"There is nothing more to say. Now, go away. I'm not dressed."

His anger was the only thing to keep him from laughing out loud.

Sarah did not show herself all that morning, and at dinnertime she sent for a tray of food. All the while, Gunn fretted about when he might have a chance to speak with her, to ask her a dozen questions that burned in his mind about what she had meant. He took several strolls around the decks, stopping by her stateroom periodically to see if she had come out. He sat in the saloon by the piano for more than an hour, hoping to see her smiling face emerge at some point.

Finally, just before three o'clock, as the *Lyoness* pulled into port at South Street, she summoned a porter and exited the stateroom with her luggage in tow, accompanied by Odah. She was dressed in a blue frock with a matching hat and a light blue hair ribbon streaming down her back. She stopped to knock on Sullivan's door.

"Daniel, are you ready? We're arriving at the dock."

Sullivan opened the door. "Be right with you, my dear,"

Gunn rushed over to her. "Sarah, I must speak with you. Please."

She tossed her mane of dark hair over her shoulder, and the ribbon fluttered in the breeze. "I think we've said quite enough to each other, don't you, Andrew? You've made yourself quite clear to me. Let's leave it at that, shall we?"

"But I want to know what you meant by that message. It's very important to me. Surely, you understand."

She looked him square in the eye. "As I said to you once before, I want what I cannot have, and I cannot have what I want. Apparently, my dear Andrew, we are indeed of like mind, after all. Perhaps more than you know. And there may be a chance, a very slight chance, that you'll realize that one day. Then we'll have something more to say to one another."

36

Sarah disappeared, along with the meaning of her message and the blue hair ribbon teasing in her wake, in the throng of the South Street seaport. She and her father vanished among the hive of other passengers embarking and disembarking from half a dozen ships along the James Street slip, busy porters and sweating stevedores, street vendors and newspaper boys.

Well, so be it. There was nothing to be done for it now. What difference would it make, anyway, to know exactly what she had meant? He was not much inclined to put stock in such hocus-pocus, though he had allowed it to trouble him at first, which he regretted. Other than the gnawing curiosity as to how she had come to find out about Thomas, and the lingering memory of her incredible allure, Gunn decided to put it all behind him. He squared the soft cap on his head, hefted his valise, and headed for the nearest cab stand.

Having no idea how to navigate the unfamiliar maze of Manhattan streets, he decided to take a taxicab, despite the added cost over the omnibus. Doing so allowed him to avoid the confusion of having to change carriers along the way. Besides, hiring a hack would mean a quicker trip uptown. His time was limited. It was an expense he could well justify.

He placed two fingers in the corners of his mouth and whistled for a passing cab. The driver pulled his hack over to the curb and stopped, which gratified Gunn and made him feel as though he somehow belonged in the largest, busiest, and most sophisticated city in the nation.

The cabbie looked down from his perch. "Ya look lost, chum. Where to?"

So much for belonging in the big city. Gunn handed up to him the slip of paper on which he had written the address. The cabbie's brow raised, and he set his worn hat back on his head.

"Gonna cost ya."

"Yes, I know."

"Hop in. Time's money."

Tossing his valise into the cab, Gunn climbed in behind it and shut the door. It banged open again.

"Problem with the latch. Spring's busted. Give the handle a jiggle."

The door shut on the second try. The driver whistled to his horse. "Move 'long, Daisy." The horse trotted off, and the cab began weaving its way north through the dense traffic of James Street.

After several blocks, Gunn was amazed at the bustle of industry and commerce everywhere he looked. He had seen nothing like it, even in the busy streets of Boston. And it made Savannah seem like a quaint, sleepy village in comparison.

The day was clear and bright, though a cool breeze gave a chill to the air. The leaves had not yet come to the trees here in Gotham. The colorful streets were teeming with wagons, coaches, carriages, carts, and drays of all sorts, not to mention the innumerable pedestrians and street urchins who apparently thought nothing of stepping out in front of a passing vehicle. The cabbie cursed and shouted at one man who dared to dart out from between a standing meat wagon and a vendor's cart, causing his horse to grunt and shy.

"Damned fool!"

The man, a tradesman by dress, made a rude hand gesture without even turning his head.

Gunn called out to the driver. "Is it always this busy?"

The driver turned halfway around, tossing words over his shoulder, "This ain't nothin'. Ya should see it once convention season starts, or like last year when they dedicated a new statuary to George Washington in Union Square. Now that was sumpin' else to see."

"Is anything going on right now?"

The cab had just made a right turn into Chatham Square, running alongside a horse-drawn streetcar on rails that ran through the center of the boulevard.

"Well, I'd stay outta this area while ya's here, Mister. Unless ya likes excitement. Of course, there ain't no livelier place to be than down this way, if you've a mind to wake snakes. Just hafta watch yer step, if ya know what yer about." The cabbie jerked his thumb behind him. "Back there a piece is what's called Five Points. The Bowery Boys and the Dead Rabbits have been stirrin' up trouble for blocks around, fightin' over who's boss."

"Who are they?"

"Two rival gangs, hate each uddah's guts. Like to beat each uddah's heads in, and anyone else whut gets in the way. Things is heatin' up. Believe you me, there'll be a war between 'em before long. Cops can't control 'em anymore. Fact, sometimes they joins in. Best steah cleah, if ya knows what's good fer ya."

"Thanks. I'll do that." His conversation with Sarah about individuals striving for what they want crossed his mind. He rode along the busy streets, watching the people rushing headlong here and there, pursuing their separate wants and needs, all the while thinking about whether it would ever be possible to fully reconcile diverse, competing desires and interests of a free people into a unified effort for the common good. He shook his head in doubt.

"Ya want I should take ya up Broadway through the middle of town? It's a little longer, but ya'll sure see the elephant."

Gunn had seen plenty of magazine sketches and engravings of the stupendous buildings along Broadway and Fifth Avenue that comprised the New York skyline. "No thanks. No time for seeing the sights. Take me straight there."

"Suit yerself, chum. It's yer dime."

The cab rode north on the Bowery, past all manner of thriving shops and restaurants, businesses and manufacturing lofts. The cabbie pointed to a large building with a columned portico on the left.

"That there's the Bowery Theater. Pretty lively place of an evenin', if ya've got the time."

"I'm only here until tomorrow."

"Pity. Everybody's in such a damned hurry these days."

A few blocks later, Gunn thought about accommodations for the evening. He wasn't sure where he'd be staying but doubted any possibility of comfort at his father's residence.

"By the way, can you recommend a decent hotel?"

"Depends on what yer willin' to spend."

"Something reasonable, but safe."

"Where ya headed tomorrah, if ya don't mind me askin'?"

"Boston. Taking the train."

The cabbie acknowledged with a nod. "Well, now. Ya'll hafta watch out for pickpockets and thieves no matter where ya lays yer head. But the Westchester," he nodded in the direction of the large hotel, "right there on the corner of Broome Street is all right. And the train station for the New York and New Haven is just a few blocks west, over on Canal Street. Easy walk."

"That sounds like the ticket."

The cabbie made a turn several blocks later east on Houston Street, then turned north again on Second Avenue. After a ride of a little more than half an hour, the cab approached what looked like a village green, divided in two, both sides enclosed by a wrought-iron fence. The avenue passed directly through center of the park. The driver turned right onto Fifteenth Street, heading the cab around the outside of the square, then turned left onto Livingston Place. He stopped in front of a high-toned, brownstone building.

"This here's Stuyvesant Square." He nodded at the building. "That's yer address."

"Are you sure?"

The cabbie raised his brow. "Look chum, I've been drivin' this hack for ten years. I oughta know where I am. Don'tcha think?"

"Of course. I just didn't expect the neighborhood to be so . . ."

"Highfalutin?"

"Exactly."

"Some punkins, ain't it? This is where all the high hats and big bugs is movin' to these days."

Gunn got out of the cab and retrieved his valise. "How much?"

The cabbie scratched his cheek with a middle finger. "Four bits."

Gunn fished a silver dollar out of his pocket. "For your trouble."

"Thanks, chum. G'luck." He slapped the reins. "Move 'long, Daisy."

Gunn walked up the steps of the brownstone and knocked on the door. Presently, a maid opened the door a crack and peered outside at him.

"I wonder, is, ah, Miss Gunn at home?"

"No, sir, not at present."

"When do you expect her?"

"Hard to say, sir, but it could be anytime."

"How about Mr. Gunn?"

"He is not at home, either. I would expect him around seven or eight this evening."

Gunn waited for her to ask if he might care to come in and wait, but she did not. He took out his watch. It was quarter to five. "Ah, all right. Thanks. I think I'll wait outside. It's such a lovely day, isn't it?"

"As you say, sir." The maid closed the door.

He sat on the stoop to wait. It really was a pleasant spring day, though not nearly as pleasant as he'd become used to in Savannah. The setting, a peaceful enclave in the midst of a bustling city, was equally as agreeable.

Both halves of the square were planted with clusters of trees and shrubs, just beginning to bud, surrounding matched fountains at the center of each. Across the square on the opposite corner rose the twin spires, their tops still under construction, of an elegant brick church in Romanesque Revival style. Most of the neighborhood, in fact, appeared to be fairly new construction. The stately homes were either of Greek Revival or Italianate architecture, their arched windows and doorways with boldly projected stone lintels and pediments highlighting their brick or brownstone facades.

Through the gate on the near side of the square, exiting the park, two women approached, arm in arm. Gunn recognized his sister immediately. The other woman peered up admiringly into Marguerite's face as they walked along. She said something in Marguerite's ear, causing both to laugh. They crossed the street together, head to head, hardly noticing a passing carriage, and walked toward him.

Marguerite saw him and started. "Andrew."

He stood, grinning. "Hello, Meg."

She stopped and pulled away from her companion. "What—how—when?"

Gunn descended the steps. "I've just arrived. Thought I'd surprise you."

"You've succeeded." She did not seem very well pleased, though she gave him a brief hug and a kiss on the cheek. "What a pleasant surprise."

"I received your letter and was able to get some leave. Thought I'd stop in on my way home."

"How marvelous."

"Aren't you going to introduce us?" Gunn said.

Marguerite recovered herself and stepped away from her companion. "Lucinda Levinson, please meet Andrew Gunn, my brother. Andrew, this is Mrs. Lucinda Levinson, my very good friend."

Moving closer to take the woman's outstretched hand, Gunn noted that she was perhaps ten years older than his sister. "Mrs. Levinson. A pleasure," he said.

The woman's quizzical expression mirrored her voice. "Brother?"

"Yes, I've told you about him."

The crow's feet around Lucinda's eyes deepened. "You have?"

"I'm the long-lost brother. I'm sure she left out the more memorable details about me," laughed Gunn. "Like how she can't help thinking about me all the time. Wondering if I'm still alive."

"Well, I do. But you write so infrequently that there is so little to tell."

"Yes, of course. How silly of me to have forgotten." Lucinda touched her forehead. "It's a real pleasure to meet you. Well, I—I'm afraid I must be getting home. It's getting late."

"Do stay," said Gunn. "Let's have time to get to know one another. I've always found Marguerite's friends so very interesting."

"If only I could."

"Lucy was just on her way home. Her husband will be arriving from work very soon."

"Yes. He usually works until late at night, but he promised to be home for supper this evening. He'll be very cross if I'm not there to greet him, I'm afraid."

"Yes, of course. What does your husband do?"

"He's a newspaper publisher. He's trying to start a new magazine to feature American writers especially rather than European ones, for a change. He's looking for investors, should you be interested."

"Splendid. Well, I'll most certainly have to keep that in mind."

"Her husband knows Walt Whitman," chirped Marguerite.

"Does he now? I'm a Hawthorne enthusiast myself. Marguerite and I both know him quite well, as a matter of fact. The Hawthornes have been our neighbors for years."

Lucinda's nose wrinkled. "Hawthorne? He hasn't written anything good in ten years."

"Yes, well. How nice it has been to meet you, Mrs. Levinson. Any friend of Meg's is a friend of mine, I assure you."

"Likewise." Lucinda cast down her eyes and then glanced furtively at Marguerite. "Well, I suppose I'd best be going."

"Let us hail you a cab," said Gunn.

"Oh no. I'll walk, thank you. It's just around the corner."

"Well, until we meet again, then." He tipped his cap.

Marguerite waved as Lucinda turned and walked away. "I'll see you tomorrow, Lucy."

Gunn eyed her. "Lucy, eh? Fast friends already. How did you two meet?" he asked quietly.

"Father introduced us. She's become a very good friend, indeed. One needs good friends in this city."

"I'm sure."

"Did he know you were coming, by the way?"

"What do you think?"

37

Marguerite led the way inside the house and directed him to a comfortable seat in the parlor. She disappeared for a short time, presumably to speak to the maid or one of the other servants, for in a house this size, there surely had to be more than one. Gunn looked around the well-appointed parlor, observing the tasteful decoration and the no-doubt expensive art that lined the walls.

When she reappeared, Marguerite had regained her composure and all of her former spunk, so familiar to him. She settled into a wing-back chair opposite Gunn.

"Long-lost brother, is it? Once lost, but now found. Well, I must say, it is indeed an amazing grace that saved such a wretch as you to return to us hale and hearty. Welcome back, dear brother, from the woebegone realms of the deep South."

"It is so uplifting to know how highly regarded I am that you would have remembered me so well to all of your friends in my long absence."

"I'm sure that I've spoken of you to Lucy before. She must have forgotten."

"You've never written of her."

"Never mind. Anyway, we've only known each other for a short while. We haven't really had time to discuss the intimate details of our lives."

"Really? You seemed very close to me."

"What are you implying?"

He shrugged. "Just that the casual observer might think you two were quite intimate by the way you were walking together."

"So what if we are? We have become fast friends in a very short while. Lucy is intelligent, well-read, and can hold a lively conversation. All things that I value in a friend."

"And so well connected."

"As I said, one needs a good friend in this city. I hope you're not implying anything untoward in our relationship."

"Far be it from me. Never mind. You're looking well, Sis. I'm glad to see it. That's a very nice dress you're wearing, by the way. Lovely."

"Thank you. Aunt May took me shopping before I left home. She said it would never do to live in New York among respectable people without suitable clothes."

"Naturally. Well, I'm glad to see that you've put away the bloomers and Syrian dress that you were so fond of last time we saw each other. Are they no longer in vogue?"

She smoothed the skirt of her crinoline day dress with her right hand, the ink stains prominent on the tips of her fingers. "They made us too conspicuous, I'm afraid. Better to appear more normal, if you will. We women can accomplish so much more if we walk among men who are completely unaware. Not that they ever really pay us any mind, unless it is to stick their noses out from behind their newspapers long enough to inform us what they think we cannot do. Whenever they do, we'll appear to them as prim and proper as you please."

He laughed. "I see now. A grand conspiracy. I take it you and Lucy share these sentiments."

"You laugh now. You won't be laughing when women at long last achieve the right to vote. Believe you me, that day is coming, and sooner than you think. Then you'll see just how much things will change.

"Change for the better, I should hope."

"In every conceivable way."

"So I have been told. We'll see."

"Never mind all that. I am very glad to see you, Andrew, though you might have let me know you were coming. How long are you staying in New York? I've told Cook to expect one more for dinner."

"I'm only staying overnight. I'm anxious to get home. Elizabeth's mother has died, and her father is not doing very well. She has asked me to come as quickly as I can."

"I'm very sorry to hear that. She is dear to me. Please give her my condolences. But you will stay with us tonight, of course."

"I am . . . prepared to take a room in a hotel."

"Father will want you to stay, I'm sure."

"I don't know. Let's not assume anything. We'll see."

"As you wish."

He swept his arm to take in the room. "Tell me. I'm very curious. How is it that he is able to afford all this? It's rather spectacular. I must say, I was expecting to find him in much more humble circumstances."

"He doesn't own this house."

"No? Is he renting it?"

"No. He lives here with the owner at his gracious invitation. We both do."

"Oh. I see. And who is that?"

"His name is Maurice Babineaux. He's a very wealthy man, a financier of sorts. A patron of the arts and a friend of the *artiste*. You might think him a strange fellow."

"I might?"

"Well, you think everyone strange who isn't just like you."

"I most certainly do not."

She laughed. "I thought that might get a rise. Anyway, he lives alone in this big house and invites others at his pleasure to stay here with him from time to time."

"Where is he now? Any chance I might meet him?"

"He is away at his estate in Syracuse, where he raises thoroughbreds. He goes every year at foaling season. His housekeeper, Mrs. Riordan, runs the house in his absence."

"Where is she?"

"I don't know. Probably attending to the needs of one of the guests."

"How many are there?"

"I suppose six or eight right now, besides Father and me."

"All men?"

"Except for *moi*."

"Isn't that awkward?"

"They don't seem to mind."

"I meant for you."

The front door opened and a man stepped into the vestibule, nearly tripping over Gunn's valise and walking stick, where he had left them. Gunn leapt up and apologized.

"Forgive me, sir. I did not mean to be so inconsiderate."

The man, quite handsome and well built, though slightly stooped, with a mane of thick brown hair and a full, dense beard, squinted at him through small, piercing blue eyes. His expression spoke at once of being intimate with both pain and pleasure. "It's quite all right, young man. Are you staying here, too?"

"No, sir. I am just visiting."

Marguerite rose and joined them in the hallway. "Allow me to introduce you. Mr. Herman Melville, this is my brother, Andrew Gunn."

"Melville. Of course. I should have recognized you right away."

Melville frowned. "Have we met?"

"No, but I've seen your face a thousand times over in newspapers and magazines. And, of course, Mr. Hawthorne spoke of you often, so often I feel like I should know you."

"Do you know Hawthorne?"

"We are neighbors in Concord. *Were* neighbors, until he moved to his post in England."

"Yes, I've just come from visiting him there."

"Is he well, I hope? And his family?"

"Well enough, I suppose. Though he has not written much of late. Seemed somewhat out of sorts."

"I'm sorry to hear that."

"It happens to the best of us. And he is the best of us."

"What brings you to New York? Are you living here now?"

"Oh, no. I am on a speaking tour, talking about my recent travels in Europe—Rome, especially. I stay here sometimes when I am in town. I'm speaking tonight at the Lyceum. As a matter of fact, I regret that I cannot stay and chat. I am here and gone, just long enough to retrieve some notes. If you will excuse me."

"Certainly. A pleasure to meet you at last."

"Likewise. By the by, Marguerite, I've just finished your story, the one about the unrequited love of a woman on the verge of destitution in a commune up in the Berkshires. Reminds me a bit of Hawthorne's *Blithesdale Romance*. You've drawn the characters, especially her poor fatherless children, with genuine pathos. Remarkable. It shows real promise. You must continue to write. Your sister possesses a true talent, Mr. Gunn."

"I won't deny that," said Gunn.

"I'm so glad you like it, Mr. Melville. You're too kind."

"Not at all. Now, I must be away. Oh, and would you kindly inform Mrs. Riordan that I will not be dining in this evening?"

He crept up the staircase, gripping and leaning on the banister. Marguerite and Gunn had just resettled themselves in the parlor when he eased himself downstairs, waving a portfolio. "Best to your father," he said upon reaching the landing. Then he was out the door.

"I wish he had been able to stay," said Gunn. "I've read through *Moby Dick* twice now. I have so many questions."

"He's a fascinating man. Very moody, though."

Gunn leaned forward in his chair, elbows on knees. "So this Babineaux fellow. How in the world did Father meet him? How did this all come about?"

"As I understand it, they met when Father was living in Philadelphia. They were introduced through a mutual friend. Evidently, Babineaux took a liking to Father, and invited him to come to New York."

As they talked, two other men walked through the front door, one a young fellow with long, flowing locks, who bounded directly up the stairs, two at a time, with the energy of a schoolboy. The other was a portly, fleshy middle-aged man, muttering to himself and oblivious to all else around him, who proceeded to follow.

"But our father is no *artiste*. What was the attraction?"

"I don't know."

"Didn't you ask?"

"Really, Andrew. Some things one just doesn't ask about."

"That's what I used to think. I have been proven wrong, many times over."

"'Twas curiosity killed the cat."

"I thought it was care."

"What?"

"Never mind. So, what does Father do here in New York?"

"Babineaux pulled some strings and secured him a position as a lecturer at Columbia College. They are in the midst of an expansion, moving uptown to Madison Avenue. Apparently, they were in need of professors."

"Lecturer? What does he teach?"

"Philosophy." She swallowed. "And ethics. But that's just temporary until they can find someone else to teach it."

"Ethics."

"That's right."

"Perfect. Hilarious."

"Don't be unkind."

"Unkind? Wasn't it unkind of him to abandon his family to seek his own wayward pleasure?"

"Can't you find it in your heart to forgive him of the past? Mother wants us to, you know. And he wants to come back into our lives."

"For what purpose?"

"Oh, come now. To reconcile. To seek forgiveness. Won't you forgive him, Andrew?"

"I've tried to. Believe me. It's not possible."

"Why not? It's the Christian thing to do, isn't it?"

"Because he hurt us, Meg. By his own actions he hurt all of us, even himself. He knows that, though he has never acknowledged it or even expressed the least bit of regret or remorse for what he has done. Look around you at how he's living now, while our mother still struggles to make ends meet every month, even with my help. So you tell me, what could he possibly understand about the subject of ethics enough to teach it to others? That's what I'd like to know."

At that moment, the front door opened, and a figure stepped through it whom he recognized right away, though he had not laid eyes on him since the tender age of eleven.

Marguerite tilted her head and offered a cockeyed smile. "Why don't you ask him yourself?"

38

His father stood in the vestibule, mouth agape beneath a foppish mustache. It was of the Bohemian style, swooping out and curved up at the ends, like horns on an ox. He slowly removed his top hat. His uncombed hair, more gray than brown now, had grown out and was pushed about wildly on his head. The only thing about him that did not appear pretentious or outlandish was his suit, which was stylish and finely tailored, though it appeared made to fit another man.

"Hello, Father," said Gunn.

"Well, hello, Andrew."

"Aren't you glad to see me?"

The professor thumbed his mustache. "Of course. What a pleasant surprise. My son. Here with us. At long last."

Gunn could not recall ever receiving the warmth of a single hug from his father or so much a sign of affection as a handshake, so it was no surprise that the man standing before him offered neither in welcome.

"Come in, Father," said Marguerite. "Sit with us. We were just talking about you."

"About me?" He attempted a tentative smile.

As a boy, Gunn had sometimes heard his mother make discreet references to his father as *Monsieur le Sauvage*. Once Gunn made the connection, he had ever since used that name on occasion in the privacy of his own mind to refer to him. The name now seemed to fit him better than the suit.

"Yes, Father, about you," said Marguerite. "We were talking about your position as a lecturer at Columbia."

Le Sauvage entered the parlor, placed his hat on a side table, and sat opposite his children on the settee. "Yes, well, I've been teaching there for several months now. The time just seems to have flown by."

"Marguerite tells me that you're teaching a class on ethics."

Le Sauvage cleared his throat and again thumbed his mustache. "Among other things, yes."

"How fitting."

Marguerite shot her brother a stern look.

"That course is just temporary, mind you, until the dean finds a more permanent solution. I teach mainly on the history of philosophy."

"I'm surprised that you're not teaching religion. As a former ordained minister, I mean."

"They offered, but I refused. I no longer teach along those lines."

"I see."

An awkward silence followed.

"Tell me," Le Sauvage said. "How is your mother these days?"

"I'm sure Meg would have a much better idea of that. I only have her letters to go by. She seems well enough. But I'm happy to say that I'm on my way to find out. I have a few weeks of leave from my ship."

"She was very well when I left in mid-February," said Marguerite.

"Yes, of course," said Le Sauvage. "So you've said."

"You might be interested to know, Andrew, that she planned to spend the last of March and all of April with Aunt May at Stormcrest. Concord can be so bleak and lonely this time of year. So you won't find her at home just now."

"Ah, well. That's certainly good to know. I wonder if she's received my telegram, then."

"No, if you sent it home to Concord, I daresay she hasn't. Your visit likely will be as much a surprise to her as it has been to us."

"I only hope she will be as happy to see me as you two have been. Your effusive joy has been just overwhelming, I must say. Somewhat embarrassing, if you wish to know."

"Now, Andrew. Imagine our shock at your just showing up unexpected on our doorstep," said Marguerite.

"I don't have to imagine at all, do I?"

"Still, it might have been nice to know you were coming. It would have given us time to prepare."

"Prepare what, exactly?"

"We are both truly happy to see you, Andrew," said Le Sauvage. "Let me assure you of that. It is very good to behold your face again after so many years. You'll never know how much it warms my heart."

"I don't doubt that. Thank you, though. I'm pleased to hear it."

"How long will you be staying?"

"Overnight. I am anxious to get home, and I have very little time."

"Will you stay here tonight with us?' his father asked. "There is plenty of room. I'll ask Mrs. Riordan to make up a room for you. Shall I?"

"No, thank you, sir. I think it best that I find lodgings elsewhere. I'm not accustomed to living in such exotic and luxurious surroundings as these. I fear that I might get spoiled and have a difficult time readjusting to normal life."

"Normal life?"

"Shipboard life, I mean. You'll understand, I trust."

"Now, Andrew, you needn't patronize—"

"Patronize? That's a big laugh, coming from you, Father."

"Of course. We understand fully," his father sniffed. "A simple no would have sufficed."

Marguerite shifted in her chair. "Does anyone have the time?"

Gunn removed his watch from its pocket. "Half past six."

His father eyed the gold watch. "I see you kept it."

"Yes, I did." Out of habit, he rubbed the smooth case as an amulet. The watch, handed down from his grandfather, was the only gift his father had ever given him, as far as he could recall. He had come to cherish it above all things.

"I'm so glad of it."

Marguerite interrupted. "Dinner is at seven. You will stay at least for that, won't you? I've asked Cook to set a place for you."

"Yes, do stay for dinner. You must. We have so much to talk about."

Gunn smiled for the first time since his father had arrived, though it wasn't much of a smile. Just enough, he supposed, to break the ice a bit. "I have gotten so used to calling it supper. Dinner for us is at noon. It's good to be up north again."

"Call it what you will. You need to eat something, Brother. You're looking awfully thin. And pale, for a sailor. I hope you're not ill. Are you?"

"A bit queasy of late. Still stumping about on my sea legs, I suppose. Otherwise, I am in perfect health, thanks."

"Speaking of sea legs, how is yours?" his father asked.

He patted his right thigh. "Nearly good as new, though it does get rather stiff now and then. My right is shorter than my left. Aches when a storm's coming, which is quite useful. I carry my walking stick mainly out of habit, though, these days. Hardly need it anymore."

"It was a nasty injury, to be sure. Most people don't survive a broken femur. We're both grateful that you've recovered so well, my son."

Gunn paused before answering. He smiled again. *Merci beaucoup, monsieur.**

At dinner, Le Sauvage introduced Gunn as his beloved, long-lost son with great flourish to the others, affecting emotion with a shaking chin, almost to the point of actual tears. He offered a toast to his returning son, to which the entire company responded in kind.

There were eight at the table. Their ensuing conversation was pleasant and harmonious for a time. The topics were light fare, mostly about academics, art, and literature, sprinkled with various cultural events occurring around town. Gunn kept his mouth shut during the meal for the most part, except to eat and ask for the salt to be passed.

The colloquy eventually turned, however, as it inevitably would these days, to the current tension and unrest in their beloved city, as well as the country at large.

"What do you think of the state legislature's attempt to establish a new police force here in the city?" asked the portly man who had entered the house earlier. "I think it is perhaps high time, don't you agree?"

"Perhaps we should best stay away from politics, gentlemen," said Le Sauvage.

"I disagree, Daniel," said the young man with flowing locks. "We are among friends, are we not? And should not friends discuss things that matter to them? But I must say that I disagree with my distinguished friend Mr. Bozeman as well, despite his obvious knowledge of the subject as a former member of our state legislature. I, for one, think the state should stay out of the matter. It is up to the people of this city to deal with the corruption of its police force, if indeed there be any, which very probably there is."

"But my dear Mr. Wilde, it is quite obvious that Mayor Wood and Tammany Hall have shown their feckless inability to do so," said Bozeman. "In fact, the city police have even become part of the problem. Tensions are mounting by the day. Things will soon get out of hand if nothing is done. Violence is bound to boil over at some point, don't you think? It's just a matter of time until the Bowery Boys and the Dead Rabbits tear this fair city apart."

"And adding a new, competing police force will fix that?" Wilde said, his eyes widening. "It's only piling corruption onto corruption in my opinion. And doing so will create an even greater divide. No, if you ask me, the problem goes much deeper than any police force. Until we resolve the immigration issues and welcome the flood of Irish and Germans to our shores, allowing them to become fully naturalized citizens, against and in spite of any objections of the kid-gloved, cologne-scented, silk-stockinged, poodle-headed, degenerate aristocracy of this city, well then, violence is inevitable, my good friend. Perhaps that is the only way. Republicans be damned."

"You can't mean that you welcome violence, Wilde," said a man by the name of Farnon, who had introduced himself as a painter.

"I do indeed, Farnon. I mean every word of it. If that's what it takes to bring proper justice to the common man, so be it."

"I consider myself a Republican," Gunn said quietly. "As well as a common man."

Everyone turned at once to look at him.

"And I think violence is rarely the answer to anything and should be avoided at all costs," he added. "Though, I would agree that it is sometimes necessary and useful as a last resort to right a wrong. But inviting it is a serious error."

Wilde brushed the hair back from his face. "And what, sir, makes you such an expert?"

"I am no expert. It is merely an observation. I have seen and heard enough of violence in recent years to know how corrosive and destructive it can be. I offer that as my considered opinion. That is all."

"Then, sir, I take it you do not believe that freedom is worth fighting for."

"I did not say so. Nor do I think so. I merely said that violence is rarely the answer. Let the fighting be done in the legislatures, in the courthouses, and at the ballot box."

"And if they should fail?" Farnon asked.

"As they will and must," said Wilde. "I give you the recent decision by the highest court in our land, a corrupted court that should be impeached and disbanded, as they have denied the very freedom and human dignity of the black man, of which there are millions in this country."

"If they should fail," said Marguerite, "then as our friend Thoreau has suggested, sometimes it is better to shed blood than to have a bleeding conscience."

"Yes, we must each follow our own individual consciences, rather than submit to the force of a corrupt state," said Wilde. "We must be willing to resist injustice wherever we find it, even to the point of pain or death."

There were grunts and head nods around the table. One man raised his glass.

Gunn stood at his seat. He spoke in a subdued voice. "Be careful what you ask for, gentlemen. I speak again from experience when I urge caution in using words whose effect is to manifest themselves in reality. You are writers, artists, and thinkers all. You should know, of all people, that words are powerful things. They derive from thoughts and imaginations, and they often lead to the very action that they express. 'As a man thinketh, so is he.' So the proverb goes. You should also realize that there are those where I have been who believe and say exactly what you are saying, but they have taken the opposite side. They are no less fervent in their imaginations, and their words are as eloquent and powerful, their conclusions as vehement. I ask you now, where does such rhetoric likely end?" He dropped his napkin to his chair. "I'm sorry gentlemen, but I have no more appetite for it. I hope you will pardon me, if I've spoiled yours."

Sequestered in the library after dinner with his father and sister, Gunn sat with his eyes closed and took a deep breath.

"That was quite a speech, Son," said Le Sauvage.

"Yes, quite the soliloquy," said Marguerite. "Perhaps you've missed your calling."

"I did not intend to say anything at all," said Gunn. He opened his eyes. "It all just came out." He took another deep breath. "The past few days have been very trying for me. I suppose everything just came to a head at once. I apologize if I offended or spoke out of turn. They are your friends, after all. I am an alien in their midst."

"Nonsense. They are all men of letters, and they appreciate a word well spoken. No doubt you've given us all something to mull over."

"Believe me, I was also speaking to myself. These are things that have troubled me a great deal over the past few years. And especially of late."

"We do live in interesting times," said Marguerite.

"Yes, we do indeed," said Gunn. He got up from his chair. "It's late. I think I should be going."

"Are you sure you won't stay?" Marguerite said.

"Yes, I think I've already overstayed my welcome. I did not come to cause a stir. Merely to see you and to know that you are well—for the time being, anyway. I do wish you the very best. Both of you."

She reached out to touch his sleeve. "Thank you for your kindness,

Andrew. I want you to know that I appreciate very much your support for both me and our mother over these many years."

Le Sauvage rose to his feet and smoothed his mustache. "Yes, Andrew. Marguerite has told me how generously you've been providing for them both. I offer my sincerest gratitude."

"Of course. How could a man do anything else?"

"Father has been supporting me, too, as well as he can, and I am now doing some secretarial work for Mr. Babineaux. I want you to know that I do expect that my latest stories will be published soon, and then I'll be able to stand on my own two feet at last. You understand, of course."

"I do."

"I just wanted to thank you again."

"Don't mention it, Meg."

For once, she did not object to his use of her nickname. "But I must. It's important to me that you know how much I appreciate your generosity. I truly value your good opinion, Andrew, and I love you dearly. I hope you know that."

He hesitated for a moment. There would never be a better opportunity to tell her what he truly thought. The time for pleasantries and platitudes had passed. "If that is so, dear sister, truly so, then I would urge you without restraint to get out of this city and go back home to Concord with all haste, as fast as your feet will carry you. For your own good. And I would gladly pay for your passage on the next train. Better yet, Meg, why don't you go with me tomorrow?"

She stopped smiling and lifted her chin. "Marguerite."

"As you wish."

Her lower lip trembled as she spoke softly but firmly. "Thank you for your wise counsel, Brother. I'm sure you have my best interests at heart, as always. But I am doing whatever I choose to do." Her voice rose in anger, and her eyes flashed. "Nobody is going to tell me what to do. Not you or anyone else. It is my life, after all, and I intend to live it to the fullest. Not in Concord. There is nothing for me there. Here in New York City, this is where my life is now, and I'll stay, if you please. Or not."

Now he was vexed, too. He usually admired her willful, headstrong nature, but this time it was taking her down a blind alley to nowhere. His fear for her welfare turned to anger. "Then so be it, Marguerite. Have it your way. But you'll do it without any further help from me."

"Just a moment," said Le Sauvage. "Don't you think that's a bit harsh, Andrew?"

"On the contrary. Consider it an act of brotherly love, Father. I think she has made a serious error in coming here to live and work, likely to lead to her own ruin unless I miss my guess. And I won't contribute to it. I simply choose not to."

"Never mind, Father," said Meg, seething. "I see how it is. He is a typical male. This is his sad attempt to control me, which is his masculine prerogative, and I won't have it. All right, then, Andrew. If that is how you truly feel, so be it."

"I assure you, it is."

39

The next morning, Gunn made his way from the Westchester Hotel to the train station for the New York and New Haven Railroad on Canal Street. As the cab driver had indicated, it was but a short walk, and it did him good to clear his head in the cool, brisk morning air, especially after another sleepless night.

He bought his ticket and boarded the train at a quarter to eight. The railroad advertised express service to Boston, leaving at eight o'clock, and stopping in New Haven, Hartford, Springfield, Worcester, and Framingham, to arrive in Boston a mere eight and a half hours later. He planned, however, to get off the train in Framingham and take a local line to West Roxbury.

The coach farthest aft was only half-full. He found an empty seat next to a window and settled in for the ride, ruminating on his visit with Marguerite and their argument about personal freedom. He regretted that it had not gone so well. She was dear to him, and he simply didn't want to see her hurt, either from the folly of others or her own. His anger had gotten the better of him, and not for the first time. He was sorry for the way he had spoken to her. He decided that he couldn't cut her off from his longstanding financial support, and he would write a letter of apology as soon as time would allow.

It was not long before a heavy-set fellow in a brown-checkered suit and a bowler hat, whose girth was nearly as wide as he was tall, sat beside him. He was perspiring and breathing heavily. He clenched a fat cigar, tipped with an inch-long ash, in his teeth. After settling in his seat, the man took the cigar from his mouth and held it in his stubby fingers. The ash fell onto the leg of his trousers, and he hurriedly brushed it onto the floor with the back of his hand as he blew smoke from the corner of his mouth.

He unfolded and spread his newspaper wide enough for Gunn to read the verso page. An article several columns wide rehashed the news about the proposed establishment of a new police force in the city. Next to that, a headline lamenting the rising crime rates. Below that, an item about a stabbing that had happened somewhere on the Bowery in broad daylight the afternoon before. Gunn sighed and turned away to look out the window.

The train left the station at precisely two minutes after eight, by Gunn's watch. It was a pleasant change to have a timely departure. Trains in the South rarely departed on time, often delayed thirty minutes or more. Stagecoach travel was even worse, especially in Georgia, sometimes delayed a few hours or even an entire day in some cases.

After a few moments, the man seated next to him looked his way.

"Headed to Boston?"

"Yes. Well, I'm actually going to West Roxbury."

"Oh? I have an uncle in West Roxbury."

"Is that so?"

"Yes, he's chief constable. John Russert is his name. Do you live there?"

"No. Just visiting."

"Where from?"

"Savannah."

The man smiled broadly, and dimples appeared in both cheeks. "Savannah, is it? You know, I used to live in Savannah, thereabouts."

"Oh?"

"It's been awhile. Used to work as a customs inspector, and later as a shipping agent. What is it you do?"

"I am an officer in the Revenue Cutter Service, currently assigned to the *Dobbin*."

"Is that so? What do you know? Small world."

"Yes, it is."

"In that case, you must know Bill Brinkman, the collector there in the Customs House."

"He just left. The new collector's name is Boston. John Boston."

"That so? Too bad. Well, it happens. What's he like?"

"I really don't know. I've only met him once."

"It really doesn't matter. They're all the same. Always on the take. Right?"

"What do you mean?"

The man chuckled. "Oh, come on, man. You are not so naive, are you? You know what I'm talking about."

"I'm sure I don't."

"No, I'm sure you don't. All right, have it your way. Say, what's your name, fella?" The man held out a sweaty, meaty paw.

"Andrew Gunn."

They shook hands.

"Jasper Russert. Pleased to meet you."

"What business are you in now, Mr. Russert?"

"Jasper, please. My friends call me J.R. I'm still a shipping agent. Importer-exporter. Sometime lobbyist for the industry. Dabble in politics. Travel kind of regular between Boston and New York these days. Down here on business, working for a client. You might know him, as a matter of fact, being from Savannah and all."

"Well, I don't really socialize that much. The service keeps me fairly busy. We're in and out of port quite a bit."

"You know the name Charley Lamar?"

It was an uncanny coincidence, hard to take in at first. Gunn blinked. "Who doesn't?"

"He's heading up a group of investors looking to buy a new ship. Asked me to help them find one, a fast one."

"A new ship? To do what, exactly?"

"Well now, I didn't ask, did I? Really none of my business, is it?

You'd have to ask old Charley. But I'm guessing he wants to do some overseas trade of some sort."

"Did you find what you were looking for?"

He shrugged and winked. "Got my eye on one."

The possibility rooted in Gunn's mind, along with other misgivings, that this jovial man, friend to all and stranger to none, might have been hired by Lamar to keep an eye on him, and this was his sly way of letting Gunn know it. It was a silly thought, to be sure, and he hated to admit having it. All the same, he couldn't help but harbor a little suspicion, given what had happened with Donnelly.

"Do you do a lot of work for Lamar?"

"Now and then. This and that. Most of it doesn't amount to much. He's one of those guys who doesn't mind spending money, until it's time to pay up. Know what I mean?"

"Why do you keep working for him, then?"

"Why not? Fella's got to make a buck. One of these times, he's going to hit it big. Huge strike. That's what he's aiming for, that get-rich-quick scheme. He's a schemer, for sure, Charley is. Got that way about him. When he does, maybe I'll be there, too. Don't you dare tell him I said that." Russert threw back his head and laughed, until he started to cough. He took another puff on his cigar and blew the smoke in Gunn's face.

"Oh, I won't. Believe me. I hardly know the man."

Russert continued to chat and smoke all the way to New Haven, regaling Gunn with stories of his travels and people he'd met along the way. It seemed that he knew people or was related to someone in every major city along the East Coast.

To test his suspicion, when the train stopped in New Haven, Gunn changed coaches to see if Russert would follow him. He did not, seeming to take no offense at his departure, or show the least bit of interest, for that matter.

It was hard to imagine such a congenial fellow, so conspicuous, so broadly traveled and as widely known, as a hireling for surreptitious purposes. But maybe that was the genius of it. In the end, he decided that such a scheme was nigh impossible. He couldn't give Lamar credit for being that clever. No, their meeting had to be mere coincidence, though he tended not to believe in those.

The miles rolled by, and so did city after city past his window. Gunn opened his valise and took out a copy of the latest installment of *Little Dorrit*, which he had purchased from a bookstore on Broughton Street before departing Savannah. Elizabeth had written to him about the series over a year ago and encouraged him to pick it up. He had enjoyed it ever since. As he opened the book, his anticipation to see Elizabeth quickened.

Despite his excitement, weariness overtook him. He read through the newest chapters until he fell asleep, his head nodding against the window. Dozing off and on, he occasionally awoke as the train lurched to a stop at the next station. Excited to be going home, he tried hard to stay awake, thinking about seeing Elizabeth for the first time in almost three years, but after a few minutes of reading or watching the landscape turn from town to farmland to woodland and back again, he inevitably drifted off. It amazed him to realize how tired he was.

At last, around quarter to five, the train arrived in Framingham. He stuffed the book back into his valise and got off there. As he passed the last coach on his way into the station, Russert smiled and waved to him through the window. He waved back.

The local to West Roxbury was scheduled to leave in another half hour. He bought a ticket and sat waiting on the platform rather than inside the station, anxious not to miss the train. The great black engine chuffed into the station about five minutes late but stayed only long enough to allow passengers to get off or on. He boarded quickly, and with a whistle, the train was off again.

Within twenty minutes, they pulled into the station at West Roxbury. There were no cabs in sight, so he walked the half mile from the station to the narrow lane where the little house with the picket fence stood, which had dwelt so long now at the intersection of his memory and imagination.

It was twilight as he opened the gate and walked up the steps to knock on the front door. He expected to see the little dog, Wallie, come bounding around the corner to nip at his heels. All was quiet. Nothing seemed to stir.

He knocked again. A moment later, the door opened. Elizabeth stood in the shadows of the hallway, dressed in black. Her eyes opened wide, and she threw herself into his arms, sobbing on his shoulder. He dropped his valise and walking stick inside the door and drew her close to him, cradling the back of her head in his hand.

"You came," she cried between sobs. "I'm so glad you came."

40

The gloom inside the Faulkner home, evident as soon as Gunn stepped through the door, surpassed anything that he might have imagined. He had never experienced anything like it, even after the death of his own brother.

As they embraced, tears came to his own eyes. Elizabeth's raw grief overwhelmed him. They stood together, rocking gently as one, for a long moment in which it seemed that time stood still. With bleared vision, he watched Marianne, the Faulkners' adopted daughter, glide slowly down the stairs and join their embrace, wrapping her arms around both of them. She, too, began to cry.

"It's so good to have you home, Andrew," Marianne said.

"It's good to be home," said Gunn.

"I'm so sorry you had to return to such misery," said Elizabeth.

"It's all right. Everything will be all right."

After a moment, he lifted Elizabeth's chin, meeting her tearful eyes with his.

"Where is your father?"

Elizabeth shook her head. "Come in and sit down, and I'll tell you all that has happened."

They entered the parlor and sat together on the settee, with Marianne on the floor at their feet. Elizabeth dried her eyes with a handkerchief, then handed it to Marianne to do the same. Gunn wiped the tears from his face with the back of his hand.

"Father is not here," Elizabeth said.

"Not here? Where is he?"

"He has gone back to Scotland."

"When?"

"Almost two weeks ago. Not long after I wrote to you. He—" She choked up.

"He what?"

"As I said in my letter, he was devastated when Mother died. Beside himself. I've never seen him that way. So sad, forlorn."

"It's understandable."

"It was just awful," said Marianne. "There was nothing we could do. We felt so helpless."

"He made arrangements the next morning for Mother's body to be embalmed."

"Really? I find that a bit surprising."

"As did we. But he said that he had promised Mother to bury her back in Scotland. It was her dying wish."

"I see. You couldn't talk him out of it?"

"I didn't even try. He was so determined. Besides, he would not come out of his room until the day the ship departed. Wouldn't eat. Didn't sleep. I could hear him in his room at all hours, talking to himself and praying out loud, crying out to God in his grief."

"I'm sorry to hear that. So when is he planning to return?"

"Well, that's the worst of it all. He is not coming back. He plans to stay in Scotland."

"For good?"

"Yes, for good and always."

"Why is that?"

"He fell into despair over that terrible decision by the Supreme Court declaring that people of African descent have no rights as American citizens. He said if that were the case, then his conscience would not allow him to lay claim to those rights, either. And he would rather go back to live in the Highlands, where at least they still valued the freedom of every man. Mother died the next day. It all happened at once, you see."

"Did he want you to go with him?"

She nodded. "He tried to persuade us, but we wanted to stay. I wanted to stay."

"Me, too," said Marianne. "This has become my home, and I have no wish to leave it."

Gunn sighed. "And your brother, where is he? Did he go with your father?"

Elizabeth shook her head. "No, Robert stayed, too. He has taken up the study of the law with Mr. Abercrombie, my father's attorney. He boards with them during the week."

"What about the house? What does your father plan to do with this house?"

"It's all so uncertain. He has left it to us and Mr. Abercrombie to settle. Father said we could stay here in the house as long as we wish or need to."

"Has he arrived safely in Scotland, do you know?"

"No, he hasn't written. He said he would write once he buried Mother in their old churchyard. He planned to reserve the plot next to hers for himself."

"That sounds fairly final, all right. What about money? How are you getting by?"

"We have no debts. Taxes have been paid for the year. With what I earn teaching, we have enough to buy food and tend to our needs. For the time being."

His thoughts turned to memories of how happy this household once was. Everything was different now, though nothing material about the house had changed.

"Where is Wallie? I noticed he didn't come round the house to greet me."

"He died several weeks ago, just after Mother got sick. I thought I'd written to you about it. But I had a great deal else on my mind, so I may have forgot."

"If you did, I don't recall. I'm sorry. I know you must miss him, too."

"We do, but nothing compares to the loss of my mother."

"Of course. I know how close you were."

"I feel so lost. Like an orphan. I know now what you must feel, Marianne. At least I've had a taste of it, though my father still lives, thank God." Elizabeth stroked Marianne's auburn hair. "You've borne up so well under the loss of both your parents. So strong. So must we all be now."

"I do still miss them," said Marianne.

"I was so sorry to hear about your uncle, the light keeper, too. He died just before Christmas, wasn't it?" Gunn asked.

Marianne nodded, lifting her gaze to meet his. "The week before."

Gunn turned his eyes to the floor. "So much sorrow, and all at once. It's hard to fathom. We must do something about all this."

"What do you suggest?" Elizabeth asked.

"I don't know. Have you and Robert talked about it? Made any plans?"

She shook her head. "Our plan so far has been just to be there for each other. Robert has his work and his studies. I have my teaching. Marianne goes to school with me each day."

"Still, I'm so sorry. I wish there were something more I could do."

"One day at a time. That's how we Scots deal with such things, you know."

"I suppose so."

"Have you eaten? We've just finished dinner, I'm afraid, but I'll gladly make you something to eat."

"It can wait. I know what. Let's go sit outside and sit in the garden. It has been such a fine spring day. A bit of fresh air will do us all good, don't you think?"

"It's almost dark outside. Besides, I have my schoolwork to finish." Marianne smiled at Elizabeth. "My teacher will be very cross if I don't get to it."

Elizabeth smiled back at her. "It can wait. She'll understand."

"No, I think I'd rather get it done, if it's all the same. I'm almost finished, anyway. You two go on."

"My best pupil," said Elizabeth. "I never have to worry about you, do I, Marianne? All right, then."

Marianne got up from her seat on the floor and gave Gunn a peck on the cheek. "So glad to have you home, Andrew. We've missed you so. I just know everything will be all right now."

"Thank you, Marianne. I've missed you, too. More than I can say. And everything will be all right. I promise you."

Marianne turned and went quietly back upstairs.

"She has become such a fine young lady," said Gunn. "She must be, what, almost fifteen now?"

"On Independence Day."

"I hardly recognize her she's grown so. You and your mother have done a fine job raising her."

"Mother, mostly. I think Marianne loved her almost as much as I."

"I doubt that."

"No, it's true. They became very close, especially this past year. Mother was so glad to have another daughter. And Marianne helped care for Mother from the time she got sick. She met her every need, even without being asked. She's awfully intuitive, you know."

The two of them arose from the settee, and Elizabeth took a candlestick from its nearby stand, leading the way through the dark, quiet house to the back door. Her hair fell to the small of her back in a French braid, just the way he liked it. The sight of it caused his heart to lope a beat.

When they opened the door and stepped into the backyard, a waxing gibbous moon hung low in the night sky. The brightest evening stars shone overhead.

She took his arm. "I'm so glad you're here at last, Andrew. I can't tell you how many times I've dreamed of this day over the past months and years. It is so good to have you home."

"And I can't tell you how often I've wished to be back in this house with you by my side, Elizabeth. This lovely garden has become one of the most delightful places on earth to me. And just look at that moon, so bright it's almost daylight. This is so much better, isn't it?"

"Yes, much. The air has a chill to it, though. I'm going to get a shawl. I'll be right back." She handed him the candlestick, but the flame went out. She laughed. "I'll bring a light. Go on into the garden and sit yourself down. I know you must be very tired after your travels."

"I slept most of the way here today."

"I don't doubt it. You must tell me everything about your trip."

Not everything, he thought as he sat on their favorite bench among the rose bushes, just beginning to show signs of life after a long winter. Images streamed through his mind of the events of the past few days. He had no idea how to explain everything that he had experienced, and no desire at all to explain some of it. In fact, he wished to forget entirely the worst parts, especially the incident with Sarah. The memory of her lying in his bed haunted him. And then there was the warning of her dream about Thomas. What could she have meant by it? Never mind. He needed to focus on what to do about the present circumstances. An idea began to form in his mind.

When Elizabeth returned, she brought with her an oil lantern, which spread a warm glow all around her. She had dried her eyes, though they were still swollen. Even so, they were alive and shining with the tenderness and love for him that he'd always known. She wrapped her shawl closely about her shoulders and sat next to him, placing the lantern on the ground nearby.

"Is everything all right, Andrew?"

"Yes, now it is."

"Are you sure? You seem, I don't know, preoccupied this evening. Distant somehow."

"Just taking it all in, I suppose. Overcome a bit."

A beguiling smile crossed her lips. "Just a bit, my love?"

Elizabeth turned toward him, placed her arms around his neck, and kissed him, her lips lingering on his.

"A lot." He pulled her closer to him, and her breathing came more rapid. Her sweet breath mingled with his as he returned her kiss, tenderly at first, then harder and with all the passion that he'd kept pent up during their long absence from each other, the way he'd wanted to a thousand times since they had parted. Every other thought and concern went out of his mind except the pleasure of being with her at this moment.

At last, she broke away, touching her hand to her hair in the tell that was so familiar to him. "I've missed you so," she whispered.

"I was afraid you might have tired of waiting."

"How could that be?"

He kissed her again, allowing no room for doubt as to how much he had missed her, until he sensed the bonds of propriety slipping away. She pressed herself against him. He stopped and leaned back, touching his hand to her warm face.

"Penny for your thoughts," she said, kissing his palm.

He smiled. "They should come much more dear at the moment."

"Be serious."

"I was just thinking—" He shut his eyes tightly.

"Yes?"

He touched the tips of his fingers to his forehead. "Well, I've had an idea."

"Go on."

"I'm sort of thinking out loud here. You might think my idea is downright rash, I'm afraid."

"I won't know if you don't tell me."

He raised his brow. "Why don't you come back to Savannah with me? You and Marianne."

"*What?*"

"We can go ahead and get married. I have been saving every dime, and—"

"Married?"

"Yes, that's what two people who love each other do. It's what we've both been wanting, isn't it?"

"Of course. I was presuming you'd soon be transferred back up north and that we'd get married then."

"I don't know when that might be, Elizabeth. It doesn't look very promising right now."

"But you wrote that your captain was going to help you. Isn't that so?"

"Not anymore, I'm afraid."

"Oh? What's happened to change things?"

"Captain Dawes died on our last patrol. Sudden heart attack."

"Oh no. Well, that does change things, doesn't it? So many tragic events these days. Not minor ones, either. Life-changing events. What's next, I wonder?"

"Well, let's do something ourselves to change things rather than wait for whatever it is to happen. Come to Savannah. Let's get married. Or we can marry now, this week. What do you say?"

She sat quietly for a moment. "Tell me about Savannah. What's it like?"

"I think you would love it, especially at this time of year. The flowers are already in bloom. They've just built a new school, the Massie School, especially for teaching poor children. It is a charming city with lovely people, for the most part. There are a few exceptions."

"But for slavery, it sounds like paradise."

"There is that. The fly in the ointment."

"It's all rather sudden."

"I know it is. I realize that. Do you want some time to think it over? We don't need to decide today."

She sat quietly for a moment, her brows knitted, staring into the deepening darkness. "No."

"No?"

"No, I don't need to think about it, Andrew." She took his hand in hers and looked into his eyes with a warm, loving gaze that allayed any trace of doubt, concern, or fear remaining in his own heart. "There is nothing in this world that I could want more right now than to be your wife."

41

Once the decision to marry was made, the rest of their plans began to fall into place. Elizabeth preferred to marry in Savannah, giving them more time to prepare. Gunn agreed.

He took lodgings in the village at an inn by the train station, which was the only proper thing to do, given that Elizabeth's parents no longer resided at the house. On Friday evening, Robert came home, and the couple announced their plans at once to Marianne and him, both overjoyed at the prospect of welcoming a new brother to the family. Robert allowed that his employer, Mr. Abercrombie, would certainly handle the sale of the house, and the proceeds would be sent to their father in Scotland.

On Saturday morning, preparations began in earnest. They had much to do to make any necessary repairs to the outside and to clean and refinish the interior. Gunn set to work on a list of projects, including repairs to the front gate latch, which had always given him fits whenever he had visited. Despite the busy preparations, the couple stole every available opportunity alone to embrace or kiss and express brief words of endearment, to the point that they had to agree to desist or else nothing would get done.

The days began to fly by. They were so overtaken by events that

Gunn had neglected the visit to his mother. On Tuesday morning, he left Elizabeth and Marianne to travel into Boston. He took the train to South Station and then an omnibus down to the ferry docks, where he boarded the boat to Hull at midday. A little more than three hours after leaving West Roxbury, he was standing at the foot of the winding driveway that led to Stormcrest, the hilltop home of his Aunt May and Uncle William Mitchell.

The gravel crunched under his feet as he climbed the steep driveway, which took him to a porte cochère at the side of the house. He climbed the steps and knocked on the door. In a moment, a servant appeared, a woman he didn't recognize, apparently annoyed that he had not come to the front door. Gunn told the servant his name and asked to see his aunt, were she at home. The servant allowed that she was and led him to the grand parlor of the house, where she bade him wait until the lady of the house could greet him. Gunn complied and sat in an overstuffed chair to wait.

In a few moments, he heard the excited voices of his aunt and his mother trailing down the main staircase, followed by their fleeting footfalls. His mother burst into the room, with Aunt May following directly on her heels.

"Andrew! Why didn't you tell us you were coming?" Eleanor cried. She rushed to him with a warm embrace.

"I sent you a telegram before I left Savannah, but I didn't realize that you weren't at home in Concord until Meg told me."

Aunt May pushed in and gave him an enthusiastic hug. "Oh, it's so good to see you, Andrew. You've seen Marguerite in New York? How is she?"

"She seems very content. We probably should talk about that."

"Yes, I keep hoping she'll decide to come home," said Eleanor.

"Not much chance of that, I'm afraid. At least not right now."

Eleanor held her son's shoulders at arm's length. "What a surprise!" When elated or startled, often her Southern accent, usually reserved, would break through. "You could knock me down with a finch feather. Let me look at you, Son. How are you? You look so thin."

"I'm very well, thank you. A little worse for wear."

"Well, you're a sight for sore eyes. When did you arrive?"

"Truth be told, I've been here for several days, but I stopped in West Roxbury before coming here."

"To see Elizabeth? Of course you did. How is she? It was dreadful to hear of her mother's death, poor thing. So sorry. Is she doing all right?"

"She's fine and as lovely as ever, Mother. I mean to marry her as soon as we can arrange it."

"What? When did you make these plans? Why am I always the last to know?"

Aunt May chuckled. "Oh, Eleanor. What makes you think that? Give your son some breathing room. He just got here."

"We've just now made plans. I'll tell you all about it, Mother. I promise."

"We were just about to sit down for something to eat, Andrew," May said. "Will you join us? You'll be able to tell us all about everything over a nice luncheon."

"Of course. Thank you. Where is Uncle William? Is he here?"

"He has been in the city on business for several days, staying at the town house in the Back Bay. He'll be home this evening, however. I hope you're planning to stay a while and spend some time with us. He will want to see you."

Gunn recalled the disagreement that overshadowed their last meeting, almost three years earlier. "I want to see him, too. I have some things that I need to say to him. We parted badly last time we saw each other. It was my fault, mostly."

"He blames himself. I think you two should talk," May said.

As usual, Aunt May put out a delightful spread, or rather her servants did, consisting mainly of a variety of fresh seafood bought that morning at the market in Hull. While they ate, Gunn conveyed his thoughts about the decision to take Elizabeth and Marianne back to Savannah with him and to get married there.

"But where will you live?" May asked.

"I don't know yet. We'll manage something. Perhaps we'll stay with Cousin Josie and Julia in the meantime, if they will have us."

"I'm sure they would be delighted . . . for a time. But you'd better ask them first, don't you think?"

"Of course. I'll send a telegram tomorrow."

"Well, I suppose I should start making plans to attend the wedding," said Eleanor.

"We will, too, presuming we're invited, of course."

"I'd be disappointed if you and Uncle William didn't come, Aunt May." said Gunn. "Mother, here's the thing. I've been thinking that you shouldn't just come for the wedding."

"Oh? Whatever do you mean?"

"I mean, why don't you come with us to Savannah? To live, permanently."

"Why, I couldn't do that."

"And why not? Now that Meg is in New York, you're left all alone in that drafty old house in Concord. What is keeping you? Come live in Savannah."

"My whole life is here."

"Begin a new life."

"I have no friends there."

"You have family. And you do indeed have one friend. Someone who seems very fond of you."

"And who might that be?"

"Daniel Sullivan."

Aunt May put down her wineglass. "Jay Daniel Sullivan? Now, there's a name from the past."

Eleanor's face flushed red. "What does Daniel Sullivan have to do with me?"

Gunn raised an eyebrow. "Why don't you tell us?"

"That was a very long time ago. Ages and ages."

"He talks as though it were yesterday."

"It was not. How do you know him, anyway?"

"We saved his life after a shipwreck. And his daughter's."

"Daughter?"

"Yes, he has a daughter, whose name is Sarah. She's about the same age as Meg."

"So he is married."

"Was. His wife died years ago."

Eleanor sighed. "I have no interest in revisiting the past."

"Are you sure?" said May.

"I am sure. The past is past. There is nothing for me there but regret."

"Why haven't you ever spoken of him?" Gunn asked.

"Some things are better left unspoken."

"Is it true that your father forbade you to marry him? And that he threatened to cut you off and ruin Daniel if you didn't stop seeing each other?"

"That is not relevant to anything that matters now."

"Why do you say so? It entirely changed your life, didn't it?"

"It is all water long under the bridge. I really don't wish to talk about it."

"He says that you left without a word, and he had no way of communicating with you."

"There was nothing more to be said. I had my reasons. Did Daniel tell you that my father forbade me to marry him?"

"Yes. Cousin Julia did as well."

"Julia?" Her tone grew sharp. "What else did she tell you?"

"Nothing, really. Only that you left Daniel behind in Savannah and got married just two months later. Why was that?"

"What do you mean, why? That's nobody's concern but mine, and mine alone. So you and Julia have been talking about me, too? I'm sure y'all had a grand time discussing my private life."

"Not at all. They simply told me the story when I found out the connection."

"What nerve. Well, you can just put your curiosity out of its misery. I'll have no more to say on the matter."

"Mother."

Eleanor's face clouded. "Nothing, I tell you. Not another word. And I'll stay at home in Concord, thank you very much. I am quite content there. And I hope your wedding is a marvelous event, Andrew. You may write to me all about it."

"Eleanor, don't be that way."

"I will be any way I choose, May Mitchell. This is certainly none of your business."

"I didn't mean to say that it is."

"Very well. Then let's have done with it, shall we? Enough said."

Eleanor folded her napkin neatly, got up from the table, and left the dining room.

"I've never seen her quite so cross. I certainly didn't mean for that to happen," said Gunn. "Maybe I should go apologize."

"I'd let her be for a little while, if I were you. I know my sister pretty well. She'll need some time to herself. You certainly managed to raise her hackles. I haven't seen her that upset since, well, since your grandfather said she couldn't marry Daniel Sullivan."

"Not even when Father left us?"

"Not even then."

42

When William Mitchell arrived home that evening, he greeted Gunn with an enthused handshake. He gave no indication of harboring any hard feelings that previously had passed between them. Rather, he peppered Gunn with questions about his experiences of the past two years, expressing great interest in his accounts of life at sea, and offering stories of his own, some of which Gunn had already heard many times.

It was always quite clear that Mitchell missed the earlier days of his own adventurous youth spent as a merchant mariner and ship's captain, and he preferred that previous life to the present one of business deals, contracts, and ledgers. The two of them had shared the bond of seafarers since Mitchell had first taught him to sail as a young boy, and it pleased Gunn beyond words that their affinity seemed unbroken now, despite the rancor of their last meeting. Mitchell's attentive audience gave him a sense of clemency that served to offset the unpleasant fact that his mother remained secluded in her room for the rest of the day and refused to come out, even for the evening meal.

After dinner, Mitchell invited him to enjoy a smoke on the front porch. Gunn readily agreed, given that Stormcrest's porch, which over-looked the approaches to Boston Harbor, was the second of his two favorite places to sit of an evening. As they settled into their chairs in the stillness of the twilight, Mitchell offered him a cigar, which he took with a smile.

"Taken up my bad habits, I see," Mitchell said as he struck a match and held the flame to the end of Gunn's cigar.

"Only one. Vice sometime . . . by action dignified," Gunn said between puffs.

Mitchell furrowed his brow. "What's that?"

"Friar Lawrence."

"Friar who?"

"Never mind. I allow myself to enjoy a good smoke from time to time, but I do try not to make a habit of it. The aroma of a good cigar has always appealed to me. I find it relaxing."

"Of course." Mitchell finished lighting his own cigar. He removed it from his lips and studied the glowing foot, as he often did when he was searching for something to say. "You know, I'm very glad you're here, Andrew. I've been wanting for some time now to sit down with you and have a good talk. Our last time together did not go so well, as you may recall."

"I regret that, Uncle William."

"As do I. As do I. The fault is mine."

"I was too harsh in expressing my mind."

"And I provoked you, I fear, by needlessly taking an untenable position to antagonize you. Nonetheless, what you said got me to thinking."

"What about?"

"About the necessity of upholding the law, even when it is not expedient for us to do so."

"Well, that is my duty, after all."

"And the need to keep a closer eye on my ships."

"I'm sorry to have threatened you."

His uncle smiled. "Admonished me."

"That was the intent."

"It worked." His cane chair creaked as he stood to take in the view, with his back to Gunn, puffing a great cloud of smoke that sat in a wreath above his head in the still night air. "I will confess something to you, Andrew. You may do with my confession what you will."

"You needn't do anything of the kind."

"But I do. You see, I know how disappointed you were in me at the time. And I found that I could not bear to leave it that way. You have always been like a son to me, Andrew. The only one I'll ever have. It pains me to have you think ill of me or doubt my character in any way."

"And you have always been like a father to me, in ways that my own father never could be."

He turned to face Gunn. "Thank you for saying that."

"I mean it."

"I thought about writing to you many times over the past couple of years. But what I have to say needs to be said in person. And it isn't something that I'd readily commit to paper and ink. You understand."

"I think I do."

Mitchell straightened and took a deep breath. "I knew that the *Parsifal* was smuggling. I knew what Webber was up to. I knew all about his illicit cargo."

"I thought so. We all did. But we had no proof."

"It's worse than that. I encouraged it. I even profited from it. Others, too."

"I see." The entire incident of the *Parsifal* sinking flooded back into his mind, along with the aching disappointment of long-standing suspicions that his own uncle was complicit in defying the law that he was sworn to uphold by smuggling goods and people aboard his fleet of ships. Now, the hurt returned, though dulled by time, along with Mitchell's confession.

"The point is, I'm done with all that. It's not worth it to me any longer."

"The risk of getting caught is great. As are the penalties."

"The greatest penalty, as far as I'm concerned, is that I allowed what I was doing to come between us. I'm truly sorry for that."

"I did not deal with it very well, either, if truth be told."

"Nonetheless, I apologize for my part. I want us to be friends again. Is that possible?"

"Most certainly. It is what I want, too, very much."

"The only act that I do not regret and will not apologize for is my part in the Underground Railroad. If that is a crime, then so be it. I am an outlaw and a fugitive from justice. And I will never surrender or turn myself in. Uncle Sam will have to stop me. I trust you understand."

"I understand. I will not argue the point, Uncle William. I will not stand in your way. But you must understand that I cannot protect you, either."

"I accept those conditions. What will you do with the information I've given you? As I said, you are free to do with it what you will. I stand ready to accept the consequences, whatever they might be."

Gunn thought for a moment. "As I said, we had no proof of your complicity."

"But now you have my confession."

"True, but there is no longer any evidence of the crime. Unless, of course, you wish to disclose whatever records you might have kept."

"I have destroyed them all. As I said, that part of my life is finished, and I want nothing more to do with it."

"In that case, I don't know a district attorney who would prosecute under those conditions. It would seem to me the principle of *corpus delicti* applies. Without corroborating evidence, a mere confession of a crime is not enough to convict. But if you'd like me to test that theory—"

"Let's not go there, shall we?"

"And what of your ships' captains? How will you prevent them from continuing on?"

"I have told each of them in no uncertain terms to cease and desist any illegal activity and if they are caught smuggling, Glastonbury Enterprises will not come to their defense."

"And what if one should he be caught, should turn state's evidence, and testify against your previous involvement to save his own hide?"

"I will take that chance. So be it. But I think the possibility is very remote. They will abide by my instructions to a man. I am sure of it. Else, they would not be captains much longer."

"Very well. But you must promise me that you are indeed finished. The son of Billy Bones Mitchell has struck his Jolly Roger for good."

Mitchell laughed. "I give you my word of honor."

"Then that is good enough for me. By the by, I've noticed that you've kept your ships out of Savannah, as I so rudely suggested you do."

"We have not sailed into or out of Savannah for over two years now. I did not wish to provoke. I must say it has been at great loss to the company. But I invite you to inspect any one of my ships, anywhere in the world. You will find them all to be completely aboveboard."

"As you know, Uncle William, the Revenue Cutter Service needs no invitation. We can do that, anyway."

"Of course you can. What I mean to say is—"

"No need. I take your meaning. And I am glad and most grateful that you have come to this position. Please don't keep your ships away from Savannah any longer on my account."

"Shall we shake on it, then?"

Gunn stood, laying his shillelagh aside, and extended his right hand. Mitchell took his hand and held it in his for a moment, then gave it a vigorous shake. The warmth of his hand seemed to flood into Gunn's arm, coursing throughout his chest and into his gut like a dram of whiskey. Tears came to his eyes.

"I see that you still carry a walking stick, Andrew. I'm sorry for that, too. I still feel horribly responsible."

Gunn picked up his shillelagh and held it in both hands, scanning the dozen or so sets of initials carved along its length. An image flashed through his mind of being tossed violently over the *Parsifal's* railing and into the roiling sea as the ship ran aground. It was the stuff of his night-mares, when he had them. "Truth be told, I hardly need it anymore, though it has become almost a part of me now. I carry it more for senti-mental reasons. As it was a gift from my former shipmates, whose initials you see carved here, I have come to cherish it more than any other possession."

He collapsed into bed that night with a lightened heart. It had been years, so long it was hard to remember when, since his spirits had been so high. So far, the trip home had been well worth the trouble of everything that had happened in the course of getting there, the events of which now had begun to fade into memory.

Despite his long absence, ended by the tragic death of Elizabeth's mother and the despair of her father, which grieved him more than words could tell, her love for him had seemed to deepen and grow. Elizabeth had turned to him above all others in her grief and had readily agreed when he suggested they should marry. Unlike on previous occasions, she had at last affirmed a desire equal to his own.

He had reconciled with the man who had been most like a father to him throughout his young life, and whom he had come to love and respect above all other men, but whose suspected involvement in illegal activity had caused great disappointment, which had driven a deep rift between them. And the cause of the reconciliation was his uncle's admission of guilt and subsequent regret, and Gunn had been right to call him on it. There was great satisfaction in that thought.

He resolved to himself that in the morning he would sort things out with his mother. He had never felt so far removed from her, though now she slept in the next room. She was angry with him, and he understood very well why she was angry. It was strange to think that what caused her anger was brought about by his involvement in events and relationships that would have remained entirely unknown to him if he had not helped save the lives of Daniel Sullivan and his daughter.

What a queer, uncanny turn of events, which now had brought needless grief and anxiety to someone he loved so deeply. He should have known that would happen, and it had been grossly insensitive of him not to realize it. Tomorrow, it would be his turn to apologize and seek forgiveness from the very woman who had given birth to him, bringing about all that had happened to him since, for better or for worse.

43

After breakfast, Gunn found his mother in the library, where she was seated in front of the great stone fireplace in a wingback chair, her Bible open upon her lap. A small, cheerful fire flickered in the fireplace, taking the chill off the room. When he entered, she placed a small silver bookmark between the pages and closed the book. She looked up and greeted him with a smile, her face drawn and wan, her eyes red-rimmed.

"Good morning, Andrew. Come, sit down."

He took the chair opposite her in front of the fire. "Good morning, Mother. I'm glad to find you here alone. I wanted to apologize to you for what I said yesterday. And I hope you can forgive me."

"Of course I forgive you. I forgave you as soon as you said what you did."

"How is that?"

"Quite simple. I was just reading here about the admonition of our Lord to forgive others of their offenses against us, even to the extent of seventy times seven."

"Even if they are not sorry for what they have done?"

"Especially then."

Gunn stayed quiet.

"Of course, you know this already. I've taught you these things from the time that you could first understand. It was a cornerstone of our life as a family, in our relationships with one another, especially between you and Thomas and your sister, as often as you quarreled and hurt each other's feelings. We all need to be forgiven from time to time. It is the essence of our Christian walk."

He sighed. "I remember."

"But . . ."

"But what?"

"There seemed to be a 'but' hidden there somewhere."

"I don't wish to get into it right now, Mother."

"Get into what?"

"A discussion that might end in disagreement."

"Well, now you have me intrigued. Have you a different understanding? Have I misstated what we taught you?"

"No, you've said it well. But I have come to a different understanding."

"How so?"

"Let's talk of something else."

"No. I want to know what you are thinking."

He shook his head at the thought of how often he had tried and failed to forgive his father, despite his mother's repeated admonition to do so. "I really don't wish to discuss it right now. I merely wanted to offer my sincere apology. Let's leave it at that, shall we?"

"All right, then. Why don't you tell me all about your trip? You stopped in New York. I'm so glad to know you took the time. Tell me how Meg is doing. I do not hear much from her."

"She seems quite happy and content."

"Oh, good. I'm glad to hear it."

"We quarreled, I'm afraid."

"You did? About what?"

Gunn crossed his legs and stared into the fire.

"About what, Andrew?"

"I don't know, Mother. Everything. Nothing."

"You two rarely see anything eye to eye anymore."

"It's not just that."

"Tell me what's on your mind, Son."

"I don't know why you allowed her to go to New York. She should have stayed in Concord with you."

"She is a young woman now. What was I to say or do to keep her?"

"I don't know. Tie her to the bedpost, I suppose."

She laughed. It was good to see her laugh. "The way you and Thomas used to do."

"It worked then."

"Well, things are different now, aren't they?"

"You can say that again. The whole world is different. Everything seems upside down and inside out these days. Everyone seems on edge. I long for a simpler time, when things were much more normal."

"And when was that? Surely, you can't say that our life has been anything like what one might think of as normal. Ever."

"Well, you're right about that. But you know what I mean."

"I think I do. But the world is not a normal place. It hasn't been since the Garden of Eden."

"Yes, but these days everyone seems to embrace and even espouse what was once not considered normal, don't they? Especially women, by the way. Surely, that's different, you must admit."

"Something is obviously troubling you. Why don't you say what it is? I wish you would confide in me."

"I'm still working it out in my own mind. I hesitate to say anything. You might find me too judgmental. You usually do, especially where Meg is concerned. You've always taken her side in things."

"Try me."

"All right, then. It's this whole women's movement thing. It seems to be based on some vain new philosophy that is aberrant at its core. I must admit that I don't fully understand where it's coming from. At first, I thought it was just a passing phase, like a waxing moon, or better yet, a flooding stream. Soon, it would likely run its course, then fade away, and things would settle. But that is not happening, is it? As it so happens, it would appear that this flooding stream is actually a tributary of a much, much larger river that has overflowed its banks. It's a river of carelessness unlike any that we've ever known, at least in our lifetimes. Meg seems to have jumped in with both feet. And it's a fairly swift current. Not sure where it will take her. Or the rest of us, for that matter."

"Marguerite has always been a free spirit, Andrew. You know this."

"Yes, of course. I do know that. But it goes beyond Meg, Mother. This is something different. Much bigger than just one person. I've seen it. Experienced it firsthand."

"What do you mean?"

He got up to stir the fire, which had fallen into embers, and added some firewood.

"Some sort of revolution. A complete turning about from what was. What always has been."

"Perhaps you're reading too much into the state of things."

"Perhaps not. I wish I could make you understand."

"I'm trying."

He turned to face her, leaning against the fireplace. "I met a young woman, very much like Meg. They could be sisters. They are certainly of the same mind. Kindred spirits, if you will."

"Oh? Who is she?"

He hesitated. "Without trying to add misery to pain, her name is Sarah Sullivan."

"Daniel's daughter?"

"The same."

His mother closed her eyes for a moment. "Go on."

"Open your eyes, Mother."

She opened her eyes and glared at him.

"What I have to tell you is difficult for me to say. You've asked me to confide in you. All right, then. I am willing to confess to you something deeply personal. I don't know who else to turn to since you, of all people, know me and know my life and the total circumstances of it. I used to have Thomas, and I wish now above all things that he was still here to share these things with. But in return for my confidence, I will need to know that you are present with me, that you are not drifting off to someplace more convenient or pleasant or desirable, as you often-times do."

"Very well. I am with you."

"If you ever breathe a word to anyone of what I am about to tell you, I will never again so much as reveal to you what my favorite color is."

"It is blue."

"Not anymore. I'm serious."

"I am, too. Go on."

Starting from the beginning, as best he could recall, and leaving nothing out, Gunn related his experiences with Sarah Sullivan, from the day of the rescue until they parted in New York. The only time his mother took her eyes from him was when he spoke of Sarah coming to his bed and that he'd been sorely tempted to take advantage of the situation. She blushed and turned aside, but quickly regained her composure. When he finished telling the story, he resumed his seat near the fire, which had fallen to smoldering embers.

His mother looked down at her hands. "Are you still attracted to her?"

He rubbed his chin. "I suppose I am. But I don't want to be. I know I shouldn't be. I love Elizabeth."

"Listen to me, Son. And listen well. You must stay away from this woman. Avoid her at all costs. Else, she will be your ruin. You must trust me on this. I know what I'm talking about."

"I realize that, Mother."

"I hope you do. What is it about her that attracts you? I mean, is it merely her physical beauty, or what, exactly?"

"She is beautiful, there is no doubt about that. I'm sure you would agree. But it's more than what meets the eye."

"What then?"

"She is so seductive in every aspect of her being, but none so much as this notion that she has of personal freedom. She insists on following her heart and doing whatever pleases her, regardless of the consequences. 'Nothing at all to hinder or bind,' as she puts it. It is all very beguiling. She claims that we are actually of the same mind, but I haven't yet realized it."

"Is that so?"

"I don't want it to be so."

"That is not what I asked."

"Honestly, it is what I fear most in this world."

"Ah. And why is that?"

"Because if I were to bend to it, succumb to it, I would become just like my father. And that is the very last thing I want to do. But it is precisely what Meg is doing right now."

"Why do you say that?"

"Because she told me so. And I observed it in her behavior. We argued about it. She refused to acknowledge what she knows to be true. It is a selfishness that knows no bounds and does not care for whatever follows. And it will eventually destroy her and devastate those around her, just as Father allowed it to do. It is this same freethinking, individualistic philosophy of mind and heart that has caused us so much pain and sorrow—which he has yet to apologize for—and that's why I cannot and will not forgive him."

"Have you tried, as I've asked you to?"

"I have. It is not possible."

"Even though our Lord commands it? Do you not recall the words of the Lord's Prayer? We must be willing to forgive others as he forgives us. For our own sakes, as well as for theirs."

"Yes, Mother. But do you understand that God's forgiveness depends on our contrition, our turning away from our sins?"

"That's very true. I never said otherwise."

"So then, how can we forgive someone who is not sorry for what they have done? Are we to be more forgiving than God?"

She waved her hand. "Perhaps you are right about that. I'll have to think more on it. Tell me, speaking of confessions, have you told Elizabeth any of what happened between you and Sarah?"

"No, not yet."

"Don't you think you should? Perhaps it is to her that you should be confessing, Andrew, not me. Any woman deserves to know the heart of the man she intends to marry before they tie the knot. Believe you me, I speak from sad experience. If you truly love Elizabeth, you will tell her. Does she not deserve to know, before you are married?"

He shook his head. "I fear the consequences. Maybe there is hope for me yet."

44

The day had dawned gray and misty. Low-lying clouds clung to the shoreline, obscuring the usual expansive vista of the surrounding islands and distant harbor, as though the heavens had descended to meet the earth for a time. The weather suited Gunn's present mood after the discussion with his mother, and he decided to set out in it for a good stretch of the legs. He borrowed a wool mackinaw from his uncle's closet and donned his slouch hat. Taking his walking stick in hand, he ambled down from the highlands into the village of Hull.

The main street was quiet as he walked along the assortment of quaint storefronts, comprising a general store, sundry shops, a fish monger, and small chandleries. An occasional wagon or carriage plodded by. He found the tiny telegraph office next to the town hall and stopped in long enough to send a telegram to Cousin Julia, informing her of his plans to bring Elizabeth and Marianne home with him, hoping that both she and Julia would welcome the news.

Anticipating a long walk into the afternoon, long enough to settle his mind, he ducked into a grocery, where he bought some hard cheese, two thick slices of ham, a pickle, and a half loaf of sourdough bread from a rosy-cheeked but dour-looking woman. She wished him a good day as she wrapped the victuals into a bundle of brown paper and tied it with twine. He answered her greeting with a grim smile equal to her own.

Tucking the parcel under his arm, he left the store and meandered through the rest of the small town until he reached the outskirts, where the cobblestones ended in a sandy lane that led along an isthmus to the dunes and outer beaches of the Nantasket peninsula. Several schooners lay at anchor in the protected waters of the bay.

By the time he rounded the higher ground of Point Allerton, which offered some temporary protection from the chill of the strengthening east wind, cold sleet began to fall, pelting his face and urging him to raise the collar of his coat and pull it close about his chin. He thought about turning around but lowered his head and pressed on. He began to recall with fondness the mild spring air of Savannah. In the distance, the foghorn at Boston Light moaned, warning ships of the hazards of the Graves, invisible in the gray mist.

The wind whipped the legs of his trousers as he walked over the crest of a large dune and caught a glimpse through a wispy break in the fog of the steel-gray Atlantic, speckled with whitecaps. He shielded his face with the crook of his elbow from the icy wind.

Down the beach a ways stood a weathered boathouse and, nestled against it, a small shack. Blue smoke streamed sideways from a stovepipe sticking up through the pitched roof of the shack. A sign nailed above the single doorway identified the hut as a shelter of the Massachusetts Humane Society, one of about ninety or so established along the coastline, manned by volunteers, to offer rescue and refuge to survivors of shipwrecks. The window exuded a welcoming, warm glow of lamplight.

Gunn eased down the face of the dune, the sand giving way under his heels. He approached the shelter, climbed the wooden steps and knocked on the door. Presently, the door opened, and a man with a hawk-billed nose greeted him.

"Hullo, young fellah. Come on in outta the weathah."

Gunn stamped the sand from his boots and entered the small, close dwelling. "Many thanks. I'm afraid it was getting the better of me. Wasn't so bad when I started out."

"Well you know what they say. If you don't like the weathah round these parts, just wait a minute."

"I am hoping it will moderate a bit, sooner rather than later."

"Come sit by the fire. Warm yourself. Take my chair. I'll get anothah."

Two other men sat around the single pot-bellied stove, which occupied the far corner of the one-roomed shack. On the stovetop, vapor rose from a coffeepot and a small black kettle, along with the mingled aroma of strong coffee and fish chowder, which filled the room. One of the men offered him a cup of coffee, and the other motioned for him to sit on the empty chair.

Among the three, Gunn recognized a familiar face, one which he knew very well. It was the severe, full-bearded visage of Joshua James, known to practically everyone who had spent any time at all in the small village. A local fisherman, James was the successful captain of his own schooner, the *Miss Esther*, though he was only about five or six years older than Gunn. Born and bred in Hull, he came from a large seafaring family who had known tremendous gains, as well as experienced tragic loss, on the high seas over the years. James had named his ship after his mother, who had died at sea within sight of shore, along with his older brother. Ever since, he had dedicated himself to saving the lives of others.

James grinned and set his cap back on his head. "Well, well, well, look what floated in on the tide. A sailor, home from the sea. What brings you to these parts, Andrew?"

Gunn shook his hand as he sat down next to him. "Hello, Joshua. Just visiting for a spell. Why aren't you out fishing?"

James whistled. "Only a fool would choose to go about in weather such as this."

Gunn chuckled. "Well, I guess that leaves no doubt about me, then, does it?"

"We were out yestiddy. Caught a mess. Figured we'd lay low tiddy. Me and the boys thought our services might well be needed down here. Fine weather for a grounding. Often happens in an easterly, especially when you can't see the bowsprit from the capstan."

"I see. I do hope you're not needed."

"So do we. But now we have an extra hand. Boys, I want you to meet Lieutenant Andrew Gunn, of the Revenue Service. He's a nephew of Billy Mitchell. We've known each other for ages. Used to sail together when we was kids. Best single-hander I ever saw."

"Pleased to know ya," said the man with the hawk-billed nose, who pulled up a chair nearby. "Jacob Richter's the name. Mate on the *Miss Esther*."

"And this is Jan Kuyper. He's our ship's carpenter," said James.

Kuyper took a bent briarwood pipe from his mouth with a puff of smoke and nodded. "So den, you're Cap'n Mitchell's nephew?"

"By marriage. His wife and my mother are sisters."

Kuyper nodded again, crossed his legs and leaned back in his seat. "Helped pull one of his ships off de shoals near Highland Light a couple years back."

"That's right," said James. "We were called in to help salvage her. The *Parsifal*, wasn't it?"

"I remember. I was there," said Gunn.

"That's right. How could I forget?" James said. "There've been so many wrecks in these waters it's hard to keep them all straight. Come to think of it, you were aboard when she went aground."

Kuyper puffed on his pipe. "You vas?"

"I was third lieutenant on the cutter *Morris* at the time. The *Parsifal* was sinking. We'd put a shot in her hull by mistake. Six pounder. It was supposed to be a warning shot after she refused to heave to for a boarding, which she finally did. We seized her after the boarding, but she was taking on water so fast that we ran her aground to keep from foundering."

"As I recall, Captain Webber, the skipper, was killed in the wreckage. Along with another crew member," said James. "Seems to me you were bunged up to a fare-thee-well, too, Andrew."

"I survived to tell the story. A little worse for wear."

"Vasn't she caught smuggling?" Kuyper asked.

"That she was. Cuban cigars. Fancy watch parts. Among other things."

"And people, too," said Richter. "Runaway slaves, wasn't it?"

"You fellas have good memories."

"Hard to forget a story like that," said Richter.

James got up and poured himself another cup of coffee from the pot. "Was your uncle involved in all that, Andrew? Seems to me he was cleared of any charges, but I've always been curious."

Gunn hesitated. "There was no evidence of his involvement."

Richter frowned. "Hard to believe he didn't know something."

"Vat of it, even if he did?" Kuyper said. "Seems to me a man makes a living on de sea any vich vay he can."

"Even so, I'd imagine it must have been a bit awkward for you, Andrew, wasn't it? As an officer in the Cutter Service, I mean."

Gunn hurried to untie the parcel in his lap. "You know, I almost forgot. I brought a bite to eat with me. Anybody hungry? It's not much, but you boys are welcome to share it, if you like."

"We've got some chowder on the stove. You're welcome to some of that as well."

They divided the food into four small sandwiches and dished out chowder into tin cups. As they ate together around the warm stove, the four men continued to trade sea stories, laughing and jibing at one another. By their free and open expressions, the others accepted Gunn in their presence as one of their own. It was good to be again in the company of men who shared the uncommon experience of life on the sea in all its pleasures and hazards.

Eventually, James told the story of the wreck of the brig *Odessa*, which occurred just a month earlier in Nantasket Roads.

"It was a late nor'easter. Miserable weather. The ship had fallen on the rocks out near Little Brewster and was getting hammered shape-less. We had torrents of rain and waves breaking over us so hard that two men had to keep bailing just to stay afloat. We took the surfboat out twice." He pointed with his thumb in the direction of the boathouse. "Hit bottom once, knocked two holes in the hull. Patched 'em with lead and went back out. Threw a line aboard the *Odessa*, which got caught in the mizzen rigging. One of the seventeen crew-men, the only ones left alive, had to climb up there to get it. He tied it around his waist and jumped into the surf. We hauled him aboard and went back for the other sixteen. By the time we got them all into the boat, we had just about swamped it. One gunnel went under water. It was just luck the other didn't. Made it back to shore by the skin of our teeth."

In turn, Gunn told his story of the sinking of the *Georgiana* and subsequent rescue of Daniel and Sarah Sullivan.

"What caused the ship to sink?" James asked.

"From what we were told, the boiler exploded in the middle of a storm. Maybe the same nor'easter as the one that hit you."

James shook his head. "Steer clear of steamships, is what I say. You couldn't pay me to sail on one."

"As for comfort and speed, you can't beat them, but I'm with you," said Gunn. "And nothing beats a vessel under sail for sheer enjoyment."

"Hear, hear," all four said in chorus.

Gunn continued his story. He included the odd occurrence of Sarah's supposed visitation by the ghost of the *Dobbin*'s dead captain.

"That woman described Captain Dawes to a tee. She said he told us we needed to go back for more survivors. But our ship was taking on water. We needed to get home. Turned out, there were more survivors, after all. More than a dozen or so, rescued by another ship. Beats anything I'd ever seen."

The three men listened, enraptured. Their only audible response was a whistle from Joshua James and Richter's grunt of astonishment. Kuyper, wide-eyed, kept quiet, but his pipe smoked like a locomotive.

Gunn went on. "This woman, Sarah Sullivan's her name, is unlike any other I've ever met. A free spirit if ever there was one. Now, get this. She claims that she wants to go to sea, wants to be a sailor, because it's the one place where she feels liberated, the most free that a person can be. Now, what do you make of that?"

Kuyper recrossed his legs and shook his head. "Pshaw."

"A womanly notion if ever I heard one," said Richter. "If you ask me, the only liberty the sea offers any man, woman, or child is the freedom to die at any moment."

"The sea is indeed a hard, demanding mistress," said James, pulling at his beard. "She brooks no foolishness, shows no pity on any man's ambitions, and gives no account for his merits. She will have mercy on whom she will have mercy."

Richter nodded, pulling at his hawk-billed nose. "God's own justice," he uttered.

45

The cold wind pressed against his back all the way to Stormcrest, speeding his steps, as though insisting on his return. A chill seeped through the warmth of his coat and settled in his shoulders. Even so, the recollections of his day with three men of like mind warmed him. He had enjoyed their company and appreciated the chance to renew an old friendship with a man he greatly admired, so much so that he'd lost track of the time, arriving back in town well after dark.

He understood these men and what motivated them to risk their own necks to save the lives and property of people they had never even met, many times without acknowledgment or proper thanks. He felt the same desire to do whatever he could to make a true difference in the world, not for the sake of vainglory, but simply because it was the right thing to do to relieve suffering or injustice wherever he found them. A rekindled sense of resolve burned within him to give his all for that purpose, in whatever circumstances he might find himself.

By the time he got back to the house, his family had finished supper and were gathered in the drawing room. His mother and uncle were seated in front of the roaring fireplace. Aunt May sat at the square rosewood grand piano, playing a folk tune and lightly humming the harmony. She stopped playing as soon as he entered the room.

"We waited as long as we could, Andrew," said May. "We were beginning to worry. Would you like something to eat? We can ring for Annabelle to fix you something."

"No, thanks, Aunt May. I'm not very hungry. I've just had the most remarkable day." He sat on the arm of the settee, next to his mother, and told them all about his encounter with the men at the rescue hut.

"He's a good man, that Joshua James," said Mitchell. "Never met a man I respect more, even as young as he is. He's done so much for the people of this town already, more than most men do in a lifetime, though they might live to be a hundred. That man is destined for greatness, I tell you."

"Word is, he's sweet on one of the Lucihe girls. Louisa is her name. She's his distant cousin, I believe. She's a little young for him, if you ask me. About half his age, if I'm not mistaken, though it doesn't seem to matter, at least not to him. But I'm sure you talked about all that."

"No, we didn't, Aunt May. Everything but that."

His mother lowered her knitting to her lap and looked up at him. "You didn't mention Elizabeth, then?"

"No, as a matter of fact, I didn't. The subject never came up."

"I swear on a stack of Bibles, I just don't know how men think," said May. "Spend all day jawing with friends and never mention anything or anyone of any importance whatsoever."

Eleanor picked up her knitting. "Well, did you at least remember to send the telegram to Cousin Josie, as we talked about? She'll want to know your plans. You know how she is, Andrew."

"Yes, Mother. Of course I did."

"Speaking of which," said Mitchell. "What are your plans, exactly, if we may ask? Seems to me your time is fairly short, what with everything you've decided to do."

"You're right about that. Time is sailing by. And I'll need to sail back next week. Tomorrow, I'll go back to West Roxbury to finish helping Elizabeth get ready. And, Mother, if you've reconsidered my invitation to come with us to Savannah, I'll gladly help you prepare as well."

"Don't be ridiculous. There is simply not enough time for me to get ready to move lock, stock, and barrel. It will be hard enough just to get myself together to attend the wedding."

"So you have changed your mind, then? You will come to the wedding, after all?"

"Of course I will be there, Andrew. Do you really think I would miss my son's wedding? Honestly."

"Good. I'm very glad."

"It's all so sudden. Have you two set a date?"

"Not yet. We still have some things to work out, not the least of which is who might accompany us to Savannah. It occurs to me that we'll need a reliable chaperone."

"But of course you will," said May. "Why don't you go with them, Eleanor?"

"Didn't you hear, May? I couldn't possibly be ready on such short notice."

"I expect the wedding will be sometime in late June, perhaps," said Gunn.

"I should be quite ready by then, I expect."

"Well, how exactly are you planning to return to Savannah?" Mitchell asked.

"By the least expensive means possible, Uncle William. I'll make arrangements tomorrow when I pass through the city on my way to Elizabeth's."

"In that case, allow me to make an announcement," said Mitchell. "I will provide transportation for you, Elizabeth, Marianne, and anyone else you convince to go with you."

"Really, Uncle William, that's not necessary. I'm too much in your debt already."

"It will be part of our wedding gift to you, Andrew. I will arrange for the *Gawain* to provide you transport. She is scheduled to leave Boston for Charleston next Friday. Will that give you enough time?"

"Well, yes. I think so. That's most generous of you. Thank you."

"Good. It's settled. A simple matter to extend the trip to Savannah. What's more, I will go with you. I can even act as a chaperone for the two of you, if you like."

"Oh? When did you decide this, husband?" May asked, an eyebrow raised.

"Just this minute."

"Heavens. Such rash decisions being made all of a sudden. Is that wise?"

"I've recently decided to begin new operations in Savannah. There is no time like the present. Strike while the iron is hot, so to speak."

"Very well, husband. As you wish. No need to consult with your wife, I suppose. I'll just continue playing in the background, then, shall I? Here is one of your favorites, Andrew."

She began playing Chopin's nocturne, the same one that Sarah had played so ethereally.

"Anything but that, Aunt May. Please."

"But I thought you loved this piece."

"Not so much of late."

The next morning, Gunn caught the noon ferry to Boston. When he arrived at the ferry dock, he decided to pay a visit to his former ship-mates on the cutter *Morris*. He walked along the waterfront to Long Wharf, where he found the ship moored alongside in her usual berth, rather than anchored in the harbor. It was good to see her there, since it meant that she had been forgiven by the city for her part in the rendition of Anthony Burns from freedom back to slavery more than two years earlier.

Gunn approached the gangway and mounted it, intending to walk aboard. He was stopped by the watch officer, in dress uniform, carrying a spyglass in the crook of his arm.

"You may halt right where you stand, sir. State your business."

"I am Second Lieutenant Andrew Gunn of the Revenue Cutter *Dobbin*. I've come to see First Lieutenant Prouty."

"You are not in uniform, sir."

"I am on leave."

"Mr. Prouty is not aboard, sir. He is no longer assigned to this ship."

"What about Mr. Miller? Captain Whitcomb?"

"Gone ashore, sir. We've just returned from a three-week patrol. All officers are ashore on liberty. I am Second Lieutenant Stephen Farley. Perhaps I can be of service to you."

"Well, you could start by allowing me to come aboard, Mr. Farley."

"Very well, sir. Come aboard."

Gunn walked the remainder of the gangway, stopped to salute the national ensign, then turned to salute the officer of the deck. Farley returned his salute and stepped closer to him.

"Would you like to leave a message, Mr. Gunn?"

"No, I just happened to stop by on my way through town. I'm just visiting family and friends after being away for the better part of three years."

"I see. Well, I'll be sure to pass the word."

Just then, Boatswain Thomas Nelson bounded up. "Why, Mr. Gunn. As I live and breathe, it is good to see you again, sir."

Gunn held out his hand. "Hello, Boats. How are you?"

Nelson shook his hand. "Fine, just fine, sir. How about yourself?"

"Never better, thanks."

"I see you still carry the old staff o' life."

Gunn lifted his walking stick. "Hardly go anywhere without it, though I don't really need it so much anymore."

"That's certainly good to hear."

"You two know each other, then?" Farley asked.

"We do, indeed. This man saved my life," said Gunn.

Nelson grinned through his salt-and-pepper beard. "It was a life worth savin', sir."

"I was hoping you'd still think so," said Gunn,

"Me and all those whose initials are carved on that stick."

"Mr. Farley here said that Lieutenant Prouty is no longer assigned to the *Morris*. Do you know where he has gone? Where might I find him?"

"Oh, Mr. Gunn. You'll be pleased to know that Mr. Prouty received orders to the *Andrew Jackson*, up in Maine. Eastport, it is. He's the new captain."

"Is that so?"

"It is. And I'm to join him early next month. Got my orders in hand."

"And sorry we are to see you go," said Farley. "How will we ever do without you, Nelson? It's beyond me."

"I'm just an old barnacle, Mr. Farley. There'll be another along soon enough to replace me, just as sure as Monday morning."

Gunn clapped Nelson on the shoulder. "That's good, Boats. You'll be a good right hand to him, I'm sure."

"Well, if it's a right hand he needs, then you should think about coming along. I know he'd be glad to have you, sir."

"I'm not so sure."

"I've heard him say it meself, Mr. Gunn. 'Course, he was asleep and dreamin' at the time. Out of his head with fever, he was."

Gunn laughed. "Well, I doubt that any such thing will happen anytime soon, Boats. Not for lack of trying, mind you. But my luck doesn't seem to be going that way. I'm stuck where I am for now. Planning to get married soon. My bride-to-be is coming to Savannah. We'll make our nest there, I suppose. At least for now."

"Well, well, well. Congratulations and solicitudes, Mr. Gunn. I wish you both very well, indeed."

"Don't you mean salutations, Nelson?" Farley asked.

Nelson grinned again. "No, sir. I meant solicitudes. I've been married nigh some ten year now. I should know what I meant."

Gunn laughed again. "Thank you, Boats. And I wish you the very best in your new assignment. Good luck to you."

Gunn departed the ship with mixed feelings. It was good to renew another old acquaintance, especially with Nelson, who had been such a significant influence in his life thus far. And he was gratified to hear that Prouty had at last been awarded his own command after so many years of waiting. Prouty would make a fine captain, no doubt, and his departure meant that a position as first lieutenant had opened on the *Morris*.

Gunn wished for the opportunity to come back to Boston under such a fine officer as Captain Whitcomb. No better ship's captain could be found anywhere on the seven seas. If he could secure the position as first lieutenant, it would mean Elizabeth would not have to leave New England to live in the South. But he also knew that the captain had a long memory, and he would not likely be welcome back to the *Morris* under Whitcomb's command anytime soon.

And that was nobody's fault but his own.

46

The house was quiet and dark when Gunn returned to West Roxbury. He sat on the front porch to await Elizabeth's arrival home after another day of teaching at the local school. A half hour or so later, she came walking up the street with Marianne, both with an armful of books. The two appeared to be in a serious discussion, but they stopped talking when they spied him sitting on the steps. Marianne opened the gate, and the two entered the yard. Gunn rose from his seat to greet them.

"You're back," said Elizabeth. "We were just wondering when you'd be home. I'm so glad to see you."

"I'll just change clothes and we can get to work. We have a lot to do before Friday."

"Friday?"

"Uncle William has offered to provide us all transportation back to Savannah aboard one of his ships. We leave on Friday next."

"Oh, I see." Her face fell.

"I'll just go on inside, shall I?" said Marianne.

"Yes, go on in, dear. Go ahead and start dinner. We'll be in shortly."

Elizabeth stood at the bottom of the steps as Marianne gave Gunn a kiss on the cheek.

"Welcome back, Andrew," Marianne said, as she opened the door and went inside.

"What's happened?" Gunn said.

"What do you mean?"

"I can tell something has happened. What is it?"

"Let's sit down together. I have something to tell you, Andrew."

"All right. I see disappointment in your face. I hope you're going to tell me that you finished painting the kitchen, but you don't like the color."

"It's much more than that, I'm afraid."

They sat together on the porch swing.

"I'm all ears."

"I cannot go with you to Savannah right now."

"Why not?"

"We've just received word from my father. He sent a letter saying that he fell very ill on the boat to Scotland. He needs help. I must go to him. I hope you understand."

The news was as disappointing as it was unexpected. Yet he knew how much her father meant to Elizabeth, especially after the recent loss of her mother. And the last thing he would want is for her father to succumb to illness because he did not have anyone to properly look after him.

"I understand completely, Elizabeth. Our plans will wait. You must go to him."

"Oh, thank you, Andrew. I'm so grateful to you for understanding."

"What do you want to do about the house?"

"What about it?"

"Do you want to continue trying to sell it? Suppose it should sell in the meantime while you are gone?"

"I hadn't even thought of that. I suppose we should do whatever else we can before I have to leave. My brother can take it from there. He will stay here to continue his studies. I see no reason not to proceed. My father will have no more use for it. Marianne and I will join you in Savannah when Father is well again."

"I will be waiting on tenterhooks for your return."

"Just a little longer, my love. And thank you again for being so understanding. It's why I love you so much."

"It certainly wasn't what I expected to hear when I got back."

"I'm sorry. But it's just a short delay. We'll still be married soon."

"We still have a great deal work to do before we leave."

"Of course we do."

"Better get to it, then."

The next several days afforded little leisure time. The waking hours were taken up with cleaning and painting projects, as well as selling off items of furniture or decor no longer needed. What small leisure they did have was taken up with walks along the footpath to Jamaica Pond, watching spring take hold and talking about their future plans together.

Gunn made another quick trip into the city, both to purchase tickets for Elizabeth and Marianne to sail to Scotland the same day as his departure and to his uncle's shipping office to inform him that he would be traveling alone to Savannah the following week. Meanwhile, Elizabeth continued teaching, allowing the school time to find a substitute.

Time passed quickly, and scarcely before they realized it, the day of their joint departure had arrived. The evening before, Robert came home, and the four of them sat in the parlor on the remaining furniture, their voices echoing against the bare walls.

"We've spent so many happy hours together in this room. It's sad to see it so empty," said Robert.

"The lack of furnishings is only part of it, too," said Elizabeth. "The whole house seems empty without Mother. And Father."

"I keep thinking I hear their voices in the next room," Robert said.

"Me, too," said Marianne.

"Yes," said Gunn. "I miss my discussions with your father over the dinner table and in his study. He always had something important to say. And he had such a fine way of leading you along a certain path without your even noticing."

"Believe you me," said Robert, "He'd let you know right well if you were straying too far from that path. I can attest to that." He grinned and rubbed his back pocket.

"You know, it's hard to think of living anywhere else," said Elizabeth. "This is the only home I can remember."

"Do you have no memory of life in Scotland?" Gunn asked.

"I was only three when we moved here," she said.

"I was but a wee bairn," said Robert, mimicking a brogue. "Life in this house is the only thing I've ever known."

"I've grown to love it here," said Marianne. "It will be very sad to leave."

Gunn leaned back and laced his fingers behind his head. "So strange to think how quickly life can change sometimes. Almost in an instant, it seems."

"And it never goes back to the way it was," said Robert. "Does it?"

"I remember thinking the very same thing when I left here almost three years ago," said Gunn. "I somehow knew nothing would ever be quite the same when I returned, even though I hoped it would never change."

"How right you were," said Elizabeth.

Robert's brow drew into a slight frown. "I've come to realize that hoping for things to stay the same is just wishful thinking."

"Sometime things can change too quickly, though," said Gunn.

"Yes, they can," said Marianne. "But there was a time, not too long ago, when I thought nothing would ever change for me. I felt sort of hopeless."

"We have to let go of the past," said Robert. "Move on. It's easy for most people to get stuck in the past and mired in old, tired customs and traditions. We must look forward to the future. That's where the stuff of life is."

"But it's important to hold on to some things, don't you think?" Elizabeth said. "Otherwise, we lose sight of who we are. And life becomes never-ending change. That's not good for anyone."

"I think it's good to hold onto some things and let go of others in favor of what's new," said Gunn. "But I do agree that change can come too fast sometimes."

"The way I see it, memory is just as important as imagination," said

Elizabeth. "That's why we have both. And it's best to use both in equal measures. Remembering the past is as essentially who we are as imagining the future. That's the only way we can live a balanced life, more centered, without spinning off like a top, willy nilly and who knows where."

"Well, I'm all for that," said Gunn. "And I will always cherish the memory of hours spent here with your family. And especially with—"

"Oh, here we go," said Robert, rolling his eyes. "Cover your ears, Marianne. It's about to get unbearably intimate in this room."

"I was going to say that I will truly miss your father. He has been a great influence in my life, both past and future. I'll be forever grateful."

"Thank you for saying so, Andrew," said Elizabeth. "He would be very pleased to hear that."

"Wait until he hears that you're getting married all of a sudden," said Robert. "That will raise an eyebrow. You know how he hates surprises."

"Why should it matter? I know he'll have something to say about it all, but I expect he'll be very pleased," said Elizabeth.

"I'm sure he will be, too," said Marianne.

Robert chuckled. "Will it make any difference if he isn't?"

"Well, certainly it would. I care very much what he thinks," said Gunn.

"Of course it would," said Elizabeth. "But I'll be sure to ask him again for his blessing, given how our plans have changed of a sudden."

"Well, anyway, I can't imagine why he would express any reservations or change his mind now," said Robert. "Andrew is still the same man he always was. Father has always praised his honesty and integrity, which is all that really matters. Nothing has happened in the meantime to change that."

Gunn dared not utter a word in reply.

47

Elizabeth trembled in his arms as he held her close and said goodbye. They stood together on the front porch, the cool night air of April close about them.

"Are you chilly, my love?" Gunn asked.

"Not as long as I have the warmth of your arms about me."

"You're shivering."

She turned her face away. "I don't know why. Not exactly, anyway. I guess I am a little afraid."

"Of what?"

"Nothing. It is nothing I can name. Just a feeling. A notion. Silly, really."

"What notion?"

She hesitated. "I'm afraid that I've made the wrong decision. That I should be going with you tomorrow, instead of going to Scotland. That we should be getting married as soon as possible, without delay. And that if we don't, something bad will happen."

"Why is that?"

Placing her head against his chest, she sighed. "I don't know. As I said, it's just a silly feeling. There is no reason for me to feel this way, is there?"

For as long as he had known her, Elizabeth had exhibited an uncanny knack for sensing something amiss, like a spirited horse wary of an unfamiliar scent or sound. He would have to tread with great care. "None that I can think of."

"Are you sure?"

"Why shouldn't I be?"

She shrugged, then tightened her arms around him. "No reason. I just feel like there is something hidden. Something I can't see, lurking in the shadows, but whatever it is shouldn't be ignored. Does that make any sense at all?"

"I've sometimes felt the same way."

"Is there anything at all that you're not telling me?"

He took a deep breath and exhaled slowly. His mouth went dry. "Like what?"

She raised her head and looked directly into his eyes. "I don't know. Has something happened?"

"Well, a great many things have happened since I left."

She shook her head. "That's not what I mean. Something seems off. What's troubling you?"

He stayed silent for a moment. A knot formed in the pit of his stomach. He knew that she would not relent, once aware of something that troubled her. He struggled to form the words that would sting like a slap, no matter how much he tried to soften them.

She raised her hand to his face and gently guided his gaze to meet hers. "Did something happen?"

He kissed her. "Nothing worth mentioning."

"What does that mean?"

"Elizabeth, the only thing that has happened is that I love you more than ever, so much that I want nothing more than to be married to you. Even right now, before another moment passes, if you like." He whispered the last sentence in her ear, his breath moving a wisp of her dark hair.

"That's not worth mentioning?"

He kissed her again, but she did not kiss him back. "You know what I mean."

"I'm not sure I do."

"Now, you *are* being silly," he said, trying to smile.

"Am I?" She searched his face with her eyes. "You have been true to me all this time, yes?"

"Yes, of course I have. Why would you ask such a thing?"

"As I've said, I have no reason. Just a feeling."

"I love you, Elizabeth. I want to spend my life with you. That's my deepest feeling. Nothing will ever change that. I don't know what else I can tell you to ease your fear."

"That's just it. I feel like there's something you're not telling me, and I'm about to get very angry with you if you refuse to tell me what it is."

The words would not come. "Let's not quarrel. Not on our last night together."

"That's entirely up to you at this point."

"Well, I for one refuse to argue." He hoped against hope that his last-ditch effort would settle the matter.

Elizabeth pulled herself away from his embrace. "Andrew Gunn, I believe something has happened that you're unwilling to share with me, for whatever reason. What that is, I can only imagine, which I do not care to do. If you love me as you say you do, tell me the truth. Whatever it is."

"The truth is that I love you."

"I want the whole truth. Please. Do me the honor of telling me the whole truth. If we are to be married, Andrew, if we are truly to become husband and wife, one in flesh and spirit, there must be no secrets between us. None. Ever. Those are my terms. If you do not agree to my terms, tell me right now. We can save ourselves a lot of heartache."

"All right. All right. So be it. I think we should sit down." He led her to the porch steps and sat beside her. He took a moment to stare at the stars shining in the night sky, altered in aspect since the last time he had done so.

Then he confessed everything, starting from the day that he had first met Sarah and her father. He told her about the rescue, about their first intimate encounter, about her visitations, her intrigue, and his fascination with her boldness and pursuit of liberation from all restraint. He ended with her visit to his bed and her warning about impending danger.

All the while, she gathered her skirts beneath her legs and hugged her knees. When he finished, she used the hem of her dress to wipe the tears from her eyes.

"Nothing happened," he said. "I swear to you, nothing happened between us."

She cried softly. "I don't know how you could possibly say that."

A veil of silence fell between them.

"Say something," he croaked.

"What is there to say?"

"I know how hurt you must be. I'm sorry. Very sorry."

"So am I," she murmured, rocking back and forth.

"I did not mean for any of it to happen."

"And that's supposed to make it better? How is that?"

"You're angry."

"Of course I'm angry, Andrew. Hurt and angry that some other woman presumed upon your affections so much that she was willing to go to bed with you."

"You have every right to be angry." He reached out to her.

She brushed his hand away. "Oh, well, thanks so much for that."

"You needn't be sarcastic."

"I knew there was something. I just knew it." She pressed her hand against her heart. "Deep down, I knew it. I've sensed it ever since you came home."

The front door opened, and an oblong shaft of light spilled across their backs. Elizabeth turned her face away from the light.

"Is everything all right with you two?" Marianne asked. "I was just beginning to wonder. Are you crying, Elizabeth?"

"Yes, sweetheart. We're just saying our goodbyes. Go on inside. I'll be in soon. Just a minute more."

"All right, then. Goodbye again, Andrew. We'll miss you."

"See you soon, Marianne."

She shut the door, and the darkness covered them again.

Elizabeth wiped her tears with the back of her hand. "I can't tell you how much it hurts, Andrew."

"I wish I could convince you how sorry I am."

"But at least you told me the truth at last. I am grateful for that. I do hope you've told me everything."

"I have."

"Do you have feelings for her, this Sarah what's-her-name? Any at all?"

He shook his head. If he ever had, they were gone now. "None whatsoever. In fact, I want nothing more to do with her."

"Do you promise me that is so?"

"I swear it."

"You must stay away from that woman. From what you have told me, she is a dire threat to everything that we hold dear. You must see that. You must feel it in your heart of hearts. If you love me as you say you do, if you value me at all, I am telling you right now, either you have nothing more to do with her, or you'll have nothing more to do with me." Elizabeth broke into full Gaelic. *"Wha daur meddle wi' me."*

Gunn knew her meaning full well. "I will steer clear of her. I promise you. Hope to die." He crossed his heart.

She managed a smile through her tears. "Believe me, you'll wish you had if you break that promise."

"You're still shivering. Let me hold you for a little while before I go."

She got to her feet. "I think you should go now, Andrew. It's late. Our ship sails early tomorrow. I must finish packing."

"How soon will you come to Savannah?"

She hesitated. "I cannot say."

He rose to meet her. "Do you still love me? Please tell me you do."

Elizabeth embraced him. "You are my heart, Andrew. You always will be." She raised up on her toes and offered him a deep, tender kiss.

His chest flooded with relief and the warmth of his love for her. He pressed her head against it and stroked her hair. A question came to mind that he hesitated for a moment to ask.

"And will you still have me?"

"How could I ever deny my own heart?"

48

After the first day at sea, the *Gawain* stopped in Nantucket to pick up a load of whale oil to round out her cargo of farming tools and machinery, all needed in the South to sustain the growth of King Cotton. On the third day out, she sailed a close reach on a steady westerly breeze, riding the long swells of the open Atlantic, headed for Charleston.

It was good to be at sea again, aboard a ship under full sail, heeled to a brisk wind. Gunn was not content to be a passenger, however, so he appealed to the captain to fit him into the watch schedule as a helmsman. The captain didn't need much coaxing to grant Gunn's request, given his relationship to the owner of his ship. Though the job was well beneath his skills and required little effort on his part, it served to occupy his mind to steer with great care, sailing full and by.

In the idle hours when he was not on watch, he tried to keep his mind focused on what lay ahead. His thoughts were filled with plans for their future, amid the countless things he needed to do to get ready for her to join him in June. The day likely would be here before he knew it.

One evening, after his latest watch, Gunn sat at the captain's table in the grand cabin with his uncle, enjoying a sumptuous five-course meal of roast beef unlike any he had tasted aboard a ship of Uncle Sam's. The conversation centered on the latest shipping news, which was no surprise to Gunn, given the company.

"You know," said Captain Corning, "I forgot to mention that I bumped into our old friend Richard Andros, the deputy collector at the Customs House in Boston the other day. He made a strange inquiry. At least, I thought it was strange."

"What was that?" Mitchell asked.

"He wanted to know if I knew of any ships for sale or if we had sold any recently."

"Why is that so strange?" Gunn asked.

"Well, the Deputy Collector of Customs isn't usually in the habit of brokering ship sales," said Corning.

"That is odd," said Mitchell. "What did you tell him?"

"I allowed that I did not know of any in particular at the moment. Unless I'm mistaken, Glastonbury has none for sale. Am I right?"

"That's right," said Mitchell. "We are currently expanding, wanting to buy, not sell."

Gunn raised his wineglass. "Here's to your future expansion. Did he say why he was asking?"

"Apparently, an acquaintance of his had been making inquiries on behalf of a third party. Said his client was looking for a fast ship. Not a large one, but of the sort that could be handled by a small crew. Had to be a sailing ship. One that could make the crossing. The faster, the better. Said he'd pay a premium for the right one."

"Now, if I didn't know any better," said Mitchell with a wry grin, "sounds something like a privateer, if you ask me."

"You don't say," said Gunn, matching his smile.

"Anyway, Andros asked me to let him know if I heard anything."

"Did he mention who the third party is?"

"Lamar Enterprises, I think it was, if I remember correctly. He handed me a card. I still have it somewhere. Now that I think on it, the card had an address in Savannah."

Gunn nearly choked on his roast beef. "Lamar?"

"Pretty sure. You know the name?"

"I believe I do, if it's who I think it is. Charley Lamar is quite the unsavory character. I'd heard earlier, on my way up from New York, that he was looking for a new ship."

"I'm not familiar with the man," said Corning.

"Neither was I until recently. Now, it seems as though I hear his name all the time, wherever I go."

"Sounds like he's very eager to get the word out and not worried a whit who knows about it."

"If nothing else, Lamar is a bold man. You might even say a bit brash."

"What do you think he has in mind for this fast ship of his?" Corning asked.

"I don't rightly know, but if it's the Lamar I'm familiar with, it can't be anything good."

"I know Charley Lamar," said Mitchell.

Gunn took a sip of wine and tried not to sound surprised. "You do?"

Mitchell gave a solemn nod. "Used to do business with him, before, well . . . you know."

"What do you know of him?"

"He's a man looking to make a name for himself. An opportunist who will seek to gratify himself at the expense of everyone around him. Unless I miss my guess, Charley would have made a right good pirate back in the day and could have given Blackbeard himself a run for his money, if it weren't for his desire to be so well thought of. I doubt that he's done an honest day's work in his entire adult life."

"That about sums it up," said Gunn. "I had a run-in with him before leaving Savannah."

"What happened?"

"He accused me of being a government spy, sent by the Treasury Department to keep an eye on him. Had me followed by one of his henchmen."

"That's a laugh," said Mitchell.

"It wasn't such a laughing matter, at least not in my view."

"That's not what I meant. It's very strange that he should accuse you of such a thing, given that it would mean his own relative sent you to spy on him."

"What do you mean?"

"Charley Lamar's cousin, Mary Ann Lamar, is married to Howell Cobb."

"The Secretary of the Treasury?"

"The very same."

"Are you serious?"

"Couldn't be more so. Mary Ann is a first cousin of Charley's father."

"How do you know this?"

"Because Charley introduced us at a party in Savannah a number of years back when Cobb was still governor of Georgia. He was real proud of his connection."

"Why would he think that his own relative would send someone to spy on him?" Corning asked. "That hardly makes sense, does it?"

"I don't know. If nothing else, perhaps his suspicions belie a guilty conscience. If I were to hazard a guess, he might think it would be to keep him from doing something to embarrass the new administration."

"Like what?" Gunn asked.

Mitchell puffed his cheeks and breathed out through pursed lips. "Something illicit is my bet. And something big enough to get noticed."

Corning winked. "Something illicit with a fast boat. Now what could that be?"

Mitchell chuckled. "Why, Captain Corning, whatever do you mean? I'm sure that I have no possible idea."

"You're suggesting that he might be smuggling," Gunn said.

"It's certainly possible, knowing Charley Lamar."

Gunn cocked his head. "Let's say you're on to something. What would he be planning to smuggle, do you think?"

"Something big enough to make a name for himself, gain some notoriety, if he could get away with it. Not unlike a modern-day Blackbeard, which I do think he fancies himself. And something that would make a lot of money all at once, most likely. Charley is always in debt and in need of a windfall to bail him out. Has been ever since I've known him."

"I see. That explains a lot. What else do you know about him?"

Mitchell raised an eyebrow. "Well, he's an avowed Fire-Eater. No question about that, and he hasn't been quiet about it. He wants to see the Southern states secede from the Union, and would like nothing better than to restart the Atlantic slave trade."

"Are you sure about that?"

"I've heard him say as much myself. He has always said that it makes no sense to outlaw the sale of slaves overseas when it is legal to sell them on the auction block in the state capital. He's not alone. There's a bunch more just like him. They're not shy about it."

"And with the recent Supreme Court decision, what better time to attempt it."

Gunn sat back heavily in his chair. "Well, smuggling slaves into the country would certainly be enough to embarrass the new administration, wouldn't it?"

"Enough to embarrass them? Probably so. Maybe even enough to start a war, I should think."

49

By the time the *Gawain* reached Charleston several days later, Gunn and Mitchell had hatched a plan to find out just what Lamar was up to. While they had only suspicions and no proof of his doing anything illicit with the new ship he was searching for, they agreed that the timing and the temptation of achieving such a grandiose scheme as attempting to challenge the federal government on the laws against the Atlantic slave trade would be too much for Lamar to ignore, given what they knew of him. And the possible consequences of his success were unthinkable. The stakes were too high for them to ignore.

Beyond that concern, Gunn had developed a deep dislike of the man. Nothing would please him more than to see Lamar in all his brash arrogance brought down a peg or two. And he believed strongly in the rule of law, which in his view formed the basis of American society, as he knew it. Though he might occasionally find fault with the law, nevertheless it was not the prerogative of any man to offend it with impunity. If he had learned any lesson from the Burns incident while aboard the *Morris*, it was that one. It seemed to him that the same lesson now had come home to his uncle as well.

For his part, Mitchell would try to reestablish a relationship with Lamar under the pretense of resuming a trading business in Savannah.

Perhaps he could even pretend to help Lamar find a ship suitable for his purposes, whatever they might be. For that ruse to succeed, the relationship between Mitchell and Gunn would have to remain below decks. For that reason, Gunn decided to leave the ship in Charleston and take the regular ferry the rest of the way to Savannah.

Meanwhile, Gunn planned to gather intelligence where he could on the waterfront among the close-knit maritime community, where it was hard to keep anything secret for long—unless of course it meant exposure to an outsider. If their suspicions were correct, after he had gathered enough information to convince others, he would notify the district attorney or whatever authorities would hear the evidence. If at all possible, he aimed to prevent Lamar from carrying out any scheme to restart the slave trade. Somebody had to.

When the ferry arrived in Savannah the next morning, Gunn reported directly to his ship, which was still in the yards. From all appearances, the repairs were almost complete. Jayjay had been true to his word. The *Dobbin* was back in the water and nearly ready to go back to sea. Things could finally get back to normal, a prospect that Gunn had been looking forward to with great anticipation. But when he arrived onboard, he soon found that things were far from normal.

The officers and petty officers of the ship were gathered in the wardroom, all in dress uniform. Seated at the head of the green baize-covered table, an officer with captain's insignia stopped speaking in midsentence as Gunn stepped off the companionway ladder, set down his belongings, and stood before them.

"Mr. Gunn, welcome back," said Bulloch. "We didn't expect you to return for another few days."

"I thought I might be needed," Gunn said, removing his hat.

"Well, you're just in time. The captain was just informing us of some changes he'd like to see."

"Changes?"

"Yes. Allow me to introduce you to Captain Robert Day. He's the new commanding officer of the *Dobbin*." Bulloch's expression seemed a little sad.

"Ah, the wayward second lieutenant," said Day with a broad, disarming smile. He was a large, burly man with a long, full beard and a shock of white hair in the gray mane brushed back from his forehead. He reminded Gunn of a drawing of Neptune he had once seen. Despite his imposing appearance, he had a congenial way about him that made his size seem less intimidating somehow.

Gunn chuckled. "Hardly wayward, sir. Just on leave. Pleasure to mcct you, captain."

"All mine, I'm sure. Come have a seat, Mr. Gunn. We were just getting started. Too bad you missed the change of command this morning. But better late, and all that nonsense."

Gunn took an empty chair at the table.

"Now then, as I was saying," said Day. "Captain Dawes was the best of men. I knew him well, liked and admired him a great deal. But it occurs to me that he always seemed lacking in initiative, if you don't mind my saying so. And I fear his ways might have caused this ship's sails to luff a bit, if you'll catch my meaning. Now, I'm not so much a by-the-book man as he was, mind you, and that all has its place. Well and good. But one thing I do require of my officers, and I will not abide the lack of it in any man. That is initiative and assertiveness. Add to that diligence and devotion to duty. There will be no slacking off, no shirking of duty while I'm aboard. And every man Jack will be expected to pull his weight when called upon. No excuses. God hates a quitter. Do I make myself clear?"

"Of course, sir," said Bulloch.

Gunn half expected to see an eye-roll from the first lieutenant, but he remained stone-faced, still, attentive.

"One more thing," Day continued. "Aweigh the anchor and make all sail, I say. Prepare to be at sea, gentlemen, more than ever before. Once this vessel is shipshape, we'll bet getting underway. A ship is meant to be at sea." He leaned forward and pressed an index finger on the table so hard the color bled from it. His smile faded as he glared at each of them in turn, his gaze landing on Bulloch last. "And you can count on this. We will not return to port if there is any chance at all that there is one more life in peril to be saved." He leaned back in his chair again. "By Jiminy, I'll make true cuttermen of you yet. So bid your fair ladies, wives, and sweethearts a fond *adieu*. They will soon learn to live without the pleasure of your soft company. But cheerily, eh? As they say, absence makes the heart grow fonder. Though I've never found that tripe to be true myself."

The sound of Day's voice faded to the background, and the remainder of his speech was lost on Gunn. It was something about keeping in mind that the needs of the service held precedence, outweighing the needs of any individual man. He chewed his lip as he thought about what this announcement would do to his plans. All of them.

When Day finished, he rose from his chair. His benevolent smile returned. The others stood with him. "You are fine men, each and every one. Welcome aboard the new *Dobbin*. I look forward to serving with you all. I'm sure that, pulling together as one, we can uphold the tried-and-true traditions of our seagoing service with the honor due them and our forebears. Carry on, gentlemen." He took his cap from its hook on the bulkhead and placed it squarely on his head. "Oh, and Mr. Gunn, I expect you'll be in uniform next time I see you."

"Aye, aye, sir," said Gunn.

The captain nodded with a grin, as though he had just wished Gunn a very happy birthday. With that, he left the wardroom, climbing the ladder to the main deck.

"Well, I guess that's that," said Bulloch, his voice low.

"Welcome back, Andrew," Grant said. "If you fellas will excuse me, I need to get back to my duties on watch."

Bulloch nodded, "Of course."

Grant clambered up the ladder, with the petty officers in tow.

Gunn mouthed, "What happened?"

"Be glad you missed the inquiry," said Bulloch.

"Was it that bad?"

"It could have been worse. But let's just say it didn't go my way. Brinkman and your new friend Lamar were there, doing their very best to make sure of that."

"Lamar is turning into quite the troublemaker. I have some things to tell you about him. He's become quite the bad penny."

"You don't have to convince me."

"So what were the findings of the board?"

"They found fault with several things, not the least of which was the loss of our anchor and other gear. The worst thing, I suppose, was that we left some survivors out there. And who knows how many? They decided we gave up the search too soon. About the only thing they didn't hold me responsible for was the death of Captain Dawes. That was deemed natural causes, thanks to Doc's testimony and yours."

"But you saved the ship."

"Yes, and that's the only thing that saved my career. Thankfully, Mr. Boston himself was kind enough to come to my defense on that score. If it weren't for him and my cousin James, things might have gone off the rails. As it is, I consider myself lucky to still have my job."

"So now we have a new captain."

"That we do. He arrived three days ago."

"What do you know of him?"

Bulloch shrugged. "He is Boston's pick. Lots of friends in high places. That's about all I know. The men seem to like him. He's a sailor's sailor."

"Yes, I gathered as much."

"So how was your trip, Andrew? I hope it was relaxing and restful."

"I'd hardly describe it in those terms."

50

The change in leadership affected many other variables, of course, one of which portended to be far more important than any other in its potential impact on the life of the ship, though it seemed insignificant at the time. Seaman Walters, the captain's steward, who had become disheartened after the death of the beloved Captain Dawes, decided not to renew his enlistment when it ran out. In fact, he had been so unnerved by the reported appearance of the ghost of Captain Dawes that he had refused to set foot alone in the cabin ever again. He chose instead to fill a vacancy as a cook at the Seaman's Inn. His departure, though relatively inconsequential to the rest of the crew, nevertheless bore considerable repercussions to the new captain. Nobody on the ship had more impact on his personal comfort or ease of mind. Despite the captain's every attempt to cajole Walters to change his mind and stay, the young seaman declined.

The captain, beside himself, expressed dismay at being unable to find a suitable replacement. Good men who could act as part cook and part valet were hard to come by these days in the booming economy of Savannah. He was quite vocal about his exasperation at Walters' intransigence and the limited choices now available to him, so much so that even Jayjay overheard him complaining about the matter as his crew finished up their work while the captain walked along the outside of the ship on a final inspection of the repairs, accompanied by Bulloch and Gunn.

"'Scuse me, cap'n. I don' mean to butt in. But if y'all be lookin' for a good man, I might jes' know of one."

The captain stopped short. "And who might that be?"

Jayjay removed his cap and scratched his balding head. "Well now, his name be Cuffee."

"And where would we find this Cuffee?"

"Well, if it ain't too late, you could find him up at Wright's."

"The slave yard?"

"The same."

"So he's a slave, this Cuffee?"

"Why, yessuh."

"What is he to you?"

"He be my cousin, suh."

"He a Gullah, like you?"

Jayjay nodded.

"And who is his owner?"

"That'd be Mistah Charley Lamar, at present. He holds the paper on Cuffee from the Parmalee Plantation. They tryin' to sell him down south because . . ."

"Well?"

"Because Cuffee done runned away. Twice."

"And what would I want to do with a runaway?"

"He need a las' chance, cap'n. His people is boat people. Best cook you ever did see. You can take my word for it. And he won't run no mo'."

"How is that?"

"Because he be deathly afraid of bein' sold down to Miz'sippi way. Slaves don' live long down there. He be ever so grateful if you kep' that from happenin'. The Parmalee only sellin' him to keep the rest from gettin' any ideas. Cuffee a good man."

Day shook his head. "I'm not in the market to buy any slaves."

"Wouldn't have to," said Jayjay.

"How's that?"

"You could hire him out."

"Hire him out?" said Gunn.

"Happens all the time. Massahs happy to hire 'em out to work for the gov'mint. Gwar'nteed to get paid."

Gunn couldn't contain himself. "Sir, I think it's a bad idea. Besides, I believe it's against regulations to bring slaves onboard."

Day frowned and shook his head. "It's against regulations to bring personal slaves aboard. There's nothing in the regulations to keep us from hiring slave labor. He'll be paid, along with his master. Happens all the time. Slaves built the Capitol building, for Pete's sake."

"Still, with the new administration, there might be some sensitivity to the issue right now, what with the hullabaloo around Dred Scott, don't you think?"

"What is it with you, Mr. Gunn? You a by-the-book kinda fellow or something?"

"Sir, I must say it strikes me as a bad idea. And it might not sit so well with the crew."

"I think maybe he's right, captain," said Bulloch. "It would seem ill-advised. Perhaps we should seek Mr. Boston's counsel."

Jayjay cleared his throat. "Bes' make up your minds quick, suh, if you won't mind me sayin' so," said Jayjay. "I heard tell Mistah Lamar plans to sell Cuffee at the very next auction, first of the month, if not sooner."

"Tell you what, Mr. Gunn," said Day. "I'll tell Boston. Hell, I'll send a telegram all the way to Secretary Cobb himself, letting them all know that, unless I hear otherwise, I intend to hire me a good steward, the best I can find. Better to seek forgiveness than to ask permission, I always say. My guess is they are too busy with other things right now to have any objection. Would that meet with your approval, do you think?"

"Sir, I—"

"Meanwhile, I'd like for you to hightail it up to find good old Charley Lamar and see what kind of deal you can work out."

"Now, sir?"

"Strike while the iron's hot, I say."

"Captain, perhaps you'd better let me do that," said Bulloch.

"Why is that?"

"Well, it's just that Charley Lamar and Andrew have developed a little dislike for each other of late."

Day looked Gunn up and down. "Nonsense. I want Gunn here to do it. I think his reluctance is just the thing. I'm thinking he'll strike a hard bargain because of it. Just the man."

Gunn pursed his lips. "Captain, if it's all the same to you, I'd rather not be sent on such an errand."

The captain did not answer. His eyes squinted to slits.

"Sir, let me do it," said Bulloch.

Day spoke in a quiet voice. "You'd rather not do it."

"No, sir. I'd very much prefer not to."

"Would you excuse us for a moment, Jayjay?" Day said.

"Mos' certainly, suh." Jayjay moved off and took his workers with him.

Day stood closer to Gunn and met him eye to eye, his breath hot on Gunn's face. "Are we going to have a problem, Mr. Gunn? You and I?"

Gunn had entered this territory before and found it familiar ground. "I hope not, sir."

"You hope not." Day took a deep breath. "I'll tell you what, Mr. Gunn. I am about to give you a direct order as the captain of this vessel. A simple order, a lawful order to go and procure an item necessary to the proper function, not to mention the good order and discipline, of my ship, as I see it. What will be your response to such an order? Before you answer, let me just say that I hope your response will be such that I am not forced to take punitive action against one of my officers before we even get underway together for the first time."

Gunn's legs felt weak beneath him. "Sir, I find the very idea of employing slaves aboard a ship of the United States abhorrent."

"Did I ask you how you felt about it, Mr. Gunn? Did you hear me ask him how he felt about it, Mr. Bulloch?"

"No, sir."

"Where are you from, Gunn?"

"Boston, sir. Concord, Massachusetts, to be precise."

"I might have known."

"All I ask is that you seek guidance from higher authority before you do this thing."

"And what if I will not?"

Bulloch intervened. "Andrew, may I speak with you a moment? Captain, could we please have a word in private?"

"Very well, you will find me in my cabin, Mr. Gunn, whenever you might choose to come to your senses. And I hope for your sake it will be very soon. I mean to sail tomorrow, and I warn you, I will not sail without a good steward. It's all on you." The captain spun on his heel and walked away.

Bulloch lowered his voice. "Andrew, you're on very shaky ground here. For what it's worth, I know of instances where other ships have resorted to the same measures. You may not like it, but that's the way of things down here."

"So what are you saying, Des?"

"I'm saying, suggesting, that you do what the captain is asking you to do."

"Ordering me to do. Against my will."

"Yes, ordering you to do, if it comes to that. Just do it, for your sake. For my sake. For both our sakes."

"Tell me, Des, would you order me to do such a thing?"

"You know I wouldn't."

"Will you obey an order to carry out disciplinary action against me, if it comes to that?"

"I'm afraid I'd have to."

"You would?"

"Reluctantly."

Gunn was more shocked than surprised. As an officer trained at Annapolis, Bulloch was very much a stickler for good order and discipline. Nonetheless, it was still a shock to hear from his good friend and shipmate that their friendship went only so far.

"I see."

"Andrew."

"No, I see where I stand, Des. It's good to know exactly where I stand."

51

As he made his way along the promenade on the Bay, Gunn heard someone call his name from behind. He stopped and turned to see Jayjay hurrying to catch up.

"Hello there, Jayjay. What's the trouble?"

"Jes' wanted to warn you, suh."

"Warn me about what?"

Jayjay paused a moment to catch his breath. "Massah Lamar, he set on sellin' Cuffee to dat man in Miz'sippi. He gon' be hard to win over."

"Then why did you even suggest that we try?"

"Have to try somethin'. Massah Lamar, he got a partner, name Trowbridge. He not as hard. Not as crafty-like. Mebbe talk to him first, if you can."

"How do you know this?"

"Got my ways."

Gunn sighed. "Well, all right. I'll see what I can do. Frankly, between you and me, I hope Lamar slams the door in my face."

"I wish you would try, Mistah Gunn. For Cuffee's sake. And mine. I'd be fo'ever grateful."

Gunn shook his head. "I can't believe I'm even involved in this, Jayjay. It's an ugly business."

"If you only knowed how ugly."

"You're right. I probably don't know the half of it. What I do see makes me sick to my stomach already."

"Believe, me, Mistah Gunn. You don' wanna know the other half. But I thank you for bein' strong agin what you do see. I wish mo' people was."

"They are few and far between down here, that's for certain. It's hard to find someone who wants to end it all. Especially now."

"You mean the court's decidin' that we ain't people?"

"Yes, that's exactly what I mean."

"It's gonna get a whole lot worse, 'fore it gets any better. And Lamar means to see to it. Need to watch out for that one."

"What are you saying?"

"That man got plans to bring in mo' niggahs."

"How do you know this?"

"He don' make no secret of it. Not much of one, anyhow. He tryin' to buy a boat right now to take over to Africa."

"That's what I thought."

"I hear tell he got his eye on one."

"Do you know which one?"

Nossuh. But I 'spect it likely won't be long till he find what he lookin' for. He pushin' real hard. And then, well then . . ."

"Tell you what, Jayjay. If you hear anything more, anything at all, you let me know. Will you? I promise you that nobody will know about it, if you are at all worried about that. I give you my word."

"Your word good 'nuff for me, Mistah Gunn."

Gunn crossed the street at Drayton and walked half a block south to a dingy brick office building with dirty, barred windows and a door that needed paint. Above the door swung a sign that read, "Lamar & Trowbridge—Brokers" in block letters.

He entered a dimly lit office that was just as dusty and drab as the outside. A railing separated the waiting area from the rest of the office, where sat two large oak desks, opposite each other. Only one was occupied, and that by a middle-aged man in shirtsleeves and a visor, hunched over a ledger. The man looked up from his work, removing the visor and squinting to see who had come in. He rose from his desk and put on the jacket draped over the back of his chair.

Gunn introduced himself, and the man opened the gate in the railing to allow him in.

"Pleased to meet you. I am Nelson Trowbridge. Won't you sit down?" Trowbridge offered him the chair in front of his desk. Gunn took a seat. "Now, how may I help you, Mr. Gunn?"

"I am here to inquire about a particular slave that you have in your custody, Mr. Trowbridge."

"Oh, and which one would that be?"

"He goes by the name of Cuffee."

"Many slaves are known by that name."

"This one comes from the Parmalee Plantation."

"Yes, of course. And what is your interest in this Cuffee?"

"Our ship is in need of a steward. I'm told he has served in such a capacity."

"He's a troublesome one. I doubt he would serve you well. A runaway, you see. I'm afraid he is bound for the open market."

"Well, that's too bad. We were prepared to offer you a very favorable contract for his services. But I guess we'll have to look elsewhere then. " He rose halfway from his chair.

"Just a moment. A contract, you say? For how long?"

"Indefinite. It would depend on how well suited he is to the work and whether he earns his fee."

Gunn could see the workings of the man's mind in his darting glances across the ledger. "What terms would you be willing to offer?"

As Gunn laid out the terms, the man's eyes widened. If the least bit smart, Trowbridge was calculating that the indefinite earnings would soon exceed the discounted sale price of a runaway slave.

"Let me just add, Mr. Trowbridge, that your property would be quite secure, given that he would have little opportunity to escape while the ship is at sea, and while in port, he would most often be under the watchful eye of the captain himself."

Trowbridge leaned back in his chair and studied the ceiling, his eyelids fluttering. "Well, now. Well, now. Let's just consider, shall we? I suppose such an arrangement might be worked out. I suppose so." He sat forward again. "Mr. Gunn, my partner will return shortly. I would need to consult with him, of course. The final say would be his, you see."

Gunn got up from his chair. "My captain is in a mad rush to find a suitable replacement as soon as possible. Perhaps I shall try elsewhere."

"Now, let's not be too hasty, Mr. Gunn. Just allow us time to discuss the matter, won't you?"

At that moment, the outside door opened, and Lamar walked into the office. The surprise on Lamar's face at seeing him made Gunn smile, despite his distaste for the man.

"What are you doing here, Gunn?"

"I've come to do some business with you, Mr. Lamar. Your partner and I were just finishing up."

"What business could you possibly have with me?"

Gunn explained the purpose of his visit.

Lamar's black beard twitched. "Get out."

"Pardon?"

"You heard me. Get out of my office. I have no interest in doing business with the likes of you."

"And why is that?"

"I know who you are and what you are about, lieutenant. In fact, I've come to learn a great deal about you. I know what happened on your previous ship and why you were sent here. And I feel no obligation whatsoever to explain myself to any Yankee, much less one who makes a point of trying to make trouble in this town. My town. The people of Savannah just want to be left alone, Gunn, free to live our lives the way we see fit, and not according to what some abolitionist sympathizers think we ought to do. And that's what I want right now. Leave me alone."

"Very well, then. Captain Day will be very disappointed, I must say. I don't know quite what to tell him."

"Bob Day?"

"You know him?"

"'Course I do. Known him a long time. He used to command the cutter *Crawford* back in the day, when I was but a boy. We all looked up to him. He has always been well loved in this community. A very fine man is Captain Day, and we welcome his return with open arms. Unlike some."

"Ah, good. I'm very glad to hear it. Maybe you could explain the situation to him for me. He was certainly hoping you'd be a bit more accommodating to his personal needs."

"He sent you up here?"

"That's right."

Trowbridge cleared his throat. "Might we have a word in private, Charley?" He nodded toward a side door. They disappeared into the adjoining room and closed the door. Their muffled voices sounded through the wall in what seemed like a brief argument, though the words were largely unintelligible. The only thing Gunn could make out was Trowbridge stressing the phrase, "get out of arrears." After a moment, they returned.

"Very well," said Lamar, smoothing his beard. "You can have Cuffee. We accept your terms."

"On a trial basis, of course."

"Yes, of course. Mr. Trowbridge here will draw up the necessary papers. The contract and so forth."

"Good. It's settled. You'll be kind enough to have him cleaned up and made presentable before you send him down to us?"

"Send him down to you?"

"Why, yes. Captain Day will expect delivery as soon as practicable. We'll sign the contract and make the first payment in advance, cash on delivery, once we see what we're getting, you understand. Today, if possible. No later than tomorrow morning."

Lamar ground his teeth. "All right."

"Any further request or comment, Mr. Gunn?" Trowbridge asked.

Gunn considered the question. He was torn. Unfortunately, it had become his duty to accomplish this distasteful task to the satisfaction of his commanding officer. Part of him, what he often considered the better part, prompted him to attend to his duty to the best of his ability. But another part, at the moment the part that wished to be unbound and forever free from constraint, hoped that somehow Lamar would break the deal and throw him out, as he had threatened earlier to do.

"Why, yes, Mr. Trowbridge. Now that we have concluded our business and I still have your attention, there is one more thing." He looked with disdain around the office. "I don't know what else goes on in this place, but it seems to me that in the present economy, any man worth his salt could make an honest, decent living at almost any legitimate enterprise without depending on the sale of human flesh. It stinks in here. You should open a window."

Rage flashed in Lamar's eyes. He snatched up his gold-headed cane and brandished it.

"Charley, don't," warned Trowbridge.

Lamar slowly lowered the cane to his side. "I will certainly take your words to heart, Mr. Gunn," he sneered. "You can be assured of that. Give Captain Day our best regards. We congratulate him on his new command. Tell him that I will soon pay my respects as an old friend. Very soon."

52

Under the light of a bright full moon, Gunn walked along River Street, passing in and out of the long shadows of the factors and warehouses along the waterfront. It was a warm, clear night, and the wharves were quiet and devoid of traffic at this hour, well after midnight. The river slurped and gurgled around the hulls of the ships moored along the wharves as the current slipped by. At last, he came to the *Gawain*, her tall masts and spars looming into the moonlit sky.

Standing aside in the shadows, he surveyed up and down the waterfront to see if anyone might observe him going aboard. Assured that he was alone, he ventured up the gangplank.

A seaman on watch, startled by his sudden presence, leapt to his feet. "Hang on there. Who might you be?"

Gunn removed the cap pulled down over his eyes, revealing his face in the moonlight. "Hello, Taggert."

"Ah, Mr. Gunn, it's you."

"I've come to see my uncle. Is he aboard?"

"Aye, Mr. Gunn, you'll find him down below in the cabin with Captain Corning."

"Are they asleep?"

"No, sir. I don't believe so. Lights still on. Just heard 'em stirrin' a minute ago, when I passed by the skylight on my rounds. Sounded like they was playin' a hand of cards of some sort."

"Good. I'll see myself in."

"Go right ahead, sir."

Gunn walked aft to the quarterdeck and climbed down the ladder into the cabin.

"Ahoy, there," he said, as his boots touched the floor.

"Well, well," said Mitchell. "Look what the cat dragged in."

"Come on in, Andrew. Pull up a chair. We were just playing a little poker. Your uncle has me at a slight disadvantage. Join us. Maybe you'll change my luck."

Gunn laughed as he sat down at the table. "No, thanks. I can't stay long. Just wanted to check in with you. I'm assuming you will be leaving soon to go back north."

"Yes, that's right. We'll be heading out tomorrow on the noon tide, as a matter of fact, as soon as we can load the cargo."

"Any luck with Lamar?"

Mitchell nodded. "It took some doing, but I managed to wheedle him into an agreement to take a small shipment of cotton to New York. We'll load up tomorrow morning. It's on trial. I'm losing money on the deal, but I had to underbid everybody else."

"That's not good for business."

Mitchell waved his empty hand. "It's a start. Don't you worry. I'll make it up later. Besides, I've got some other prospects, too."

"Were you able to find out anything about his plans for buying a ship?"

"I told him that I'd heard he was looking and asked if he might be planning to compete with the likes of us. He said that I needn't worry as long as we stick to coastal trade. He was looking at foreign markets. That's all I could get out of him. What about you?"

"I've got a source who tells me that Lamar definitely plans to bring more slaves in. He seems pretty sure of his information."

"Reliable?"

"I'd say so. He's a man of his word. And he knows his way around the waterfront."

Mitchell squinted one eye. "Mind telling us who he is?"

"He's a shipwright over at Willink's. Goes by the name of Jayjay."

"Jayjay Johnson?"

Gunn nodded. "The same. Why? Do you know him?"

Mitchell and Corning exchanged knowing looks.

"We do," said Mitchell. "We are old friends. Jayjay often has been very helpful to us in our past efforts to, uh—"

"Ship northbound freight otherwise proscribed," Corning said.

Mitchell cleared his throat. "Extra-manifest. If you catch my meaning."

"I understand," said Gunn, shifting in his chair. He knew exactly what they meant.

"So what are you going to do?" Mitchell asked.

Gunn shrugged. "Nothing, for the moment. Don't want to tip our hand, so to speak. Until I have some evidence to show, I don't want to risk making any kind of accusation. Lamar will just deny it, anyway. His word against mine. We know who would win that battle in this town."

"What about telling your captain?"

"I will when the time is right. I'm not too sure of him yet, to be honest."

"Probably best. Well, listen. Captain Corning will be returning with the *Gawain* in about a month or so. I might come back with him. Maybe not. But let's keep in touch through him, shall we? I trust him implicitly to keep things quiet. Can we count on you, Tom?"

Corning raised his right hand. "Certainly. You can count on me."

"And you'll help us gather more information?"

"Yes, of course," said Corning. "I want to stop this menace as much as you do. I can't think of anything that will tear this country apart quicker than starting up the Atlantic trade. The man is a lunatic. If Lamar is successful, it will open the floodgates. Others will soon try. If that's what he's about, then he must be stopped at all costs."

"Good. That's settled."

Gunn shifted in his seat. "Would you do me a favor, Uncle William, while you're in New York?"

"Sure. What's that?"

"Look in on Meg for me. I'm worried about her. We parted on bad terms when we last saw each other."

"Will do. What about your father?"

Gunn dropped his gaze to the shadows on the floor. "You needn't bother with him."

"As you wish."

When Gunn left the *Gawain*, the moon was low in the western sky, the light diffused by a thin veil of clouds. Gunn picked his way along the waterfront in the darkness, avoiding the various obstacles and pitfalls along the way back to the shipyard. When he reached his own ship about twenty minutes later, all was quiet except for the lone figure of Foster, who remained on watch at the gangway.

Foster saluted him. "Mornin', sir."

"Good morning, Foster. All's well?"

"Aye, sir, it is."

They both turned as they heard a stifled cry off the port quarter. A ship had ghosted in and was rounding up, getting ready to anchor, about three hundred yards from the *Dobbin* and a hundred yards from Lamar's cotton press. The ship, a three-masted barque, under minimal sail, was dark. Ashore, lights were on inside the warehouse and a single lamp with a red lens shone from a post in front of the press.

"What's this?"

"Dunno, sir. Odd time to come in, ain't it?"

"I'd say so."

The ship dropped anchor and settled back on her rode, the stern swinging away from the slight wind. It was all very neatly done.

"Get me a glass, will you, Foster?"

The seaman scrambled up the steps to the quarterdeck and soon returned with a spyglass, handing it to Gunn. Putting the instrument to his eye, Gunn focused on the bow, where the trailboard affixed to the hull displayed the name of the vessel in bold script: *E.A. RAWLINS*.

The barque's crew doused the sails in darkness and went about squaring the yards, securing the ship from sea, while making as little noise as possible. Soon, they lowered a boat into the water with four men at the oars. Three other men, one of them presumably the captain, climbed down into the longboat and settled themselves on the thwarts.

Without a word, the boat crew started rowing toward shore, their oars squeaking in the oarlocks as the only accompanying sound.

Three men emerged from the warehouse of the cotton press. Gunn turned his spyglass on their faces. One of them was the bearded visage of Charley Lamar. The man next to him was Trowbridge. The short figure standing behind them turned out to be Donnelly.

The boat reached the wharf, and a hollow thump sounded as it came alongside. The crew shipped their oars and made the boat fast, and the three passengers climbed out onto the wharf. Lamar approached them and slapped the tallest one on the back. Their laughter rang across the open water, but their words were unintelligible. One thing was clear, however. Though in the wee hours of the morning, the arrival of these men and the ship that bore them was quite expected and most welcome.

53

In the light of day, it was quite clear that, though the *Rawlins* had sailed neatly into harbor under the power of her own sails, the shabby old ship was the worse for wear and in dire need of repair. Some of her rigging was missing, the hull had been badly patched, and the paint was peeling in places, not to mention that the main topmast appeared to be sprung and leaning to the right, the starboard shrouds sagging and swaying in the breeze like a cobweb. It indeed had required skillful seamanship to sail that hulk unassisted up the river and into the harbor in the dead of night. Gunn surmised that this was the ship that Willink had been anticipating, and the reason that it was so urgent for the work on the *Dobbin* to be completed on time.

After breakfast, Gunn mentioned his concerns to Bulloch and his new captain as they stood on the main deck, surveying the new arrival.

"She came in during the morning watch, well before dawn," said Gunn. "I don't like the looks of her, sir. Something's off."

"Not from around here," said Bulloch. "Leastwise, I don't recall seeing her before."

Day frowned. "I wonder who she belongs to."

"The captain went ashore at the cotton press. Charley Lamar met him at the wharf. They seemed fairly chummy."

"Is that so?" Day said.

"We could board her and find out," said Gunn.

"No, that would be a waste of time," said Day. "She's obviously not hauling cargo at the moment. In for repairs, most likely. None of our business, really, at least for now."

Just then, a tugboat approached with the *Gawain* at the hip, nosing slowly between the *Rawlins* and the *Dobbin*, heading for the wharf at the cotton press.

"Now, there's one to board," said the captain.

"Why is that, sir?" Gunn said.

"I just don't like the cut of her jib, lieutenant. Something about her. Dunno. Makes about as much sense as what you said earlier."

"She came in a few days ago," said Bulloch. "I asked about her at the Customs House. Belongs to a fleet owned by a man in Boston, name of Mitchell." He shot a furtive glance at Gunn. "Her captain checked in on arrival, nothing to declare. Last port of call was Charleston. Nantucket and Boston before that. She does strictly coastal trading, far as I can tell."

"Boston, eh?" the captain said with a raised eyebrow. "Know anything about this Mitchell or his fleet of ships, Mr. Gunn?"

Gunn nodded. "He is known as a legitimate trader for the most part, though his ships have on occasion been caught smuggling in the past. However, I have it on good authority that he has cleaned house over the past couple of years."

The captain eyed him. "Whose authority?"

"Mitchell's. He is my uncle, sir."

"Uncle?"

"Yes, sir. By marriage. He's married to my mother's sister. He has been steering clear of Savannah until recently, but he is trying to restart regular business here."

"Why now? And why should he steer clear of Savannah, anyway? Why shouldn't he want to trade here?"

"Previous conditions were not favorable, I suppose, sir. Savannah is now in the midst of a boom. Things change."

"Wait just a cotton-picking minute. Is this Billy Mitchell you're speaking of? Is Billy Mitchell your uncle?"

"Yes, sir. The same."

"I knew Billy Mitchell back in the day, when I was here on the *Crawford*. He was under suspicion then, as I recall."

"As I said, sir, he has assured me that he has cleaned house."

Day scoffed. "He has assured you, has he, Mr. Gunn? His nephew."

"Well, it looks like he's headed in to take a load of cotton from Charley Lamar," said Bulloch.

"Nothing amiss there, I suppose," said Day. "Still, I'd like to keep an eye on that one. Maybe we'll follow her out, just to see what she's up to. That all right with you, Mr. Gunn?"

"Of course, sir."

"And by the way, I thought you said everything went well yesterday with Lamar."

"It did, sir. Mission accomplished. Are you not pleased with Cuffee?"

"He cleaned up real nice. And he's actually got some manners to boot, more than most white men that I know. Not to mention that he cooks eggs just the way I like them. He'll do fine, I expect. Just what I wanted. That's not the issue. No, I'm talking about Lamar."

"What about him, sir?"

"When Mr. Lamar delivered Cuffee to the ship last night, we had a little talk. He said you were quite rude to him, so much so that he just couldn't let it slide. He told me all about your encounter. Demanded satisfaction."

"Satisfaction? Did he tell you that he was rude to me first?"

The captain slammed the rail with his fist. "That is not the point, Mr. Gunn. Charley Lamar is an upstanding member of this community. He has served the people of this town well as both an alderman and an elected member of the state legislature. I have known him and his father longer than you have been alive. I expect that you will treat him in all instances with the respect he rightly deserves. You are to put aside this nonsense between you. When you see him next, you will apologize for your behavior toward him. And from here on out, you are to conduct yourself with decorum and common courtesy, not just with him, but in all cases, as befits a federal officer and a gentleman. Are we clear on that, mister?"

"Yes, sir."

"Are we *clear*?"

"Aye, aye, sir."

"Good. I sincerely hope we're not going to have many more of these little discussions. Are we, Mr. Gunn?"

"No, sir. Not if I can help it."

"Most excellent. See to it. Now, Mr. Bulloch. If you please, let's get this ship underway. Time's a-wastin'."

The same tug that had towed the *Gawain* to the cotton press pulled and pushed the *Dobbin* away from Willink's dock. Once clear, the cutter hoisted sails and moved off into the approaches to the harbor, where the captain ordered that the new starboard anchor be dropped. There she sat, biding her time, while waiting for the noon tide and the anticipated departure of the *Gawain*. It was just as well, for not long after she had anchored, the breeze died away, unlikely to return in full until afternoon.

Meanwhile, the crew busied themselves making final preparations for spending several weeks at sea. A lighter came to the ship to deliver fresh provisions and the latest mail and took back with it a packet of mail from the ship, which included a letter from Gunn to Elizabeth, again begging her forgiveness and urging that she should soon join him in Savannah as soon as possible. A new foretopsail, which the sailmakers had been late in delivering, also arrived with the sincere apologies of the chandlery's owner.

Bulloch and Gunn surveyed the work from the ship's waist.

"Well, Des. It seems I've put my foot in it once again," Gunn said quietly.

"You seem to have a knack for it, my friend."

"I know. Can't seem to help myself."

"I'd advise you to try a little harder, especially where Lamar is concerned. As you can see, he has connections in this town and elsewhere. You should tread more carefully."

"I find that increasingly difficult, I must admit."

"Try harder."

"Des, can I tell you something in confidence?"

"I should hope you'd know by now that you can."

"I mean, it's very important that this information should stay between us at the moment."

"Go on."

"I believe that Lamar is making definite plans to reopen the Atlantic slave trade."

"That's just noise. Lamar loves to talk. You know this."

"But it's not just talk. He is looking to buy a ship intended just for that purpose. I know this to be true."

"How do you know?"

Gunn told him about his encounter with the shipping agent in New York, his discussions with Mitchell, and the intelligence from Jayjay.

"Jayjay?" Bulloch said incredulously. "You'd take the word of a . . . of a yard worker? What has gotten into you, Andrew? I think this obsession with Lamar has gone a bit too far. You need to back and fill."

"I'm convinced of it, Des. I can feel the truth of it in my bones. I think Lamar has purchased the *Rawlins* to outfit it for the slave trade."

"That old scow?"

"He probably can't afford much better. I think he's in financial trouble, and he's getting desperate. Think about it. Bringing in a cargo of slaves would give him just the windfall he needs."

Bulloch shook his head. "He'd be crazy to try it. Anybody would. Most people, even in the South—leastwise those in their right minds— don't want the trade reopened. None of my friends do. My own father, who owns slaves, thinks that it would be the ruin of our country. Not to mention that it is still a capital crime."

"If you ask me, Charley Lamar is just crazy enough to try."

"That's the thing, Andrew. Nobody is asking you. Leave it alone before you get yourself into real hot water, like you've never ever seen before."

54

When the *Gawain* set sail and left the harbor on the tide, the *Dobbin* weighed anchor and followed. For the next five hours or so, all the way downriver, the cutter stayed about two hundred yards astern, mimicking every move the *Gawain* made. As they neared the mouth of the river, a figure appeared at the brig's stern, waving his arms overhead in a broad arc. As the watch officer, Gunn drew a spyglass to his eye. He immediately recognized the figure as his uncle. He was grinning, taunting them.

Gunn sighed and muttered to himself. "Oh, Uncle William."

The captain noticed, too. He turned to Gunn with a wry smile. "Mr. Gunn, it would appear that the vessel ahead is signaling some sort of distress. Set a course to overhaul her. As soon as we clear the mouth of the river and enter safe water, I want you to order her to heave to. We'll conduct a boarding, to ascertain how we may be of assistance."

Twenty minutes later, the two vessels stood out to sea, nearly abreast of each other, the *Gawain* about fifty yards downwind. Gunn picked up the speaking trumpet.

"Give that to me, Mr. Gunn," the captain said.

Gunn handed him the trumpet. The captain walked to the port rail.

"Ahoy, the *Gawain*. This is the captain of the *Dobbin*. Heave to and prepare to be boarded."

Mitchell waved an arm, acknowledging the order. A minute later, the *Gawain* began rounding up into the wind. Her sails shivered, and shouts from the quarterdeck ordered the crew to shorten sail and back the jib. The *Dobbin* followed suit, all the while keeping the same relative position off the *Gawain*'s starboard side. Both vessels slowed to bare steerageway.

Captain Day directed Bulloch to assemble an armed boarding party of four men, which he promptly did. Meanwhile, the crew lowered a longboat on the leeward side, and presently the boarding party climbed down into the boat.

The captain called down to Bulloch. "Give her a good going over. No stone unturned."

"Aye, aye, sir. Will do," Bulloch replied.

The boat crew rowed over to the *Gawain*, and the boarding party clambered aboard. Gunn kept a close eye as Captain Corning met Bulloch and his party at the gangway. Corning nodded agreement and ordered the main hatch to be opened. The boarding party disappeared below decks.

A half hour later the men emerged from the forward hatch, brushing loose cotton from their uniforms. Corning escorted them to the stern of the ship, where a crew member opened the lazarette for inspection. Bulloch and one of his men went down through the open hatch into the lazarette, while the other three waited on deck. Through it all, William Mitchell smoked a cigar, reclining on a settee against the captain's coffin, aft of the ship's wheel.

After the boarding, the party returned to the *Dobbin*, soaked with sweat and covered in grime and tufts of cotton fiber. Bulloch saluted and reported.

"All clear, captain. She's got a full load of cotton. Manifest is clean. Next port of call is New York. We found nothing amiss."

Day returned his salute. "Very well, Mr. Bulloch. Have the men lay below and get something to eat."

A shout came from the other ship. "Ahoy, *Dobbin*. Good hunting, captain." The voice belonged to Mitchell.

"What's that?" Captain Day called back.

"I say . . . good hunting." The voice, more deliberate this time, echoed over the open water between the two ships. "Try the *Rawlins* for luck."

Day turned to Gunn. "Now what in blazes does he mean by that?"

Bulloch shot Gunn a warning glance.

"I'm sure I don't know, sir," said Gunn.

"Never mind. Fill the sails, Mr. Gunn. Steer south by southeast."

"Aye, aye, sir."

The *Dobbin* set sail and left the *Gawain* in her wake, headed in the opposite direction. It was not long before nothing but her masts showed over the horizon, then she disappeared entirely in the twilight.

True to his word, the captain kept the ship at sea as much as possible for the next month, other than an occasional port visit to replenish supplies, patrolling up and down the coastline between Jacksonville and Charleston, boarding every inbound vessel within the three-mile statutory limit to inspect their cargos and manifests. On an average day, they boarded ten to fifteen ships. The goal, as usual, was to intercept smuggling ventures from foreign ports intended for the United Sates, attempting to circumvent the customs duties that were the primary source of revenue for the federal treasury.

Since colonial times, the attitudes of Americans toward smuggling had always been mixed, given that the act of smuggling goods from Europe, South America, and the Far East, though illegal, was considered by many as an acceptable way of avoiding unfair taxation by an overbearing or tyrannous government. Even good citizens were inclined to turn a blind eye on occasion, especially if they might benefit from it. Those same attitudes persisted to the present day, a fact of which Gunn was acutely aware.

On the other hand, American industrialists and manufacturers were keen to prevent their profits being undercut by a market flooded with illicit foreign goods, dulling their competitive edge. They demanded protection from the federal government and were in favor of stiff tariffs, the higher the better. And the fledgling federal government, still relatively new to the competitive world at large, could not survive without those tariffs.

These opposing attitudes were nowhere more prevalent than in the Southern states, Georgia and South Carolina in particular. Of course, nobody in their right mind would attempt to undercut the production of cotton by importing more of the stuff. However, tobacco, sugar, molasses, and alcohol products, which could be produced more easily, less expensively, and in greater volume elsewhere, presented a real threat to Southern planters and manufacturers. The threat to them grew with each passing year as the cost of domestic slave labor constantly increased due to the outlawing of the Atlantic slave trade, limiting the supply.

Rumors of an illicit slave trade persisted, with most of the suspected activity centered not in the South, as one might expect, but in New York City, of all places. The suspected traders operated vessels outfitted there in the center of American commerce, though not daring to bring slaves from Africa directly into the United States. The piracy laws passed in 1820 demanded no less than capital punishment by hanging for any malefactors caught importing slaves. Instead, the traders would purchase slaves in Africa and transport them by ship to Cuba, where the trade was legal. And Cuba, situated only ninety miles from the coast of Florida, presented a convenient locus from which slaves could be smuggled into the states along the Gulf Coast.

Of the scores of suspected slave trading ventures over the past decade, only one had been prosecuted to conviction by federal authorities, and the Supreme Court had overturned that case. Though some ventures may have been successful, nobody really knew how many. Nevertheless, the demand for more slaves over that same period of time had risen considerably, given the recent expansion of slave states and territories, and the prospect of more to come due to the exercise of popular sovereignty, established by the Kansas-Nebraska Act three years earlier. The pressure to break the law and smuggle more slaves had heated to the boiling point along with that demand. A few Southern newspapers in Charleston and Savannah recently had even suggested repealing the ban, although most Americans remained adamantly opposed to it, as Bulloch had pointed out. Even most slaveholders opposed it, faced with the prospect of their property losing value in an expanded market.

These issues occasionally occupied Gunn's mind during this month at sea, especially during a dull watch, when his thoughts sometimes strayed to imagined scenarios, given his growing suspicions about Lamar's intentions and the opportunities represented by the stealthy arrival of the *Rawlins* in Savannah. The other officers on the ship seemed far less concerned about the prospect of interdicting a slave ship than he was, however, given how improbable it was to encounter any along the East Coast. They focused instead on the far greater possibility of confiscating an illegal cargo of fine cigars from Cuba, or expensive French brandy, or exotic silks from China and the Far East. Accordingly, the piqued interest of all settled on a schooner named *Express,* heading north just off the coast of Georgia early one morning, a little before dawn.

Gunn had the morning watch, and he was the first to spot the ship's sails just over the horizon. The captain had commended his sharp eye. The schooner hugged the shoreline a half mile or so east of Saint Catherine's Island, nearly obscure against the darkened outline of the lowlands. As soon as she spotted the *Dobbin,* she turned and headed south. The *Dobbin* had the advantage of a stronger offshore wind and quickly overtook the slower, heavily laden ship. Gunn hailed the weathered vessel and ordered her to heave to. The *Express,* flying the flag of the United States atop her mainmast, rounded into the wind and complied without a fight.

It was Grant's turn to conduct the boarding. He and Foster, along with two others, lowered themselves into the longboat and the crew rowed them across the stretch of water that separated the two vessels. When they reached the *Express,* they nimbly climbed aboard, as most of them had a thousand times before. Seven or eight sailors surrounded them at the gangway, armed with knives in their belts. One remained on the helm.

After a brief interaction, a sailor led the boarding party to the main hatch. Several others opened the hatch, then stood aside as Grant and one of his men went below into the hold. In a few minutes, Grant emerged. He engaged the same sailor and then motioned for his men to remain while he took to the longboat. The boat crew rowed him back to the *Dobbin*. He climbed aboard and saluted Captain Day.

Day returned his salute. "What did you find, Mr. Grant?"

Grant smiled. "Well, sir, the man who claims to be the mate says the captain is not aboard."

"Not aboard? Where is he?"

"Went ashore on Saint Catherine's, so he says. Santa Catalina, as he calls it. Speaks Spanish, mainly."

"What's he doing ashore?"

"The mate says he doesn't know, best I could make out. Said he'd be back by morning."

"Is that so? What was their last port of call?"

"Nassau, Bahamas, he claims."

"Aha. And where are they headed?"

"Says he doesn't know. We'd have to ask the captain. Seemed like a joke to me."

"This is no joke. I hope he knows that. So then what is their cargo?"

"Well, it's marked as tea from British Ceylon." Grant grinned. "But there was a real strong smell of tobacco. I had them open one of the crates. Full of cigar boxes."

"Well, now. Cigars, is it?"

"Aye, sir. Cubans. Thousands of them."

"Did they give you any trouble, Mr. Grant?"

"No, sir. Not the least. Very helpful. Allowed that we could look wherever we wanted. Said they are just simple sailors who do what they're told to do."

"Likely story. My bet is that you were talking to the captain himself."

"I believe so, sir," said Grant.

"Well, sir, assemble yourself a prize crew. You can handpick your men. I want you to go back and seize that ship in the name of God and country. Arrest the crew. Are they armed?"

"Just knives, sir."

"Well, disarm them and put them in irons, every last one of them. Simple sailors, my foot. You'll sail the ship back to Savannah under our escort. Well done, Mr. Grant. Well done."

"Aye, aye, sir."

That afternoon, as the two ships sailed in tandem toward the mouth of the Savannah River, the *Dobbin* tailing her prize, Captain Day strode the quarterdeck, pacing on the weather side, smoking a pipe. With each puff, the smoke trailed over his shoulder and vanished in the wind. Gunn approached him to request permission to relieve Bulloch for the dogwatch. The captain stopped in mid-stride and smiled broadly at Gunn, removing the pipe from his mouth.

"First patrol and we've hit the grand prize. Eh, Mr. Gunn? How about that?"

"Yes, sir. It's quite the prize."

"Indeed it is. I'll tell you what's what. As long as we're out here, leastwise while I'm in command, anybody who thinks they're going to slip one by on the old *Dobbin* ought to think twice."

Gunn's thoughts raced to the one person that he thought might try. He couldn't resist the opportunity.

"I might know of someone who could be thinking about doing just that, captain."

"What? What's that you say?"

Cuffee approached the captain, balancing a mug of steaming coffee on a tray.

"Ah, Cuffee. You read my mind. Just what the doctor ordered. You really are a gem."

Gunn hesitated as Day took a tentative sip from the mug. "It concerns Charley Lamar."

"Not again."

Cuffee glanced at Gunn, took a step back and waited. "Anyt'ing else, Cap'n Day?"

"No, Cuffee that will be all. Thanks."

Cuffee bowed from the waist, took his tray and departed toward the galley.

Day scowled at Gunn. "Now, what's this about Lamar?"

"Well, sir. I should perhaps wait until I've gathered all the facts, but I believe Mr. Lamar is up to something."

"Meaning what? Out with it."

"Meaning I think he has a plan to smuggle contraband into the country. Maybe even Savannah."

"That's utterly preposterous. What cargo?"

"Slaves. African slaves."

"Impossible. That's damned crazy. I know Charley Lamar, and even he is not that stupid."

"I think he has bought a ship for that purpose."

"What ship?"

"The *Rawlins.*"

"Nonsense. That ship isn't fit to sail across the river, much less across the Atlantic."

"Even so, I think he might try."

"That's enough, Mr. Gunn. I'll hear no more. You sure know how to ruin a fine evening, don't you?"

"I'm sorry, sir. I didn't mean to—"

"Never mind that. The one I want you to apologize to is Charley Lamar. And you'll not forget to do that as soon as we tie up to the dock. Will you, Mr. Gunn?"

"No, sir. I won't forget."

55

Beneath a brilliant sunset, resplendent in shades of vermillion, gold, and violet, the two ships anchored about a mile south of Tybee Light to await the dawn. The pilot boat, standing another mile offshore, sailed in to meet them like a curious swan, but once close enough for identification, she turned about and sailed off again, her sails catching the wind and the radiant colors of the evening sky.

After supper, Gunn again assumed the watch. The captain took to the quarterdeck long enough to receive various reports on the condition of the ship, then retired below into his cabin. Presently, Cuffee emerged from the cabin after assisting the captain to settle in for the night.

Cuffee passed Gunn, politely greeting him on his way toward the forecastle. Just before he reached the quarterdeck steps, he turned about and approached Gunn where he stood at the starboard rail.

"Mistah Gunn, suh? May I please hab a word?"

"What is it, Cuffee?"

"Well, suh, I don' mean to step out my place."

"Go on. Say what's on your mind."

"I wouldn't, 'cept I heared other men talk, and dey say you a trusty man."

"I try to be."

"Well, I heared what you was talkin' to the captain 'bout dis mornin'. Couldn't help it."

"What about?"

"'Bout Massah Charles."

"Lamar?"

"Yessuh. De same."

"What about him?"

"Dat he up to no good."

"I'd appreciate it if you don't repeat that, Cuffee. I don't want it spread around."

"You don' hab to worry 'bout me, Mistah Gunn. I won't say a word. But it already done spread round."

"What do you mean?"

"My people know what he up to. He done bragged 'bout it. Says we gon' soon hab lots of company."

"When did you hear him say that?"

"Up at the slabe yard. He like to make fun."

"I see. I'm not surprised. Thanks for letting me know."

"You won't tell the captain I told you?"

"No, Cuffee. You can trust me."

"Yessuh. I know. Jayjay said so, too."

"Jayjay?"

"He my cousin. He Gullah-Geechee, like me."

"Yes, I know. Can I ask you something, Cuffee?"

"I guess."

"Do you know anything about a woman called Odah? Works for a white man by the name of Sullivan."

Cuffee's eyes widened, and he didn't answer.

"She's Gullah, too. Do you know her?"

"I heared tell."

"What do you know of her?"

"She a kind of queen."

"What do you mean?"

"She hab many powers."

"What kind of powers?"

Cuffee lowered his voice. "I don' like to say, bein' a Christian man."

"Please, Cuffee. I need to know. If you know, you must tell me."

"Debil powers, Mistah Gunn. She a boo hag. Best stay away. Dat's all I got to say."

"Boo hag?"

"Ebil spirit," said Cuffee. "Gullah call dem boo hag."

Gunn tried to search his face, but it was impossible in the darkness. "You're not serious about that. Are you? I mean, there's no such thing as a boo hag, is there? Not really."

Cuffee appeared uneasy. He fingered the necklace of indigo beads and sea shells that he wore beneath his open shirt collar. "Oh, yessuh," he said. "Dey all around we, like de wind in de tree. And dey be much stronger dan we be, too. I believe dat only Jesus have de power ubber de ebil ones. He will deliber us from ebil, if we jes trus' him." He touched his necklace again.

Gunn's mind conjured images of the night aboard the *Lyoness*, when Odah had hissed at him in the shadows. He wondered if she had cast some sort of spell. Maybe that would explain how things had been happening to him of late.

"Thank you, Cuffee. Good night."

At first light, the two ships weighed anchor and sailed upriver, the *Dobbin* in the lead, with Bulloch navigating the way. They arrived in port at midmorning, and the *Dobbin* moored in her usual spot on Moore's Wharf at the head of Bull Street, while the *Express* anchored in the harbor.

The deputy collector stood on the wharf to greet the ship. As soon as the brow was put over, he climbed aboard. The captain and his officers met him at the gangway.

"Welcome home, gentlemen," James Bulloch said. "The watch at the Exchange spied you coming up the river. Looks like you've brought something with you."

"A small gift on our return," said Day, beaming. "A load of contraband Cuban cigars, disguised as tea. We've seized the boat and arrested the crew."

Bulloch nodded approvingly. "Should fetch a fine price at auction. Well done, indeed. Congratulations, Captain Day."

"It is a good haul, if I do say so myself," said Day.

"I'm sure Mr. Boston will be very pleased."

"Where is he? Why didn't he come down to meet us?"

"He had some urgent business. Sent me down instead. Besides, I have some good news that I wanted to convey personally to Mr. Gunn here. Something I think he'll be very glad to hear."

"Oh? And what is that?" Day asked.

Gunn stepped forward. "What's the news, James?"

"We've received a letter from Washington. It's final. Your request for transfer has been approved."

Day wore a perturbed expression. "What's this? A transfer?"

"And that's not all. Captain John Prouty, the new captain of the *Andrew Jackson* up in Eastport, Maine, has asked for you personally, Andrew."

Flabbergasted, Gunn said the first thing that came to mind. "He was our former first lieutenant on the *Morris*."

"Why didn't I know of this transfer?" said Day.

"I made the request through Captain Dawes, sir," said Gunn. "Long before you arrived."

"Quite frankly, it was such a long shot we thought it not worth mentioning," said James Bulloch.

"See here, now. That's all well and good, Mr. Bulloch," said Day. "But I'll need him to stay until you find a good replacement. And not one of those nincompoops who can't tell the business end of a sextant. Too many of those around. Give me a man worth his salt."

"Of course, sir. The bureau says the captains should work out the transfer dates."

The first lieutenant spoke up for the first time. "Well, that's two reasons to celebrate, eh? Who will join me in the bar at the City Hotel this afternoon? First round is on me."

"You don't have to twist my arm," said James, grinning.

"I'm in," said Gunn.

Day held up a palm. "Before anybody does any celebrating, we've got a lot of work to do." He faced Gunn and pointed a finger. "Especially you, Mr. Gunn. Among other things, you've got promises to keep, as I recall. Best get to it."

As the two climbed the steep cobblestones of Bull Street, past the Exchange, James Bulloch glanced over his shoulder at the ship. "What's with you and Captain Day, Andrew?"

"What do you mean?"

"I mean that I sense a bit of tension between you."

"Is it that obvious?"

"Like a hawser in a stiff breeze."

"I'm afraid I've managed to get on his bad side."

"Already? What happened?"

Gunn explained his interaction with Lamar as best he could, short of accusing him of smuggling.

"Apparently, Lamar and Captain Day are old acquaintances. So I'm on my way now to apologize for my actions."

"I see. Well, as it turns out, maybe your transfer is indeed the best thing that could happen right now."

"Not soon enough for me," said Gunn.

They crossed the Strand and Bay Street together, then parted ways, Bulloch for the Customs House and Gunn for Drayton Street and the offices of Lamar and Trowbridge.

Lamar was just exiting the office when Gunn arrived. Following him out the door was none other than Daniel Sullivan. Lamar closed and locked the door, then turned to face him. Sullivan approached with a smile and extended his hand.

"Hello, Andrew. It's good to see you," said Sullivan as they shook hands. "How've you been?"

"I'm well, Daniel, thanks for asking."

"What are you doing here?" Lamar said flatly.

"I've come to offer an apology."

"I'd better go," said Sullivan.

"No, Daniel. Stay, please," said Gunn. "It would be better if you did, I think."

Lamar half closed his eyes, peering down his nose at Gunn. "An apology? For what, pray tell?"

"For my rude behavior last time we met."

"What brought this on?"

"I was simply out of line. And I regret it. Let's just leave it at that."

"Better men than you have come to regret insulting Charley Lamar. I should have called you out, you know."

"Again, I am sorry. It won't happen again."

"He did apologize, Charley," said Sullivan.

"All right, then. So be it," said Lamar. "Let bygones be bygones, I always say."

"Good," said Gunn, extending his hand. "Thank you, sir."

Lamar hesitated before shaking his hand. "You know, Sullivan here tells me that you're a good enough chap, though until now nobody could have convinced me of it. I think maybe we could be friends, you and I, under the right circumstances. I'm known to be very good to my friends. And my friends are very good to me. Now, I'd say it could be we simply set off on the wrong foot. Maybe we should start dancing to the same tune. What do you say, Gunn?"

Gunn hesitated. His gaze passed from Lamar to Sullivan, then back again.

"I'm afraid that my dance card is quite full at the moment, Mr. Lamar."

Lamar sucked his teeth. "Too bad." He polished the gold tip of his cane with a gloved hand. "For you, not for me, Mr. Gunn." He turned to Sullivan. "Let's go."

"You go on, Charley. I'll meet you at the bank."

"Suit yourself." Lamar stiffened his back and walked off.

"Guess he can't take a joke," said Gunn.

"He's not in a joking mood at the moment."

"Is he ever?"

"He's got himself in another bind. Never mind." Sullivan pursed his lips. "You should watch yourself with him, Andrew. He can be very vindictive, you know. Especially when he's cornered."

"Might I say the same to you, Daniel? For the life of me, I can't understand why you have anything to do with that man."

"I told you. I handle his business affairs—for his father's sake, not his."

"Are you aware of his plans to smuggle slaves, then?"

"What?"

"You heard me."

"I don't know of any such plans. That's quite the accusation. What proof do you have?"

"None. Yet. But I intend to get it."

"It would be insane for Charley to even think about doing any such thing. It would amount to an act of piracy. The penalty would be death. Charley can be foolhardy, but he's not crazy. It's all bluster."

"We'll see about that. Has he purchased the *Rawlins*?"

"Yes, but—"

"Any others?"

"Well, I'm not at liberty to say, really."

"What for?"

"He has plans to expand to foreign markets. Said something about importing wine."

"Really? You buy that?"

"Things are getting pretty tight these days. The markets are down. He is looking to diversify, find new sources of income."

"I'll bet."

"Look, I think you should take a step back. Be a little more circumspect, Andrew. You could get yourself into some very difficult legal trouble if you're not more careful. Just some friendly advice."

"Thanks. I'll take it under consideration."

"For your own good."

"Everyone keeps saying that."

"You should listen to them."

"Noted."

"Listen now, why don't you come by the house for supper sometime this week? Sarah has been a little depressed lately. As a matter of fact, she's been down in the mouth ever since we returned from New York. It might cheer her to see you again."

"Thanks. But I'm fairly busy this week. Perhaps another time."

"Well, you're welcome anytime. You know that."

"Thanks again. By the way, how's Casimir?"

"Who?"

"The little stray terrier that I gave to Sarah."

"Oh yes, of course." Sullivan shook his head. "Sad, really. Apparently, he ran away while we were gone. He hasn't returned. Too bad. Sarah had taken a liking to him. She loved having him around the house."

"Yes, I can see why. He was a clever little dog. Very smart."

56

It was not unusual for Gunn to feel a sense of the world rushing at him whenever he returned from sea. For the first few days after any deployment, the news seemed to come like a passing summer squall. On this occasion, however, he couldn't wait for the news to get to him. He was anxious to know if any word from Elizabeth had arrived in the month since he'd been away. After completing his business with Lamar, he decided to pay a visit to Josie and Julia, who always served as a good source of news—mostly reliable.

As he walked down Bull Street through the center of town, busy with noonday traffic, just beyond Johnson Square an open carriage rode by on the near side of the street. In it sat Sarah Sullivan and Caroline Lamar, and opposite them facing backward, the lone figure of Odah. The carriage passed by, and Sarah glanced over, then turned away, chatting with Caroline, who laughed and nodded. Caroline made a point of looking directly at him and bowed her head with a simpering smile. He tipped his cap to her. Odah glared at him, then averted her gaze, busying herself with a large black umbrella, which she held up to shade the other two women from the sun. The carriage hurried down the street and around Wright Square, soon out of sight. Just as well.

As he walked along, looking at the grand houses on the street, the thought occurred to him that it was just as well that he was finally going to be transferred. Though he had begun looking for a place in which he could afford to live with a new wife and her young ward, he'd found to his dismay that it would not be easy to find in this economy, as decent housing was so limited and expensive.

Ten minutes later, he climbed the steps of the house and entered to find it quiet and dark. He called out, but nobody answered. Presently, Mrs. O'Reilly came from the back of the house and greeted him.

"Where is everyone?" Gunn asked.

"Miss Josie has taken to her bed with lumbago, and Miss Julia has gone to fetch some medicine from Doctor Arnold."

"Ah, well, I'm sorry to hear that. Is Miss Josie awake?"

"I believe so. You can go on up, if you like."

Gunn climbed the stairs, went to Josie's bedroom door, and knocked. She bade him come in and sat up in bed as he entered the room. He walked to the bed and kissed her cheek.

"I'm sorry to see you doing so poorly, Cousin Josie."

"It's just a fact of life these days, I'm afraid. But thanks for your concern, my boy. Glad to see you back again safe and sound."

"I came by to catch up on the latest news. Any mail for me?"

She stayed quiet, wincing as she repositioned herself in the bed.

"Cousin Josie?"

"I'm afraid there has been some bad news, Andrew."

"Bad news? What is it?"

She hesitated. "You should sit down." She patted the side of the bed, where he sat, balanced on the edge.

"It's your father. He has died, you see. I'm very sorry to be the one to tell you."

The news left him speechless. He sometimes had wished his father dead, but now that it had happened, he found himself grief-stricken, without knowing why.

"Your mother sent word last week in a letter."

"I see. I just saw him, little more than a month ago. He seemed fine then. Was he ill? How did he die?"

"I understand that he was killed three weeks ago. Murdered by an unknown assailant. Both he and an acquaintance. Apparently, they were in a bad part of town after dark. Someplace called the Bowery. That's all we know."

She reached out with her gnarled hand and touched his.

"How is Mother?"

"As well as can be expected. She is concerned now because she has lost touch with Marguerite. It's all in the letter. You can read it, if you like. She sent one to you as well. They are over there on my desk." She motioned toward the desk on the far wall. "There's another one from Elizabeth. Came last week, too."

"Thank you." He got up and retrieved the letters from the desk.

"Will you be staying with us for a while?"

"Yes, off and on, as I can. I expect the ship will be leaving again on patrol in a week or so."

"Make yourself to home, as usual, Andrew. Your bed is made, and there are fresh linens in the closet."

"Thanks again, Cousin Josie."

He took the letters upstairs to his room on the third floor and lay down on the bed to read them. First, the letter from his mother, which repeated everything Josie had just told him, though she expressed her concern for Meg's welfare in much more explicit terms. As it turned out, Meg had been named as correspondent in a lawsuit and divorce proceedings filed by a Mr. Jeremiah Levinson, a prominent magazine publisher, against his wife, Lucinda, on the basis of marital infidelity. His mother's letter enclosed a newspaper clipping from the *Times*, given to her by Uncle William, which described the circumstances in more lurid detail. Mitchell had looked for her in New York at her former address and elsewhere in the city but was unable to find her. It was hard for Gunn to determine which news was more shocking: the sudden, unexpected death of his father or the scandal involving his sister.

Gunn propped himself on an elbow and opened the letter from Elizabeth. He hoped for better news but was quickly disappointed. She had written to tell him that her father had been very ill with a heart condition but seemed to be on the mend, with the help of a good doctor. She expressed deep regret that she would not be able to join him right away, which she fully intended to do, but that she would come as soon as possible, whenever her father had made sufficient recovery. She had no idea how long a period that might be, but she hoped he would continue to understand. Sent her love and many kisses until then. All in less than a page.

The combined news of his father's untimely death, his missing sister, and Elizabeth's indefinite delay was more than he could bear. Grief swept over him in waves, and weariness overtook him. He lay back on the bed and wept silent, bitter tears. There was nothing else for it.

He returned to work on the *Dobbin* in a daze. By then, the seized vessel had been moved to moor alongside the cutter. Customs surveyors and inspectors swarmed the decks and the hold of the *Express*, tallying the illicit cargo as the stevedores offloaded it, heaving the crates ashore with the help of the *Dobbin's* crew. The federal marshal removed the prisoners and carted them off in a hired cotton wagon.

At the end of the workday, when about half of the cargo had been unloaded and carted to a warehouse for safekeeping, and the two ships were tidied up and secured, the captain was the first to leave the ship, accompanied by Bulloch, both heading up to the City Hotel to celebrate their success. Gunn lingered behind, not certain whether to join them, given his want of a celebratory mood. But Grant, who had quit drinking years earlier due to an almost ruinous bout of alcoholism, urged him to go and have some fun, offering to stay on the ship and keep watch.

When Gunn arrived at the hotel, the bar was crowded and noisy. A cloud of cigar smoke filled the room and billowed out into the lobby. Through the haze, Gunn saw a cluster of men that included Captain Day, the two Bullochs, Boston, Judge Nicoll, and Joseph Ganahl, the district attorney. Others mingled around them, and they moved about, laughing and joking, drinking and smoking. At a table nearby, Daniel Sullivan sat with Lamar, sipping a whiskey and tapping the ash from his cigar. Lamar had hold of Sullivan's sleeve, smiling and sniggering around a long cigar stuck in his mouth.

Gunn sat down with them. "Mind if I join you gentlemen?"

"If you must," said Lamar, his grin fading.

"Well, I could sit elsewhere," said Gunn.

"Nonsense," said Sullivan. "Have a seat, Andrew."

He sat across from Lamar, who took pains to relight an already lit cigar.

"You made it," Sullivan said with a smile.

"Yes, I wasn't sure I would," said Gunn. "Not in a very jubilant mood at the moment."

"Why is that?"

"Got some bad news."

"Nothing terrible, I hope."

"Bad enough. Rather not talk about it, if you don't mind."

"Suit yourself. I think you could use one of these." Sullivan held up his empty glass.

"I could use one with something in it."

Sullivan threw back his head and laughed. He turned and waved at Duke, holding up three fingers. The bartender nodded.

As they waited for their drinks, Gunn observed the celebration with a touch of disdain. The feeling came over him almost unnoticed. He wondered at himself and how it was that he couldn't seem to join in what should have been a cause for celebration among men who did their utmost to uphold the observances of law and order that formed the basis of a civilized society.

"What's with you, Gunn?" Lamar said.

"What do you mean?"

"You look like you've been sucking on a lemon."

"I'd rather not say."

"Cat got your tongue?"

"No, I'd just rather keep my thoughts to myself."

"Well, maybe you've wised up at last. Will wonders never cease."

Gunn let the comment pass. Duke brought their drinks.

"Cigar?" Sullivan asked, offering a spare.

He shook his head and sipped his drink. It was one of the better bourbons.

"Tell me, Gunn, why aren't you celebrating with the rest of them?" Lamar asked.

"Maybe I think there is little to celebrate."

"Then why are you here?" Lamar asked.

"I'm not sure I should be."

Lamar snorted. "You're free to leave. Nobody put a gun to your head."

Gunn moved to leave. Sullivan held his sleeve.

"Wait a minute, Andrew. Where are you going? Stay and finish your drink."

"Aw, let the man go, Sullivan," said Lamar. "He'd obviously rather be elsewhere."

Though reluctant, he sat.

"Now then, tell me what's on your mind," Sullivan said, smiling.

Gunn looked over his shoulder at the celebration. "Just not sure what all the fuss is about," he said. "It's not like anything real has been accomplished. There will be another shipment next week. Another prat miscreant will pop up and attempt to make illicit profit at the taxpayers' expense."

Lamar laughed. "Is that all? Get a grip, Gunn. Don't be such a stooge. It's all a game of cat and mouse. Why, this country was founded by miscreants. You're from Boston, aren't you? I hear tell they're real fond of illegal tea parties up your way. Isn't that right?"

"That happened long before the rule of law was established by our Constitution. And nobody is above it now, Mr. Lamar. Not me. Not anybody. Not even the likes of you."

Lamar puffed on his cigar. "What's that supposed to mean?"

"I think you know."

"Maybe you should explain it so there is no mistake."

"I think there are some men among us who are planning to do great harm to this country. They want to do something that most Americans would find intolerable."

"Yeah? What's that?"

"They plan to violate the law by bringing in new slaves from Africa. They hope to make a huge profit by doing so. And maybe they even hope to provoke a war, if necessary to make it all happen."

Lamar sat silent for a moment, rolling the cigar in his fingers. "That so? And why would they do that?"

"Because they wish to cause the Southern states to secede from the North."

"And what does any of that have to do with me?"

"Why don't you tell us?" Gunn said.

"Andrew," Sullivan warned. "You'll have to forgive my young friend, Charley. Sometimes, he tends to be rather blunt in his manner."

"I should say," said Lamar. "Not very gentlemanly, if you ask me."

"My apologies, sir," said Gunn. "The circumstances of life have forged my manner. It can be somewhat blunt at times, I know. But I find that, like a good hammer, it saves time when trying to drive home a point."

A crooked smile crossed Lamar's face. He turned to Sullivan. "I'm thinking your friend here has an overactive imagination. You should advise him to get some rest. He's obviously overwrought. Working too hard, no doubt. Strung tight as a fiddle. Not good for his health to dwell on such flights of fancy."

Lamar rose from the table, dropped his cigar to the floor, and ground it out with his heel. "If you'll excuse me, gentlemen, I'd like to offer my congratulations to someone who has worked very hard all his life to gain the reputation as a true man of the people. Unlike some among us."

He picked up his whiskey glass and walked over to stand next to Captain Day, draping an arm over the other man's shoulder and raising his glass in a toast.

Gunn's eyes followed his movements. A flash of anger pulsed through him.

"Tell me something, Daniel."

"What's that?"

"How is it that, no matter what I do or where I turn in this town of late, there's Charley Lamar right smack-dab in my field of view? I swear it's true."

Sullivan raised an eyebrow. "I don't know. But maybe you should try your very best to avoid him from now on."

Gunn shook his head. "I think I'd prefer to wring his neck. Be done with it. Problem solved. I've come to really dislike that man."

Sullivan squinted one eye. "Listen to me carefully, Andrew. You're putting yourself in real jeopardy, especially by throwing about some cockeyed innuendo."

"It's nothing of the kind. You saw his reaction, that smug smile of his. He wanted so much to admit it."

He watched as Lamar called Donnelly over from the bar, then whispered in his ear. Donnelly nodded and left the bar.

Sullivan also glanced at Lamar, watching as he downed the last of the whiskey from his glass. "As a friend, I'll say that I understand your sentiments toward him. I can even sympathize. But as an attorney, I'm warning you one last time to stay away from Charley Lamar."

Gunn leaned forward. "I tried. Look, I hear you, Daniel. I heard you this morning. And I will heed your good advice. I promise."

"Please understand. I only have your best interests at heart. I don't want to see you hurt in any way. Best just steer clear."

"I do understand, Daniel. Thank you. I'll do my best." The thought occurred to him that he might return the favor. If he couldn't convince Sullivan of Lamar's nefarious intentions, he might at least persuade him to consider the dangers right under his own nose. It astonished him to know how difficult it could be for supposedly rational people to acknowledge what they did not wish to see. Perhaps the same was true of himself. "Now, let me give you some advice, well intended, friend to friend. Perhaps you will heed mine."

"Fair enough."

"Odah."

"What about her?"

"You should be rid of her. I believe she is a bad influence on your household, especially Sarah."

"Nonsense. Why would you say such a thing?"

"Because it is true."

57

The two men left the hotel together. Outside, a cabbie waited at the curb, no doubt on the prospect that, at any given moment, a guest of the hotel or an inebriated patron of the bar would emerge in need of a ride. Sullivan invited Gunn to share the cab.

"Ride along with me, won't you? Tell me more about what you've observed in Odah that causes you so much concern. I'm not quite sure I understand what you're saying."

"All right, though you very well might conclude that I've lost my senses. But I'll take that chance."

They entered the cab and settled in. Sullivan gave the cabbie the address of his home, and the cab trotted off, making a full turn in the Bay, in the midst of traffic, to head south at the corner on Whitaker. Another cab, a little farther down the block, copied the move, presumably to avoid the several squares of Bull Street. The cab fell in behind them.

"Now, start from the beginning," Sullivan said. "Tell me everything."

After a deep breath, Gunn began describing his first encounters with Odah on the *Lyoness*, relaying her cryptic warning to him, along with Cuffee's admonition, and ending with her vicious glare just that morning.

"And that's all I know," he concluded. "Take it for what it's worth."

They rode through the lesser traffic of Whitaker Street in silence for a block or so. The scent of spring blossoms drifted through the open windows, along with the dust of the street.

"So you're saying she's some kind of witch?"

"Priestess. Cuffee called her a queen. He seemed to be very much afraid of whatever black arts she can conjure."

"I don't doubt your sincerity in what you're telling me. But the only indication of the truth of it that I can recall is Sarah used to tell me about an occasional game she would play with Odah, when she was a child. She called it 'Whispers.' It sounded like a sort of séance. They would attempt to speak to her dead mother. But I never paid much attention to it, you know. Thought it was harmless child's play. I knew how much Sarah missed her mother, and I thought it might do her some good to pretend to talk to her. Her mother was an ardent spiritualist, but I never thought . . ."

"I think Odah's influence goes well beyond childhood games. It might even be the reason for Sarah's nightmares and visitations. Have you thought about that?"

"I daresay it never occurred to me."

The cab slowed and made a left turn at the corner of Jones Street, heading east. The rays of the setting sun swept across the interior of the cab. The other cab kept pace, following maybe fifty yards behind them and making the same turn. Gunn thought it odd.

"Why not free Odah?"

"I've already told you. She'd have to leave the country. She wants to stay."

"Why do you suppose that is? Don't you find it odd that she would choose to stay with you all these years after the death of your wife, when she could have had her freedom in Liberia?"

Sullivan frowned and shook his head. "Nothing unusual there. Reports from Liberia are not very inviting. Rather dismal, in fact. I read in the paper not long ago that a former slave returned from Liberia and begged his master to take him back. Besides, we've always treated Odah as family. And she's forever been very devoted to Sarah's care."

"But what if there are other reasons?"

"Such as?"

"I don't know, Daniel. It's hard to even guess. At the very least, you provide her access to the world at large, greater than she would have otherwise. Perhaps it gives her some sort of access that she needs."

"What sort of access? And for what purpose?"

"I don't know. I don't pretend to know. I do know this, however. She does not strike me as a force for good in this world. Far from it."

"But what could she hope to gain by doing us any harm?"

Gunn thought of the unspeakable harm that his own father had done, and the harm that had come to him in the end. And all for what?

"There is evil that walks among us, Daniel, which seeks to do us harm. That I do know. I've learned the hard way. Just look around. It is evident everywhere you look, even sometimes sitting across a table, smiling, enjoying a casual afternoon drink and cigar among friends. Why would anyone seek to destroy what is good in the world or to bring about harm to anyone else? The answer to that question is as elusive as the wind and as near to us as our own hearts. We must fight against it as hard as we can, wherever we see it, and however it manifests or it will overcome us, I'm afraid."

"You're right about that, of course. I'm beginning to understand now."

"Understand what?"

Sullivan smiled. "Why you so readily disregard my best lawyerly advice."

Gunn laughed. "I don't pretend to have all the answers. I would merely urge you to watch carefully. See for yourself. You've admitted to being an indulgent father. Don't be so blind to the influences on Sarah, both bad and good. On both of you, for that matter. If I am right, Sarah could be in real danger. So could you."

The cab came to a stop in front of Sullivan's town house.

"Let's say you're right. What exactly do you suggest we do about it?"

"I think if it were the safety of my daughter at stake, I'd rid the house of her as soon as I could. Tonight, if possible."

"You would, eh?"

"I think I would."

"That seems rather harsh after so many years of faithful service. I wonder . . ."

"What?"

"We all have our prejudices, don't we?"

"Come now, Daniel. You know me better than that."

"Do I? How well do any of us know ourselves? I'm just saying."

Gunn lowered his head. "I've said my piece in good conscience. Take it for what it's worth, my friend."

"That'll be two bits, mister," said the cabbie.

Sullivan got out and paid the driver. The front door to the house opened, and Sarah stepped onto the stoop.

"Been wondering when you'd get home, Daniel," she called. "Supper is getting cold."

Sullivan waved to her. "Sorry to be late, my dear. Won't you come in, Andrew?"

"I should get back to the ship," Gunn said.

The cabbie swiped his nose with his sleeve. "You want I should take you to the docks, mister?"

Gunn looked around for the cab that had been following, but it was nowhere in sight. He presumed it had turned the corner at Bull Street. "No, thanks. It's a fine evening. I believe I'll walk."

"Suit yourself."

He stepped out of the cab and shut the door. The driver slapped the reins and the cab lurched away.

Sarah called down to him, brushing a wisp of hair from her eyes. "Aren't you even going to say hello?"

He stood fast. "Hello."

Sullivan climbed the stairs and gave Sarah a kiss on the cheek.

"I left supper on the table for you," she said as he went inside.

Gunn turned to go.

"Wait a moment, please, Andrew," she said.

He stopped and turned back. "What is it?"

She came down the steps and stood before him. Up close, her face was pale and drawn, her eyes bloodshot. Dark circles made her eyes look deep-set. The sparkle was gone.

"I've missed you. Haven't you missed me?"

Gunn didn't answer.

"You're angry with me," she said, her eyes narrowing.

"I'm not angry. I just think it would be better if we did as your father suggested and stay away from each other for a while."

"I will do what I want to do."

"So you've said. I've heard that wind blow before."

She crossed her arms. "Still getting married to your sweetheart?"

"That's the plan."

"Here or there?"

"Well, I'm not sure. Things are rather uncertain at the moment."

"Uncertain?"

"Yes. Things are, well, uncertain."

One corner of her mouth lifted in a smile. "Good. I'll take uncertain. For the moment."

"I'd better be going."

"All right. Nobody's keeping you."

She turned, mounted the steps, entered the house, and shut the door silently behind her.

The shadows had lengthened and twilight was creeping in as he walked back down to Whitaker and turned the corner north, headed for Perry Street. He intended to stop by to see how Cousin Josie was faring and to ask Julia if she had any further news to share, hoping she might know more details about what had become of Meg.

As he walked along, the vague feeling that he was being watched made the hairs on the back of his neck stand. He passed a vacant lot where the foundations of a new house had been laid. Piles of lumber, bricks, and construction materials cluttered the lot. A small, dark form that looked like a little dog darted behind the corner of the foundation, just a blur in his vision.

"Casimir? Is that you?"

A sudden surge of joy passed through him. Gunn hurried to the corner where the shape had disappeared. He searched about but saw nothing.

"Casimir?"

A voice came from behind him. "Casimir ain't here. But we are."

Two men tackled him to the ground, knocking the wind out of him. He fell face-first into the dirt, his hat and cane crushed beneath him. One of the men straddled him, pinning his arms behind his back. The other put a knee on his head, pressing it into the ground.

He breathed in quick, shallow breaths, blowing dust and bits of pebble away from his open mouth. Through eyes squinted with pain, he saw someone leaning over him, his head covered by a burlap hood with eyeholes cut in it at odd angles.

"You like to live dangerous like, don't you, Gunn?"

He couldn't answer.

"Cat got your tongue? No matter. You just need to listen. Listen good." The man pressed harder with his knee. "You listenin'?"

Gunn tried to nod. He thought he recognized Donnelly's voice.

"Some folks would like it if you left this town. Sooner rather than later. You're not welcome here anymore. Understand? Not welcome no more." He emphasized each word with his knee. "Blink twice if you understand."

Gunn blinked.

"Good. Now, if you don't leave on your own, you're gonna get some help. And no guarantees whether you'll be alive or dead when you do. Savvy?"

"Yeah," Gunn grunted.

"Good." The man released the pressure of his knee from Gunn's head and stood up. "Let him go."

The other man got up and kicked him in the ribs, then stepped over him. The hooded man pulled the cane from beneath him and feinted a blow to his head. Gunn flinched. The man tried to snap the walking stick across his knee, but it wouldn't break. He hurled it across the lot.

The agony in Gunn's side left him almost senseless, but he felt relief at hearing their departing footsteps as they left him alone.

"See ya around, Gunn. Not for long, though, if you know what's good for you."

The men ran off and disappeared down a nearby alley in the gathering twilight. Gunn rolled over to a sitting position, holding his ribs and trying to catch his breath. He tried to stand but fell back, resting on his elbows.

A shadow passed over his right shoulder. He looked up to see Odah staring down at him.

"Odah. Did you see those two men?" he panted. "They came out of nowhere . . . "

Her face contorted in a grimace. She raised her left hand, forking two fingers, just as before.

"Hoonah stay 'way from dis place. Neber come back."

"What did you say?"

"Hoonah hear me. Stay 'way from dis place. Bad t'ings happen. I put a curse on eh haid." She spat at Gunn's head but the spittle missed. "Neber come back here, else hoonah die."

He tried to shout, but it was hard even to catch his breath. He scooted back with his heels, sprawling in the dirt. "Get away from me, woman. Leave me alone. I know what you're about, no mistake."

She hissed at him in perfect English. "Foolish man. You'd like to think you're so smart. You know nothing. You have no idea what is happening everywhere, all around you. You have eyes but do not even see."

"Don't be so sure. I have a pretty good idea what you're doing to Sarah. And I intend to stop you. So help me Almighty God, I will."

Her jaw twitched. "Then you will surely die. And no god will help you."

"So you do speak English."

Her lips curled into a snarl, revealing her protruding front teeth. "I speak now so you will understand and remember when you see it all happen before your dying eyes. But then it will be too late. Even now it is too late."

"What are you talking about?"

She moved close alongside, as though daring him to touch her. "New niggahs will come soon. Do you hear me, white man? More and more niggahs from Africa, big and strong, and more than you can number. War is coming, too. Coming like a mighty wind. Nobody in this world can stop it. Terrible war. Brother against brother. Father against son. Women will weep for the thousands upon thousands left dead and rotting in the fields. And slaves will be free in the last days, free to do as they will. And they will all rise up, gather together, and make a new land. Of people who are free at last." She nodded with grim satisfaction. "Den lick back all de bad t'ings eber done to we. Tarrify de buckra."

"Buckra?"

She leaned over him and pressed a leathery finger, cold as a corpse, to his forehead, forcing his head back to look her in the eyes. They burned with a fierce light.

"Buckra," she sneered.

58

Cousin Julia opened the front door and took his arm to steady him.

"I saw you coming up the walk from my chair. You look horrible, Andrew. Why are you limping so badly? And what in the world happened to your face?"

"I was attacked by two thugs. Took me by surprise."

She took his crumpled hat and cane, helped him inside, and guided him to the nearest chair.

"Did they rob you?"

"No. It was a message."

"A message from whom?"

"Not sure, but I suspect it was Charley Lamar."

She rang a bell for Mrs. O'Reilly, who appeared in a matter of seconds.

"Mrs. O'Reilly, would you please bring Mr. Andrew some water and bring me a wet towel?"

"Right away, Miss Julia." She hurried off to the back of the house.

Gunn held his side and groaned.

"What makes you think it was Charley Lamar?" Julia asked.

"It just makes sense. They told me I should make myself scarce or they'd do it for me."

"Oh my. What are you going to do?"

"I'm not afraid of them."

"Maybe you should be. I thought you wanted to leave and go back home. This might be the right time, Andrew."

"Cousin Julia, I have no intention of going anywhere at the moment. Something is happening. Something very bad. I think I know what it is. Time will surely tell unless I can find somebody in this town who will listen to me, who will try to stop it first."

"What is it?"

He told her. Her eyes grew wide as he told her what he knew.

"That's crazy. Why would Lamar do that?"

"For money, of course. He's desperate for it and will do anything, *anything* to get it. But if you ask me, there's much more to it than mere greed."

"Really? Like what?"

He hesitated. "I think he is trying to start a war. He wants the South to secede, and he has grandiose notions that he'll be the hero who causes it."

"Who in his right mind would want to start a war? You can't be serious."

"I wish I weren't. Nobody in this town seems to take me seriously, though."

"I do."

Mrs. O'Reilly brought a dripping glass of water and a wet towel.

"Thank you, Fanny," he said. "You're an angel."

"Not at all. I'm awfully sorry to see you in such a state, Mr. Andrew."

"I'll be all right. Not to worry."

"I'll gladly make you something to eat. What would you like?"

"Nothing, thanks. I couldn't eat a thing right now."

"Well, you let me know if you change your mind, won't you?" Mrs. O'Reilly bobbed her head and left the room.

He took a gulp of water. Then another. "Something else, Cousin Julia."

"What's that?"

"There are other forces at work, too. Dark forces conspiring to make it all happen. Evil forces. Like nothing I've ever known or seen before. And somehow, it seems connected to whatever Lamar is trying to do. I can't really explain it all."

He winced as Julia began dabbing the raw scrape on his face with the wet towel. The towel came away bloody.

"What in the world do you mean?" Julia asked.

He told her in the briefest terms about Odah and her influence on the Sullivans, then about her prophecy of a coming war and the ensuing destruction.

His narrative finished, he repositioned himself in the chair, grimacing in pain. She placed a pillow behind his back.

"Are you all right? What have you got yourself into, Andrew? I don't know how you can stand all this, especially given all that's happened with Marguerite and . . ."

"And my father."

"Yes. It's just too much all at once."

"You can say that again."

"Maybe you should just go on up to bed."

"I'm sorry to burden you with this. But nobody else will listen or give me the time of day. It feels good just to say these things out loud."

"I'm very sorry about it all. You must feel a bit, well, discombobulated, I would think."

"That's a good word for it."

Julia sat in her chair by the window. "What are you going to do? Maybe you should speak with Reverend Axson."

"You think he might help?"

"Couldn't hurt. I don't know what else to suggest at the moment. Where else to turn in time of real trouble? I think you're going to need God's help to see you through all this."

"Maybe so."

She inclined her head and lifted a brow. "Maybe so?"

"You're right, of course."

"Tell me, have you heard any more from Elizabeth?"

"One letter saying she intends to stay in Scotland indefinitely."

"Oh dear. I'm sorry to hear that. What else can possibly go wrong?"

"I don't think I want to find out."

"Dear me."

Silence fell between them for a moment.

"Do you know what is strange in all this, Cousin Julia?"

"What's that, my dear?"

"It's just hit me that, with all this chaos that's been swirling around me right now, I would think the news of my father's death would have mattered most to me. But somehow it doesn't. I was sad, of course, when I first got the news, but now it almost seems like an enormous relief. I know that sounds terrible, but it's the truth."

"Understandable."

"I feel so disconnected from what happened to him. Almost like it happened to someone else's father. Terrible news. So sorry it happened. But . . . nothing. Why is that, do you think? Is it wrong of me?"

"I think you must be very tired."

"I am, but that's not the point."

Julia's gaze drifted away. She seemed preoccupied. "It's not so very surprising, really."

"Why? What do you mean?"

She looked out the window. "The streetlamps are being lit. Must be close to bedtime."

"Julia? What did you mean? Why is it not surprising?"

"I should not have said that. It's all too much for now. Better left alone."

"What is it you're not saying?"

"We can talk about it in the morning."

"Julia. I want to know right now. What did you mean, *not surprising*?"

"I should not be the one to tell you."

"Now, you must tell me. I will not let you leave this room until you do."

Julia sat forward, wringing her hands in her lap. A pained look came over her face. She took a quick breath.

"You might as well know. Daniel Gunn . . . is not your real father."

"What? How can you say that?"

"Because I know it to be true."

"Who told you so?"

"Your mother."

"My mother? When did she ever say such a thing?"

"Before you were born, dear. She wrote a letter to me, which I have long since destroyed."

He looked away and shook his head, staring at the floor. "Well . . . did she tell you who is, then?"

She breathed a long sigh. "It's Daniel Sullivan."

"That—that's just not possible. Incredible." He reached into his vest and removed his gold pocket watch, the one his father had given him and that had been his grandfather's. He flicked the case open and took out the miniature of the man he'd thought was his father, until this moment. "Look. Look, Cousin Julia. We are spitting images of each other."

She took the miniature and held it to the lamp. She returned it to him, shaking her head. "I don't see it."

"Don't see it? Must be the lighting. Do you need your spectacles?"

"No, dear. You are mistaken."

"Don't be ridiculous. I am not mistaken. Mother has always said that we bear a striking resemblance."

"Then it is the power of suggestion, I'm afraid. If your mother has always said that, perhaps it's because she wanted it to be true. I do see her features in your face, but truth be told—"

"This is sheer nonsense. Unbelievable. Look again."

"Have you ever taken a good hard look at yourself in a mirror?"

"I don't own one."

"Really? How do you brush your hair?"

"Like this." He ran his fingers through his hair and smoothed it down.

"Well, maybe you should. I don't know how men can do without a looking glass. But that explains a lot, doesn't it? Most men today always look as though they need a good combing out."

"This has been one horrible day, I must tell you. If what you are saying is true, this really puts the gravy on it."

"I would not lie to you, Andrew, especially about something so serious as this. My only regret is that I opened my big mouth to begin with. I should never have said anything. It was not my secret to tell. Then again, now that he's dead, perhaps it's best." She gave a tentative nod. "I just didn't want you to keep punishing yourself."

The sudden shock of learning the identity of his true father was overcome by a sense of profound gratitude that took hold in his mind, displacing all other thoughts. Somebody at last had spoken the truth to him. "Then I wouldn't have it any other way, Julia. And I'll thank you for telling me the truth. I only wish someone had told me years ago. It might have saved me a lot of grief."

"I'm sure it will grieve your mother, now that you know her secret."

"But why the secrecy?"

"Come now, Andrew, you must know. She was with child when she left home. An unwed mother, especially one who has been forbidden to marry by her father, has few choices other than to run away and keep secrets. Forever, if possible."

"But my father—Daniel Gunn knew. He must have known, don't you think?"

"I would expect he did. The man had his faults, but stupidity wasn't one of them. He certainly could count to nine."

"Come to think of it, that explains an awful lot."

"Such as?"

"Why he seemed to hate me so much."

"I don't think he hated you, Andrew. He cared for you. I'm sure he loved you in his own way."

"He had a funny way of showing it, then. Do you think anyone else knows the whole story?"

"Your mother said she never told anyone but me who your real father was, and she swore me to secrecy. She thought someone should know in case anything ever happened to her. She didn't trust her own sister to keep her mouth shut. She trusted me, and now I have broken her trust. I wonder if she'll ever forgive me."

"It all tends to make more sense now. It's no wonder she married so soon after arriving in Boston."

"And it seems she traded one Daniel for another. Maybe that name held a sentimental meaning for her. Maybe it was just fortuitous. I don't know."

"Do you think Daniel Sullivan knows?"

"I don't know. He might suspect, I suppose."

"I think he does."

"Why do you say that?"

"When I think back now on certain things he's said and done, it just makes sense."

"You may be right. But the poor man didn't even know where she was. Your mother didn't want him to know, for fear that he would come for her, and her father would ruin him. She knew that her father would use their illegitimate child to do it. Your grandfather was just that kind of man, I'm sad to say. Oh, Andrew, I'm so sorry. I shouldn't have ever used such a horrid word as *illegitimate* to describe you. Such an ugly word. I didn't mean to. Please forgive me."

He took both her hands. "Easily forgiven, my dear Julia. I've been called far worse. I have been called a son by a man who never was my father."

59

At Julia's insistence, Gunn spent the night at the house on Perry Street. When he awoke the next morning, aching and sore, it was a short walk to Chippewa Square, then north on Bull Street to the Independent Presbyterian Church on the corner of South Broad. The spire, rising above all others in town and visible for blocks around in any direction, made the imposing white marble church easy to find from most anywhere in the city.

Gunn climbed the steps, tried the massive wooden doors to find them open, and entered the sanctuary. It was still very early on a Tuesday, but he hoped to find Reverend Axson there.

The sanctuary was silent and still. Soft morning light filtered through the tall Federal windows on both sides. He stood for a moment on the black-and-white checkerboard floor, admiring the magnificent raised pulpit made entirely of dark mahogany. Overhead, the graceful curves of the balcony, supported by Corinthian columns, skirted the huge room on three sides. And upward from that, an oval domed ceiling, centered on a finely detailed plaster rosette, soared high above the rows of straight-backed, boxed pews. In no other church throughout his many years of attendance had he ever felt more inspired or nearer to God than here.

Reverend Axson poked his balding pate through a door at the front of the sanctuary. He opened the door wider and held it ajar. His preaching voice echoed clearly across the expanse.

"I heard the outside doors open but thought perhaps it was my imagination."

"I'm sorry, reverend. I didn't mean to disturb."

"Not at all. May I ask, are you a member here?"

"I'm Andrew Gunn, cousin to Julia Moore."

"Of course. Dear Julia. How may I be of assistance?"

"I know it's very early, but I could use some pastoral advice."

Axson closed the door and stepped farther into the room. "In that case, come right in. You are most welcome at any hour."

Gunn walked down the aisle and met him at the front of the sanctuary. Axson offered a seat on the front pew and sat his slight frame nearby.

"Now, what brings you here so early? I've just finished my morning prayers. Not used to having visitors when the day is so young."

"Well, it's a rather long story. I will try to shorten it."

Axson's middle-aged features broke into a kind smile. "I've heard a great many in my time. Why don't you start from the beginning?"

With fits and starts, Gunn told Axson about his chance meeting with Sullivan and Sarah, her disturbing visions and visitations, and his latest encounters with Lamar and Odah. He reserved, for the moment, the recent revelation about his relationship to Daniel Sullivan. He had barely had time to admit that knowledge to himself, much less explain it to someone else. All the while, Axson listened intently, nodding now and then, frowning on occasion. When Gunn had finished, after about ten minutes' time, he simply stopped speaking and shrugged.

Axson shifted his position in the pew and cleared his throat. "Quite a perplexing story."

"I've left out some parts, but I think you get the gist. The thing is, I can't help but feel that all this is related somehow. I sense that I'm up against something much bigger than I am, perhaps more than I can handle. Yet I feel compelled to do something about it. And I can't seem to help myself. In a word, I've become kind of obsessed by it all. I can't seem to just let it go, which is what everybody else urges me to do."

"Yes, I see. Tell me more about this Odah person. You say she is Gullah?"

"That's right. Some sort of priestess. Apparently, very influential among her people."

"I've had the privilege of preaching among the Gullah on many occasions over the years. They are a very religious people, though quite superstitious for the most part. A few genuine believers in the gospel among them, as is the case in many of our own societies, but most have mixed Christian beliefs with other pagan religions. I have known one other like this Odah, but he was more a witch doctor of sorts. He was possessed by truly demonic powers."

Gunn nodded vigorously. "That's what I fear."

"I'd warn you and anyone else to avoid her, if at all possible, but I'm sure you already know that. And how do you see her as being related to this Mr. Lamar?"

"Do you know him?"

"Only by reputation. I have been here in Savannah only a few months. But one hears things. I do try my best not to prejudge people, however."

"I can't prove anything, but they both seem intent on bringing in more slaves from Africa."

"That would be against the law. It's a capital offense. Why would they do so?"

"Maybe to start a war, among other things."

Axson recoiled, mouth agape. "That's an outlandish allegation, sir. Are you sure of it?"

"It sounds insane, I know. And as I said, I've no proof, other than what they've said to me and others."

"Frankly, I find it hard to believe such an allegation."

"You're not the first to doubt it."

"But this is a very volatile moment in our history. It would not take much of a spark to set off a conflagration, I'm afraid. A plot to reopen the slave trade could certainly do it."

"That's one of my greatest fears, reverend. Slavery will be the ruin of our country yet."

"It is a most difficult issue, and the cause of much division, to be sure, even in the church."

"My future father-in-law, another man of the cloth like yourself, just left the country permanently to return to Scotland over the Dred Scott decision."

"I'm sorry to hear that."

"I imagine you must be somewhat of the same mind."

Axson hesitated. "I agree that it is a thorny issue, indeed, on which men of good conscience and sound doctrine can readily disagree."

"What are you saying? Are you not against the institution of slavery?"

"Scripture does not forbid it."

"But surely an appeal to good conscience does."

"Many of our congregation, men of good conscience as you say, own slaves. My own family has owned slaves. I do not condemn them, nor judge them harshly. Neither should you."

"You don't? Would you care to explain?"

"God is our supreme judge in the affairs of men. Only he can condemn. I see it this way. Slavery has existed as long as there have been tribes on earth. Every society in the history of mankind has used slavery to some extent to build their legacies. Is it evil? Just as in other human institutions, at times it can be and often is. Sometimes, however, it has been used by God to accomplish his sovereign purposes in this world. Joseph, for example, was sold into slavery by his own brothers because they were envious of him. To what end? God used Joseph to save his brethren, his father, and all the people of Egypt from sure starvation. Was that evil?"

"Surely, you don't—"

"Slavery is the natural state of man. Rousseau was wrong, of course. He had it exactly backward. We are not born into freedom. Rather, we are all born in chains, slaves to sin. Slaves to our own passions, the lust for power, and the pride of life. But if God should elect to enliven our hearts, we then become slaves of Christ Jesus, who frees us and calls us brothers and sons of adoption. This is what the Scriptures teach us. Do you believe this to be true, Andrew?"

"I have been taught that. Yes, of course."

"Then why should it offend you to know that the world at large reflects the natural state of man? Most men, though they may vigorously protest, secretly desire someone to tell them what to do. Indeed, we all wittingly or unwittingly bend the knee to someone or something greater than ourselves."

"But, Reverend—"

"Hear me out, Andrew. Real freedom is dangerous and unstable, and it always will be while we are yet on this earth. It can easily devolve into abject evil. We know this to be true. The French Revolution proved it beyond any shadow of doubt, *n'est-ce pas*? This is why God has instituted governments among men and placed masters over them. Most people don't realize how dangerous freedom can be, because they are not really free and never have been. But they sense that it is so. Men of all colors and creeds will labor under the most oppressive conditions and actually fear to be free, though loath to admit it, so long as their basic needs are met and their lives are not threatened. Most will readily trade their freedom for safety and the security of a warm bed and a hot meal. You'll remember that Esau traded his birthright for a bowl of stew, and so 'the elder served the younger,' as we are told in Genesis. It is a rare soul who thinks and acts otherwise. Can you not attest to it yourself in your own heart of hearts? If nothing else, the slave serves to illustrate to us our natural condition in stark relief and to teach us all to yearn for our true liberation. That being our freedom in Christ, the most sublime liberation."

Gunn could not keep the edge out of his voice. "Some have had a rather harsh lesson, don't you think, pastor? More severe than others, perhaps."

"The Scriptures adjure masters to treat their slaves with good will as unto the Lord, and slaves likewise to obey their masters with fear and trembling. If they do not, they are indeed doing evil in disobedience to his will."

"So what shall we say then? Slavery should increase, that grace may abound?"

Axson frowned knowingly. "God forbid. My sincere hope is that one day every slave in every nation will be set free, to the glory of God himself."

"We at least agree on that. But I did not come to argue about slavery, Reverend Axson."

"And I did not intend to launch into a sermon, Andrew. You asked a question. I've tried to answer your question honestly. What is it that you would like me to do?"

"I don't know. Tell me, if you can, how to handle what I seem to be up against. I feel like my life is in danger to some degree. And not mine alone."

"Does your fear have anything to do with the wound on your face?"

"In just the last day, I've been beaten, kicked, cursed, and spat upon."

"That is of real concern. I'm not sure of the answer. Perhaps the police can help, though they will be of little use where spiritual matters are concerned. And I will remind you that your struggle in part truly is not merely against flesh and blood, but against the powers of this dark world and spiritual wickedness in high places, as the apostle Paul warns us. But I can also tell you this. God has prepared you for this moment. He will strengthen you for what is to come. You should perhaps pray about it. Seek his help. Ask the Holy Spirit to guide you."

"Sometimes, I wish God would just speak to me aloud. Tell me what to do. Like in a voice from heaven, or something."

"He will, if you will but hear."

Gunn leaned forward. "Hear what?"

The reverend thought for a moment, running a hand over his bald head, as if to smooth an absent strand of unruly hair. "As a sailor, you're very familiar with the wind, aren't you, Andrew? How it speaks, whether loudly or quietly, and acts unseen to send you sailing off in one direction or another?"

"You can't sail against it, that's for sure."

"Well, the original language of the Bible uses the same words for spirit and wind." Axson sat back with a smile, looking very satisfied with himself.

"Meaning what, exactly?"

Axson sighed. "Heed the Spirit, Andrew, the true wind. Trust in him. In all your ways acknowledge him, and he will indeed set your course."

60

Gunn shook his head and smiled to himself. The observation was not lost on him that a man grasping for sense clings to a metaphor as a castaway holds fast to a fragment of flotsam. It had often occurred to him that much of the Bible was written in metaphor, perhaps to that end. And no wonder, after all. The literary device tended to make the hard places plain. Several times before in his life, notably in situations most crucial, he had received useful, salutary advice given as metaphor. Even his old friend and former shipmate, Boatswain Thomas Nelson, as rough and unlettered as any rude sailor might be, had admonished him once in sheer poetry to "find the wind's eye and sheet home." Nelson's meaning, though perhaps obscure to the casual ear, had rung crystal clear to Gunn at the time. He had laid hold of the advice and followed it to his very real benefit.

So it was now as he left the church, trying to grasp the meaning of Reverend Axson's somewhat nebulous admonition. Gunn prayed the entire way down to the ship, asking God for guidance and wisdom as to what to do and for protection in the face of the recent threats to his life. He was not necessarily afraid for his own life, but he did fear that if he did nothing about the threats, other people and his beloved country would suffer in ways that he had difficulty imagining. He was compelled to resist those destructive forces with the strength of every sinew in his body. By the time he reached the wharf a quarter hour later, he had resolved in his mind to stay in Savannah and do whatever he could to fight against this present evil.

When he boarded the ship and went below into the wardroom, Bulloch greeted him with astonishment.

"What in blazes happened to you?"

Gunn touched the wound on his face. The truth was too incredible and hard to explain. "I—I tripped on a cobblestone. Fell flat on my face."

"Looks horrible. Where have you been? The captain has been looking for you."

"I stopped on the way in to take care of something. Sorry to be late. What does the captain want with me?"

"He wanted to let you know that he is on his way to speak with Boston to protest your transfer."

"I might have known. Did he say why?"

"Something about good order and discipline."

"Do you think he will succeed?"

"I don't know. It's likely that he'll at least manage to delay it further."

"Well, I suppose that's that."

Bulloch handed him an envelope. "This telegram came for you last night. I hope it's not more bad news."

Gunn took the envelope and opened it. The message was from his Uncle William.

SORRY ABOUT YOUR FATHER STOP SENT A MAN TO LOCATE MEG STOP ALL SIGNS POINT TO PARIS STOP NEWS ON OTHER FRONTS LATER STOP CHIN UP.

Gunn crumpled the telegram and the envelope and tossed them in the waste bin.

"Everything all right?" Bulloch asked.

"My uncle has sent someone to look for Meg. She is missing."

"Your sister? Since when?"

"Several weeks ago. God only knows where she is. He thinks she has left New York and gone to Paris."

"Why Paris? What's going on?"

"I don't know, Des. I wish I did. But I'd rather not talk about it right now, if you don't mind."

"Of course. Let me know if I can help."

"I will."

Captain Day returned a half hour later and summoned Gunn to his cabin, along with the first lieutenant. Gunn stood before them.

"I've some bad news for you, Mr. Gunn. You're going to be with us a little while longer than perhaps you may have anticipated."

"That's fine by me, sir."

The captain cocked his head. "What's that?"

"I no longer wish to be transferred, sir. I withdraw my request."

"Oh, ho. What brought this about?"

"I've come to like Savannah, very much, in fact. And I am needed here. I can see that, now. I want to be of service to my country, to this ship, and to you, Captain Day. There is no better place for me at the moment than on this ship."

"I don't understand. Why the change of heart?"

"I've invited my fiancée to join me here. She has agreed. We hope to be married soon."

"Married?" Day and Bulloch echoed the word together.

"Yes, sir. As soon as possible."

"Are you sure this is what you want, Andrew?" Bulloch asked.

"Yes, sir. Quite sure."

"Very well, then," said Day. "So be it. How the wind has shifted."

"Indeed, sir."

"I hope it doesn't mean a storm is brewing."

"Not if I can help it, Captain Day. By your leave, sir?"

Day nodded his assent.

Gunn assumed the watch from the third lieutenant, and the ship continued the work from the previous day to complete the offload of contraband from the seized vessel after customs officers finished the careful inventory. Other contraband was revealed along the course of their work. They discovered barrels of rum marked as molasses beneath the crates of cigars. More cause for celebration. When they had finished, a tug came to tow the *Express* out to an anchorage in the harbor.

That evening after supper, Gunn noticed that his journal was missing from among the personal items in his sea chest. He searched every corner of his stateroom, the wardroom, and anywhere else that came to mind, thinking that perhaps he had misplaced it or carelessly laid it aside in some unusual spot. He questioned Grant as to whether anyone had entered the wardroom without permission, or whether anything of his own might be missing. Grant said he hadn't noticed anyone unauthorized entering the wardroom or seen anything else amiss. Bulloch said the same when Gunn queried him. Not wanting to cause a stir, and unwilling to make unfounded accusations against his friends and fellow officers, Gunn decided to let the matter drop, hoping that it would eventually turn up.

He went to bed that night still troubled about his missing journal, recalling the incident when it appeared that someone had rifled through his belongings while the ship was on the ways at Willink's. Nothing seemed to be missing at the time, other than one letter from Elizabeth, which he thought had been left at the house, though he had never found it. The memory was unsettling.

So much had happened in the last day or so. His head hurt to think of it all as he rehearsed the events in his mind. It would have been nice to have his journal to set out his thoughts, especially the new knowledge about his real father. He fell into a fitful sleep as he thought about these things and awoke several times during the night doing the same.

The last time, he awoke with a start. It was still dark in his stateroom. Nothing stirred above decks. He couldn't imagine what had awakened him, other than a sense of unease. A strange smell, not unlike a struck match, hung close about. He raised himself to his elbows to investigate.

At the foot of his bed hovered an ebony form, almost shapeless, like spilled ink on dark cloth. It seemed transparent, yet somehow blacker than the surrounding night. In an instant, it coalesced into the shape of a shrouded woman. Then he blinked, and it was gone.

He jumped out of bed, hitting his forehead on the bunk above. Stars exploded in his head. He yelped and swore in pain and fell back on his bunk, rubbing the knot that immediately began to rise. Struggling to his feet, he searched about for any sign of whatever it was he had seen. Nothing had been disturbed. There was no indication that anyone had been there. Even the odd smell was gone.

On impulse, he opened his sea chest. There, on top of his other belongings, lay his lost journal. He picked it up to find that the leather cover and the pages inside had been singed and blackened around the edges.

He lit a small oil lamp on the washstand at the head of his bed and sat down to inspect the journal. Pages had been torn out here and there. Anywhere that Elizabeth's name occurred, it had been stricken out with charcoal. He turned to the last written page. A blot of what appeared to be blood appeared after the final entry. All the empty pages after that had been removed, torn out.

Bulloch stumbled to his stateroom and pulled back the curtain.

"What the hell is going on? I heard you cry out."

Gunn looked up. "Nothing. I found my journal."

At noon the next day, Gunn asked the captain for an hour's liberty to take care of some personal business. The captain, pleased with Gunn's recent change of heart and apparent willingness to comply with his wishes, readily granted his permission.

Gunn soon broke a sweat in the humid midday air, already quite warm in May. He hurried through town, deciding to take Abercorn to avoid the slave market taking place at the county courthouse on Wright Square. When he arrived at Sullivan's law office on the corner of East York Street and Abercorn, he could hear the auctioneer's braying chant from a block away. It enraged him even to think about the abomination occurring within earshot, as accustomed as though it were the sale of common farm animals on market day.

He entered the office in a fury and found Sullivan's secretary, Oliver Brimley, at his desk in shirtsleeves. The man hastened to put on his coat, and greeted him with a dazed, but polite smile. When Gunn asked to see Sullivan, Brimley offered a perfunctory apology, explaining that Mr.

Sullivan was with a client. Gunn barked that it was urgent and he would wait.

In a few moments, he heard raised voices, followed by muffled shouts from behind the office door. Seconds later, the door opened and Charley Lamar burst into the outer office, nearly bowling Gunn over as he stormed out with a scowl on his face. The outside door slammed shut.

Sullivan came to the open door of his office, dabbing his face with a handkerchief.

"Come in, Andrew. I only have about thirty minutes before I must leave for court, but you are welcome to them."

"It will take less than that to say what I came to say."

"What in the devil has happened to your face?"

"That's part of what I came to see you about."

"Do tell. Well then, let's not waste a second. Come in and sit down."

"I'll stand, if it's all the same."

Sullivan closed the door behind them. "Now I am intrigued. What's on your mind?"

"Several things. First, what have you decided to do about dismissing Odah from your household?"

"Nothing yet. It's not quite so simple as dismissing her, Andrew, as I have explained. You must understand. The law—"

"She is a real threat to me, and I think she is a danger to both you and Sarah. As long as she remains in your house, you are asking for trouble."

"Slow down. Tell me what's happened. How did you get that ugly scrape?"

Gunn explained what had occurred the previous day, only a few blocks from their house. Then he described what he had seen last night.

"I don't know what to say, Andrew. You've caught me entirely off guard. Do you realize how utterly crazy this sounds?"

"Yes, believe me, I do."

"Let's discuss this matter when we both have more time. Why don't you come over for supper tonight?"

"I won't step foot in your house while Odah is still there."

"That's quite the ultimatum."

"I mean it."

A woman's voice sounded in the outer office, chatting with Brimley. The door opened, and the secretary stuck his head through the opening. "Your daughter is here to see you, sir."

"Ah. Send her in."

Sarah walked through the door and kissed Sullivan on the cheek.

"Hello, Daniel. I just stopped by on my way to—why, hello, Andrew. What a surprise to find you here. What's happened to your face?"

Gunn greeted her, trying to smile, ignoring her inquiry.

"Andrew was just telling me about some disturbing encounters that he's apparently had with Odah of late. He claims we are in danger, my dear."

"How queer. What on earth?"

"You need to be rid of her, I'm telling you," Gunn said. "But that's not what I really came to talk to you about."

"Andrew, let's talk when I have more time," said Sullivan. "Come to supper tonight? Join us. Eight o'clock."

Sarah raised a forefinger. "I'm afraid I have other plans for the evening, Daniel. I'm meeting Desmond Bulloch in town for supper. That's what I came to tell you."

"And I'm afraid I can't. Won't. Not until Odah is gone," said Gunn.

"Really, Andrew," said Sullivan.

Gunn shot Sarah a glance. "Desmond?"

"Yes, Desmond. Any objections?"

"No. Not at all." He felt a headache coming on. "Look, let me just say what I came to say, now, to both of you, before I lose my nerve."

"And what, pray tell, might that be?" Sarah asked.

Gunn glared at Sullivan, then softened his gaze. "It's about us. The three of us. I suspect your father has a pretty good idea already about the subject. I think perhaps he has all along."

An awkward silence prevailed.

Sullivan shifted on his feet. "I'm not sure I know what you mean, Andrew."

"I think you do, sir. And it's high time we deal with it, don't you agree?"

"Perhaps we should all sit down for a moment," said Sullivan. Sarah and Gunn took seats in front of the desk, while Sullivan settled into his desk chair.

"Daniel?" Sarah queried.

Sullivan's nostrils flared. "I had hoped for a better or more convenient moment. But I suppose there is no better moment for the truth to be spoken than the present, is there?"

Sarah fidgeted. She glanced at Gunn. "What is it?"

"It's not easy to . . ." Sullivan closed his eyes for a moment. "I guess there is no other way. Andrew is very likely your half-brother, Sarah."

An expression of wide-eyed incredulity came over Sarah's flushed face. She said nothing.

"It's true, my dear."

"Who?" she uttered.

"Andrew's mother, Eleanor, and I were . . . we loved each other very much, many years ago."

"How long—how long have you known?" Sarah whispered.

"I've suspected it was true for quite a while," Sullivan said.

"Not you," she said. Her gaze shifted to Gunn. "Him."

Gunn cleared his throat. "Day before yesterday. My cousin Julia told me it was true."

She bowed her head and lowered her eyes, staring at her lap. Her lips moved, but her voice was silent.

Sullivan sighed. "I'm sorry, Sarah. I should have told you sooner, but I didn't really know for certain. I want to apologize to both of you. I know this comes as a great shock."

Her eyes welled. Her lips parted, and her hands began to shake.

Gunn had never seen her so undone. He wanted to go to her and comfort her. He started to rise, but she put out her hand against him, and he dared not.

"I hope you both will find it in your hearts to forgive me," Sullivan said.

The three of them sat in stony silence for what seemed like several minutes before Sullivan excused himself to prepare for his court appearance. Still stunned, Sarah and Gunn got up from their seats. Gunn managed a weak smile, which Sarah ignored. He opened the door as she sidled past him into the outer office. Standing to one side, Odah awaited her distraught mistress.

"Let's go, Odah," Sarah snapped. "Hurry, now. I'm late."

A wry, crooked smile, barely evident, crept onto the old woman's wrinkled face. They all exited together. Gunn stopped outside the door and watched Sarah and Odah walk briskly down the sidewalk and around the corner.

Although he had heard Sullivan's confession firsthand, it still seemed so unreal to him. The man had asked for his forgiveness, which was more than the one who had pretended to be his father had ever done. Gunn was willing to forgive, but it would take time to reconcile his mind to the mere facts of the matter. He could only imagine how troubled, even mortified, Sarah must be, given what had passed between them.

The thought of their mutual embarrassment caused a chill to run down Gunn's spine, making him cringe as he walked into the bright, warm afternoon sunshine.

61

That evening, as the sun was setting, Gunn was wavering in his mind about whether to join Sullivan for supper. He had dressed for it, but then hesitated at the gangway before departing, as though waiting for a sign.

The breeze picked up as he peered off into the deepening shadows of the bluff overlooking River Street. Someone was lurking there, pressed against the side of a warehouse.

He sought out the ship's gunner, who was also the designated master at arms for the month.

"Doc, give me the keys to the small arms locker."

"Sir? May I ask what for?"

"Just give them to me. Hurry. I'll explain later."

Doc gave him the keys, and he opened the locker to remove a revolver.

"Sir, where are you going with that?"

"There is someone hiding in the shadows out there. I aim to find out who it is and what they want."

"Shall I go with you, Mr. Gunn?"

"No need. You stay here. I'll be right over there, between those buildings." He nodded toward the warehouse. "If I'm not back in five minutes, come looking for me."

"Aye, aye, sir."

Gunn left the ship with the revolver tucked beneath his coat, trying to look as nonchalant as the thumping heart in his chest would allow. He passed the warehouse, looking the opposite way. As he passed by, he heard someone whisper his name.

"Mistah Gunn."

He stopped in his tracks and walked toward the warehouse, his hand on the pistol grip.

"Who is it?"

"Jayjay, Mistah Gunn. Over heah."

Gunn joined him in the shadows.

"What are you doing here, Jayjay?"

"Was hopin' you'd be leaving the ship sometime this evenin'. If you hadn't, I don' know who else to trus' with what I got to say. I don' want nobody else to know I be givin' it up."

"What is it, then?"

"Been workin' on that ship, the *Rawlins*. You know the one?

"Yes. I've seen it."

"Well, suh, they be makin' changes to de inside, see. Things you can't see from the outside."

"What kind of changes?"

"Big water tanks. Hold mo' water than the crew ever need. Take out bulkheads down below, makin' room for mo' cargo, see."

"That's very interesting."

"That ain't all. I heard Massah Lamar talkin' bout makin' her sound 'nuff to sail plum to Africa and back. One time. That's all he need, see. No extra money to fix her right."

"How long before you finish?"

"Two, mebbe three weeks at mos'."

"Well, well. Thank you, Jayjay. I am indebted to you."

"You won't tell who told you?"

"You have my word."

"Good 'nuff fuh me. If I can ask, how Cuffee doin'?"

"He is doing well, from all appearances. The captain seems very pleased with him."

"But how he doin'?"

"I don't rightly know. But I'll check on him for you."

"Be 'bliged."

"Go on now, before someone else sees you."

Jayjay stole away and melted into the shadows.

Gunn returned to the *Dobbin*, replaced his weapon in the small arms locker, and returned the keys to the gunner. He was just about to go below when he spied the captain returning to the ship, occasionally stumbling on the uneven wharf. He sent Foster, the duty messenger, to meet the captain, who at first refused his help but soon relented. Foster steadied him by the elbow and guided him up the gangplank.

"Foster, go fetch Cuffee," Gunn said. He took over, helping the captain toward the stern and easing him down the ladder into the cabin. The smell of whiskey surrounded them.

"Thanks, Gunn. You're a good man," the captain slurred. "Anyone ever tell you that?"

"On rare occasion," Gunn replied. "You've caught me on a good day."

"I'll be up directly . . . to give the night orders," said Day, his eyes half-closed.

"Take your time, sir. Everything is under control."

Day nodded, belched, and stumbled toward his bunk.

Gunn exited the cabin. Cuffee ran into him in his haste to attend to the captain.

"S-Sorry, Mistah Gunn."

"It's all right, Cuffee. You'll find him in a sad state, I'm afraid. He'll need your help getting ready for bed."

"Won't be de first time," said Cuffee.

Gunn grabbed his arm. "Cuffee, how are things going?"

"What do you mean, suh?"

"I mean, is everything all right with you so far?"

"Who askin'? Did de cap'n say sumpin' bad 'bout me?"

"No, not at all. He seems very happy with you."

Cuffee cocked his head. "Not sure how you it mean, den, suh."

"How are you?"

"How should I be?"

"I don't know. How do you feel about things?"

Cuffee cast an anxious glance toward the light of the companion-way. "We be, suh. Das all." He wiped sweat from his brow.

"I guess that pretty much sums it up, doesn't it?"

"Suh?"

"Never mind." He let go of Cuffee's arm and watched him disappear into the cabin.

Gunn decided to remain onboard the ship that night and several nights thereafter.

Four days later, the *Dobbin* departed for another patrol. Before the departure, Gunn mailed a long letter to his mother, telling her how he'd learned the truth about his father, and expressing anger that she had not told him before now. Such betrayal indeed would be very hard to forgive.

Meanwhile, he debated with himself over what to do about the *Rawlins*, finally concluding that he should wait until the work on the ship was completed and the alterations unmistakable. At that point, a single boarding would provide all the physical evidence needed to prove the purpose of the venture beyond a reasonable doubt. He only hoped they would return to port before the *Rawlins* could begin her voyage.

The days passed in steady routine. After almost three weeks at sea, it became quite apparent that shipping traffic along the seaboard had slowed considerably since the last patrol. The number of boardings per day had diminished to four or five, sometimes none at all. It was light work, though dreadfully dull.

Nevertheless, the captain exhibited relatively good spirits all the while, apparently still pleased that their seizure of the *Express* had brought such praise and adulation from Boston, as well as Mayor Screven and other notable citizens of Savannah. Not to mention the glowing, congratulatory telegram he'd received from Secretary Cobb himself. He ordered the ship to anchor one evening within sight of

Tybee Light to allow the crew to relax and enjoy a cribbage tournament, organized by Mr. Grant to pass the time, while guarding the approaches to the river. The four officers sat around the wardroom table, discussing the lack of activity.

"I've been reading in the papers that the latest boom in the economy has caused an enormous glut in commerce," the captain said, tossing out two cards and pegging his points on the board. "Now banks are overextended, and all the markets are beginning to cool. Seems like business is truly beginning to dry up. I hate to see it coming, but we may be in for a real bad dry spell."

"Yes, sir. I've heard the same," said Bulloch. "It all seems to be happening very quickly. I hope there isn't a hard crash. Could be devastating."

"One might hope that the cost of housing would come down as a result," said Gunn brightly. "I have my eye on a small flat above a hardware store on Broughton."

"Well now, that would be a bit of a silver lining, wouldn't it? Especially for a young man contemplating marriage and setting up a household," Bulloch said with a wink.

Gunn grinned. "It has crossed my mind. Maybe you should try it. Come to think of it, I understand you recently had supper with Sarah Sullivan. Any spark there? Maybe you should ask her to the Independence Day Ball. Who knows what it might lead to?"

Puffing on a cigar, Bulloch plucked two cards out of his hand, placed them on the table, advanced his peg, and counted out the points. "No matter. It's not even worth mentioning. She seemed a bit out of sorts the whole evening. I might blame you for that, Andrew."

"Why me?"

"She said you were the cause of her foul mood."

"What did she mean by that?"

"I dunno. When I asked that question, she only said that you weren't the person she thought you were. Wouldn't say anything more. What do you think she meant?"

Gunn shrugged, staring at the cards in his hand, trying to maintain a poker face. "I'm sure I don't know."

"Well, anyway, other than that, we did seem to have a good time. But if you're implying that there's half a chance the two of us might develop some sort of relationship, you should know by now I'm not really the marrying type."

Gunn laughed. "You're a perfect match, then, believe me."

"No true sailor is the marrying type," said Day. "No offense, Mr. Gunn, of course."

"None taken, sir."

Day continued. "It's just that, well, I prefer going to sea more than anything else in the world. Not conducive to a good marriage, though, wouldn't you agree? Give me a stout ship and a good crew, and I'm a happy man. No, sir. I'm bound to the sea, and she to me."

"You can love a thing too much, perhaps," said Gunn. "No offense, sir."

"Now, that's why I've come to like you so much, Mr. Gunn. Never afraid to speak your mind, eh? You remind me of someone else I knew as a younger man."

"Despite the hazard, sir, I've learned that to do otherwise often leads to misapprehension, then to resentment, and unnecessary conflict," said Gunn.

"Oh, ho. Well said, sir. Well—"

Blake's booming voice called from the companionway. "Flares sighted, cap'n. Two of 'em, fine off the starboard bow."

Day pushed his chair back and rose immediately. "Time to get to work, gents." He grabbed his cap from its hook and climbed the ladder, buttoning his coat on the way. "You have the watch, Mr. Gunn," he called over his shoulder. "Hop to it."

Gunn hurried to follow him. Dawkins was already on the helm, and the crew scampered about the decks, getting ready to weigh anchor and set the sails. Within minutes, the *Dobbin* was underway, sailing south toward the sightings. The quartermaster had taken a bearing on the flares when the sighting first occurred, and Gunn steered the ship in that general direction.

Flare sightings offshore, though uncommon, usually meant that a vessel was in distress. Sometimes, fishermen used them to communicate between their boats when locating schools of fish. On occasion, smugglers had also been known to send up flares to set up a rendezvous for a surreptitious offload of illicit cargo. No telling what the case was on this particular night.

Several of the crew, those not involved in tending the sails, kept a sharp lookout for any sign of distress or dishonest activity. After an hour of searching without result, Gunn began to consider another possibility. As he knew from experience, sometimes smugglers would send up flares to distract and divert cutters away from an area where their presence was unwanted.

He caught the captain's eye. "Captain, it could very well be that we've been had."

"I was just thinking the same thing, Mr. Gunn. I hope we're both wrong."

A shout came from the forward lookout. "Cap'n, off the starboard bow. There's a boat in the water. Looks to be adrift."

Gunn steered the ship toward the direction of the lookout's outstretched arm. Ten minutes later, the cutter was alongside. Blake held a lantern over the boat to illuminate the contents. Sprawled in the bottom of the boat lay the figure of a man face-up, a bullet hole in the middle of his forehead. Blood obscured the features of his face and covered the bottom boards beneath his head.

No other vessels were visible in the surrounding area, as far as the horizon on any side.

The crew retrieved the body, carefully wrapped it in spare canvas, and placed it in the hold. They fastened a towline to the boat and headed back north, toward the mouth of the river.

"Well, as much as I hate to admit it, I suppose we'll have to return to port early," the captain said, his brow furrowed. "This is obviously a crime that must be investigated. Better set a course for home, Mr. Gunn."

"Aye, aye, sir."

Gunn was glad for the opportunity to return early. Nothing worried him more at the moment than that the *Rawlins* might be ready at any time to escape and sail off to Africa to commit what he considered could become the worst crime of the century—worse than any murder, as bad as that was. He was tempted to order on all plain sail, as much canvas as the ship could carry. But the hazards of sailing upriver at night would not allow it, and they would be back soon enough, he knew.

Six hours later, the *Dobbin* was moored at the wharf in Savannah. It was still very early in the morning, before working hours. The captain sent Gunn up to the Customs House to wait for it to open so he could notify the district attorney about what had happened.

He waited in the wan morning sunlight on the marble steps of the building. At eight o'clock sharp, Mr. Ganahl turned the corner from Bull Street and climbed the steps.

"Well, halloo there, lieutenant. What brings you here at this time of the morning?"

"I've the unfortunate duty to inform you of a possible murder that happened sometime last evening, just north of Ossabaw Island."

"Oh? That is unfortunate. I do appreciate your letting me know so expeditiously. Where is the body?"

"Still on the ship, sir. Shot through the head."

"I'll send Marshal Stewart down to investigate."

"There is a boat, too. A small one. No cargo, however. Nothing but what appears to be personal belongings and some tools."

"Any weapons?"

"None that we found, sir."

"Curious."

"Yes, sir."

From their first meeting, Ganahl had impressed him as an intelligent and sincere young man. Despite his youth, he had gained a reputation as an insightful and clever prosecutor. Gunn decided to take a chance.

"While I have you here, Mr. Ganahl, there is another matter I'd like to discuss with you, if you have a moment."

"Something important on your mind?"

"Very."

"Why don't you come on up to my office, then, and we can talk about it?"

Gunn followed him into the Custom House and up the winding staircase to the second floor. Ganahl unlocked the office door, hung up his stovepipe hat, and motioned for Gunn to take a seat, which he did.

"Now then, what can I do for you, Mr. Gunn?"

"I'm flattered that you remembered, my name, sir."

"Let's dispense with the sirs, shall we? I take it we're roughly the same age, *n'est-ce pas?* My young bride, Harriet, tells me that's French for 'ain't it so?' She's from New Orleans, so I guess she'd know."

"Are you newly married?"

"Just so."

"I'm hoping to marry soon, myself."

"I recommend it as the natural state of man. At any rate, the name is Joseph. Harriet calls me Joe, leastwise when she isn't mad at me, and so do most of my friends. Why don't we start there, Andrew?"

"Fine, Joe." He took a deep breath. "You might find what I have to say rather fantastic. Most folks do."

Ganahl forced a thin smile. "Try me."

"It involves Charley Lamar."

"Most things around here do of late, it seems."

"That's what worries me, Joe. You see, I think he's getting ready to upset the apple cart for the city, the state, and the entire country at large."

"Do tell."

"Yes, sir."

"Joe."

Gunn acknowledged him with a nod. "I think he has plans to sail a ship to Africa to restart the slave trade."

In the silence of the room, one could have heard a whispered prayer outside the closed door.

"How do you know this?"

Gunn told him what he had learned from Jayjay and others.

"Do you have any hard evidence, other than what others have told you? It's sad to say, but the word of a colored man against a white won't cut any ice in this town."

No, I'm afraid not. Not yet, anyway. I think evidence would be rather simple to get, however."

"You do? How is that?"

"A good thorough boarding should do the trick."

Ganahl cleared his throat. "We've done that already. Two days ago. Boston sent two inspectors and the marshal."

"And?"

"They've cleared the *Rawlins* for departure. Soon as repairs are completed."

"That's impossible."

"It's so. Ask John Boston. Lamar has been pressing for weeks now to get a port clearance. Up until yesterday, Boston refused. He seems to think what you think. Lamar complained to his cousin Howie Cobb that Boston was being unfair. Claims he just wants to start shipping wine from Madeira, or some such nonsense. Cobb sent a wire yesterday telling Boston to let him go. And that's that. *Finis.*"

"Incredible. So you've known about it for a while."

"Trying to keep it under wraps as best we can. Folks getting wind of even the suspicion that Lamar might actively be trying to reopen the Atlantic trade to Georgia could set off a powder keg. We've still got our eye on him, though. Never can be too sure what he's up to these days."

"I'll gladly help collect whatever information you might need. I'll go spy on him if you want me to.."

Ganahl raised both palms. "Hold on, hold on, now. Don't go off half-cocked."

"Why not? He's been spying on me. Turnabout is fair play."

"What's this?"

"He's been having me followed. Two of his thugs roughed me up a couple weeks back." Gunn pointed to the dark patch on his cheek, just about healed.

"Now, if that's true, you should have let me know."

"I've been trying to let people know. Remember? I said so at the Sullivans' party. Nobody has believed me up until now."

"Even so, don't make the mistake of taking things into your own hands, Andrew. That would not work out well for you. You have no authority, either as a federal officer or a private citizen, to spy on anybody without a legal warrant. You got one?"

"No."

"Well, then. Do yourself a big favor. You just let us handle Mr. Charles Augustus Lafayette Lamar. All right?"

"All right. But I'm not convinced anyone truly can."

62

Rumors circulated that the dead man had been identified as one of Charley Lamar's dockhands at the cotton press. Later that day, the rumors were confirmed once the marshal made inquiries among the other workers. Why he would have been found shot to death in a skiff offshore, nobody seemed to know.

A quick scan of the harbor with a spyglass assured Gunn that the *Rawlins* was still at Willink's, although no longer on the ways. Workers were busy bending on new sails. He had no doubt that work was nearing completion. It was just a matter of days, perhaps even hours.

Storm clouds formed in the western skies, and the glass began to drop, forecasting a change in weather. The wind veered to the south-southeast and began to pick up. Just before noon, Gunn was surprised to see the *Gawain* enter the harbor under shortened sail and drop anchor. He decided to skip the noon meal and, with the captain's permission, took the dinghy out to meet her. He figured there was no longer any need for continued secrecy, now that it was apparent Lamar would be acting with seeming impunity.

He rowed over the chop in the harbor, nestling in the lee of the *Gawain*, and tossed the painter to a ready crew member, who made it fast to the side. His uncle's grinning face appeared over the rail.

Gunn called up to him. "Stand by to be boarded, sir."

"Again? I'm telling you, I intend to notify my congressman. I consider this to be nothing but intentional harassment."

"Permission to come aboard sir?"

A rope ladder tumbled down the side of the ship, and Gunn climbed aboard. His uncle shook his hand and hugged him, smiling from ear to ear.

"Have I got a surprise for you. Come on."

Mitchell took his arm and urged him aft toward the cabin. As he climbed down the ladder, the voice of Captain Corning greeted him.

"Well, well. Look who they've sent as a welcoming party."

Gunn turned to see him, standing next to a beaming Aunt May and behind her, his mother. She wore a timid smile on her face.

There was no hiding his surprise. He was completely taken aback and somewhat displeased about it. "Why, hello there. Knock me over with a feather duster. What in the world are you all doing here?"

"Hello, son. It's so good to see you." His mother made a tentative movement toward him, then stopped short. He went to her and embraced her.

She whispered in his ear. "I'm so very sorry. I should have told you."

He broke the embrace and held her hands. "Hello, Mother. You're early."

Tears came to her eyes. "I know. We'd had no word, no idea how much longer Elizabeth might be in Scotland tending to her father in his illness. But I came for other reasons, of which I'm sure you can guess."

"We'll talk later. Welcome to Savannah. Where do you all plan to stay?"

"We're staying at the Pulaski House," said Mitchell.

"And I've wired Cousin Josie and asked to stay with them," said his mother. "I begged her not to say anything so we might surprise you."

"You've succeeded. She never said a solitary word to me about it. Little surprise there. Well, don't let me keep you. There's a storm brewing. You need to get ashore and get settled as soon as possible. I have the watch tonight, so I'll see you maybe tomorrow. We can talk more then."

"Before you go, I have some information that might interest you," said Mitchell.

"By all means."

"The ladies will need to get themselves together. Let's go up on deck, shall we?"

The wind whipped around them as they climbed topsides. Mitchell drew him to one side, in the shelter of the wheelhouse.

"I haven't shared this with your mother yet, because I'm afraid she would worry more than she already has. But I knew you'd want to know as soon as possible. My man has traced Meg to Paris. As you may have guessed, she went there with a woman by the name of Levinson, with whom she is mixed up in this terrible scandal. The woman apparently has her own fortune, so money is no issue for them. From there, the trail goes cold, but he believes they've traveled to the South of France somewhere. He will continue to search, until I tell him otherwise."

Gunn shook his head. "I just don't know what to make of it. I never dreamed."

"My other news is no better. Brace yourself. My man tells me that your father was killed by a mob, some of the Dead Rabbits street gang. He was with a young man by the name of Wilde, of all things. The circumstances were rather unsavory, I'm afraid. They were both beaten to death. Their bodies were unrecognizable. The police said that Meg apparently had to identify him by a birthmark on his left hand. You can imagine."

"I really can't. How horrible. No wonder she left town."

"I'm very sorry, Andrew. Again, I haven't shared these details with your mother. She's been distressed enough. But I thought you should know."

"Thank you for telling me. The truth is always best."

"I'm glad you feel that way."

"And on that note, Uncle William, please tell me, truthfully, honestly, were you aware that Daniel Gunn was not my real father?"

Mitchell pulled at his beard. "You've caught me off guard, Andrew. I must say, well, we suspected as much, May and I, but we honestly didn't know for certain until your mother recently confessed it to us. These are not topics of polite conversation, you understand. Apparently, you found out somehow. Eleanor regrets not telling you, very much so."

"I regret it, too. More than I can say."

"One last bit of news. This one less shocking. Or at least I'm sure you won't be shocked to know that Lamar is planning to buy another ship. My contacts in New York tell me that this one is a racing yacht by the name of *Wanderer*. She's built on the same lines as the *America*. Very fast. She's being refitted to haul cargo."

"*Wanderer*, eh? Well, that settles it in my mind. You don't buy a racing yacht to haul cotton. You buy it to outrun anyone who might try to chase you down."

"My thinking exactly."

"The *Rawlins* is almost ready."

"I figured as much."

"Lamar got clearance to leave port as soon as the repairs are complete. The release came from the Treasury Secretary himself."

"The man has connections."

"Don't I know it. The port collector suspects that he's up to no good. He tried to put Lamar off. But the rascal complained to Cobb of unwarranted treatment."

"Of course."

"I wish we could find a way to stop him. He's going to get away with it, you know. I can feel it in my bones."

"I wish I could say otherwise."

"How long are you staying this time, Uncle William?"

"I plan to be here for about a month to drum up some new business. Things are getting tight these days. That load from Lamar turned out to be last year's crop. It was moldy throughout. Cost me dearly. Good thing wind is cheap. Anyway, Corning is dropping us off and heading up to Charleston and then on to Norfolk. That's why we didn't take a mooring. He'll be back in three weeks to pick us up. That is, unless there is a wedding in the offing." He winked.

"Your guess is as good as mine, Uncle William. I really have no idea at this point. I do try to keep my hopes up, though."

"That's the spirit."

"Thanks for the information. I'll be going now so you all can get safely ashore." He lifted his chin skyward. "That storm won't hold off much longer."

The deluge broke about an hour after Gunn returned to the

Dobbin. The rain lasted all afternoon, with rolling thunder and lightning, coming down so hard that at times River Street flooded so deep it indeed resembled its name. The storm was just beginning to let up when Foster called down through the wardroom companionway, where Gunn was reviewing the smooth logs for the previous month.

"Mr. Gunn, there is a coach out here. Man says he would like to speak with you."

"Who is it?"

"Dunno. Looks like a muckety-muck."

Gunn went topsides to see a horse and coach that resembled Sullivan's. The driver hunched over in his slicker, rain pouring from the brim of his hat.

He left the ship, holding the collar of his coat over his head, and ran to the coach, dancing around the huge puddles in the street. The door to the coach swung open and he hopped in.

Sullivan and Sarah greeted him. Her eyes were red and swollen. She looked like she needed sleep.

"What's the matter?" Gunn asked.

"I took your advice," Sullivan said, gravely. "We confronted Odah about the things you said. She admitted to everything. Seemed to be rather pleased with herself. And she even admitted that she's been working with Lamar and feeding him information, too. I don't know what they are up to, exactly, but it is not good."

"Is she gone, then?"

Mitchell nodded. "I told her that she could leave on the next ship to Liberia, if she wished. Or I would sell her south if she refused to leave. She laughed at me. Hideous laugh. Said I was bluffing. I assured her that I was not. We were not prepared for what happened next."

"I'd never seen anything like it," said Sarah, her hands shaking. "I was terrified. It was all so horrible."

Gunn put his arm around her. She calmed herself and continued. "Odah screamed that she would see us all dead. She ran around the house breaking and smashing everything that she could lay hands on."

"It was a horrific scene," said Sullivan. "Like she was possessed by a demon."

"She cursed us madly and said she would see that we all burned in hell. You, too. She claims to know all about you. And Elizabeth. And Thomas. And . . . and your father. And she would use it all against you."

"She knows these things because she has seen my journal."

"How did she manage that?" Sullivan asked.

"I find it hard to understand how myself."

Sarah looked up at him through tears. "Remember the story you told me about the seven sisters being chased by the Follower? And the one sister who hides?"

"The Plaedies and Aldebaran. Yes, of course."

"That's how I feel all the time, Andrew. Something or someone is always following me. I feel like I must hide."

"I think that's a very good idea."

"But Elizabeth is in danger, too, Andrew. You must protect her. Believe me. I've seen it in a dream. I'm so sorry. I'm so sorry about everything." She threw her arms around his neck and hugged him. "Everything," she whispered.

He rocked her gently in his arms. "I am, too, Sarah. But I am not sorry about one thing. I'm very happy to have gained another sister."

Her embrace tightened. "And I a new brother," she mumbled into his shoulder. "Can you ever forgive me?"

"With all my heart." He turned to Sullivan. "Where is Odah now?"

"I don't know," muttered Sullivan. "Without proper papers, she'll need to hide somewhere, else the slave traders will catch her. Maybe she has gone to the offshore islands. Maybe not."

"She is still a threat, then."

"That's just the thing. We're here to tell you what happened, but as soon as we leave, I'm taking Sarah to meet the six o'clock train to Augusta. I have a brother there, who will make sure she's safe, at least for the next couple weeks, until we know Odah's gone for good. I know I can count on him."

"What about you?"

"I'll be all right."

Gunn got quiet for a moment. The rain drummed on the roof of the carriage.

"So I have an uncle?"

Sullivan smiled. "As a matter of fact, you do. And I'll wager that he'll be very pleased to know at long last that he has a nephew."

63

That evening, Gunn remained aboard the ship as the officer of the watch. The rain had finally subsided, and the watch section assembled at the end of the workday on the foredeck. The reedy melody of a harmonica mingled with occasional shouts and laughter as the men teased one another, trading stories or bragging about their latest exploits during the brief respite in town.

Raucous laughter erupted, and Gunn couldn't help but find out what was so amusing. He strolled forward to the foredeck, trying to appear nonchalant, not wishing to invade the privacy of these men who had so little of it to spare.

Sitting in the midst of a circle of his former shipmates, Matthew Walters, previously the captain's steward, regaled them with his stories of life as a civilian.

The men started to rise as Gunn approached.

"Sit, sit. Don't let me disturb you. Good to see you, Walters. You're looking well and happy."

"I was just tellin' the fellas about some of the lunacy that I've seen up there at the Seamen's Inn. When folks gets drunk on easy rum, no tellin' what can happen. I've seen all kinds of goin's-on."

Dawkins laughed and shook his head. "You wouldn't believe it, Mr.

Gunn. Some idjut stripped plumb naked and was dancin' a jig on the tables, his bits all janglin' about."

"An image we can all live without, Dawkins. Thanks for that. Must have been some potent rum."

"Oh, it was the best, Mr. Gunn," said Walters. He was a winsome lad, with a wide, toothy grin, not hard to like. "Straight from Jamaica. Had some myself."

"Jamaican rum?"

"They was practically givin' the stuff away."

"Who was?"

"Some huckleberry, called hisself Donnelly. Said he worked for Charley Lamar. Told everybody drinks was on the house, and there was more where that come from. They brought barrels of it in, right under Uncle Sam's nose. Braggin' he was. He was pretty corned up, if you ask me. Hollerin' loud enough to wake snakes. Cavortin' and wavin' a pistol around till he was plumb tuckered out. Said he'd use it on anybody who looked at him cross-eyed. Claimed he shot a man in the head, just 'cause he talked back. 'He ain't talkin' no more,' he said. Plain lunatic."

"Did he mention when they brought it in? The rum."

"Not exactly. Few days back, I reckon. That's when all this happened."

"I'd keep my distance from that man, if I were you," said Gunn. "Would you be willing to tell the marshal what you just told me?"

The question was quite sobering to the mood of the group.

"Golly, I—I don't know, Mr. Gunn. I'd be afeared that I might find myself in a shallow three-by-six if I was to do somethin' like that. I'd sure as hell lose my job. Folks don't take too awful kindly to—"

"I understand. Think about it. I'm sure he would like very much to hear your story. Sorry to spoil your fun. Carry on."

The next morning, Gunn awoke to find the *Rawlins* gone. He searched the entire harbor with the spyglass. Lamar's white tugboat, the *C.A.L. Lamar*, usually tied up at the wharf near the cotton press, was also missing. There was nothing for it, no way to prevent what was now almost surely going to happen. The only thing he could think to do was to tell Ganahl what he had learned about Donnelly and hope that somehow the information would lead to the arrest of both Donnelly and his boss. He had just decided on that course of action when Ganahl himself, along with John Boston, hailed the ship and came aboard.

"Where is Captain Day?" Boston asked. "We have some urgent news."

"He's in his cabin, I'm sure," said Gunn. "Allow me to take you to him."

They followed him aft to the companionway and descended the ladder. Captain Day sat at the table, just finishing his breakfast, as Cuffee cleared away the dishes. His eyes were bleary, and the sweet-sour smell of fermentation filled the room. He dabbed his beard with a napkin and rose to greet them.

"Hello, gentlemen. What brings you here so early of a morning?"

"Bad news, I'm afraid," said Boston. "We've just received word by telegram from Washington that Charley Lamar has commissioned the *Rawlins* to sail for the coast of Africa."

"I thought the *Rawlins* was cleared to sail to Madeira."

"Not anymore," Ganahl said. "There is now no doubt that he intends to bring in a shipload of slaves, and he's even bragging about it to Secretary Cobb himself."

"He sent a telegram late last night." Boston pulled a folded telegram from his pocket and read from it. "'Let your cruisers catch me if they can.'" He slapped the telegram with his fingertips.

"Is he aboard the *Rawlins*?" Gunn asked.

"No. I confronted him at his office not a half hour ago. He just laughed and dared us to try to stop the ship. He's a lunatic, I swear."

"I don't believe it," said Day. "The temerity of the man."

"Take a look." Boston held out the telegram, which shivered in his hand. "See for yourself."

Day scanned the telegram, stroking his long beard. "Well, I'll be . . ."

"You'll be underway within the hour, Captain Day" said Boston. "The *Rawlins* left sometime last night. She can't be too far ahead. I want you to catch that ship and bring her back here. Is that understood?"

"Yes, sir," said Day.

"There is no time to spare, captain. Bring back that ship, or there will be hell to pay."

Gunn started to tell them about Donnelly. "Mr. Boston— "

"No time, gentlemen. The clock is ticking. There will be time for discussion later."

"Aye, aye, sir."

The ship sailed twenty minutes later. The previous day's storm had swept through, leaving in its wake a fresh, northwesterly breeze, perfect for a transit downriver. With an ebb tide, the Dobbin reached the mouth of the river in less than five hours.

Presuming a southeasterly course, given the *Rawlins'* intended destination, the captain laid down a rhumbline on the chart for the watch officers to follow. With the wind fair behind her, the *Dobbin* flew along that track for several hours with nothing in sight.

As early evening approached, the forward lookout spotted a sail on the horizon, dead ahead. The captain ordered Gunn to set all plain sail in pursuit.

Gunn had just given the orders to the boatswain when he happened to glance over his shoulder to see a single red flare arcing high in the western sky behind them. It appeared to come from the same general direction in which they had spotted the flare off Ossabaw Island. He reported the flare to the captain, who immediately scanned the horizon with his binoculars. After a moment, the captain lowered his glasses, brow knitted.

"About ship, Mr. Gunn."

"Captain?"

"You heard me. About ship."

"But, sir—"

"Must I say it again, lieutenant?"

Bulloch approached. "What's going on?"

"Flare sighting," the captain said, nodding toward the horizon. "Could be a ship in distress."

"It might have been a flare," said Gunn.

"Was it, or wasn't it?" Day demanded.

He pointed. "I saw what I thought was a red signal flare near the horizon."

Spyglass in hand, Bulloch scanned the horizon, blinded somewhat by the setting sun.

"Can't see a thing."

"We can't take the chance that it's nothing. Mr. Gunn saw the flare. We have no choice but to respond."

"It could be a ploy to draw us off, sir," said Gunn.

"Could be. But I'm not willing to risk the loss of life if you're wrong, Mr. Gunn."

"Des, what do you think?"

"What's that? Day boomed. "Who do you think is captain of this ship, Mr. Gunn?"

"Sir, I just thought—"

"You are not paid to think, lieutenant. You are paid to follow my orders. And that's exactly what you'll do or regret the consequences. What'll it be?"

Bulloch heaved a sigh. "Sir, perhaps we should—"

"Do we have a mutiny on our hands? Look to reason, gentlemen. We are in a stern chase. It will take us hours, perhaps an entire day to overhaul the *Rawlins*, if we ever do. Once she catches sight of us and puts on more sail, or catches a fair wind, it's goodbye, Nellie. And that's all presuming the ship ahead of us is indeed the *Rawlins*, which we do not even know and cannot be certain of. Now, we have a choice to make, don't we? Either we pursue a potentially fruitless chase, or we save lives. How can I make it more clear?"

"You're right, captain," said Bulloch.

"Well, I'm so very glad that you agree, Mr. Bulloch. How terribly amenable of you." Day turned on Gunn. "Now, about ship, mister. I'll not say it again."

64

Sarah's dire warning haunted him. In the still hours of the morning as he lay awake on his bunk, he thought of the premonition that she'd given him about the danger to Elizabeth and himself.

When he slept, he a had wild, fragmented dream about Elizabeth being pursued on a windswept beach by a great, predatory seabird, her long brown hair tangled in its claws, while he was trapped in a nearby lighthouse, powerless to do anything to stop it.

In the daylight hours, between watches, he drew great comfort from the reminder that Elizabeth was safe in Scotland. This present evil couldn't touch her there. Perhaps things had worked out for the best, after all. For once, he was glad that she wasn't with him.

These things still occupied his thoughts as the *Dobbin* sailed upriver toward Savannah after searching through the first night of the flare sighting and for nearly two days thereafter. The search had turned up nothing.

Day paced the quarterdeck like an aging lion measuring the limits of his cage, occasionally stopping to look wistfully over the stern and out to sea. Gunn wondered if the captain had stayed out so long searching because he dared not return to port so soon without the *Rawlins* in tow.

Many other thoughts passed through his mind during those many hours. How strange and life-changing the last few months had been. The chance encounter with Sullivan and Sarah. The horrible, senseless death of the man who he'd thought was his father. The disappearance of his sister. The discovery of the truth of his own beginnings. It was all too much to take in at once.

Bulloch joined him at the ship's rail and offered a cigar.

"Peace offering?"

Gunn refused. Bulloch pressed it into his hand.

"Have one with me."

Gunn hesitated as Day glowered at them both from the quarter-deck. Then he smiled and took it. "Why not?"

"You were right, you know," said Bulloch.

"About the flare?"

"About everything. I shouldn't have doubted you. I should have pressed the issue."

"Then we'd both be in the doghouse. Or worse."

"Been there before."

"We could have stopped them, you know."

"I know. We'll get them when they try to come back."

"Maybe so. I hope you're right. But I have a bad feeling about it all."

"How so?"

"Just do." Gunn puffed his cigar. "You know, it's almost as though the captain wanted them to get away. Like it was supposed to happen that way."

"What are you saying?"

"I think you know."

"Pretty serious. But I think you're wrong about that."

"You just finished saying how right I was. But I do hope that I'm wrong."

They smoked quietly for a moment.

"Something else on your mind?" Bulloch asked.

"What do you mean?"

"You seemed pretty deep in thought. Like you were mulling something over."

Gunn shook his head. "If you only knew."

"I wish I did. You can tell me, you know."

"I'm just not sure how you'll take it."

"Try me."

"It's about Sarah Sullivan."

Bulloch scowled. "Now, wait a minute. You told me you had no interest in her."

"You said the same thing. Apparently, you do, though."

"Maybe a little. All right, a lot. But don't tell me you've changed your mind, too."

"I haven't. My interest in Sarah is not romantic."

"What then?"

Gunn took a deep breath. "She's my half-sister, Des."

"You have lost your ever-loving mind, my friend. Must be the cigar. It's gone to your head. Better put it out."

"It's true."

He told Bulloch what he had learned about Daniel Sullivan and his mother.

"That's incredible. I just can't even begin to imagine how you must feel about it all. How long have you known?"

"I've suspected for a while. Daniel himself admitted it was true. My mother confirmed it when she arrived in town a few days ago. Until then, I didn't really know for sure."

"Well, how do you feel about it? Does Sarah know?"

"She knows. I told her. No doubt that's what she was brooding about at supper that night."

"Ah, yes. When she said that you weren't the person she thought you were."

Gunn nodded. "I still can't seem to wrap my mind around the idea, though I must admit I'm kind of warming to it."

"And Sullivan?"

Gunn shrugged. "Says he's sorry that he didn't tell us sooner. But he wasn't sure until now."

They both grew silent. Bulloch turned to face him with a half-smile.

"Thanks for telling me."

"You're the only one I've told, outside my family."

"I'm actually relieved to know."

"Why is that?"

"I thought maybe I'd end up having to fight you for her. And I know how you feel about duels."

Gunn laughed out loud for the first time in days.

At last, the *Dobbin* arrived back in port. Once the ship was tied up, Captain Day headed uptown to tell Boston the bad news. He instructed Bulloch to grant liberty to the crew once everything had been secured from sea.

Gunn decided to head to Perry Street to greet his mother properly at last and to talk about all that had happened. They had much to discuss.

He walked through town, making his way south along Whitaker Street. As he passed through Broughton, he had the growing sensation of being followed, much like before. He looked back over his shoulder to see the stubby form of Donnelly duck into a storefront. He took a firmer grip on his walking stick and continued down the street.

After several more blocks, he slipped into a narrow alley, between a hat shop and an Irish pub. He walked behind the pub and hid behind an outhouse at the rear. Flies buzzed overhead. He brushed two from his face. The stench made him gag.

A few moments later, the sound of boots on gravel reached his ears. Gunn crouched into a stance like a baseball batter and waited. As soon as Donnelly passed into view, he swung his shillelagh as hard as he could into the man's belly. Donnelly doubled over, crying out in surprise and pain. Gunn hit him hard again behind the knees, and he dropped to the ground with a grunt, rolling onto his back.

"Too bad you came alone this time, Donnelly."

"I didn't," Donnelly groaned between clenched teeth. He reached beneath his coat. Gunn saw the butt of a revolver in his hand as he withdrew it. He stepped on Donnelly's arm before he could aim it. Donnelly grimaced in pain, as Gunn wrenched the weapon from his hand.

"I'll just take that, shall I?" He walked over to the outhouse, opened the door, and dropped the pistol into the hole. A splash echoed in the dark void.

"You'll want to clean that before you try using it again, or it might backfire on you. Now, get up."

Donnelly struggled to his feet. "You're going to regret this, Gunn." He spat into the dirt. "Mark my words."

"Maybe so. But not half as much as you'll regret it if I ever again find you following or threatening me or anyone else that I care about. I swear that I won't be nearly so gentle next time."

"You have no idea what you're up against. I'll have a warrant sworn out before Judge Nicoll for your arrest on charges of assault and battery."

"That's just fine by me. The district attorney will have to decide which one to take up first, either that or the charge of murder against you. I have a witness who'll testify that you bragged about killing that poor dock worker from the cotton press."

"You're lying."

"Am I?"

Donnelly was silent as he shot furtive glances to either side.

"You'd better find a good place to hide, Donnelly. I know all the usual holes. Maybe another state might suit you better. Now, get out of my sight while you still have the chance."

The defeated man picked up his hat, dusted it off, and limped away.

Gunn called after him. "And tell your stupid boss the same goes for him, too."

Donnelly snarled over his shoulder. He bumped into the side of the building, swore loudly, and disappeared around the corner.

Gunn brushed himself off and continued his walk, wary the entire way of anyone else around him. By the time he reached Perry Street, he had begun to cool down.

He entered the house, expecting to see his mother and cousins seated in the parlor, chatting. Instead, he could hardly believe the vision that met his eyes.

Standing next to the window, bathed in its soft evening backlight, was none other than Elizabeth Faulkner. He stood in the doorway of the parlor, dumbfounded.

"I saw you coming up the walk," she said.

His heart was racing, his pulse beating in his ears. "Elizabeth. How? When did you get here?"

"Yesterday," she said.

"How?"

"We took a steamship from Greenock.

"We?"

"Marianne and I."

"What about your father?"

She dropped her eyes from his. "He died a few days after I sent my letter to you. Took a sudden turn, and he was gone."

"I'm so sorry."

"It will be all right." She looked at him again with tears in her eyes, her lower lip trembling. "He said we should not mourn him. We should rejoice that he is happy in heaven with my mother." She wiped a tear from her cheek with the back of her hand. "He asked me to tell you that he wants us to be happy, too, just as they are."

"I just can't believe this is happening."

"Well, come over here and I'll prove it to you." She smiled through her tears.

He put down his cane, rushed over and took her in his arms. "I was beginning to think this day might never come."

"Me, too." She kissed him before he could say anything more. Then she laid her head on his shoulder, held him tight, and took a deep breath. "Let me just breathe you in." After a moment, she raised her face to his. "I smell salt air." She wrinkled her nose. "And cigars."

He chuckled. "You'll have to take the good with the bad, I'm afraid."

"I'll take it all, and for all time."

"So when is the wedding? Everybody seems to be here now."

"That's true enough, except for Robert, but let's not wait any longer. Marianne says it should be a day to remember forever. She wants it to be on her birthday."

"When is that again?"

"The Fourth of July."

He grinned. "Can't think of a better day. Whatever day suits you tickles me plumb to heaven."

65

The Fourth of July fell on a Saturday. The ten days leading up to that day were full of frantic preparations. There was much to accomplish, most of which fell upon Elizabeth and his mother, of course. May got involved too, insisting on hiring the best seamstress in town to make a wedding dress for Elizabeth, along with a good deal of her trousseau, as a gift to her.

They planned the wedding to take place on Saturday afternoon at the Independent Presbyterian Church, officiated by Reverend Axson, who had kindly agreed to postpone a trip to visit family in Augusta at Cousin Julia's request. The party consisted of a very intimate gathering of family and a few friends, followed by a late dinner or early supper at the house on Perry Street, hosted by Josie and Julia. Later, with the exception of Josie, they would all go to the town's Independence Day Ball to celebrate the marriage as well as the birth of the nation.

Much of Gunn's time, meanwhile, was taken up by his duties on the ship, which went about the usual business in and out of port. He lived on the ship while Elizabeth and Marianne took his third-floor garret in the house on Perry Street.

Captain Day seemed reluctant to spend much time at rest during those days. However, he had promised the officers and crew that they would remain in port for the Independence Day festivities, to include an annual parade, a midnight fireworks show on the waterfront, and the ball on Saturday evening at the Pulaski House, which was an affair not to be missed by anyone who mattered in Savannah.

There was ample time, however, during his visits to Elizabeth in the evenings for Gunn to explain to her everything that had happened since they had last seen each other. She was astounded to hear about all that he had to tell her, especially about who his real father was. But she was most interested in what had transpired between him and Sarah in the meantime, not to mention relieved and gratified that she now enjoyed the prospect of having another sister-in-law rather than a potential rival for his affections. It was all rather amusing now, once she'd had time to think about it.

Toward the end of the week before the wedding, the *Gawain* arrived in port a little later than expected, having weathered a bad storm at sea on the return trip. Captain Corning told Mitchell that she'd lost a fore-topmast yard when the topsail backed in a sudden wind shift. Mitchell asked Gunn if Willink's still provided good service, and Gunn assured him that the yard was top notch, and that Jayjay would certainly take good care of them in time for sailing early the following week, after the wedding.

The special day arrived at last. Gunn dressed in his best uniform, as did Bulloch, who had agreed to be his best man. Rather than walking to the church in the burgeoning humidity of the afternoon, they left the ship and got into a rented carriage at Bull Street, after waiting impatiently for the parade to pass.

The last float in the parade carried Mayor Screven and Charley Lamar, dressed in period costume as George Washington and General Lafayette, as they had in many previous years. They saluted the excited crowd lining the street, who cheered as the float passed by, while waving flags and singing "The Star-Spangled Banner," somewhat off-key and in modulated unison with the fife and drum corps farther down the Bay. It was a grand spectacle and an auspicious start to the bright, sunny afternoon.

When they arrived at the church, it was still early. Uncle William and Aunt May had not yet arrived in their carriage with the bride and

Marianne. Josie and Julia were already there, and seated in the sanctuary in the third pew from the front, along with his mother. A few friends from the membership of the church also had come early. Gunn and Bulloch took their places in an anteroom at the front of the church, from which they could see the later arrivals through the cracked-open door. They did not have long to wait.

Aunt May arrived and sat next to Eleanor. A few minutes later, just before one o'clock, Daniel Sullivan walked through the doors. Gunn was surprised and happy to see Sarah on his arm. They nodded pleasant hellos to the other guests and took seats behind Josie, Julia, and his mother. Eleanor turned in her pew and beamed at Daniel. He smiled, leaned forward, took her outstretched hand, and kissed her cheek.

Reverend Axson passed through the anteroom, motioning for Gunn and Bulloch to follow him to the front of the sanctuary, which they did. The organist in the balcony at the back of the church began playing a rendition of a trumpet voluntary by Handel. At precisely one o'clock, the church doors opened and in walked the bride, on the arm of William Mitchell, whom she had asked to walk her down the aisle. Marianne preceded them, strewing rose petals from a basket the entire way.

Dressed in lavender, Elizabeth was crowned with a floral veil, the lace provided by his mother. She carried a bouquet to match the flowers in her hair. The two paused for a moment at the back of the sanctuary, then proceeded down the aisle in measured steps. As she got closer, Gunn could better see the elegant simplicity of the silk taffeta dress. Her appearance was more lovely and graceful than his imagination had ever allowed. Her bouquet was as beautiful and tasteful, accented throughout with dried Scottish thistle, a bundle of which she had brought with her from her native land. Tears streamed down her beaming face.

She took her place at his side. Mitchell gave her away and took his seat beside May. The rest, other than their vows, was a blur to Gunn. Axson preached a brief sermon, taken from the book of Ephesians, chapter five, calling upon husbands to practice sacrificial love toward their wives, caring for them as Christ did the Church.

Then, in what seemed a brief, suspended moment in time, it was over. They walked down the aisle together and exited the church to greet their small party of guests outside amid exclamations and tears of joy.

The only awkward moment came when Gunn introduced his bride to Daniel Sullivan and his new half-sister for the first time. He didn't quite know how to describe their relationship but stumbled through it just the same with a bit of nervous laughter to cover the embarrassment of confusion.

An open carriage, provided by the Mitchells, awaited the couple in the street. Their guests gathered round while Gunn helped his wife in, and she settled into the seat facing forward. Marianne got in and sat across from her, smiling with happiness he had never seen in her face before. As he readied himself to join them, a small dog bolted from beneath the carriage, dancing at his feet.

"Casimir! Where have you been?"

The dog begged to be picked up, which Gunn promptly did. This time, Casimir did not resist. "Where did you come from, little one? Are you still lost, all this time?" Casimir licked his hand.

"Oh, is he lost? So cute. Can we keep him, Andrew? Please?" Marianne cried. She reached to take the dog from him.

"He's a bit dirty and smelly, I'm afraid," he said.

"That's all right. I don't mind. Can we?"

He looked at Elizabeth for affirmation. She nodded, smiling. Then he sought out Sarah in the gathering.

Sarah grinned and shrugged. "He apparently always liked you better, anyway."

"I don't see why not, then," said Gunn. "Happy Birthday, Marianne. Let's go."

Marianne squealed with delight. He climbed into the carriage and sat next to Elizabeth, taking her hand. She smiled, her eyes brilliant. Marianne hugged and stroked the little dog. The driver clucked to the horses, and the carriage moved down the street.

Gunn had never felt so happy or so complete in his entire life.

66

The remainder of the day flew by, charged with excitement and anticipation, first with the early supper, and then getting ready to attend the ball that same evening. Anticipating the ball, Aunt May had arranged for the dressmaker to provide Elizabeth a matching evening bodice, allowing her to wear the same frock, along with a cashmere shawl that had been her mother's to cover her bared shoulders in the chill of the evening. Josie lent her a small diamond necklace to complete her exquisite attire. Gunn was sure that she would be the most beautiful woman in Savannah that night.

Their party arrived at the ball together, though in separate carriages, with the exception of Cousin Josie, who elected to stay at home. Casimir, who had been properly bathed and groomed, happily remained with her, although he seemed a bit happier about it than she.

It promised to be a splendid evening. The ballroom at the Pulaski House was festooned in red, white, and blue bunting, with matching floral arrangements. The small orchestra played almost incessantly.

All of Savannah society attended, most of whom were unknown to Gunn. The dignitaries he did recognize included Mayor Screven, Doctor Arnold and his wife, the Nicolls, the John Bostons, Joe Ganahl and his young wife, Harriet, and James Bulloch. Captain Day congregated with the other military officers and their wives. Even Captain Corning attended, dressed in his best finery. Gunn introduced his new wife to them all.

People came and went as the night progressed, dancing waltz after reel and an occasional polka, until exhaustion. The only couple conspicuous in their absence were the Charles Lamars.

As the newly married couple danced their third waltz, Elizabeth asked, "Which one is Mr. Lamar?"

Gunn surveyed the room. "Not here."

"From what you've told me, after all that's happened, maybe he's too ashamed to be seen. Perhaps he is finally developing a conscience."

He laughed. "Charley Lamar? Hardly. More likely just fashionably late."

"Or maybe they've arrested him. Do you think it's possible?"

"No, I saw him just this morning in the parade. I only wish it were true. But bragging isn't a crime. Neither is insanity. More's the pity. He hasn't really committed any provable crime so far, other than sending his ship out of port without a proper clearance. The penalty for that is a mere fine."

Gunn danced exclusively with his new bride throughout the evening, although his uncle, his friend Bulloch, and his new father all took turns cutting in for an opportunity to dance with her as well.

At one point, while Sullivan took a turn around the dance floor with Elizabeth, Captain Corning and Mitchell approached Gunn and took him aside. With a wink, Mitchell spoke in a conspiratorial tone.

"Once again, Jayjay has been very helpful, indeed, in responding to our every need."

"Glad to hear it. I knew he would be. Repairs all made?"

Corning nodded. "Yes, he fixed us right up. We're all shipshape, and the *Gawain* is ready to sail on a moment's notice."

"When will that be, do you think?"

"As early as Monday."

"So soon?"

"Yes, we have taken on a special cargo that could easily spoil the longer we stay," said Corning.

"What on earth would that be?" Gunn asked, intrigued.

"Cuffee," Mitchell whispered.

Gunn inclined his ear. "Coffee, did you say?"

Mitchell shook his head. "Your ship's steward, Cuffee."

"I don't understand."

Mitchell glanced side to side. "Jayjay asked us to take Cuffee up north, away from Savannah. As I told you before, we've been friends a long time, now. He was of some help to us. And he asked us to do him a favor. One good turn deserves another."

"If things went as planned, he is already onboard," said Corning.

Gunn cast an incredulous eye toward Captain Day. *"What?"*

"He's coming with us. Free passage." Mitchell looked very pleased with himself. "Just thought you should know."

Gunn took Mitchell by the arm. "Are you crazy, Uncle William? Do you know what will happen if you get caught? When Captain Day discovers Cuffee is missing, the catchers will be looking for him everywhere in this city. They'll not leave a hank of cordage unturned."

"I'll take that chance. We have ways of hiding things we don't want found. I warned you, it's one part of my old business that I just won't give up. No matter what."

Gunn thought for a moment. "I don't know how you managed this. Maybe it's best that I don't. And as I told you earlier, I can't protect you if things go sour. But I won't stand in your way."

The evening progressed. Gunn tried his best to relax, given what he had just learned, distracting himself with the festivities and the company of his friends and family. For his part, Bulloch had taken up with Sarah, who wore a stunning indigo gown with a sapphire necklace. Despite all her charm, she was no match for Elizabeth, though the glow had returned to her face and her smile was ready and genuine. Gunn was pleased to see that they made a delightful couple, seeming to enjoy themselves with each successive dance, although she, too, was the willing partner to other admirers.

Best of all, Daniel Sullivan danced with Eleanor as often as she would allow. When not dancing, they sat together in the chairs that lined the walls of the ballroom, talking and smiling.

It was proving to be a wonderful, marvelous evening and the end of a lovely day. Toward ten o'clock, the orchestra took a hiatus, and refreshments were served in an adjacent room. Talk was of the fireworks show to be held at midnight along the waterfront and how it was sure to be the best yet.

A commotion erupted in the ballroom. Gunn turned to see Charley Lamar enter the room, staggering drunkenly, with Caroline tugging at his sleeve. He brushed her away with a scowl as rude as his gesture.

"Happy Independence Day, everyone," he slurred. "We've arrived. Better late than never, I always say. We would have been here sooner, but my lovely wife did not really want to come. Did you, my dear? Never mind. She can be forgiven. Where are the drinks?"

Caroline blushed. Sarah went to her side.

Elizabeth turned to Gunn and whispered, "Is that the man?"

Gunn nodded. "In the flesh."

"He looks drunk."

"I imagine he is. I've had just about enough of his antics. Somebody needs to put a stop to this."

She clutched his arm. "Not you, though."

"Why not me? If not me, who else? The man is a monster who should be put in a cage. It's about time."

Gunn released her grip on his arm and walked over to confront Lamar.

"I think you should leave, Mr. Lamar. You're obviously drunk."

The surrounding guests grew quiet.

Lamar regarded him with disdain. "Says who?"

"All decent folk."

"And you're one of them, eh? That's a laugh." He broke into loud guffaws.

"I think it's time," said Gunn quietly.

"You gonna make me leave? You little Yankee worm. I'd like to see you try. I've had just about as much of you as a man can take. You don't have the guts. None of you do. You and all the other so-called decent folks in this room." He raised his voice. "Let me tell you about decent folks. Especially this . . . this vermin." He dismissed Gunn with a waved hand. "Behold, if you dare, a man who would sleep with his own sister."

An audible gasp swept through the crowd, followed by utter silence.

"That's a lie, and you know it," Gunn said.

"Is it? Not what I've been told." He pointed first at Sarah and then at Gunn. "I have it on good authority that you two have had intimate relations of late, and prolly more'n once, is my guess." He spun slowly, steadying himself, addressing the crowd now gathered around them. "And did you all know they were brother and sister? Bet you didn't. Well, you do now. That's another nasty little scandal all its own."

Sarah glanced at Caroline, a look of utter horror on her face. "How could you, Caroline? You are my friend. It's just not . . ."

Caroline apologized with her eyes, looking down at the floor.

"Don't look to her, Miss Sarah Sullivan, belle of Savannah." Lamar said. "She's not the only one who spilled the beans. Your own house-maid, Odah, swears she saw you go into this man's room in the middle of the night, when most good people are asleep in their own beds. My wife merely confirmed it, my dear, based on what you yourself told her."

"What you imply is simply not true, sir, and you well know it," Elizabeth said, her lips quivering. "My husband would never do such a thing."

Lamar sneered. "Husband? I'm sure you very well wish it weren't true, my dear. I hear congratulations are in order, by the way. Or were. Perhaps you'll reconsider your position, after tonight."

Sullivan stood next to Gunn. "That's quite enough, Charley. You've gone too far."

Gunn saw the anguish in Sarah's wide eyes, like that of a wounded animal, as well as the hurt in his wife's face. He turned on Lamar, as his anger broke free of its frayed bonds. He had never wanted to injure someone so badly in his life. At that moment, he could have strangled Lamar with his bare hands. "It's all a dirty, rotten lie, Lamar," he shouted. "You are nothing but a liar and a scoundrel. And so is your wife."

"Now, them's fightin' words, Yank."

Gunn took a step forward. "Name the place and time, you coward."

"Don't," Elizabeth whispered.

"Coward, is it?" Lamar wore a gruesome grin. "Why don't we settle this outside, like gentlemen?"

Elizabeth grabbed his arm. "Andrew, please don't do this. Not on our wedding night."

67

Outside the grand hotel, at the corner of Bull and Saint Julian Streets, on the northwest corner of Johnson Square, a small crowd gathered to witness the confrontation. Much of the crowd consisted of what had been the happy wedding party earlier in the day. The disapproving face of Captain Day was among them.

The two enemies stood in the street, apart from the spectators. They were joined by five other men. Desmond Bulloch, Daniel Sullivan, and William Mitchell flanked Gunn. Captain Joseph Claghorn, dressed in the uniform of the Chatham Artillery, and another military officer whom Gunn did not recognize backed Lamar.

Lamar spoke first. "Well, Mr. Gunn. I must say you have gumption. But you're not very smart to call me and my dear wife liars in front of our friends. I will have satisfaction. Tonight."

Gunn squared off. "I will fight you here and now, Lamar. It's about time somebody taught you a lesson you won't soon forget."

"I'm surprised at you. Gentlemen do not engage in street fights, Gunn. But then, you wouldn't know that, being Yankee scum, now would you?"

"Name the place and time, then."

"All right. Meet me an hour from now at midnight in the Colonial

Park Cemetery, under a large oak tree near the Bulloch monument. Your friend there should know where to find it." He chucked his chin at Desmond.

"To do what?"

"You know very well what. And tell your other friend there, my *former* attorney, to bring that handsome brace of dueling pistols that he's so proud of. You know the ones, Sullivan. They should do just fine for our purposes."

"I have never been your attorney, Charley," said Sullivan. "I work for your father, not you."

"You can go work for the devil himself, Sullivan, for all I care. You'll have nothing more to do with me."

Gunn scoffed. "You can't be serious, Lamar."

"Deadly serious. Captain Claghorn here will be my second. Name yours."

"This is my wedding day."

"Just as I thought. Gutless."

"Make it a minute after midnight, Lamar. And don't be late."

Lamar turned on his heel and retreated to the door to retrieve his wife from the small knot of spectators, then ordered his carriage to be brought around.

"Andrew, don't do this," said Bulloch. "You don't know what you're up against. That man will think nothing of putting a bullet right between your eyes."

Gunn shook his head. "Who else, then, Des? And when? This may be the only chance we have to stop the madness that this lunatic intends to bring down upon our heads."

"All right, then. If you're determined to go forward, at least let me be your second," said Bulloch.

"No. No, I want you and Sarah to escort my wife and Marianne home, Des. Please see that she gets there safely and stay with her until I return. I will have Daniel as my second, if he is willing."

Sullivan frowned. "I'd rather talk you out of this foolishness. But if you are intent on going through with it, Son, I will stand by you."

"Good. Thank you.

"I will go with you, Andrew," said Mitchell. "I insist."

"Very well, then. Let's be off."

Sullivan called for his carriage. Gunn went to the door of the hotel, where Elizabeth waited.

"What is going on, Andrew?"

"I'm going to fight him."

"Fight Lamar? Where? How?"

"He has called me out to fight him in a duel."

"A duel?" She shook her head. "You can't. I won't allow it."

"I have no choice, Elizabeth. Please understand that. If I refuse to fight him, he will win."

"And if he kills you, he will win. And we will lose everything we've been hoping for."

"Somebody has to stop him before it is too late."

"Does it have to be you?"

"I don't see anyone else willing to do what must be done. Listen to me, now. I have the opportunity to stop him. If I don't take it, and others suffer greater loss as a consequence, how could I live with myself? Don't you see?"

She bowed her head. "I don't know what else to say to convince you. It breaks my heart. What if you do kill him? Can you live with having taken another man's life? And what about the law? Dueling is illegal in Georgia, isn't it? If not, it ought to be."

"I have thought of it. If it comes to that, I will seek mercy from the courts and from God. But unless I miss my guess, Lamar will not even show up. The man is a bully and a coward at heart, as all bullies are."

She raised her gaze to meet his, her eyes moist. "Then come back to me, Andrew Gunn. I will be waiting for you. I will not budge from this spot until you return."

He kissed her lips tenderly. "Desmond will see you safely home. Wait for me there. I will join you soon. I promise."

He got into the carriage with Sullivan and Mitchell, and they drove off. They rode the entire way to Sullivan's house on Jones Street in somber silence. When they arrived, the first words were spoken by Sullivan, expressing surprise that the front door stood wide open.

"Strange. Who on earth left the door open? I'm sure it was shut when we left this evening."

"Be careful going in," said Mitchell.

"Don't you worry. I will," said Sullivan. He alighted from the carriage and climbed the steps, pausing before he entered. A few minutes later, he returned with the case containing the brace of pistols in hand, a horn of gunpowder held beneath his left arm. A leather bullet pouch dangled from his fingers. The butler shut the door behind him.

"Nobody knew the door was open, not even Doyle," Sullivan said, as he climbed into the carriage. "Strange. I don't know what to make of it."

"Anything missing?"

"Impossible to say. I didn't have time to look."

He told his driver to head toward the cemetery. The carriage moved off along Jones Street. The three men again spent the next few minutes in silence, alone with their thoughts in anticipation of what was about to happen.

Gunn broke the silence, trying to avoid saying what they might all be thinking, namely what might happen should he not prevail. "So, Daniel." He pointed to the case with the firearms. "Did those really belong to Andrew Jackson?"

Sullivan smiled. "I have no idea. That's what the dealer claimed, the man I bought them from. They are very likely from the period of the war. I just liked the look of them. It makes a good story, doesn't it? I paid the man fifty dollars for the pair."

"Do they still work?" Mitchell asked.

"Only too well."

"Maybe you should have sold them to Lamar while you had the chance," said Gunn. "Could have doubled your money."

"And give him the satisfaction? Charley Lamar just can't stand to not have something he wants, something he can't have. There's no way I would give up that enjoyment."

Mitchell chuckled. "Too bad, if it isn't true. I mean the part about them belonging to Andrew Jackson. He has always been one of my heroes."

"Mine, too," said Sullivan. "A flawed man, indeed, but one of real character and determination. They broke the mold."

"Indeed."

"You know, Andrew," said Sullivan. "I had hoped for a better time to tell you this. I never imagined it happening this way. But I am glad to have a witness, because I want you to know that I'm speaking the absolute truth. When your mother and I were young, when we loved and cherished each other, before . . . well, you know. I once told her that I wanted very much, if we ever had children, to name my firstborn son Andrew Jackson Sullivan."

Gunn was speechless. He recovered soon enough to croak out a few words. "So you've known all along."

"Since the day you told me your full name. I've had a pretty good idea, but I wasn't quite sure."

"You never gave it away. Why didn't you say anything?"

"I think that's pretty obvious."

"No wonder you didn't want Sarah and me to be together."

"I think that's pretty obvious, too. I could see how much you liked each other. I hope that now you'll have the opportunity to love each other—in a different way, of course."

"Thanks very much for telling me now. It means a great deal to know it."

"And know this: I am so very proud at last to call you my son. I couldn't have wished for a better one."

Gunn nodded. "I hope I don't disappoint you tonight."

"You won't, no matter what happens."

"Are you sure this is the right thing to do?" Mitchell asked. "We will both support you if you want to back out."

"Absolutely," said Sullivan.

"I'm as sure as I can be," Gunn said. "A man I greatly admire once said something I'll never forget. 'In truth, there is no such thing in a man's nature as a settled and full resolve, either for good or evil, except at the very moment of execution.' I believe he was right."

"Who was that?"

"My good friend Nathaniel Hawthorne."

The carriage turned on Abercorn and arrived at the west gate of the cemetery a few minutes later. The three men got out and entered through the gate. They meandered through the marble headstones and brick vaulted tombs in single file along the pathway, under a waxing gibbous moon, hanging like a lantern low in the night sky. A light breeze rustled the leaves of the live oaks.

"I think we're early," said Mitchell.

"Good," said Gunn. "I don't want him to think I'm afraid of him. He needs to see me waiting when he gets here."

"Where is the Bulloch monument?"

"On the far side. I know where it is."

"Is this Bulloch related to your friend Desmond?" Mitchell asked.

"Great-uncle. One of Georgia's great patriots. He comes from good stock, that one."

"No wonder you chose him as best man."

"He's one of the best that I know."

They arrived at the site. Sullivan loaded the weapons in the moonlight with Mitchell's help. The midnight fireworks show started in the distance, sending up multi-colored plumes of light, exploding in showers of sparks, followed by muffled pops. The bell in the watchtower at the Exchange began to chime.

"That's midnight. He's late," said Gunn.

"Maybe he's not coming," said Mitchell.

"No, wait. That's not just midnight. Listen. The bell is ringing in groups of five. That's a fire."

"Some nitwit on the waterfront has set the place on fire, no doubt," said Mitchell.

"No, it means the fifth ward. That's where I live."

They all looked in the direction of Sullivan's house, where a pillar of smoke rose above the treetops, surmounting an angry orange glow.

"I hope everything is all right," Sullivan said.

Lamar arrived a few minutes later, followed by the two men who were with him earlier, along with Dr. Arnold, who sniffed nervously several times.

"So you decided to show some courage after all, eh Gunn?" Lamar said. He had sobered up some but still had the bravado of a drunkard.

"I'm not afraid to face you, Lamar. Never have been."

"We'll see. Shall we?" He stepped unsteadily into the clearing between the large oak tree and the monument and turned to face Gunn. "Ten paces, as per custom?"

"Let's make it five," said Gunn.

Lamar laughed. "Suit yourself. It's your funeral."

They each took a weapon from Sullivan, then faced back-to-back. Gunn's hand shook as he cocked the pistol. He had never experienced greater fear in his life.

"Now, gentlemen," Captain Claghorn intoned in a deep, solemn voice. "Take your places." He counted off five paces as the two men drew apart.

They turned about to face each other.

"Any last words, Gunn?"

"None that a gentleman would utter."

Lamar's grin beamed in the moonlight as he raised his pistol.

"Hold on there." Bulloch's voice boomed in the darkness. He ran up to Gunn, breathless.

Sarah followed a few paces behind him. "Andrew, please stop!" She sank to the ground, panting.

"Let me do this," said Bulloch.

"What's going on?" Lamar said, lowering his pistol.

"I'm standing in for my friend," said Bulloch.

"You are not," said Gunn.

"Over my dead body," said Lamar.

"Have it your way, Lamar," said Bulloch.

"You'll do no such thing," said Gunn.

Bulloch lowered his voice to a whisper. "Let me. I'm a better shot."

Gunn matched his tone. "How do you figure that?"

"My hand is steadier. I have a lot less to lose. Let me."

Bulloch grabbed the muzzle and pointed it at his own chest, then wrested the weapon from Gunn's hand and turned to face Lamar.

"Such gallantry," Lamar mocked. "Almost makes me want to weep."

"You'll be crying soon enough," said Bulloch.

A far shout rang out. "You there. Stop. Stop this minute."

"By the laws of the state of Georgia, cease and desist." It was Granahl's courtroom voice. He arrived with Mayor Screven, Judge Nicoll, James Bulloch, and Marshal Stewart, wielding a drawn sidearm.

"In the name of the people of Savannah, put down your weapons," the mayor said.

"The people of Savannah can kiss my arse," said Lamar.

Stewart leveled his revolver at Lamar's chest. "Don't make me use this, Charley."

Lamar dropped his weapon on the ground with a clatter. Bulloch uncocked the other pistol and did likewise.

"Charley Lamar, you never cease to amaze me," said Judge Nicoll. "You'd better get home to Caroline while she'll still have you. I wouldn't blame her a bit if she threw you out on your ear."

"She knows better than that, judge."

"Go home, Charley," Nicoll said. "If y'all leave right now, Marshal Stewart has agreed not to press charges. Let's all leave in peace. What do you say?"

"I'll do anything I damned well please, old man. What kind of free country is this if a man can't even defend his own honor? I ask you."

"Marshal, arrest that man," said Nicoll.

The marshal moved toward Lamar.

"All right, all right. You win." Lamar nodded and departed with his men without further protest. The mayor's delegation followed them toward the gates of the graveyard.

James Bulloch approached Gunn and held out an envelope. "New orders, Andrew. Mr. Boston signed them not ten minutes ago. You are to depart as soon as possible and proceed without delay to Eastport, Maine. The Revenue Cutter *Andrew Jackson*. Captain Day sends his regards and would prefer it if you'd catch the first boat out of Savannah. Your sea chest will be waiting on the dock for you."

Gunn was utterly astonished as he unsealed the orders. It was too dark to read in the moonlight. He had to take the man's word for it.

Desmond said, "May be for the best, my friend. I wish you all the luck, Andrew. I mean that."

"We can sail tomorrow, if you like," said Mitchell. "I still owe your new bride a free ticket."

"Fire!" The shout split the night air. "Fire!" It was Doyle, the butler from Sullivan's house, gasping for breath as he ran toward them. "They told me where to find you, Mr. Sullivan. Your house is on fire, sir. Odah set fire to it not a half hour ago. Flames are high up to the third story already. Hurry. Please come, sir. *Hurry.*"

"Is everyone safe?" Sullivan asked. "Please tell me everybody got out, Doyle."

"Yes, yes, sir. We even got the horses out the stable. I took one and ran up here as fast as I could to find you."

Sullivan's shoulders slumped. "Odah. I might have known." He drew Andrew to him, as Sarah rushed to his side.

"I'm terribly sorry, Daddy," Sarah said. "I feel like it's all my fault."

"It will be all right, Sarah. Let it go. Let it go. We can rebuild. All that I hold dearest now is right here with me."

"Andrew, we should go," said Bulloch. "Elizabeth is waiting. She will be worried."

"Yes, Elizabeth said to hurry home, Andrew," Sarah said. Her voice quieted. "She said to tell you she'd have the bedclothes turned down for you."

Gunn peered at her in the dim light of the setting moon. "Why, my dear sister, if I didn't know any better, I'd swear you're blushing right now."

68

FINALE

—Eastport Maine, Christmas Eve, 1858

Nothing gratifies a seafarer more than a stalwart vessel and shipmates worthy of her, no matter the destination. It is only left to him to measure up, as a man strives to do with the woman he comes to cherish above all others.

To be sure, the Revenue Cutter *Andrew Jackson* was not a stalwart vessel by any measure. She had her flaws, as all ships do. As one of the oldest in the fleet, her hull leaked profusely, requiring frequent bailing. She had been moved to her current homeport in Maine, relegated to a quieter life, to reduce the strain on her limited capacities.

Her crew, however, was more than worthy of her. They kept her going as best they could. Gunn knew Captain John Prouty to be a man of high integrity and one of the finest seagoing officers he'd ever met, who previously had taught him the finer points of navigation and seamanship. Likewise, the boatswain, Thomas Nelson, though a bit rough around the edges, was as stalwart and true as any man might be. He had trained the crew well.

Gunn was glad at last to be back among them.

The afternoon waned, and evening hurried on. The *Jackson* had returned from patrol a day earlier, and the captain had just granted the crew well-deserved liberty to celebrate the holiday. He lifted a glass of Madeira in his cabin, toasting his officers and petty officers.

"Uncle Sam will forgive me for this little indulgence, I'm sure," he said, smiling. "I want to wish you all a very merry Christmas. Go home to your families, wives and sweethearts, with my best wishes for their continued prosperity and happiness."

"Hear, hear," they said in unison. They emptied their cups and placed them on the table. One by one, they started up the ladder to the deck above.

"Hold on, Mr. Gunn," Prouty said. "You, too, Nelson, if you will, just a moment."

The two stayed behind.

Prouty cleared his throat. His eyes were misty. "I just wanted to say to you two in particular how much I appreciate us all being together once more. It has been my privilege, one that I do not deserve, to serve as your captain this past year."

"Likewise, I'm sure, sir," said Gunn.

Nelson's broad grin showed through his heavy beard. "It's been a banger of a year, cap'n. I'm just grateful that you allow an old cabbage-head like me to serve alongside you, sir. You and Mr. Gunn here. Can't say how much tickled I am. Surely." He blushed a little through his tan.

Prouty shook both their hands. "Merry Christmas to you both."

The two climbed the ladder to the quarterdeck.

"Oh, Mr. Gunn. I almost forgot." Nelson reached his beefy hand into his coat pocket and pulled out a perfectly wrapped monkey's fist. "I made this myself. For the little one."

"Why, that's very kind of you, Nelson. Thomas will love it, I'm sure."

Nelson beamed a smile at the mention of his own given name. "He's welcome to it, I'm sure, sir."

"Merry Christmas to you, Thomas."

"And to you, sir."

As Gunn left the ship, a light snow had begun to fall, along with the evening twilight. He walked the several blocks through the old coastal fishing village, his boots kicking up the dusting of snow, until arriving at his seaside cottage on Water Street. Lamplight shone through the windows of the small wooden dwelling, and smoke spiraled up from the single chimney into the still night air.

He felt his separate pockets for the packages he'd tucked away there, assuring himself that he hadn't forgotten them, along with Nelson's gift.

He stamped his boots as he came through the front door into the warmth and glow of the house. Casimir danced around his feet, barking his greeting.

"All right, all right. I'm home. Here I am."

"Take your boots off, Andrew," Elizabeth called. "It's getting late. Dinner is almost ready. Take Tommy for a minute, will you? He's past hungry."

He removed his overcoat, hat, and boots, entered the kitchen, and picked up his son from the highchair, then kissed his wife on the cheek, with Casimir underfoot the whole time.

"It's good to be home. Smells good, whatever it is."

"You're later than I thought you'd be. It's Christmas Eve. What was Captain Prouty thinking?"

"We had some work to do. No shortage of that, even at Christmas."

"Well, I shouldn't complain. At least you're home for this one."

They ate their supper to the constant babble of their son, laughing at his attempts to mimic their own words to each other. When they finished, Elizabeth asked him to take Tommy into the parlor and play with him while she cleaned up.

"He'll be ready for bed shortly," she said. "He didn't have much of a nap today."

"Well, no wonder. It's Christmas Eve. He's too excited, I imagine."

He took his young son into the next room and knelt on the floor with him to play. The boy crawled around the room, with Casimir following, sniffing his backside.

Gunn laughed. "Oh, it's that way, is it?"

Tommy fell into a heap on his stomach, only to get back up again and head toward the blazing fire. Gunn lunged to pull him back before he could reach it.

"Let's not go there, little man. Here, Tommy. Look, I've brought you something." He reached into his coat pocket and pulled out the monkey's fist. "Merry Christmas."

Tommy squealed with delight, took the ball and promptly threw it, missing Gunn's head by inches.

"What an arm. All right, now. That's enough of that. Here's something else I think you'll like." He went to his coat where it hung by the door and reached into an inside pocket to retrieve a small package wrapped in brown paper.

Elizabeth entered the room and sat down in her sewing chair. "What's this?"

Gunn helped Tommy open the package. "It's my Christmas gift to him. His own copy of Hawthorne's *Twice-Told Tales*." He held the book up for her to see.

She laughed. "He's only eight months old, Andrew. He'll just tear the pages out, one by one."

"I know. I'll read it to him. I want him to know early on what good literature is. Nothing like a good story, is there? Every young man should be so lucky."

She chuckled again and shook her head. "Well, it's this young man's bedtime. And he needs a changing." She wrinkled her nose. "Can't you smell that?" She rose from her chair to pick him up, but he squealed and crawled away from her. "Thomas Faulkner Gunn, come back here, you little scamp." She caught him and swept him up in her arms, before he could escape again, nuzzling his cheek. "Come on, little man. Let's get you cleaned up and ready for bed. Let your daddy relax for a minute."

Elizabeth carried the boy to the bedroom as Gunn took a chair and settled himself in front of the warm fire. Casimir curled up nearby. A stray glove, one of Elizabeth's, lay on the floor. He picked it up and draped it on the arm of the chair.

He sat a while and watched the flames die to embers, thinking about how many blessings they had enjoyed in this house for the past eighteen months or so. They were so far removed on this little island, isolated from all the previous troubles they had endured. Though, word from his mother and others reached them by mail on occasion, of course, despite the distance between them.

His mother had written to tell them of her intention to sell the house in Concord and stay in Savannah, living with her cousins in the spare room, at their invitation. She was pleased to report that Sarah and Daniel Sullivan were doing well, though they had moved to Augusta, near his brother. But Daniel had made frequent trips since then back to Savannah, mainly to see her, of course. She seemed very happy.

Sarah Sullivan had confirmed as much in her occasional letters to him. At present, she was staying at a cloister near Dublin under the watchful eye of Father Martin, trying to sort out how best to proceed with her young life. She had stopped having wild dreams.

He thought of Marianne, now attending classes at the Normal School in Framingham, training to become a teacher, just like Elizabeth, and spending weekends and holidays with his aunt and uncle in Boston. Her many letters were full of longing to be with them again next summer, sprinkled with inquiries about Casimir.

A half hour later, Elizabeth returned. She came to him and sat in his lap, placing his arm around her waist. She had let her hair down into a braid that fell to the small of her back. He played with the bow that held it in place.

She picked up the glove from the arm of the chair. "You found my glove."

"It was lying on the floor."

"I've been looking everywhere for that thing. Casimir must have been playing with it." She handed him an envelope. "A letter came for you today. It's from your Uncle William."

Gunn opened it and quickly scanned the letter. "Good news. They've finally found Meg—in Lisbon, of all places. She was in a very bad way. Abandoned with no money by her so-called friend. She's now on her way back to Boston to live with William and Aunt May. At least for now. What wonderful news. Oh, and at latest word, Cuffee is no longer in hiding. He is now safe and free at last somewhere in Canada."

"Does he say where?"

"No, he is careful not to say. He refers to him only as 'our prized cargo, delivered.'"

"I'm so very glad. That's welcome news to be very thankful for this Christmastide."

"Yes, indeed. What's this?" He unfolded an enclosed newspaper clipping from the *Boston Herald*, dated several weeks earlier, and read it aloud. The article told the scandalous story of the schooner *Wanderer*, suspected of importing a shipload of slaves from Africa and landing them in late November on Jekyll Island, off Georgia's coast. Most of the slaves were still at large, but authorities expected that as many as four hundred had landed. They placed blame for the outrageous venture at the feet of one Charles Augustus Lafayette Lamar of Savannah.

"Can you believe it? He did it. That madman actually pulled it off. If only I could have been there to stop him. I tell you, we'll be lucky if we're not at war with Georgia this time next year. Think of what that will mean."

"You certainly tried stop him, my dear."

"I should have shot him when I had the chance."

"Now, what kind of thing is that to say on Christmas Eve? You tried your best to prevent it. When nobody else would, you tried. That must be enough, at least for now."

"I suppose you're right, Elizabeth. As usual, you're right."

"Let's just enjoy the evening, here by the fire, and celebrate in peace, shall we? God's grace and peace toward men of goodwill." She rested herself against him.

"As you wish, my dear. That reminds me. I have something for you," he said, reaching into his pocket for the third package. He pulled it out and gave it to her.

"Oh, what is it?"

"Open it and see."

She unwrapped the narrow, flat package. Inside the box was an amber cross pendant, trimmed in delicate silver filagree, on a necklace made of leather cord.

"It's just lovely, Andrew," she breathed. "Thank you."

"I'll be able to afford the silver chain to match next Christmas. I hope."

She wrapped her arms around his neck and hugged him. "Put it on for me," she whispered.

As she turned away, he draped the pendant around her graceful neck and tied the ends.

She kissed his lips deep and hard. Then she got up from his lap and took his hand, her lovely eyes beckoning him to follow. "Let's go to bed, husband. Right now."

"It's early yet. And don't you have a gift for me?"

She smiled softly. "Yes, but you'll need to help me think of a name for your gift. A girl's name, I hope. And it can't be Elizabeth. That's too easy."

He returned her smile and gave her palm a tender kiss. "Perfect."

She pulled him out of the chair by the hand and led him to the bedroom.

~

He awoke from a sound sleep with a start to the sound of Casimir's bark. The dog stood at the foot of the bed, the hair on his back raised, and barking incessantly. Elizabeth groaned, rolled over, and covered her head with a pillow.

"Your turn to take him out," she muttered. "Hurry. He'll wake the baby."

"What in this world are you barking at, Casimir?" Gunn said. "Be quiet, will you?"

For an instant, in the darkness of the room, Gunn caught sight of the same ominous form that he'd seen once before, lingering just there at the foot of the bed. The hairs on the back of his own neck stood up. He rubbed his eyes, threw the covers off, and jumped up, but before he reached the spot where it hovered, the shapeless form was gone. Casimir stopped barking.

He put on a robe, picked up his shillelagh from its perch behind the bedroom door and hurried to the next room to check on Tommy, with Casimir at his heels. The door was ajar. He entered to find the boy sound asleep in his crib, breathing softly on his back. He searched the rest of the little house but found nothing out of the ordinary. The faint glow of embers in the hearth gave little warmth to the deep chill in the parlor.

Returning to the bedroom, he padded over to the nearest window and peered into the front yard. A gust of rising wind whistled through the old oak just outside. A branch tapped gnarled fingers against the frosted windowpane. The snow had stopped falling, and the sky was clear. A half-moon hung over the tree line, its light glistening on the shroud of snow and illuminating the rail fence that surrounded the house.

On a fencepost near the front gate perched the silhouetted form of a large dark-and-white bird, about the size of a raven. It was a seabird—a great shearwater, from the shape of the long, hooked bill—artlessly preening its mottled tail feathers. The sight surprised him. A more superstitious man might have considered it ominous. In all his years at sea, Gunn had not witnessed a lone shearwater so far from the open ocean, except after a bad storm. Even more odd, he had never known any to overstay a seasonal migration to the South Atlantic for the winter nesting months.

The bird suddenly seemed aware of being watched. It uttered a startled cry that sounded of mad laughter and lifted its long, stiff wings in flight, disappearing into the darkness of the night.

"Stunner," he muttered.

"What is it?" Elizabeth sat up in bed, drawing the down comforter about her.

He shivered. "Nothing. I thought I saw something. Just my imagination, I think. Go back to sleep."

"Well, come back to bed, won't you?"

She lifted a corner of the bedclothes, inviting him in. He removed his robe, crawled under the warmth of the blankets and lay back against the pillow. She nestled against him, beneath the shelter of his arm. Casimir curled up on the foot of the bed and sighed.

"Is it Christmas Day yet?" Elizabeth murmured.

"I think it must be."

"Your son will be awake soon. Merry Christmas, my love."

"And to you, my dearest one."

He kissed her forehead and hoped that the bliss of quiet rest would soon return. Despite his unspeakable joy in the present solace of hearth and home, he lay awake until daybreak, knowing deep inside, in places he could not name, the uncertain dread of what was yet to come.

— The End —

ACKNOWLEDGMENTS

Many thanks to my editor, Jenny Quinlan, without whose deft touch this book would be far less worthy of the reader's kind attention.

This book is a work of fiction in its entirety. Although it is based on a true story, the historical elements have been filtered through my imagination. Anyone seeking historical facts about the conspiracy to restart the Atlantic slave trade in the years leading up to the Civil War should look elsewhere to factual sources, as I did. In particular, I am most grateful to my friend, Jim Jordan, author of *The Slave-Trader's Letter-Book*, an excellent and reliable source, whose generous guidance in telling this story was invaluable.

I am also indebted to the fine librarians and staff of the Georgia Historical Society in Savannah, Georgia, who made accessible their fine collection to me.

As always, I am blessed by the encouragement and faith of my lovely wife and constant muse, Gwendolyn Cheryl Bull.

Ad dei gloriam.

ABOUT THE AUTHOR

A retired Coast Guard officer, Alton Fletcher enjoys sailing almost as much as writing, and sometimes regrets he can't do both at once.

He became enamored with books and the sea as a boy, upon first reading Robert Louis Stevenson's *Treasure Island*. Since then, he has found nothing more enjoyable than a good sea story well told.

He and his cherished wife of forty-nine years make their home in Virginia.

Look for the further adventures of Andrew Gunn to be published soon.

For more books and updates: www.altonfletcher.com

X x.com/altonfletcher16